THE SILVER TONGUE

THE
SILVER
TONGUE

HOLLY M. PFEIFFER

ABOOKS

Alive Book Publishing

Additional copies may be ordered from the publisher for educational,
business, promotional or premium use.
For information, contact ALIVE Book Publishing at:
alivebookpublishing.com, or call (925) 837-7303.

This is a work of fiction. Names, characters, places and incidents are
either products of the author's imagination or are used fictitiously.
Any resemblance to actual events, locales or persons, living or dead,
is entirely coincidental.

Book and Cover Design by Alex P. Johnson

ISBN 13
978-1-63132-145-0

Library of Congress Control Number: 2021914968

Library of Congress Cataloging-in-Publication Data
is available upon request.

First Edition

Published in the United States of America by ALIVE Book Publishing
and ALIVE Publishing Group, imprints of Advanced Publishing LLC
3200 A Danville Blvd., Suite 204, Alamo, California 94507
alivebookpublishing.com

PRINTED IN THE UNITED STATES OF AMERICA

10 9 8 7 6 5 4 3 2 1

To Cassidy

CHAPTER 1

It was a night like any other in Palace Marzine. Nobility with powdered faces and prim button-downs wandered the halls, looking for dinner engagements. Servants rushed from room to room, making sure no mouth was left unwiped and no dish was left untaken. But one place was empty of servants—of nobles, too. And that was the palace's main dining hall. Instead, it was occupied by the royal family of Marzine. Addison, his wife, Lyra, and their son, Cornelius, sat stiff-backed with Cornelius' betrothed, princess Isabel of Andria. Looks of polite boredom were shared as they began their meal.

Prince Cornelius wasn't one to hold his tongue, but holding his tongue was all he could do in the present moment. He was holding onto his tongue for dear life. While the others admired the light the moon cast, Cornelius stared into the lusterless eyes of the salmon that lay untouched before him. He wouldn't dare break eye contact with the fish, for he might risk *making* eye contact with his father. Cornelius feared few things. Perhaps only one: his father's eyes. One couldn't help but be wary of them. The line of gold rimming around the pupil gave the king a surreal look. Cornelius, in contrast to his father, had shallow blue eyes. The defect wasn't noticeable beside the rest of him, though. Sitting there in an elegant high-backed chair, he looked painted. His figure was slim and muscular but not from hunger or overwork. His hair was done up with perfumed grease, perfectly coiffed, as was the style. Everything about him was purposed, perfected. It was relatively easy to forget his eyes in comparison.

And other than his looks, he was seemingly well-rounded and, to be frank, delightful. All good men of noble descent were as pleasant as he, so he was only keeping up. He spoke each of the five languages present on the continent, though these tongues were classroom-taught and held no culture. To be fair, he'd hardly been outside of palace Marzine's obsidian walls, let alone to other parts of the continent. The farthest he'd ventured was Sirensea, the capital city across the bay from his home on Addison Island. But he wouldn't be well-rounded if language study was his only interest. So other than his cultureless linguistics, he practiced swordplay and dabbled in horseback riding. And, most notably to him and least notably to his father, he was a classical musician. He played a variety of instruments, but his penchant was for the viola. Strangely, his least favorite instrument to play was the violin, but only because he'd failed to play a concerto for an audience once. But even classical musicianship wasn't enough to get him ahead in high society.

Though he didn't flaunt it before his father, he was silver-tongued, a natural-born wordsmith. If he so desired, he could stage a coup with words. And perhaps he would someday if he ever got bored enough. The only thing that nullified this nation-leveling charm was his father's presence. Somehow, the man's eyes turned his lilting phrases to subdued mutterings. He would be flirting with his betrothed and charming his mother if it weren't for his father. Without the king, his words were enchanted, his disposition beguiling. He could manipulate anyone to do his bidding. But there was another thing that set him off. And that would be his name.

"Gale, look. It's a grand sight. I'm certain you wouldn't wish to be rude in the presence of her ladyship," his mother said, the slightest implication of disappointment in her tone. Another misnaming. His name was Cornelius, for the love of God. But that name had long been dead. It was even inscribed on a tombstone in the necropolis gardens. He didn't know why he was still hurt by the name "Gale." He'd even agreed to change his name. There were some pains he couldn't hide behind a smile, though.

Cornelius wanted to reply to his mother, to assure her that he would look at the moon as if he wasn't some petrified-of-his-father fool, but those eyes just wouldn't allow it. He made his head lurch towards the scene, however. It took all the force of will he would ever have. The moon was indeed marvelous in all its luminosity. He relished the brief moment of gazing, the blood-curdling fear nearly subsiding. Everyone knew the best moons were in Marzine. The opaline tinge that lit the sky was a treasure to Marzine's citizens. Cornelius, his betrothed, and his parents regarded the moon together at that moment, all of life's woes vanishing. But then, Cornelius noticed the golden ring around it. What was the old literature? Ring around the moon, sailor's doom. Clear night, sailor's delight. To Cornelius, the halo meant something else, something more. And, of course, this something was his father's eyes. Because Cornelius' world revolved around them.

The others gradually returned to their fish, the tentative sound of cutlery against plates beginning again. Cornelius took a long draught of honey wine from a crystal glass, praying that the alcohol would soothe him. But the silence made him wary. He turned his gaze to the midnight purple furniture that surrounded them, the silver intricacies playing into the moon's embrace. He had always admired the color of midnight purple. But before he could take an even breath, his mother dismantled his carefully crafted calm.

"Gale, my son, why aren't you eating? Do you have a stomachache? You've thinned out lately. You should eat." His name was Cornelius. His mother meant well, but her attempt at pleasantries only served to anger him.

Cornelius hoped his betrothed, Isabel, was enjoying the royal family's unspoken discord. He certainly would've had he been in her place.

Lyra of Marzine's ice-blue eyes narrowed in on him, and she bore a resemblance to a vulture about to consume the entrails of a dead man. If Lyra wasn't violently mad, he might have resented her for her misnamings and ridicule. But she was indeed violently mad, and he couldn't blame her for it, what with her husband being the man at the end of the table. He would be violently mad, too, if he had to marry a man like Addison.

Isabel of Andria sat across from him. Even in her agitation, she was beautiful, her eyes blue like sapphires, her blonde hair in ringlets. Isabel wore layers and layers of powders to impress her new betrothed, but the princess didn't need them. Cornelius didn't think so, at least, though he did acknowledge how much effort she'd put into the soft curve of her eyeliner. He always ended up poking himself in the eye when he experimented with it.

Earlier in the evening, there was a party to celebrate the engagement. Cornelius had first met Isabel during the party, with hundreds of eyes piercing them. He'd smiled suavely and kissed her hand, which was the custom for suitors. She'd blushed. He did look particularly dashing in his Sleetalian-made suit, a novelty in royal Marzine. She looked fair in her traditional Marzinian gown. Blue suited her. They'd danced, their figures close to one another. She'd smelled of lavender, and he'd complimented her choice of perfume.

For the remainder of the candlelit evening, he'd lavished her with compliments, and she'd tried her best to do the same, though Cornelius' charm carried the conversation for the most part.

To make her feel special, he'd snuck her out of the ballroom with him. They ran hand in hand down the palace's echoey corridors until they came upon Cornelius' favorite music room. There, in the fleeting sunlight surrounded by classical instruments, he'd kissed her. He could feel the relief in her lips, too. Every royal expected to live a lovelorn life, though many didn't want to. She knew she wouldn't be alone then. He'd made her blush. He'd made her smile. He'd made her feel safe. Safe, in the music room, where he brought all his lovers. It was all so ironic. Her life wouldn't be lovelorn, but with him, it would be teary.

It was a routine of Cornelius' to bring lovers to the music room. It was a well-practiced routine, too. It could be pretty dull being locked away in a secluded palace on a remote island with a sheltered sea surrounding it. There wasn't anything better to do than romance the guards. Cornelius didn't wish to be wed, at least not yet. He was only seventeen, after all. Being bound to a single person for the remainder of his life was daunting. He wouldn't revoke his fate, though. His duty as crown prince was to take a partner who would benefit the kingdom with their parentage. The marriage he was entering would establish a trade agreement with the other continent. He would only have to be more secretive in his ways. It was immoral, sure, but he was the type to make amends after the deed was done. Giving Isabel a repentant grin, he finally spoke.

"What do you do in your s-spare time, lady Isabel?" Cornelius inquired, collecting all the luster he could to ignore his father. Shame flooded into him. He never stuttered. But at least he was making an effort to be courteous. Isabel gave him a questioning look, remembering the romantic who'd kissed her in the music room and comparing him to this dullard. Cornelius sucked in a breath of air when it took her a full moment to reply.

"I enjoy reading, thank you. I'm entertained most by the classics. My favorite is *The Tale of Alexander*. Well, Alexander himself is my father, so I suppose I'm biased, but his bravery is undeniable. And…" Cornelius didn't hear past that. His father was staring intently at him, wires of blue lightning arcing in his eyes. It felt as if someone were poking and prodding at the base of his spine. After his betrothed finished her monologue, his mother would most certainly scold him again.

Cornelius broke his gaze as his betrothed's reply reached completion. He instead looked out the large, rounded windows at the end of the long hall to see the sky's twilight blue and the pale light of the moon. He saw something strange beyond the panes. There was a small boat, probably a triple-level, skimming the surface of the clear, cerulean sea. Hardly any boats passed the royal island of Addison, named for his father. The ship's helm and body were crafted from dark spruce wood, and the bowsprit of the vessel was rounded. These characteristics were Sleetalian, not Marzinian.

In most cases, his father would point out the ship, but his attentions were fixed on his son. Cornelius found his situation too dire to be too distracted by a strange ship, though. He passed it off as another captured rebellion ship with rare goods. It would be offered as a tribute.

"Other than the viola, what do you enjoy doing in your spare time, prince Gale?" Isabel asked Cornelius after the silence grew to be too much. Usually, Cornelius would return with a flirty retort. *Spending time with lovely ladies like you. But to clarify, you're the only lovely lady worth spending time with.* That's what he would say. He could almost hear her response. But instead of his flirty retort, he gave voice to an unfathomably unintelligent phrase.

"I… I like… knitting." It was the truth, but as soon as the words left his lips, searing embarrassment coursed through him. He enjoyed knitting, but only after nights such as these to calm himself down. The repetitive motion of the knitting prongs helped him relax.

The knife his father was using to chop his salmon into small bites dropped from his hands. He could imagine his father's expression but didn't dare glance up. Others had died for less at the fingertips of Addison of Marzine.

Isabel frowned. She also knew how to knit. It was more of a

feminine hobby, she had to admit, but everything was a little odd in Marzine. She was told not to judge these people and their customs. There were already enough strange occurrences to keep her pondering through the night, like how this lovely linguist could hardly speak in the presence of his parents.

"Alright, perhaps we could knit together sometime." She had meant to be gracious with her invitation, but it only irritated the king.

"Honestly, Gale, you should at least try to present yourself as the sovereign you are," his mother said through a bite of salmon. Cornelius' heart stopped. *Gale again. My name is Cornelius!* Cornelius usually wasn't so opposed to the name "Gale." He'd accepted the name as his own a few years previous. If they wanted him dead and his brother back, so be it. He would be Gale. But sometimes, it was too much. Sometimes, he couldn't remember who Cornelius was.

Cornelius gazed at his mother's moon-illuminated face. Her scorched red hair was pinned up neatly in a bun atop her head, a few plastered tendrils hanging down. He observed the creases in her forehead from many years of burden and torment. Torment at the hands of his father, who'd made her like this. Addison of Marzine had killed Gale, after all. Killed Gale, given Cornelius his name a few years later, and inscribed that name "Cornelius" on his brother's headstone. It was too much. Just too much. So Cornelius finally let go of his tongue.

"My n-name is Cornelius, the name you chose for me," Cornelius said in the ghost of a whisper, a shadow to the candlelight. His mother's eyes took on a disapproving darkness. Isabel watched on in bewilderment. She chopped her salmon a bit too finely as she watched.

"Didn't I tell you to speak louder, Gale?" His mother asked, no recognition of fault in her eyes. Cornelius searched her face, however. He strived and journeyed over the ridges in her skin for some inkling, some hint that she knew he was her second son. His heart cracked when he couldn't. It seemed everyone else in the Marzinian court called him Gale but knew he was Cornelius. Only his mother was truly insane enough to believe his father's lie.

"My name is Cornelius, the name you chose f-for me." His voice was slightly less shaky as he repeated himself. His phrasing was more robust, his voice a forte. His father's methodical chopping had ceased again.

"Speak with more emphasis, Gale," his mother commanded, her tone stern, her gaze void of recognition for the second time. Cornelius felt a hand at his throat, choking him until tears sprang from his eyes. Any other day he could endure it. But not today. Anger boiled within him. Cornelius stood, his upholstered seat sliding backward in his wake. Isabel released a soft gasp, a pale hand covering her lips.

"My name is Cornelius, the name you chose for me!" He could use plenty of emphasis if he wanted to. His silken words returned to him, his confidence invigorating him. Isabel found herself admiring his anger; it was somewhat similar to the passion she read of in her drab romance novels. She found her fists clenching as she watched. She'd never seen anything like him! So spontaneous!

"Cornelius?" his mother queried, utter confusion in her eyes. She placed a subtle hand on her chest in surprise.

"*Cornelius?*" he mocked cruelly, imitating her gesture. He felt bitter. His own mother didn't recognize him, and now he was throwing a tantrum about it before his betrothed of all people. And the king of Marzine.

"But… But your late brother passed, Gale." This was how his mother saw him. Dead. He was dead to her. He was a rotting, worm-eaten corpse to her. He opened his mouth to speak, but someone interrupted him.

"You can't blame her for the state of her mind, Cornelius." Addison's brazen voice spoke. It sounded like the rumble of an earthquake, a mountain crumbling into the abyss. Cornelius finally looked at his father and crumbled, just like that mountain.

"If you'd excuse me, I need to use the powder room. I'd prefer it if you'd be so kind as to have a servant show me where it might be. In fact... I think I'll retire for the evening." Isabel rushed over her words hurriedly, staggering to her feet. She was far too flustered to continue on through the duration of the evening. A servant slunk from the shadows of the room, a grim look on his face. He motioned for her to go before him, and she gladly obliged, her spectral blue gown swaying in turn. Cornelius paid her no mind.

"I don't blame her. I blame you," Cornelius said hatefully, looking into his father's eyes. He was too furious to feel the fear that usually drowned out other things when he looked at his father. Addison of Marzine leaned back against his chair, loosening his cravat. Cornelius slammed his fists down against the ornate table, the clatter of cutlery following his wild motion. His mother only stared. He waited. A moment, another... A full quarter-hour passed without a reply from his father. The lion-like man just sat motionless, staring at Cornelius as if he were a spectacle at a circus. Finally, Cornelius gave in.

"I think I'll retire as well," he whispered after his father finally returned to his chopping. He strode away, sinking back into himself. A sea breeze blew through the room from the open corridor as Cornelius dared to glance back. His father's shoulder-length silver-blonde hair curled in the wind, his eyes still fixed on his son. Then, he merely looked away, which hurt more than the misnamings ever would.

He was out in the open corridor with its high ceiling and velveted floors, his hands toying with one another. His breathing became sharp and painful, and his chest burned. Burned like he wished the world around him would. That way, he wouldn't have to live in the dubious dark anymore, wondering when he'd be happy again. That way, he would have a blank slate, neither of his two names written down anywhere.

There was still a glimmer of hope in him that hadn't been singed away by the flames. He had yet to see the world, so how did he know if it deserved to be burned? And how could he ever learn? His duties were here in Marzine. His father would never permit him to leave. So he decided. He knew only Marzine deserved to burn. He would save a few others from the flames, but everyone else could burn. He would watch from some distant cliff as the ashes rose into the sea air, the moon's light invisible beside the light of the flames. He would charm himself with his own words, allowing himself to believe that he wasn't at fault for the disaster. He would play his viola until he fell asleep. Then, he would rise from the ashes and see what was beyond the burnt remains of his kingdom. The conjecture abated his pain, and he was granted composure once again.

His chambers were a medley of mint greens and vibrant scarlets, the lavish furnishings welcoming. A dying flame was alight in a hearth, and he sunk to his knees before it, warming his sea-chilled hands. A servant had left a kettle of rose tea on the fire. He had difficulty finding sleep during solitary nights, and the rose tea pacified him. He gingerly poured himself a cup and positioned himself in an armchair so that he was facing a window, the sea just beyond the glass. He heard the melody of the waves as he sipped the sweetened liquid.

He calmed himself further with the notion that the day was over and never would there be such a day again, soothed himself as one comforts a child, for that was all he needed. Maybe that was the reason for his arrogance, his narcissism. Nobody would care for him but him.

As the small hours of the morning came about, Cornelius unbuttoned his shirt and clutched his viola to his chest as he positioned himself atop his bed. The shape of the viola replaced that of a body, for the bed felt too large when he was alone in it. He pulled the silken covers over him and his instrument, the hush of sleep falling over him.

He would find himself somewhere different only an hour or so later. He would find himself in bearings from which he could judge the other four nations, see if they needed to be burned. The journey he was about to embark on would be one he would remember vividly for the rest of his life, however short or long it was.

CHAPTER 2

The two shadows crept along the base of the wall, their footsteps muted against the sand. The shadows had their minds focused on one person and one person alone: Cornelius, prince of Marzine. Before that hour, the discussions between them had been both numerous and vigorous, a plan forming. With every detail perfected, there was no room for error. Even the slightest miscalculation or misstep could result in sudden or drawn-out death. But if either of them lost sleep over their deaths, they didn't show it, at least not to each other. A mission meant leaving fear to die in one's place.

Mikka Savva wore a bleak glare behind his mask. He surveyed the scene, his midnight gaze breaking down the scenery. The massive obsidian wall that surrounded the palace compound, in most cases, would be impassable. No person in their right mind would attempt to maneuver their way around the ample guards and stark defenses. Mikka wasn't entirely in his right mind, though. He was also slightly drunk, which was customary for him. He admired how the smoothed obsidian reflected the alabaster light of the moon, less daunted by the task than he should've been.

Unlike himself, his partner Pia still had a few brain cells to her name. She thought it was too precarious an approach, scaling the unscalable obsidian wall. Mikka was the leader, though, and she had no real say in it. Though she lived her life in a perpetual state of rolling the dice, she was more hesitant about their current job. For one, they would die if they failed. Like, die-die. In any other situation, they could escape unscathed. But if something went wrong, all there was waiting for them were two shallow graves. She knew fear was supposed to be left to die in one's place. But with her few remaining brain cells, she decided that she should at least warn Mikka.

"Mikka, we can still turn back," Pia mentioned in accented Sleetalian. Her words sounded odd, demure. Sleetalian was a brash language, and though she'd been speaking it for a while, some of her words were still sloppy. Mikka shook his head. He was as stubborn as ever.

Pia wasn't built for climbing. Her frame was sturdy and reliable. She made a formidable opponent in a fighting ring, but her form would drag her down when scaling the obsidian wall. She would have to rely heavily on her instincts for this mission, not brute force and smackdowns that would make the angels sing. Mikka, however, was fit for climbing. He was tall and lean, his muscles strong. He was a cat; he would always land on his feet. She was more of an elephant. She was the exact opposite of Mikka, having dark hair while his was light. His eyes were blue; hers were golden. And, most notably, she was short, and he was tall. Their friendship was unlikely but closer than most.

"You can use your first language. I understand you fine," Mikka replied in stilted Emberan. He was trying to learn her language as she had his. She thought it sweet but also quite stupid at such a critical moment. Still, it was adorable. She gave in and spoke her native language, Emberan.

"Alright, alright," she responded. His eyes crinkled at the corners in a smile, and he motioned her forward. She removed a leather bag from her back and placed it on the coarse sand. Mikka tugged a ravel of rope from the pack and heaved it over his shoulder. His gloves were custom-made for climbing smooth surfaces. He'd had them tailored in the nation Wilkinia beforehand, anticipating the wall. They'd done a fair amount of groundwork for this mission. The wall was somewhat of a relic. Many scholars visited to study it. Nic Murray, a partner of theirs, had studied it weeks earlier. Murray had found the obsidian wall's most vulnerable point and mapped it all out for them. For a quiet man, he could be pretty descriptive.

Mikka began his arduous ascent. He was silent, another piece of obsidian in the exterior. Despite the wall's apparent sleekness, Mikka could see the small rivulets and scratches in the rock. There was only enough leeway to pinch between two fingers, but Mikka had worked with less in his days. Once a sharpshooter in the Sleetalian army, he'd gotten familiar with the word "unscalable."

He found imperfection after imperfection in the slightly weathered surface. Every once in a while, he would glance down to see Pia, her anxious face glowing in the light of the Marzinian moon.

Sentries stood atop the obsidian wall's lookouts, each sturdy individual balancing their weight in the wind. The shift would change once the moon reached Saturn. Pia would have only moments to scale the wall with the rope Mikka was carrying with him. From there, they would have an hour to take the prince and leave the palace compound. Their ship, *The Vault of Heaven*, would have to be out to sea by dawn for the kidnapping to be successful.

Mikka reached the wall's crest, waiting just below the sentries. He was like a spider, seemingly clinging to nothing at all. Just as the guard gave a final survey, Mikka edged his way up. Pia's golden eyes shone with doubt. Could she scale the face as Mikka did? At least she would have the help of the rope around her waist. It was still a wonder how Mikka's hands fit so perfectly into the grooves in the barrier. She'd seen him brave many a wall but never had she seen him scale such a smooth, slick surface. So the obsidian wall of Marzine wasn't as impervious as the literature made it out to be. She smirked, emboldened.

Though his spidering was extraordinary, it wasn't his only

strength. One with a trained eye would see the outline of a pistol at his belt, the fine weapon made of silver no less. Though he carried the silver pistol, his skill was in sharpshooting. He had a rifle back on the ship. His shooting was exceptional no matter the handle, though. Mikka was easily the most precise person she'd ever met, even with the drinking. He saw the world in detail, noticing the thread holding buttons to a sweater, not the sweater itself.

The rope slithered down the wall, and her heart was pounding faster than it had been only moments before. She sighed heavily and wrapped the length around her waist and legs. She tried to be as silent as she could, as silent as Mikka. But the farther she scaled, the more she doubted the mission.

Halfway up, her angst subsided. Pia thought she was making good time. She had been worrying over this all day. Resting midway up the slick exterior, she breathed a sigh of relief. Mikka was a bit less pleased. She wasn't going nearly as fast as she believed herself to be, for her standards had been lowered significantly by her doubt. Mikka glanced in both directions nervously. The next shift would be arriving soon. He whispered a hurried warning down to Pia, but the deafening sound of the wind drowned out his plea. Pia was three-quarters the way there when Mikka saw the guards approaching. His breath caught in his throat. There was only one thing he could do. The next shift would arrive in a matter of seconds.

Mikka's act was an act of salvaging, a crude Hail Mary. A sighting of the pair would compromise their entire mission. Mikka unfastened the taut rope from a particularly rocky edge of the summit and fastened it around his waist. He weighed almost twice what Pia did, so she would catapult upward if he jumped off the great obsidian wall. It was a plan to defy all logic and maybe even physics. Mikka prayed to whoever would listen to help them withstand the constructs of the universe. They would both die if it failed. But if it worked, they would be saved from another death, a court-sanctioned death. So with fear's claws at his throat, he slipped over the other side of the wall. Pia felt a sudden tug on the rope. Her body soared upwards at break-neck speed. Mikka shoved a fist in his mouth to keep him from crying out, his teeth digging into his flesh. Lord, he would need—no, deserve—a shot of raska after this. Pia caught herself on the rock's edge. Her arms were strong enough to hold her there until Mikka found his way to the ground beneath safely. She hung limply until the guards were at their posts. They were none the wiser. Mikka coiled the rope again from the bottom and tossed it up to her. Pia caught it with immense effort and tied herself to the edge again. She slid down silently as Mikka had. His fear-provoked Hail Mary had worked. He slumped down against the side of the obsidian wall and pulled off his mask, taking gulping breaths of sea air.

Pia was panting as well. She gave Mikka a withering glare. "What?" she asked with a mixture of fury and relief.

"It's your fault for being slow," Mikka murmured, a smile playing at his lips.

"You're insane," she retorted, stretching her panic-stiffened limbs.

"I'm well aware," he drawled. She sighed and shook her head. There was no time to waste. A vast garden stretched out before them. Many exotic, poisonous plants grew on these sea plains, both beautiful and deadly, like Pia. Mikka couldn't help but stare at her as she surveyed the gardens, discerning the pathways. He soon pulled himself from her gravity, though, for the night was new. There was a lot more peril to deal with, and neither one of them could be distracted. She may have been as alluring as the Marzinian flora, but she was poisonous as the fronds.

They wound their way past countless stone sculptures and vibrant plants, each tainted with an edge of the sea. Pia couldn't stand the sea. She hated everything about it. Pia was stable, and the sea was not, always mercurial. Now that she was on solid ground, the sea still affected her surroundings. It irked her.

Patrols of King's Guard circulated periodically through the area. The King's Guard were the order of guard that served the king directly. Their crewmate, Lara, had a vast knowledge of the nations, even knowledge of what was behind the obsidian wall. She had taught them about the King's Guard's order and how they made a star pattern with their troops. Mikka and Pia took evasive measures to avoid those. Every so often, Mikka glanced up at the nebulous sky to see the position of the moon. He could tell how much time they had left to capture the prince.

They reached the palace ten minutes after entering the gardens. That would leave them twenty to find the prince. The palace was hulking and extravagant, the moon making the marble walls shine white. He thought the prince's quarters were in the leftmost tower. Lara's source wasn't entirely certain, but it was the best shot they had so that they would take it. They walked through the gardens to the tower. There was a set of stairs winding around the narrow building up to the prince's private terrace, to be used for emergencies. Mikka led Pia up the stairs silently, realizing how they were suspended above the waves. The steps became steeper the higher up they went. There was no railing, and Pia felt like hurling. The waves crashed against one another below them. Any number of sea monsters could be waiting below to snap her up. She wouldn't be some creature's midnight snack, at least not tonight. Pia missed the sea-touched gardens they'd been in previously. A touch of the sea was better than the sea itself.

"Pia, we have to hurry," Mikka whispered in Emberan. He wouldn't give in, would he? She could hardly understand his slurred speech, but that same sweetness made her grin as she deciphered his phrase.

A terrace appeared up ahead. The pair could only hope guards had deserted it out of pure complacency. The space was large and flat, a welcome change to the steepness of the stairs. Posts stood on either end, supporting a cross-hatched pattern of leaves and flowers blooming above their heads. Ornate furniture lay spread out across it. Even a bath! Mikka marveled over the lack of privacy. Marzinians and their riches. Marzinians and their immodesty. Marzinians and their... He could go on. Mikka hated the Marzinians, especially their siren monarchy. "Siren" was a term used in the Sleetalian military to poke fun at the Marzinian attackers. Equating them to the creatures that lured mariners to their demise diminished the guilt of ending their lives in combat.

"Should I kick it in?" Pia asked readily, a smile edging at her lips. Mikka glowered.

"No. I have a lock pick, remember? And besides, I could just shoot it open with a muffler on my pistol if we really can't wrench the door open."

Pia's smile disappeared. She sighed and seated herself on one of the overstuffed terrace couches to wait. Mikka set to work on the door. He tinkered at the lock for a moment, his left hand brushing at the sand-crusted wood. How could sand get up so high? Marzinians and their sand.

The door opened with a metallic click. Inside, birch trees stood erect in the four corners of the room. There was more ornate, upholstered furniture in this room. But the most beautiful piece in the space was a slender, wooden desk. Its curves were more graceful than her own. Pia had the sudden urge to steal the desk and leave the prince. They were kidnapping him for money, after all. This desk would fetch a pretty price if they sold it in darker circles.

"This must be the prince's study," Pia observed as she stepped into the room, her feet silent against the polished floorboards. Mikka stared her to silence, and she realized she shouldn't be making idle conversation in the middle of a mission. She wasn't used to this. Her tasks usually included healthy doses of bang and large amounts of boom with a touch of arson here and there. Mikka only needed her to keep himself calm and to carry a prince, perhaps. He drew his pistol, the familiar embrace of the metal against his fingers. He got Pia behind him, and the pair started forward. Pia drew her own gun. She had never enjoyed guns much. Killers didn't earn deaths caused by firearms like deaths caused by hands. And something as sinister as death had to be earned, in her eyes.

They walked on their heels to ensure nobody heard them. Pia pulled her bird mask higher on her face. The bird masks symbolized the Masked Birds, the resistance they belonged to. It was a touch too literal for Pia's taste, but she wore her mask proudly. Mikka, however, didn't. A few months after joining the Masked Birds, Mikka's pa got in trouble with the Marzinians. He had stolen a raska bottle or something. He was tried in the Marzinian court harshly. Too harshly. He was sentenced to life in state prison. Life, for petty theft! Marzinians and their corruption. Mikka didn't love his father, didn't even like him. He was a mean drunk who took out his rage on Mikka. But he couldn't just let his pa waste away in prison. So, he had Shadrach, the leader of the Masked Birds, pay off the authorities. In return, Mikka owed Shadrach everything. Mikka didn't like to owe anyone. The bird mask was almost like a collar to Mikka, and he was merely a mutt with the debt hanging over his head.

It was soon apparent that the prince had favorite colors: scarlet and mint. The papered walls were mint green, and the baroque furniture was the most violent shade of scarlet. There was a great deal to marvel over in the prince's tower chambers, not just the mint and scarlet decor, though it was loud. There were fine instruments and bookcases with fancy glass doors. There were paintings, usually of the abstract style. And then, there was trouble. A servant girl was mopping the wooden floors in a vault Mikka had thought to be the prince's bedchamber. Soon, they had her bound with a small length of rope and on her knees like a prisoner to be executed. She cried silently, for Mikka's long fingers were around her throat. It had all happened so fast that the young girl hadn't had time to so much as blink.

"Where is the prince?" he asked, his voice monotone in Marzinian. His icy fingers hung limply at her throat, ready to choke her if she cried out. He held his gun in the other hand. She whimpered for a moment, trying to get her bearings. Pia felt a twinge of pity in her heart but snuffed it out as soon as she sensed it. They shouldn't feel sympathy for these wretched people after all they had done.

"I-I," she sniffed, her eyes alight with shock.

"You stuttered. I didn't tell her to stutter, did I?" he asked Pia.

She shook her head, unbothered.

"Do you have a death wish?" he threatened.

Pia relaxed slightly.

"N-No... take a left a-at the next hall and then t-take a right. It's the first door. It's bright r-red. You c-can't miss it," she told him, shaking.

"If you're wrong, it's your head with a bullet through it," Mikka said, pressing the gun against her skull. She buried her face in her palms and began sobbing hysterically.

"Mikka, you know what we have to do." It was only an obligation, telling him to kill her. Never would she wish death on an innocent.

Mikka gazed into the girl's eyes. She looked fifteen or sixteen, the flush of youth present in her cheeks. She had so much life left to live. She still had many happinesses ahead of her. Mikka couldn't take that away. If this made him soft, it wasn't softness he feared.

"We'll spare her. Let her tell her king. Let Shadrach throw a fit about it. We did our job to the best of our abilities." His eyes glinted. Her gaze warmed. She still disapproved of his decision.

They both knew what kind of punishments Shadrach doled out. Neither of them were looking forward to it.

After locking the girl in the vault, continued, following her instructions. There it was, a brazenly red door. It towered high above their heads, almost as if it had stretched to fit a ten-foot prince. Mikka gulped. The unknown frightened him more than all things. Marzinians and their mystery…

"Would you go first?" Mikka asked Pia bashfully. His timidness made her chuckle to herself. Mikka squared his shoulders in an attempt to make himself seem unafraid, but Pia knew just how fearful he could be. They'd fought a war together, after all.

"Yes, Mikka, of course, I will," she pledged with sarcasm as brazen as the red door. She shuffled towards the scarlet entryway, her hand against the gilded knob. The door turned open silently, moonlight spilling from within.

"This is it?" Mikka whispered incredulously. Pia appraised the room with a raised brow. The color scheme was much the same as the outer corridors, mint, and scarlet. Mikka cocked his pistol despite the lack of imminent danger.

The chamber was lavish enough, but Mikka had expected diamond curtains and emerald fire stones. The view had all the glittering jewels the room lacked. It was breathtaking. The moon was bulbous among the stars, its light paving a moondust path in the sea. The room made him want to curl up and fall asleep, a sense of peace settling over him. It smelled of roses and rain.

There was a bed against the far wall. Cornelius, known as Gale to anyone but vagabonds and knowledge-seekers, lay asleep in it, his expression as serene as the decor. His curly hair glowed in the moonlight. His features were relaxed in sleep but were still regal and Marzinian. He was everything Mikka had imagined, save ten feet tall and awake. He was just so defenseless. Pia chuckled.

"It's the Siren Prince of Marzine, Mikka," she whispered,

gesturing carelessly at the boy. Mikka allowed himself a chuckle as well. Mikka would have no trouble carrying him, but he was still worried. Pia removed leather cords and a line of cloth from her pack to bind and gag him, but what he was cradling in his arms made her hesitate. Mikka scowled. The prince appeared to be embracing some sort of string instrument, a fiddle of sorts? He couldn't tell only from the outer case. Marzinians and their music...

He delicately tried to pry it from the sleeping boy's arms, but he stirred whenever Mikka touched it. Pia sighed and took a syringe out of her bag. The needle was filled with a sleeping tonic brewed by Shadrach himself. They were supposed to administer it only if he was awake, but the string instrument wasn't going anywhere without muscle relaxants. She injected it into his wrist, but they still couldn't pry the instrument from his arms, which seemed to be in some state of living rigor mortis.

"Should we just... take him and the instrument?" Pia suggested. Mikka quirked a brow. If they were going to make it, they had to leave now. Mikka nodded, and they strung the leather cords around the instrument and the prince, fastening him to his fiddle. Mikka carried him bridal style, which was profoundly uncomfortable for him.

They navigated their way back to the servant's entrance, unbothered by anyone. Mikka felt as if it was a miracle given the previous occurrence. They scaled the wall. Pia watched the prince while Mikka constructed the makeshift pulley system they'd devised back on the ship. They slipped over the edge of the obsidian barrier as the watch arrived. A jovial-looking man with an oily handlebar mustache glanced over the edge, but they weren't in his line of sight by the time he had the sense to look.

Pia's heart was thudding in her fingernails by the time they reached the bottom. She let her teeth grind together in her mouth. There'd been too many close calls that night. She thought back to the girl they'd spared the life of. Would someone find her, or would she just be left to rot? Pia shook it off and continued ahead into the moonlight. Mikka's heavy grunting, the sea crashing against the shore, and the occasional snore from the sleeping prince were the only sounds. Relief settled over her as they entered the hidden alcove where *The Vault of Heaven* sat waiting for their safe return. Mikka was alive. She was alive. Pia took solace in that thought as the adrenaline wore her down.

The rest of the group were waiting on the main deck. Rodrigo Reyes, Pia's twin brother, leaned against the ship's railing. He smiled at her, but she chose to ignore him. He'd always reminded her of a mewling pup. Mannon, one of the three mariners they'd hired to help Nic Murray captain the ship, pushed Rodrigo down to the deck with a chuckle.

"So you found him!" Rodrigo exclaimed, scrambling back up. They all spoke Sleetalian and had communicated with it during their time together at sea. They shared another language, too. Marzinian. But they would never speak the language of those who'd taken their countries from them.

"Indeed they have," confirmed Lara, her Wilkinian accent present over her Sleetalian. She stood to her full height, far taller than Mikka and far taller than all of them. She pulled her dark hair into a knot at the nape of her neck. A beaded hair clip held it in place. A beaded hair clip was the closest thing any one of them could get to fancy. Mikka laid the slumbering prince on the deck. He furrowed his brows in his sleep, his fingers curling around his fiddle case.

"That's not... my name," he cried in his sleep. The crew began to chuckle as they gathered around him. Only Rodrigo didn't laugh. He only looked concerned. Pia rested her elbow nonchalantly on a crate.

"Ladies and gents," she sighed. "I present to you the Prince of Marzine, Gale or Cornelius, whatever his pa likes to call him these days."

Only moments later, *The Vault of Heaven* left the alcove and sailed into the beyond.

CHAPTER 3

Cornelius felt the conscious sensation of another in his arms, perhaps that young ambassador from Wilkinian Marzine or that nobleman's daughter who had been staying at the palace. He couldn't recall which of them, though. That was awfully strange. Usually, he could remember who he'd courted the day previous.

As his senses sharpened, he couldn't help but notice how stiff the other was, whoever they might be. It could even be his betrothed, he realized. None of his usual lovers was this stiff. Isabel of Andria was a pretty girl; he was at least sure of that. But he wasn't seductive enough to bring a foreign princess to bed with him. Something was wrong, but he couldn't remember what. Murky memories floated through his mind like pond scum, and a blaring headache was beginning to take hold. It took a couple moments to pry his eyelids open and a few more after that for his vision to clear, only to see the moon above his head. But something was off. Bars were intersecting his line of sight.

Finally, he began to link his seemingly nonsensical memories together. He'd had enough that evening, becoming a stuttering wreck for his betrothed, and he'd yelled at his less-than-sane mother for calling him by his dead brother's name even though she wasn't lucid enough to differentiate him. Worst of all, when he closed his bleary eyes, he was met with his father's hostile stare, gold rimming the pupils of his primordial eyes. All of last night's chaos had caused him to fall asleep embracing his viola instead of Isabel of Andria or the handsome ambassador from Marzinian Wilkinia.

If that wasn't enough to muse on, why were there bars over the moon? When Cornelius tried to lift a hand to massage his aching temple, he found that his wrists were closed in irons. Yes, something was definitely wrong. He wasn't in his sleeping chambers, nor was he under bedclothes. He wasn't even in the Marzinian palace compound. Yes, he felt it now—the gentle rocking of ocean waves against the underbelly of a ship. He estimated the boat was a triple-level, long and narrow as the Sleetalians made them, from the sway frequency. Being both a Marzinian and a prince, Cornelius had spent many an afternoon on ships or studying. Marzine was a sea-faring country, the most sea-faring of the five nations.

Another memory struck him as he regained his bearings. He recalled glancing out the circular window of the dining hall, only to see an out-of-place ship, triple leveled and small with Sleetalian characteristics as he assumed this one to be. The wheels in his mind turned. He, the most ensconced person on the continent, had been kidnapped. The shock made him bolt upright. Breathing was excruciating.

"Where... Where..." was all he could manage as he tried not to succumb to the dizziness.

Lara was startled by the sudden movements of the Siren Prince. He'd sat up abruptly, the instrument still clutched tightly to his chest. His eyes were a surreal blue in the waning torchlight of the brig. His curls were golden red, and his form was angular yet slim. He was handsome, but only in a superficial way.

The group had decided it was best to keep him locked in the brig until they knew he was compliant. Lara, an optimist, thought that perhaps they could work out some sort of agreement with Cornelius-Gale and maybe, just maybe, their sea voyages could be more pleasant travel than being on the lam. Mikka had told her to cast all hopes of that over the side of the ship, but Mikka hated Marzine with the passion of a thousand suns. Cornelius was the prince of that very nation. Marzine had displaced everyone in one way or another. The seeds of his prejudice had sprouted from that, watered by his own fears and assumptions.

"Are you Cornelius or Gale? None of us really know," Lara asked in fluent Marzinian, her tone wary. But Cornelius noticed the undertones. He had spent enough time studying the nuances of speech to tell she resented him. For what, he didn't know. Everyone loved the prince of Marzine, granter of boons, and charmer of all. Then he remembered the irons holding him in his viola's embrace and the sway of the boat. He remembered how he had been taken in his sleep. So he made himself lie back. Struggling against his captors and his restraints would make his ordeal worse. He instead scrutinized the girl. Her hair was dark like the stygian-sanded beaches of Sleetal. Her eyes were a lighter shade, caramel or something similar. It seemed to change ever so slightly when she blinked. When flattering someone, complimenting their eyes was one of the most effective methods of doing so. He wondered if flattery would help him out of this. Perhaps he would have to learn another style of flattery. The prospect excited him. And though he knew it shouldn't, he had been ever so bored in palace Marzine.

All he could deduct about the girl from his scrutinization was that she was very, *very* tall. Beautiful, but not in a superficial way.

"I prefer Cornelius, thank you very much. Don't worry, you kidnapped the right man." As soon as he spoke, his chronic charisma came back. "And, if I could be so bold as to ask, where am I and what is your business with me?" he inquired, his tone sickly-sweet. He held up cuffed wrists for her consideration.

The girl's thick brows rose. She stood slowly and drew a dagger from one of her pockets, her handling hateful. She didn't seem to know how to wield a dagger, holding it more like a quill. If he could only be freed from his bindings, he could disarm her and make her his captive. He supposed he could hear her out before that, though.

"My name is Lara, and you should be grateful I'm granting you that. You'll get nothing else from me until tomorrow," she replied, sounding as pretentious as a noblewoman. The girl, Lara, crossed her arms over her narrow torso, glowering. Cornelius leaned back. So she didn't like him. He was confident in his abilities, though.

"I am grateful," he said airily. "Thank you, Lara."

"I know damn well you aren't," she retorted. A strip of her curly black hair slipped from its knot and slithered down her neck.

"Alright, well, it's obvious that we aren't friends. This isn't a friendly situation. I'm restrained in a room that resembles a prison cell, not in my chambers where I fell asleep." He kept his tone light, unopposing. He was as obliging as a sleeping sea monster. As dangerous as one as well. "Also, I assume you meant sunrise when you said tomorrow, for it already is tomorrow," he said. He had never been in this sort of danger. It was enthralling. He relaxed his shoulders and stretched out.

"You've got some nerve, Marzinian," Lara breathed. She passed the dagger through her fingers.

"I meant not to offend, only to state the obvious," he said with a conniving grin. They returned to their previous silence and staring. Cornelius could think of a thousand remarks, but she had a blade. He had to select the most fitting of the thousand, the least offensive. Finally, Cornelius decided. He would tell her his favorite colors to see if she was the one who'd taken him from his chambers. His decor was mint and scarlet. It was a longshot, but she might brag about seeing the colors mint and scarlet during his kidnapping. And talking about colors, though it may seem like a foolish waste of words, was safe. It was the wisest choice.

"My favorite color is scarlet, although mint is a close second," he told her. She raised a brow.

"I know. Mikka said as much when he told us about that gaudy tower of yours. But there'll be no more gaudy towers for you unless we decide to throw you off one."

Cornelius smiled in victory. Who was Mikka? Well, this Mikka must've seen his chambers. Mikka was the one who'd taken him, the bastard.

"He must have regaled you with the harrowing tale of my capture in great detail for you to know the color of my decor," he responded idly.

"Quiet," Lara said, picking the dirt from beneath her fingernails with the dagger. Another few moments of silence passed as Cornelius became accustomed to the feeling of the waves rocking the narrow Sleetalian ship. She sat down on the metal chair in the corner of the brig again. Cornelius decided to press further.

"Mikka sounds like quite the con artist, penetrating the Marzinian palace compound and all." He'd found a thread, and he would cling onto it as long as he could. Lara was more intelligent than he believed, though. More intelligent than most people knew her to be.

"Damnit," she swore with an accusing glare.

"What seems to be the problem? I was merely making conversation as we wait for the sun to rise, Lara." He smirked.

"I told you about Mikka after you, like a boy on the first day of primary school, told me your favorite colors. Now you know more than you did moments ago. Mikka's gonna murder me and make it look like an accident." She sighed.

"I'm sorry about that. I hope Mikka makes it quick, cuts the proper arteries and all that. I'll miss you dearly."

His self-serving smile made her want to toss him overboard. She stood again. "I know all about you and your siren song. I studied you day and night for this, read all the newspaper clippings, and noted down all the barroom gossip I could. You're just a little boy who hides behind big words. I could make sure you never speak again." Her dagger glinted maliciously in the half-light.

His charming smile dropped, but he wasn't done yet. Nobody could silence him, especially not Lara, who'd made the mistake of asking him his name.

"My tongue is my finest attribute. I'd be such a boring hostage without it," he said petulantly. "You wouldn't want a bland captive, now would you? That's what I am, a captive. Now, if I were a betting man, I would wager that you and Mikka and whoever you associate with mean to sell me back to my father." He straightened his posture and continued. "My tongue is my finest attribute," he repeated. "I'd be useless without it. He wouldn't pay the ransom if I were without my tongue. In fact, I doubt he'll pay it at all. He could simply sire a new heir with a younger consort." he said. "So, if it's a grand sum you're after, then allow me my tongue and, thank you." He finished with an air of animosity. The girl was speechless.

"Mikka'll straighten you out, siren," she spat.

He flinched. If Cornelius knew how to do one thing, he knew how to inspire discord.

Lara left. Mikka could deal with the Marzinian. Yes, Mikka could handle him. Mikka could take anything. She stepped out into the corridor, her footsteps echoing through the entrails of the ship. Cornelius had made her experience something she had denied herself for the longest time; anger. She was a natural-born thinker, philosopher, questioner. So Lara questioned and thought and philosophized. Why did she let him speak? Why had she listened to him at all?

She strode up the metal stairway to the crew quarters. Mikka would know what to do. Mikka, however, was in a foul mood. He needed a night off and had fully intended to take one. His quarters were the largest, the captain's quarters, even though Nic Murray was the captain. They were still modest but more extensive than the rest of the crew's dwellings. He had his own bed with his own coverlet knitted by his late mother. He had his own chest of drawers, even his own chair that he could sit on and stare aimlessly through the porthole at the choppy waves beyond.

Mikka had brought only a few belongings with him. In his hands, he held *The Tale of Alexander*, a classic that almost all households had. It was his mother's copy. She'd written little notes in the margins of the yellowed text. He had already numbed himself with an unholy amount of raska, half of a cheap bottle gone.

When Lara barged into his room, he was less than pleased to see her. It was dark, save the lantern on the floor beside his bed. The look on Lara's face wiped away any trace of anger, though, for Lara herself seemed to have enough rage for the both of them.

"I need you to deal with him. He's quite the smooth talker." She spoke in her native tongue of Wilkinian, something she rarely did. Mikka had learned conversational Wilkinian in the Sleetalian army, but he could hardly understand her at such a rapid pace. He could only comprehend the contempt in her voice.

"Did he hurt you?" Mikka asked hurriedly, rising to his feet. His woolen coverlet fell from his form, and he was left exposed, his abdomen wound with muscles. Lara glanced away as Mikka pulled on his trousers and undershirt. She only answered when he was decent again.

"No, he only deceived me. You told me not to tell him anything until morning, but my tongue slipped, and I told him it was you who captured him."

Mikka carefully tucked the worn copy of *The Tale of Alexander* under his pillow as Lara started ahead of him. He'd never once seen her angry, nor had he heard her speak to him without being made to. Mikka knew nothing about her other than her name and the fact that she read way too much. He thought of her as a library of sorts, an overflowing pool of knowledge. Still, he didn't want her to have to suffer some Marzinian scoundrel. He buttoned his trousers and followed, carrying his silver pistol with him.

As they trudged down the metal-inlaid corridor, Mikka felt that familiar fear of the unknown. He didn't know how the prince would act, nor did he know how he'd be affected by it. He squared his shoulders and puffed out his chest, attempted to make himself look and feel as big as possible. He'd built walls for a reason.

The brig was two levels down. Its ceiling was open and barred to allow natural light and air in. The lowest level was dank and dark. Nic Murray's quarters were down on the lowest level beside the brig, and they reminded Mikka of a casket. It was so cramped and cold, dark and dreary. He supposed the man was made for it. He was silent, a ghost of a person, hiding behind his own eyes. Lara unlocked the sturdy door, and they entered.

Cornelius had had a laughing fit once Lara left him alone. He couldn't help himself. This was the most fun he'd had. Ever. There were actual stakes. High ones as well. Cornelius had finally relinquished his viola, at last, shuffling it awkwardly out of his arms and nudging it down beside him on the flimsy cot as if it were a friend, for he cared deeply for it. Then, he'd straightened himself up. He'd tried to button his shirt, but he only got halfway up his torso before the irons stunted his range of motion. A large Sleetalian man appeared in the doorway wearing a stern expression, stubble dotting his cheeks.

"You must be Mikka. My name is Cornelius, not Gale, and I must congratulate you on my capture. Very subtle, very silent. In fact, I think this is the best sleep I've had in years." As soon as Cornelius finished his pleasantries, he felt the cold press of metal against his lips. A silver pistol glinted in the moonlight. Cornelius could taste the death and on it. He knew they wouldn't kill him, and he was calm from his fit of laughter, so he did the unimaginable. Cornelius kissed the barrel like he would a maiden's hand, all while staring up at Mikka. "Truly the kiss of death," he whispered, smiling listlessly up at the man.

"Be silent," Mikka commanded, a harsh accent hovering over his Marzinian. He took a step back, staring at the prince.

"Only for you," he said in classical tutor-taught Sleetalian. His sickly-sweet tone made Mikka's eyes widen. He felt as if the prince were mocking him, and he would never stand for that. Mikka punched him square in the eye with all his might. Lara winced, closing her eyes tightly in the corner. The prince, to his credit, was silent. But he did smile lazily. And the smile said all the words he didn't. If he could manipulate the pack's leader, he could manage the rest of these mongrels.

"I told you to be silent," Mikka whispered in a deadly monotone.

"I was merely acknowledging your request. You've known me for mere moments, and you've already smacked me. How violent, how vile. I thought you, of all people, would have more sophistication, Mikka. After all, you did infiltrate the palace compound." Cornelius' words were poison. The sound of his own name being spoken by the Marzinian angered Mikka further, but he turned his back. He didn't want trouble, in all truth. He didn't want another mission of danger. He, like Lara, wanted to do some nice sightseeing for a boat-load of gold coins. So the man removed himself from the room. He left and trudged up to the upper deck of *The Vault of Heaven* and fired a few whittled-down raska bottle corks into the open sea from his pistol, the wind wrapping itself around him.

It woke everyone. One by one, the crew introduced themselves to Cornelius. Only Nic Murray and Rodrigo Reyes didn't end up slapping him. And when he was alone again, Cornelius drowsed fitfully, his viola again in his embrace. This would be fun.

CHAPTER 4

It seemed as if Cornelius had only dozed off for only a second when he woke to see Nic Murray, the russet-haired man he'd met earlier in the night. He couldn't really call it a meeting, though. There wasn't really an exchange of words, per se. Cornelius had introduced himself as amiably as he could, but the effect of his smile was tainted with the new mark on his eye. A bluish-red bruise had risen around it in the shape of a crescent. Despite his best efforts, Nic Murray had only nodded back at him, his hands buried deep in the pockets of his long leather coat. He only knew the mariner's name because of Pia Reyes, who came before Nic Murray. She'd given him the man's name because she knew he wouldn't tell Cornelius himself.

"Good morning. I met you earlier," he greeted him, straightening his posture. He glanced around quickly to see if they'd taken his viola while he was dozing, but it was still right beside him where he'd left it. How he'd slept, he didn't know. He felt groggy, the same headache from before blaring. The tall Orenian leaned against the grey-blue wall on the opposite side of the brig, observing Cornelius with a sage eye.

Murray had been just beyond the brig's door when Mikka hit the prince. The sharpshooter angered easily, but not that easily. Obviously, the Siren Prince wasn't one to trifle with, but Murray wasn't planning on trifling with him. In truth, he could care less. He'd rather be on the bridge standing behind the wheel, the wind in his hair, his eyes on the sea. This mission was beyond him.

After hitting Cornelius, Mikka ordered Murray not to

indulge the prince in conversation. Nic Murray wouldn't have done so for the world. He was content just to stare. He could tell a lot about a man by the way he carried himself. Words weren't needed to learn about those around him. But Cornelius spoke without being prompted, and his tone of voice was like that of a merchant. He was trying to sell himself with every lilting word.

"You're Nic Murray. Pia Reyes spoke to me before you. She gave me your name." Murray was in all manners stoic. He didn't give Cornelius so much as a nod or a raised brow. To Cornelius, this was a new challenge. How does one get a rise out of a statue? Impossible, right? No, only improbable. He remembered with wariness the brush with Mikka. Nic Murray didn't strike him as one to give beatings, even if his victim was cuffed, but Cornelius would still be cautious.

He leaned his head against his viola case and looked up through the ceiling bars. Stars winked in and out of existence as dawn broke over their heads. The penumbra that consumed the room was gone, and the whole of the man was revealed to him. His hair was darker than one would expect from an Orenian, and he looked like a metallic statue that had been tarnished over time. Fitting for his demeanor. Even his eyes were grey, steely, again like a statue's. Cornelius, not one to hold his tongue, voiced his thoughts.

"You look like a statue," he murmured in a tone he tried to make veiled. Cornelius hated being overlooked. He leaned closer to his instrument. "A handsome one, to be exact," he joined, the implication of flirtation hidden between his words. He found the thread he was going to follow. "I can see how much time and intention the artist put into every line in your face, every nuance of your stoic eyes. I can see how he labored over you, how much he cared for you. It probably took his mind when you actually got up and walked away."

Nic Murray went rigid. The improbable had been done.

Cornelius had gotten a rise out of a statue.

Nic Murray's heart soared into a state of palpitations. Murray and Cornelius were different individuals with different ways of being. He favored being alone, ignored, forgotten. Cornelius was contrary to his everything. As he stared at the pleased-by-himself Cornelius, he felt so evident that he only wanted to flee, to escape up to the ship's bridge to stare at the sea. The sea was ever-changing, and that change was the one thing he could rely on.

Murray had never been called handsome before, not in that way. He had never been called a work of art, never had anyone mention his eyes. He'd never been told he was to be longed for, never told he'd taken someone's sanity. This is what Mikka, Pia, and Lara had warned him of. This was what poor Rodrigo had liked about the prince. It was... intriguing... and repulsing. The silence in the brig was stony.

Cornelius wasn't a flirt. He had standards. He wouldn't say the things he did to just anyone. And, perhaps he could gain an ally this way. Cornelius was about to add to his previous remark, but Murray began to unchain him before he had the chance. Wow, his words had never worked *that* quickly. He wasn't complaining, though. He allowed a complacent smile onto his face. It disappeared when he realized he was being dragged out of the brig with a detachable chain, used to hang Marzinian prisoners by their wrists when the Sleetalians lay siege on the coast. His feathers were ruffled by the thought.

Before he was too far away from the flimsy cot, he slipped his chained arms around his viola. He didn't want them to take it from him. There wasn't exactly a lot he had on a ship going God knows where with Lord knows who.

He was led out into the main corridor for the first time, his legs a bit wobbly from sitting for so long. From what he saw, the ship was definitely a triple-level and Sleetalian, as he'd surmised. The metal plates bordering each wall, the dark color of the panels, and the irons at his wrists proved its heritage. It was indeed the ship he'd seen while tending to his betrothed and family. It was an astonishingly tiny ship, but not inconspicuous in the slightest. It would be noticed at any port, and the King's Guard would be alerted. His kidnappers weren't only enemies of the empire; they were idiots. But then he recalled his own train of thought. It was too conspicuous to be noticed, he realized. He'd thought it was a captured rebellion ship, too outlandish to be anything else. They were either idiots with tremendous luck or highly intelligent. When he considered the circumstances of his capture, he knew they were the latter.

Cornelius' pace had slowed, but Nic Murray didn't mind trudging a bit. The sentinel didn't want to face Mikka or anyone else. He was far too flustered by Cornelius.

After the dismal saunter through the ship's underbelly, they ascended a metal stairway to the first level. There were portholes on this level, and Cornelius could see the churning turquoise waves beyond the glass. Nic Murray looked as well, a fondness in his eyes Cornelius couldn't put into words.

The galley was… cozy. That was the kindest thing anyone could say about it. The walls were paneled with the same wood and metal as the corridors and quarters. There was a small stove and two bolted-down metal tables: one for cooking and supping. An array of sharpened knives hung on the far wall. Cornelius had a sneaking suspicion that those knives weren't used for the delicate art of chopping vegetables. The room was as antiquated and obsolete as the map that hung beside the single porthole. The nations were separate instead of conjoined as they were currently, vivid colors displaying their distinction. Cornelius stared at the map. He agreed the countries should keep their cultures, but they shouldn't be divided. Sleetal was now Marzinian Sleetal. Embera was now Marzinian Embera. The continent was one nation with a variety of cultures as it should be. At least, that's what everyone he knew said.

Rodrigo Reyes, the sweet-hearted boy he'd met before, stood beside the stove, a pot of something boiling with blue flames licking its sides. He had a pretty smile. He hadn't seen the other crew members smile yet. Only Rodrigo and Rodrigo was smiling at him. He nervously smiled back.

Rodrigo was cooking spice soup for his fellows, various vegetables boiling in the pot. He'd chopped them meticulously with the knife set that hung on the far wall, which was indeed used for chopping vegetables. Some of the broth had stained his shirt, but he didn't mind. The color had already faded from many years out on his family's farmland with Pia. He would scrub it out later when he did the week's laundry.

Murray looked miserable, dredging forward step by step, and Cornelius looked... pleased. One would think it would be the other way around.

Then, unfortunately, Rodrigo looked closer. He could see the fear plain as day beneath the smile. He held an instrument near to his chest in the same manner a child holds a stuffed bear. Rodrigo's only fault was his undying kindness. He could never hate another person, even if he was the crown prince of the nation that had made so many suffer. He felt for the Siren Prince. Cornelius saw the unwavering goodness in Rodrigo's eyes when he turned to look at them. Cornelius saw an opportunity. Oh, he was having so much fun. He would be near gleeful by the time someone bothered to explain his kidnapping to him.

Murray bent down and wrapped the chain around one of the table's legs, locking it tightly like Mikka had instructed. Mikka and Pia entered the room, both as miserable as Murray. Rodrigo began pouring his spice soup into small bowls he'd brought from home. He was the only one who seemed less than pained. Cornelius' smile had faded. Even the hired mariners, Mannon, Tolmas, and Joan, looked worn. He now wore a glare. He had nothing against the others, only Mikka. Mikka had given him a ring around his eye. He'd pressed his pistol to Cornelius' lips.

Worst of all, he'd tried to silence him. Lara entered last, looking profoundly tired. Her eyes were half-closed, and her arms hung limply at her sides. She'd read up on Marzine's sovereigns until the sun rose, yet she still couldn't comprehend Cornelius.

Rodrigo was the last to sit. He had placed a bowl of spice soup in front of everyone else before finally serving himself. He pulled a chair out before him and straddled it, his arms resting on its back so he could face the group. Mikka and Cornelius were staring at each other with contempt. Large swirling clouds swam over the sea. A storm was brewing, both figuratively and literally.

"Hello again. We made introductions very early this morning," he said curtly, his posture straighter than all others in the room. "By the way, Rodrigo, was it? Thank you for the soup. It smells heavenly, and I'm absolutely famished."

Rodrigo's eyes crinkled at the corners in a warm smile. "Oh, wow. I'm, uh, glad you think so. And thank you. I do all the cooking and cleaning, so if you ever want something to eat, I can—"

Mikka cut his phrase short with a single stare.

"Rodrigo, this isn't the time nor the place for niceties. He's the prince of Marzine. We do not make friends with the prince of Marzine." Rodrigo had no response for him. It was true that the Marzinians had treated Mikka like river bilge, but he didn't need to take up that kind of behavior in return.

"I'm sure he's starving. Please just let him have some soup," Rodrigo said, giving Mikka a pleading glance. Mikka was more impervious than the obsidian wall.

"I'm the one calling the shots. The Marzinian doesn't speak, nor does he eat," Mikka snarled. He swept Cornelius' bowl off the table. Cornelius watched it shatter mournfully. He was as famished as he said he was. He hadn't eaten since the engagement banquet yesterday afternoon.

"Let's just begin," Pia said quietly, placing a hand on Mikka's arm. Pia looked at the Marzinian prince in his unbecoming button-down. His eyes were large and shallow like a reef. His mouth was poised, ready to smile when given the barest sliver of a reason to. She felt the same sort of pity that Rodrigo did, the same kind of conviction as well. There was only one difference; she knew whose side she was on.

Mikka seated himself with a barbaric grunt, his hands curled into fists. Cornelius observed them mutely, and obviously to him, not so obviously to them, they were madly in love with each other.

"Lara," Mikka spoke through gritted teeth, "could you brief the hostage now?" Lara looked up, her eyes shadowed but eager. She stood, moving to stand before the knife-adorned wall. Everyone, save Mikka, turned their attention to her. He already knew what she was going to say, so he stormed out of the room as he had the last time he'd spoken to Cornelius. This time, he shot more corks into the ocean than he ever had. This time, his *raska* bottle would be drained. As soon as he left, Rodrigo moved to the stove to get another bowl for Cornelius. He ladled a more generous helping this time, for he felt bad that the first portion had gone to waste.

"Alright," Lara spoke in Marzinian. "We'll discuss our course later. The captive is not to be trusted yet." Her voice was cold. Cornelius felt fear flood him as he heard the word "captive" again. It was painfully evident that he was a captive, but the word inspired a fear that he couldn't abate. The prince took a precarious sip of the spice soup, cradling the bowl with awkwardly cupped hands. Flavors burned his nostrils as he savored the soup. He nodded at Rodrigo, a smile spreading across his face.

"Cornelius, Prince of Marzine," she said, addressing him.

"Lara, Lily of the Valley." It was an aged term but a significant part of his vernacular. He found that ladies preferred when he used older terms of endearment. The moniker "love" towered over aged terms, but Lara didn't seem to be the kind to appreciate that while acquaintances. She scowled at him, her eyes narrowing. But then she shook her head and sighed, choosing not to indulge his childishness. And he admitted it; he was childish. But he was also on a ship he didn't know the name of being held captive by fellow teenagers. They were all childish. This was childish. If things could be solved less childishly, princes wouldn't have to be kidnapped. Wars wouldn't be lost or won.

"Once we know you can be trusted, you'll stay with Rodrigo in his quarters. The king wants you alive and unharmed. We'll care for you as long as you're compliant."

Cornelius felt like a zoo animal or a trading chip. He was exactly that to them, but his fear still felt far-flung, vague. He finished his spice soup hurriedly after that.

"You will not harm or kill anyone aboard the ship, even if they first harm you. You will not speak unless spoken to." Cornelius felt his heart beating in his fingertips, his pulse livid. His tongue was his greatest attribute.

"You will not engage in conversation with anyone at the ports we stop at."

Cornelius felt as if hot wax was dribbling down his face, sealing his lips shut.

"You will not attempt to escape or signal the Marzinian authorities. If you break any of these rules, there will be consequences."

"How will you know when to trust me?" he asked while he still could.

"When you lose it for the first time," Nic Murray said in an odd, high-pitched tone. His words resounded through the room. Everyone, even the hired mariners, whirled around to stare at him. Cornelius had a sneaking suspicion that his crew members had never heard him speak before. But why was he speaking now of all times? That, it seemed, was a popular question. Lara's eyes blazed.

"Murray…" she said with perverted curiosity.

"A normal person would have panicked by now," Murray spoke a bit louder, his voice surprisingly high for his stature. Lara had never heard him speak.

When no one replied to him, Murray spoke again. "He thinks he can find a way out of this in which his father won't lose any coin. He'd be narcissistic in thinking that if he weren't as charming as he is. And, if you all haven't noticed, he's having fun," he finished, folding his hands together resolutely. "Just think, he's flirted with each and every one of us, but not out of attraction. He's just seeing who he can get a rise out of, like a schoolyard bully. He called you Lily of the Valley. He called me a statue; please don't ask. He thanked Rodrigo. And though it saddens me to ask this, who would ever thank Rodrigo? When he first met Pia, he told her that she was as beautiful as the amber-crested mountains of Orenia. He's never even seen them. And the one I found most amusing was when he kissed Mikka's gun." If anyone in the galley wasn't already beside themselves, they were then. For a moment, the quiet burbling of the pot on the stove was the only sound. "And also, didn't anyone bother to check his violin case? I looked while he was asleep. There was a damned knife!" Murray exclaimed spitefully.

"That's to sharpen pencils! And it's a viola, thank you very much!" Cornelius said. As Murray turned to look at him, Cornelius felt something eerily familiar. He feared looking into his metallic eyes. Nic Murray knew him better than his own mother did. Nic Murray knew his name and his game. Nic Murray was just like his father.

"Oh joy, he's panicking," Murray said in perfect monotone. "Remarkable timing. A storm's brewing and he'd be soaked to the bone in that rotten brig. That fancy little button-down wouldn't help him much either." No. It couldn't be. Murray wasn't like his father. He didn't have those eyes. Murray didn't... He couldn't...

"He's gone all quiet," Rodrigo said, kneeling beside the prince.

"He's panicking," Nic Murray said simply, a shadow crossing over his eyes

"You were right, Murray," Lara murmured as she strode closer, scrutinizing the prince like a test subject. Cornelius looked up at them all, his gaze jumping over Nic Murray. He needed to escape. He would submit to any terms so long as Murray stopped staring at him.

"Alright," he conceded, his tone so subdued that Rodrigo had to lean in to hear him.

"He's panicked. Now we can trust he'll only break the speaking rule because there's no way he's following that. And... and I think I've thoroughly frightened him. He's scared of me. So if he ever does break any other rules, I can just... just speak again." Nic Murray said, voicing his thoughts for the benefit of the group. His throat felt raw.

"Nic, I don't think I've ever heard you speak before," Rodrigo said with bemusement.

"Please call me Murray. I just don't like you enough to let you call me by my first name," he said, letting a sigh seep through his lips.

They led a silent Cornelius to Rodrigo's quarters. It wasn't the most luxurious room. It was used as a storage area for crates of salted cod and mead kegs, just in the off chance that they got marooned on an island and wanted to drink themselves to death. The room consisted of a cot for Rodrigo, a colorful woven blanket hanging neatly over it. He also had a bolted-down nightstand, a lantern balanced atop it. A worn copy of the holy book sat beside it and a mat for his knees while praying. He kept his things rather neat, for there weren't many of them. Even his clothing was tidy. His shirts hung from rusted hooks beneath a shelf on which his trousers were folded. On the other half of the spartan room, crates and kegs were piled. The porthole obscured behind them. A mattress had been placed on top of two larger boxes for Cornelius to sleep on. And from the looks of it, he wouldn't be sleeping for the next however long they decided to keep him.

Cornelius seated himself on the mattress, his viola clutched to his chest as it always was. Rodrigo unlocked his chains and gave him a concerned look. Cornelius only stared at the peeling wall, his bunkmate shuffling around, rearranging his meager belongings to accommodate the prince. Rodrigo even gave two of his own shirts and a pair of his trousers to Cornelius, laying them over his shoulders like a clothing rack. All the scattered Cornelius could do was accept the cook's charity, his senses slowly coming back to him.

As the morning dragged onward, Cornelius slowly realized that he wasn't safe, that this wasn't just some child's game. He *was* a captive, a trading chip, a zoo animal. He was among enemies instead of possible allies. Worst of all, he was being watched. As noon struck, a smile curled the edges of his lips upward, his empty eyes glinting. He would only have to try harder.

CHAPTER 5

Pop… Pop… Pop… While his pistol was intended to shoot bullets, Mikka could just as well load it with whittled-down corks. During their travels aboard *The Vault of Heaven*, the crew had accumulated quite a few stoppers. He was only ridding them of the remains, releasing stress as he did so. The air around him was light and blustery, his close-cropped hair windswept. He wasn't cold in the least, for he had his flask to warm him. Raska was his poison of choice. And because it had grown so popular during the war, it was everyone else's, too.

When Mikka was fourteen, there wasn't anything he wanted less than to be like his father. The man was a bastard with a drink-rounded belly and violent tendencies. His hair was greasy, and his hairline had receded well back on his scalp. The man reminded him of an angry bull. Mikka's own hair had been long the last time he'd seen his father. It was a Sleetalian custom for young men to grow out their curls until they joined the army or killed their first fellow man. The two were interchangeable. He had worn it in a long, gleaming braid. He was proud of it, for every boy was proud of their braid. Young Sleetalian men were required to join the army upon their sixteenth year, but then the continental war began. At first, nothing changed. The other four nations believed the Marzinian court insane. Marzine had waged war on every other country without rhyme or reason. When Embera fell, the other three nations got antsy. When Wilkinia fell, the required age was lowered. Then every young man fourteen and older had to join the army. Mikka's braid was shorn off whether he wanted it to be or not. In fact, his father had to hold him down while the barber chopped it.

Pop… Mikka shot another cork, a pocket knife in his free hand to alter corks with. When he was drafted, he'd been stripped of belongings, for the youngest were sent to the front lines. It was unspoken, but everyone knew they weren't going to live. Marzinian might grew, and war tension in Orenia spread to Sleetal. Mikka was given his soldier's greatcoat. It smelled metallic, but all the bloodstains had long since been bleached and dyed away. It had been taken from a fallen soldier and sewn back together, for Sleetal's coffers were all but exhausted. Donning the garb gave him a feeling of foreboding. He felt as if he would have the same fate as the one who wore it before him, to die on the stygian-sanded beaches of Sleetal during a Marzinian raid. He felt naked in the uniform, altered like the corks in his pistol. His youth had been taken from him, and he would be exposed to war before it was right to be.

In basic training, he'd gained his first skill. The martinet taught him how to shoot, put a second-hand rifle in his hands, and bloodlust in his soul. He didn't need much drilling, in truth. He was immediately skilled, his fingers moving deftly against the metal as he fired. He could reload faster than any of his peers, and for that reason, they had him train to be a sharpshooter. He and the few friends he had were brought to another fort. He again surpassed his peers and earned a higher position in the game of war. He was a rook. If one let their focus waver for only a moment, Mikka's bullet would strike them down.

There were times of guilt, too. Times when he huddled behind a bluff and held himself, weeping. The tears would freeze on his eyelashes, freeze his eyes shut. But he would still hit his mark. Every. Damned. Time. Those days were cold, and it was as if the blood in his veins had frozen, his heart motionless. As summer came, his guilt melted away. He found comrades. He poked fun at the Marzinian sirens who had fallen in his wake. And, if the blame did happen to freeze him again, he melted it away with raska. During the winter, he was given a flask by a nameless soldier. And though Mikka hadn't wanted to believe it at first, the man had offed himself the next day. It was an unwritten law to pass one's flask on to another soldier when deciding to quit drinking or end one's own life. For the man who'd given Mikka his flask, it was, unfortunately, the latter.

Pop...Pop...Pop... **Pop**... He closed his eyes, reloading with a sigh. He could still see them behind his eyelids. He saw the face of a young boy, horror deep in his blue eyes, the same horror Mikka had felt at the sight of those blue eyes. They were the same age, fifteen by that time. And then he was gone, another Marzinian soldier lost to the war. They called those lost in the war the "deficit."

A consequence of gaining power. It was a cruel title. The godforsaken "deficit" of all things, like an amount someone owes!

There was also an older man. He was a Marzinian soldier as well, made to fight despite his age. He was dying from a bayonet stab wound, blood seeping through his faded uniform. His eyes were glazed over with pain. Mikka had helped that man, make no mistake. He would've died in far more agony if it weren't for Mikka. There were many others he saw too. But the young boy and the old man were the closest to his heart, the faces he always saw when he closed his eyes. The raska blurred their faces. The raska melted the guilt, made him warm.

Pop... Two years he'd spent in the Sleetalian army, one of those spent drinking raska and killing only for the sake of killing. Those were the darkest times, and it certainly didn't help that the Siren Prince of Marzine was the uncanny image of the young boy he'd shot. Now seeing the phantom that had plagued him since his fifteenth year, he was furious. His liver would pay dearly for the following months, for he would consume unholy amounts of raska to numb himself, keep him from killing the young boy all over again. Yes, that's what he'd do. The gold he would get in the end would outweigh his sorrows. Then he could buy himself a new liver.

Pop… But he could only really hope it would outweigh his sorrows. He didn't know if it indeed would. He untucked a handkerchief from his pocket and cleaned the barrel of his gun, the cloth gliding smoothly over the metal.

"You'll never believe it, Mikka!" Pia exclaimed, the corridor door slamming loudly in her wake. She strode across the deck and climbed the step ladder to the deck the crew had named "Mikka's shooting deck." She was grinning broadly, her eyes warm with amusement. Mikka turned, hooking the pistol on his belt.

"What is it? Everything alright?" he asked her, eyes still clouded with memories. Her smile only grew wider as she joined him on the deck. It lit up the deck more than the sun ever would. Mikka blushed. Not from the cold. Not from the raska.

"It's better than alright. Nic Murray *spoke*." For a moment, all that could be heard was the constant seething of the waves, a sea bird's cry here and there. Mikka was almost startled silent.

"Very funny," he said sharply. There was no chance in hell Murray had spoken. The sentinel had been mute as long as he'd known him.

"I swear on my life. And he just said all these things about the Marzinian, and the Marzinian just lost it. Caved in on himself or something." Pia chuckled.

With that, Mikka's eyebrow arched. His hands dropped from his hips, the clouds above casting a shadow over his face.

"No joke?" he asked suspiciously.

She nodded.

"Are you and I thinking of the same Nic Murray?" Mikka's voice was almost accusatory, and Pia took a step back, her smile still just as zealous.

"Yes, the same Nic Murray. He just opened his mouth and boom! Words!" Pia's own words were hurried and a bit jumbled. This was how she got when she was worked up. Mikka felt a smile tugging at the corners of his lips.

"Unbelievable. So that odd little man got to him more than my pistol could. A testament to how much we don't know about those goddamn sirens," Mikka said speculatively.

"Oh, stop it with that crap. Cornelius is just all-around strange. After all, an average hostage would be pleading for their life, not betting on it."

Mikka crossed his arms, his muscles bulging under a loose-fitting sweater. The clouds had joined together into a veil above their heads, the sky overcast.

"We should go in before we're drenched." His chapped lips cracked into a smile. They descended the ladder and strode by the hired mariners, who were tending to the mast before it rained. Mikka held the door open for Pia, who, in return, punched him in the stomach. He doubled over, still smiling. Her laughter echoed down the undisturbed hall. He hoped the others could hear it. He'd made her laugh, and he wanted everyone to know it.

They decided on having the leftover spice soup made by Rodrigo. Mikka didn't make the mistake of holding the door for Pia as they entered the galley. She instead held it for him. The worst he could give her was a sarcastic "thanks" and a smile. His grin dropped as his eyes swept the room. The bowls from earlier were left strewn on the table, and the shards from his little outburst were still on the floor.

"You would think Rodrigo would've cleaned this up by now. He's already taken on the other chores," Mikka said sourly.

"He's trying, Mikka. Rodrigo already does so much for us. Besides, he has to quarter with a Marzinian." Pia bit her lip. If any other person picked on her brother like he did, they would earn a hard punch to the teeth. It was Mikka, though. In some ways, Mikka was closer to her than her brother. She'd known him since her regiment went to the Southern Islands of Sleetal to help fend off the sirens. Rodrigo had stayed at home in Embera instead of joining her. And in addition to their service together, she and Mikka had worked as a duo for a year following the war's end. They knew each other's ins and outs. They never spoke of the wartimes, but their experiences were shared. Again, Rodrigo had stayed in Embera. He didn't know half of what the soldiers went through. He didn't know the constant, gnawing fear.

"He only came along because of you. He has no real purpose other than to cling to your shirtsleeves," Mikka told her, interrupting her thought.

She dished out the remaining spice soup while Mikka kicked at the shards, his gaze disinterested.

Mikka stacked the bowls and crammed them to the edge of the table as Pia seated herself. She slid a bowl across the metal to Mikka, and they drank their soup in silence. It was always quiet after they spoke of Rodrigo.

"He cleans. The ship would be a swamp without him," Mikka remarked as he noticed the frown that had stubbornly taken root on Pia's face.

"He came as a cabin boy," Pia huffed. Mikka glowered at the soup.

"But this isn't some pleasure boat. And what even is a cabin boy anyway?" he asked skeptically. Both of them chuckled. Mikka took a long sip of soup, savoring the warmth. He wiped his mouth on his sleeve.

"An imaginary title I made up for him so he could feel helpful," Pia conceded with a shameless smile.

"Why did you let him come? He's only a hindrance." Again she glared, drinking heavily from the bowl so she wouldn't have to answer.

"He's not a hindrance..." she said softly. "I let him come

because... because he cried." It pained her to say it. "He cried the night I set out for Wilkinia to meet Shadrach."

Mikka raised an eyebrow but held his tongue. He didn't want to fluster Pia again. She could harbor a nasty grudge.

"I was going off on another 'suicide mission.' He told me I was selfish for putting myself in danger, for not staying at home where I could do nothing to help. He told me he was sick of sitting by the door late at night waiting for me to return." Pia shook her head at the thought, glancing out the window at the swirling clouds. "He's never once been angry at me like that, and it... it disturbed me. I would've done anything to get him to stop crying."

Mikka stared at her with condescension. Why would she care? If he was able-bodied and didn't fight for his country, she should disregard him, not drag him along with her.

Pia looked up and met his judgment, a flicker of regret in her eyes.

"Anyway, when will we reach Orenia? I wanna get myself one of those Orenian talismans for good luck or something. Gives me something to look forward to, you know?" Her rapid change of subject was heeded, but Mikka thought it best to lay the topic of Rodrigo to rest for the time being. He wasn't good with... sensitivities. And though the ideas he was raised with were now called "antiquated," he thought they worked just as well as any other philosophies.

"Murray's navigation charts say two or three days. Since when were you superstitious?" he asked. Pia, in return, gave an equally half-hearted laugh. No more was said between them.

Soon, Pia was quietly washing the disarrayed dishes so her brother wouldn't get grief from Mikka later on. Mikka had simply left, not knowing what to make of the conversation. He'd exhausted their cork supply, so he had nothing better to do than return to his quarters and sift through the pages of *The Tale of Alexander*, trying to find something profound and bright among the other dreary phrases. It was like searching for a needle in a haystack.

In the quarters beside Mikka's, Cornelius was waking from his panic. "And that's why my mother uses hair clips instead of knotting her hair," Rodrigo finished, plopping down on his cot. He wore a broad smile and seemed rather pleased with himself. It was unfortunate Cornelius had missed the entire story. He certainly wanted to hear why Rodrigo's mother used hair clips instead of knotting her hair. Murray's eyes were still blazing in the back of his mind. Needless to say, he'd been distracted.

"Rodrigo," he said suddenly. Rodrigo looked over brightly. "I would like to thank you for taking me into your quarters." He eyed the room with veiled disdain, his lips turned upward in a smile. Rodrigo could easily see through the glamor, but he knew where Cornelius was used to living. He would be put off in the same way if he was suddenly made to sleep in a palace.

"It's my pleasure," he replied. Rodrigo hadn't expected someone his sister had kidnapped to be thanking him, but Cornelius seemed like an unconventional man. Only moments ago, he'd been a husk of what Rodrigo had seen before. But now, he was as charming as ever, his silver tongue fabricating lie after lie behind his lips. He was charismatic to a fault, but he could get whatever he wanted from his talent, and Rodrigo was a willing target. No one he knew would simply thank him as Cornelius did. Nobody would smile at him as Cornelius did. Nobody at all seemed to like him. So, who cared if it was only a fabrication? It couldn't hurt to give the prince what he wanted, an ally, as long as he got what he wanted. The deal was made without words.

"If I could be so bold as to ask, why are you here? You don't seem like the lawless type." Cornelius asked after a long pause, his eyes meeting Rodrigo's. Rodrigo began toying with one of his shirt buttons. If he tugged any harder, the button would pop off, and he would have to sew it back on.

"We're not lawless," he said unobtrusively. And he was right for the most part. They were revolutionaries. Shadrach, leader of the Masked Birds, had been the king of Sleetal before his nation's surrender. See, the Masked Birds weren't really a resistance group; they were a kingdom of people pledged to the Shadrach of Sleetal. They would do everything in their power to put him back on the throne. So yes, the Sleetalian King had sent a scruffy group of vagabonds to take the Marzinian prince hostage and hold him for ransom. He was using his enemy to fuel his own cause, and it was ingenious. He would've sent proper soldiers to do the job, but they were either in prison or six feet under, three feet under if Marzinians had buried them.

"Not lawless? Well then, I must be on a luxurious riverboat drifting down the Sirensea Straits with a fruity drink in my hand, not a captive on the filthiest rustbucket sailing the seven seas." Rodrigo laughed warmly.

"How dare we deprive you of your fruity drinks? You know what, maybe we are lawless. But they don't like me very much. I don't think I'm part of the 'we,'" he admitted with a small smile.

"That makes sense. It's just hard to believe that if I ran right now, you would try to stop me," Cornelius said reasonably, sizing up Rodrigo's smaller stature.

"But where would you go? We're on a tiny little ship in the middle of a brewing storm. You'd die before you saw land," Rodrigo said, eyes glinting with an iniquity Cornelius hadn't yet detected.

"See, that's what I was looking for. You do have some darkness in you, sunshine."

"You seem to have enough for the both of us, jaded prince." Rodrigo laughed.

"You can believe anything about me you'd like. Your only job is to keep me alive long enough to glean some gold from your sister. I mean, you're a hardened criminal after all. So lawless that it makes me cower in terror." Even he couldn't make it sound convincing. Rodrigo was just... soft.

"Well, I'm tired. I'm going to get some sleep," Rodrigo said, a warm feeling settling in his chest. Cornelius heaved a crate to the side and peered out the porthole.

"It's only late afternoon," Cornelius said, gesturing toward the gap he'd made.

"I wake up early to clean and such," Rodrigo told the prince, wrapping himself with his blankets. "Try not to off me in my sleep. Your other captors will have your head," he said with a faltered yawn. Cornelius was unchained now. He could hurt Rodrigo if he really tried, but he didn't want to find out what Mikka's punishment would be, not that they would kill him. The prince swept a hand across his bruised eye, the skin still raised and painful. He'd already made an ally and an enemy. He thought of the sad cook who lay in the cot opposite his own. All Rodrigo wanted was affection. If that was his wish, Cornelius would grant it. Then, he would take his leave. Never see the soft little soup-pusher again. And the eyes of Nic Murray, he would gouge them out along with his father's. This was not a game.

Mikka sat alone again. He was out of raska but not desperate enough to tap into their mead store yet. He had one hell of a headache, though. For once, he just wanted his warm nightshirt from home. He was freezing and sore, blisters forming on his blisters from altering so many corks. The sway of the ship had become more violent against the waves, but he knew Murray had it covered. The sentiment didn't help his nausea. He wondered if the prince and Rodrigo had gotten friendly. He wondered if they were plotting against the rest of the group. He wondered if they should've kept him in the brig after all.

Most of all, he wondered if Pia missed him like he missed her. On nights like this one, when they were both inevitably restless, they would sit in the galley. Even if they didn't speak to one another, they weren't so alone. Her presence nullified his fears, and he needed that more than ever now. He thought the hard part would be over once they'd taken Cornelius, but it was only just the beginning. The prince was more treacherous than he looked.

CHAPTER 6

S
he could see them in the distance now. A gathering of mountains lay in *The Vault of Heaven's* path. A very prominent gathering. She'd seen countless paintings and sketches, read numerous tales and handwritten journals with ink blotches and misspellings about these peaks. These were the Orenian Barrier Mountains, the most illustrious crags on the continent. The sight of them was one of the only reasons she'd taken the Glorified Tour Guide job when it was offered to her by Shadrach.

For the sake of evading the law, they would have to be in a constant state of displacement. That meant she would get to see four of the five nations, Marzine left out for obvious reasons. It had always been her dream to see the world. Now, she would be paid to do so. All because of Cornelius, her ticket to travel the Earth.

The murkiness lessened as the sun rose higher above the waters. The amber-crested peaks gleamed. The bare surface stones weren't as valuable as those deeper down, but they were still just as dazzling to the onlooker. The local folklore sainted these gems as boons from God to compensate for the peaks' hardships. Lara loved Orenian folklore. Well, she loved all legend. And this place reeked of it. She wished she could share her joy with even one person, but she was alone on *The Vault of Heaven*. Someday, she would have someone to tell her tales to. And if she didn't, perhaps she would immortalize them in journals like sojourners before her.

Then, she felt someone behind her. She turned her head

sharply to stare at him. Nic Murray stood before her, looking vaguely bored. His steely eyes traced the peaks, mapping them out in his mind. After recovering from the initial shock of his presence, she remembered Orenia was his homeland. It must be good to return. She considered asking him about it for a moment but decided it was best to stay silent. She didn't want to disturb him as he stared at the mountainscape. She hadn't wanted to be disturbed.

Nic Murray strode over to her, his height a bit beneath her own. He looked like some sort of odd emaciated ghost at times. Other times, Murray looked like a fierce Orenian warrior. He was constantly disproving and proving himself. He'd been silent for months, and suddenly, he'd decided to speak.

He wore a blue tunic, which looked out of place beside his regular button-down and leather coat pairing. It was a Marzinian soldier's uniform. If they wanted to remain unnoticed on their supply run, they would have to look like a group one wouldn't want to bother, pretend to be a troop of soldiers going on a supply run. Despite their different nationalities, they would be as ordinary as any other troop. All sorts had joined the Marzinian army after the capture of their countries. The act secured the well-being of their families. It also paid well in a time when work was scarce.

"You're here for directions?" Lara asked, finally acknowledging Murray when the amber-crested peaks felt much closer. Lara had researched alcoves and unmarked areas on various maps and charts before they'd departed Wilkinia. She'd choose a covert spot on each nation's mainland when they had to get supplies or meet with Shadrach. Nic Murray nodded. His eyes swept the scene before them yet again, but this time Lara saw something different. Was it a trace of remorse? Sorrow? Whatever it was, it gave Murray's eyes the most melancholy tinge.

"Alright, so steer the *Vault* due northeast, and you'll see a collection of cliffs in the shape of a..." Lara took a moment to study a chart she had brought from her quarters. "A turtle." she finished, looking at Murray expectantly. He simply nodded as he had the first time and turned back to the doorway he'd entered through. Nic Murray was an enigma. There was already enough to deal with as it was, and Lara didn't care who he was, so long as he played nice.

She soon followed Murray as she felt the ship veer northeast. They would be on Orenian soil soon, and she could hardly contain her excitement. Her wanderlust was running rampant. Before meeting the others on the main deck, she hurried back to the quarters she shared with Pia to collect her bag. She had taken the bottom bunk, her blankets splayed across the yellowed mattress. There were travel journals, scrolls, and large volumes on each nation packed into the room's corners and a metal desk for her studies, leaving hardly any room for Pia. Pia's blankets were tucked in military corners, her pillow neatly at the head of the bed. Lara rushed around the room, collecting her things and wrapping a tattered cloak around herself. It wouldn't be as balmy as it was in Marzine. But wet, yes.

Mikka had made it mandatory to meet on the main deck before going on land. It was compulsory for everyone, save Murray and his three hired mariners, who were doing the work of bringing them to shore. Lara flitted down the cold corridor like a butterfly. She hefted her bag closer to her as she stepped out of the passage and into the wind. None of her scrolls would be ruined by the weather. She would make sure of that.

Mikka was the only one out on the main deck. His eyes were on his boots, dark circles hovering beneath them. His head snapped up to look at her, an ever-present glower on his face. That glower only ever lessened when he looked at Pia. He was desperately in love with her, a surprise to no one.

"You're late," he grumbled. She glanced around at the empty deck. If she was late, then Mikka was the king of Sleetal.

"So are the others, then," she said, motioning to no one beside her.

"Fine." It seemed he'd woken up on the floor, not the wrong side of the bed as he did most days. Pia had mentioned something about a disagreement with Mikka before they fell asleep, which was odd in itself. She was never in their quarters when Lara fell asleep. Pia arrived in the small hours of the morning, waking her with the metal door's creaking.

When she'd first met Pia, she had her own suspicions of where the girl might go, but then she'd gotten to know her better and heard of her nightly routine with Mikka and how close they were. They would go to the galley and just sit. They sat quietly unless Mikka had a bottle of raska from which he could fill his flask. But the night before they arrived in Orenia, Pia had returned before midnight, her feathers having been thoroughly ruffled.

"Hey... so we match," Lara said, trying to lighten the mood.

"Yeah, we all do," he bit back, sullen. Lord, he would have lines in his face by the time he was thirty. She stayed silent after that, allowing a sea bird's call to fill her ears.

Rodrigo led the Siren Prince out of the corridor door by his metal cuffs, looking optimistic as ever. Cornelius was laughing loudly at something Rodrigo had said. It was a hollow, laudatory laugh, a cocktail party laugh. Of course, Rodrigo would consider the enemy a friend, even if the enemy didn't reciprocate his feelings.

Cornelius wore the tattered clothes of a prisoner, but it was more a costume than anything. They were some of Mikka's old clothes. He was a prisoner, but he would be masquerading as one as well. They couldn't leave him to himself on the ship. He would find his way out of his irons and slash the sail. Hell, he'd probably capsize it.

The laughing quieted as they joined the line. Mikka glared down at Cornelius, and the prince exiled the smile from his lips.

He didn't want to be hit again or, worse, shot in a non-fatal area. He wouldn't put it past Mikka. What he did know was that they needed him alive. He wouldn't be injured to the point of death, but there was a lot the human body could endure before dying.

"What do you think, Andrian tuck or full tuck?" Cornelius asked. The silence was unbearable, so suffocating that the prince felt his heart would stop if he didn't say something. He tucked half of his overlarge shirt into his pants. Lara's brows knit while the others, save Mikka, looked on with interest.

"What's an Andrian tuck?" Lara asked finally, giving in. Andria was the place she most wanted to travel to before she died. It was on the mysterious "other continent," after all. If he knew something she didn't, she was obliged to talk to him.

"It's something my betrothed taught me. Isabel is from the other continent, Andria, to be precise. We're engaged to establish a trade route between our continent and the other."

Rodrigo admitted a cough of surprise. God help that poor girl. If she had to marry a man like Cornelius, then her romantic life wouldn't be kind. Exciting maybe, but never kind with Cornelius.

"Betrothed? Andria? That's fascinating," Lara told him truthfully. "Did she tell you lots about the other continent? I've always wanted to know more, but there aren't very many texts on it, at least not in Wilkinia. Let's see… Andria, Walsia, and Hyvern? Those are the obvious ones from *The Tale of Alexander*, but I'm sure there are others." Lara tended to rant when passionate about something.

"Yes, those are the ones. Isabel's traveled to all. And get this, her father is Alexander," he said with a wide smile.

Lara's expression was beyond price. "You're lying! Didn't the man take his own life after his lover died?" she asked.

"No! He took a wife and ruled his kingdom. He's alive and well, at least according to his daughter," Cornelius exclaimed with some conspiracy in his voice. He'd found her weakness:

knowledge. The prince had studied Andria before his betrothed had arrived, so he had some familiarity with the other continent. Little had he known that this familiarity would help him in a hostage situation.

"Quiet down!" Mikka yelled. Cornelius opened his mouth to protest but remembered the purple lump beneath his eye. Lara sighed and returned to her spot in the lineup. She glared at Mikka, readjusting the scrolls and books in her bag. Cornelius went with the Andrian tuck. It was more stylish, and he wouldn't sacrifice any comfort he could offer himself in such a comfortless position.

Pia was last to leave through the corridor door. Her knuckles were wrapped in strips of linen, leather gloves covering over the bandages. The girl lived her life from fight to fight. That was why she'd joined the Masked Birds with Mikka.

The ship had reached the shore, the underbelly rising over the sedimented sands. At sea level, the fog was as subduing as a kick to the gut.

Murray seemed pleased with himself, if only slightly, as he stepped out onto the main deck. Nic Murray's three mariners lowered the gangplank, Mikka leading them down. Each step creaked mournfully. Cornelius suddenly felt ill at ease, as if he were walking through a ghost. Their anchor drop was just a few miles out from Conaire, a misty port town. They would stop in Conaire and get their supplies, and for Mikka, more raska.

Lara could only see a step ahead of her, her boots getting wedged between stones frequently. She led the group, their glorified tour guide, forever and always. She gripped a lantern tightly in the crook of the arm that wasn't clutching her bag.

Murray walked at the end of the line holding a similar lantern. He was undaunted by the fog. Being brought up in Orenia had familiarized him with the gloom.

Lara knew of a path that wound through the crags. It had a name, some long, complicated string of words in Orenian.

Murchadh Mac Niadh, if she recalled it correctly. There were only a few wood planks here and there to allow travelers a better range of passage. It was better than a vertical climb, she supposed. They ended up clutching the back of each other's tunics to stay together. Rodrigo couldn't keep up with Cornelius. He was breathless in the first moments. After a few well-worded complaints from the prince, Rodrigo unchained him and let him walk ten steps ahead.

Their pace was harsh as the crumbling pathway began to rise. At times, Lara feared they were off course. She had to consult the map every few minutes to assure herself. Each plank of wood was too spaced out, and it was difficult to keep her composure. There was a thrill to it, however. It made her want to abandon her maps and charts entirely and just roam through the haunted mountains, conversing with only spirits and wild things forever and ever. She filled her lungs with misty air and continued forward.

The higher they climbed, the more visibility they gained. The sun began to break through the gloom, and Cornelius could see the back of Pia's neck for the first time. There were other aspects of the journey that became more precarious, though. The trail was only a ledge on the face of a cliff now. It hadn't been trodden in many years, so rock and precious stones crumbled off the side at their heavy step. One time, Lara felt a painful twinge in her heel. A particularly pointed gem had nearly broken through the sole of her boot. She sighed and kicked it off the edge. A splash sounded below.

It had been an hour of walking. Cornelius was beginning to wonder if they planned to kill and eat him at the mountain's summit, hopefully in that order. He knew they were in Orenia. He'd made Rodrigo tell him. What could he say? He was curious. And Rodrigo was just so simpleminded. He'd learned much about Rodrigo in the two days he'd stayed in his quarters, if one could even call them that. Rodrigo was achingly kind and trusting to a fault. And despite both of those traits, nobody cared for him. Not even his own sister. Cornelius wasn't sure Rodrigo's parents had even loved him with the amount of people-pleasing the boy did. Well, to be fair, he wasn't sure if anyone loved anyone after the war. It had brought out the worst in people, put demons in display cases. Brothers turned against brothers. Nations rose and fell. Rodrigo loved to help others, losing himself as he did so. There was no place for such a person in war.

Finally, after all of them had abandoned hope of ever reaching Conaire, their descent began. They sank back into the fog, but this time they did so enthusiastically. Maybe if Mikka was in a better mood, they could get a hot meal and some tea while in town. Rodrigo had packed soup for the journey back, if not. At least, he hoped they would drink it on the trip back. He'd offered it to them many times that day. Nobody had wanted it, although Cornelius had thanked him for taking the time to prepare it. The prince was sick of Rodrigo's soups. Slow-roasted Orenian lamb crusted in herbs was what he hungered for. His mouth watered at the thought.

They began to make out shapes in the distance, profiles of a town. Lara almost whooped for joy, but then she remembered herself. She was playing the role of a soldier. A grim, war-hardened soldier. She plastered a Mikka-like frown on her face and hunched over. Mikka pulled a jar of muck from his sack, dregs of coffee grounds, and charcoal from his lantern. He held Cornelius firm while Murray rubbed it on his face. It would hide his identity and make him look more prisoner-like. Cornelius remained silent as Murray worked, his whole body stiff with fear.

"It'll be alright," Rodrigo whispered. He was so strange to Cornelius, someone who wasn't kind without some sort of endgame in mind.

It was brighter in Conaire's lantern-lit glow. There were

many wooden posts from which lanterns hung, illuminating the worn path. Conaire was as bustling and lively as any port town, trades and bargains happening at every street end despite the foul weather. All the houses were dilapidated. No repairs had been made since the war's end. Orenia had been last to surrender, so they had the highest military presence and the highest taxes. Patrols of Marzinian soldiers walked the streets just as they did, a prisoner or two in tow. They weren't as noticeable they'd expected. Cornelius was back in chains and led by none other than Nic Murray. He felt the cold, judicious presence of Murray's eyes on his neck. Only days ago, the prince had flirted without personal reproach. Now, he was as fearful of Nic Murray as he was his father.

Cornelius watched the bustling crowd more closely to distract himself from the chains around his wrists. He saw the dark shadows beneath their eyes, saw how frail and tired everyone looked, how grey they seemed. And most of all, he noticed how the Marzinian troops treated them with an utter lack of respect, beating whomever they thought was out of line. This wasn't... this couldn't be Marzine's doing. He heard the cries of a child, and he closed his eyes. He was painfully aware of how Murray's grip traveled to his wrist. He had to escape, he had to get away right then. What if he burned too when the world went up in flames?

He heard two soldiers speaking in hushed Orenian. "The prince of Marzine was kidnapped. Some bloke scaled the obsidian wall for the Masked Birds. A message was sent from the Raven King demanding ransom money."

"Got what was coming for him, I'd say. I'm not one for politics, but the king cut our salary again. Maybe if my purse was a bit heavier, I'd be inclined to look for the little bastard.",

A flicker of hope blazed in his chest. It was a wild thought, a frenzied attempt following close behind. He was desperate, desperate to get Nic Murray away from him.

"I'm him! I'm the prince of Marzine!" Cornelius yelled, flailing against his restraints. Nic Murray clapped a hand over his mouth and pulled him back into an alleyway before the two soldiers could look over. After a moment, they left to join their troop. Cornelius still struggled though, he fought and fought until Mikka and the rest doubled back into the alley, a few suspicious glances received along the way.

"So you choose now to lose your pretense? Now, in the dead center of Conaire?" Lara asked furiously, her Sleetalian halting. Mikka stood there silently for a moment, his eyes ablaze. Then, he kicked Cornelius. The blow was aimed directly in the jaw, the pain nauseating. Cornelius spit blood on Mikka's boots bitterly, giving him an acrimonious stare.

"Back off," Murray said reluctantly. Mikka turned his gaze to Murray. This was the first he'd heard from the man. Ever. Just the fact that he'd had spoken scared him, immobilized him. And… just this once, he decided to listen. He moved away from a groveling Cornelius, nodding indignantly at Murray.

"Fine then, you have to stay with him while we get supplies. He won't try anything with you."

Murray only nodded, shifting back into the shadows. They stood there in a chaotic circle for a moment, Cornelius centerstage like an offering waiting to be burned. Lara was utterly confounded by his behavior. One moment he was confident and at ease, flirting with the godforsaken air, but the next, he became a shadow of what he had been. It was strange, and only Murray seemed to trigger it. Mikka had made the right decision by entrusting the prince with him.

"Well then, we came here for goods and supplies, did we not?" Pia said lamely, staring at the shaking Siren Prince.

Mikka's lips were curved in a frown. She hadn't spoken all day. Why now? And why not to him? He sighed. Mikka knew he would have to apologize to her for his slanders against her brother. He… he needed her. That was all he cared to admit.

Nic Murray let out a sigh of his own. Of course, he was being made to sit miserably in an alleyway and watch some pompous fool cry. There was no use for him on land other than that. Still, this was more interesting than slithering down the streets of Conaire with a group of snakes. He knelt down beside the prince to console him.

"Cornelius... wait... should I address you as a sire or something? No, no, I shouldn't," he murmured to himself. The whole speaking thing wasn't as easy as he'd anticipated. "Cornelius, get up before I make you." Yes, it was definitely better if "sire" wasn't included in that sentence.

Cornelius pulled himself up into a sitting position with the assistance of a crate, rubbing his jaw. He cast a sidelong glare at Murray's boots. He didn't want to be made to do anything but would oblige Murray so long as he wasn't stared at anymore. The sentinel yawned, and Cornelius spit out more blood, worried a tooth had come loose. The last thing he needed was a fragmented smile. The prince stood gingerly, and at his full height, he felt nauseous. Murray caught him as the world tilted left. He was suddenly so cold, so hatefully hard. There were hands on his wrists, his back pressed into Murray's leather coat. He saw long, pale fingertips on his skin.

"Be still. You might fall again, and it's already taken this long to get you up." His words were monotone. It sounded like he was reading from a script.

Murray hauled him to the farthest reaches of the alley, any light obscured either by fog or overlapping roofs. There were more crates back there, more pipes as well. Murray bound Cornelius to a rusted pipe, sitting him on the trunk beside it. He sat beside Cornelius on a crate made of Sleetalian spruce.

"Why?" he asked. The simple word stole the breath right out of Cornelius' lungs. "Why are you afraid of me?" he finished. Cornelius wanted more than anything to remain silent, to shrink into nothingness. But, sadly, he wasn't one to hold his tongue.

"You stare," Cornelius said. He met Murray's gaze, his eyes drowned in fear.

"Elaborate," Murray said.

"I didn't realize it at first, but it's as if you aren't real. You're an actual statue. You watch from the shadows, standing sentinel, always vigilant. I can't stand it, knowing I'm under constant scrutiny."

Murray nodded, a lusterless look on his face. "So I'm inhuman to you?"

Cornelius swallowed and finally met Murray's steely eyes.

"Yes," he whispered. There was a long pause as Murray found his words.

"It's my birthday today. I'm seventeen. Gay, also. Does that make me more human? Does it make me less human to like watching and listening, to like being invisible? And if I told you about my dreams, would that make me more like you? If I joked and jested and flirted, would you not fear me like I'm goddamn Lucifer? If I told you about my little sadnesses and the things that keep me up at night, would that amend me in your sight? If I showed my defects and begged for love like Rodrigo does, would you stop making me feel inhuman? I came on this mission to leave the inhumanity behind, to be out at sea, not for you." He stood. He couldn't bear to remain seated. "You should be ashamed of yourself for not fearing me because I'm your captor, but fearing me because of my eyes, my *eyes* of all things. You're conceited," he ended.

Cornelius was envigored with each word he spoke, each flaw he revealed. Flaws lead to threads, and threads lead to ropes, and ropes lead to ways out.

"I like both men and women. And though so many think I'm flirtatious for that reason, I'm not. That's just how I am. Happy birthday! I'll raise Rodrigo's soup to you on the way back to the ship I'm being held for ransom on. Oh, and let me tell you why I fear your eyes. You remind me of my father. My father stares at me because he wants me to be my dead brother, the dead brother he killed. So it's reasonable that I fear you. I fear you like Lucifer's odd cousin, not Lucifer himself. The devil's fear is reserved for my father. My little sadnesses and things that keep me up at night are the same as yours, so I'm not interested. We all have them. And Rodrigo may be a little less intelligent than you, but that doesn't mean you should be unkind to him. I will never stop making you feel inhuman because that's how I make everyone feel. And your eyes… they're the most beautiful I've ever seen. But they're so much like my father's." Cornelius leaned back against the walls of one of the alley's buildings. "You stare at me, that's all. You don't see me like others do. That haunts me," he said in the gloom, the smell of Orenian street food drifting through the fog.

"Nobody has wished me a happy birthday since I was thirteen," Murray said.

"Well… just don't stare at me, and I'll sing for you. I'd play the birthday song, too, if I had my viola," Murray snorted. They sat in comfortable silence. It had been so quiet for so long that the prince had fallen asleep beside him. Murray allowed himself to get lost in his own thoughts.

CHAPTER 7

Pia started off ahead of the rest of the group in a fury. There was a noticeable distance between her and the others, and Mikka had to run to close the gap, forehead creased in annoyance.

It was close to midday, and the sun was finally working as it was intended to. The fog had cleared, but Pia wished the streets would've remained hidden after it had. The sight was just dreadful in broad daylight. It was indeed as bustling as any port town, but people were just lying in the thoroughfare, sick and sallow and near their deaths. The ones that could stand were just as sickly as those who'd collapsed. It was not a sight for sore eyes, nor any eyes at all. It looked like a plague had struck the port town, all herbs, and medicine given to the Marzinian army to make up for the "deficit." These people were utterly helpless, their tired bodies made only to work off a debt. Pia grimaced. She had sworn to help these people, and she would do just that... once she had the means.

Not even the buildings were sound. The port town was facing the sea, winds striking the modest wooden structures with brutal force. The drafty rooms wouldn't help those who still had homes recover from their sickness. Both houses and people were plain and dull, all semblance of color and individuality stripped from them. The only difference she could note was a painted sign on a storefront. Oh, a storefront. This is what they were looking for. Her insistent step slowed. The heat of the day began to set in, the air around them growing thick and syrupy with the fog's leftover moisture. She turned to the others.

"Looks like a viable candidate," she said, motioning towards the door.

A man lay on the rotting porch, his cap lying on his chest. This far back in town, both spindly and sturdy trees could be seen surrounding them. Birds sang, rejoicing in their full bellies. The worms were well-fed on the bodies of the dead, so the birds were, too. The man sang, also, though his melody was contrary to that of the birds. His was disturbing, off-tune. His keening broke off into a high note, harmonizing with a particularly outspoken bird. Glancing up, he pulled his leather cap out of his eyes. They were black, black like bottomless pits—black as the eyes of the birds. Muddied water dripped from the porch's awning. *Drip... Drip... Drip...*

"We should go in instead of squandering our time out in the street," Lara suggested, her voice low so the man wouldn't hear. Again she clutched her bag closer to her. They'd all felt the same ghostly shiver.

"Um, a-alright." Rodrigo gulped, trying to rein in his flight or fight response. Orenia was known for its jewels, but also for its stories, ghost stories to be precise. Rodrigo had a great fear of the supernatural, and he was none too pleased to be where he was.

The windows had been boarded up with discolored wood planks, but the door was open with its colorful "welcome" sign. As Mikka stepped up onto the porch, the rotted planks gave way beneath his weight with a low crunch. He glowered, knee-deep into the porch. There was an airless laugh from the man with the black eyes.

"Serves you right." His voice was bone dry. "Go lick king Addison's boots, you mock siren." The man chuckled. Pia thought Mikka would blow a gasket, but he proved her wrong, keeping his composure.

"I'm sorry to have disturbed you, sir," Mikka answered in

faltering Orenian. He nodded respectfully at the man, a pensive sadness in his eyes.

"The new ones always start off like you. Soon you'll learn about the benefits that come with the job—the power. Soon you'll forgive Marzine and turn on the country that you were failed by, Sleetal by the looks of you. You and your troop are the same as the rest, just a little greener. I'll be right here at the same time next year. If you're still good and *honest*, I'll repair this porch with my own two hands."

Mikka only sighed. Rodrigo awoke from his stupor and helped Mikka up.

"I'll be back," Mikka swore as he stood to his full height again. The man spat in the porch's hole.

"Sure. And I'm the Virgin Mary," he said after a long moment. The only sounds were the creaking of waterlogged wood and the singing of the tree birds. Each crewmember navigated around the gaping hole, entering through the half-open door of the storefront. They'd heard the dark-eyed man's words and knew them to be true. Marzinian soldiers were being brainwashed and turned into slaves of the empire. Mikka knew the process well.

Pia saw him place his hand on his pistol for reassurance, saw the way his jaw tightened. She saw how his hands shook when he wasn't natant in a sea of *raska*. And if he went on in the same way for much longer, he wasn't long for this world, and most definitely wouldn't have the mind to return in a year.

The store was dusty and narrow, each wall packed with shelves of shriveled up, nasty goods. Only the jewelry was kept in good order. Tables were crammed into the floor space. The boarded windows were covered by various trinkets and baubles. As Pia surveyed the room for the second time, she noticed something wildly different from each building's exterior in Conaire: there was color. On the shelves, talisman after talisman made of precious Orenian jewels lay waiting to be bought, necklaces and brooches beneath those. Each more vivid than the last. There were rings of all sorts, wedding, engagement, and gift. The store was more of a dragon's hoard than a heap of refuse, now that she thought of it. The crowning jewel to reign over all others was a tiara made from the clearest of jade stones. It gleamed, even by lantern light.

There was a vacant post for the bookkeeper, along with a little bronze bell for ringing. Lara was enraptured by a bundle of scrolls in the back of the room. Rodrigo was with Mikka, picking out provisions, Mikka berating him with every breath he breathed.

Pia went to the jewel-piled shelves in the back. She'd joked with Mikka about buying an Orenian charm for good fortune, and maybe she would. Her eyes fell on a small talisman on a high shelf. The color depended on how the light struck the stone. Was it azure blue, or was it the yellow of the sky before a blizzard? The first time she'd seen a blizzard's first moments, she'd been with Mikka in Sleetal. They'd huddled together in a Sleetalian pub's dingy upper room to wait out the tempest before returning to one of their various jobs. They had played cards by candlelight as the wind howled against the boarded-up windows.

Pia turned around, feeling hot breath on her neck. Mikka stood there, a color in his eyes she'd never seen before. His eyes were deep, dark cobalt before. Now they were indigo, midnight purple flecks centering around his pupils. Like the talisman, his eyes had changed.

"I'm sorry about Rodrigo," he murmured in the most accented Emberan she'd ever heard. He was so close to her. If anyone but him had been so close, close enough to kiss, she would have punched them in the gut. But his eyes were too pretty, too sad to make her feel vulnerable. He was so... so suffocatingly close. She could smell the alcohol in his breath. Of all things sweet and sordid, his kiss would taste of *raska*.

"You better be," she riposted, inhaling in a sharp breath. She turned back to the talisman but still felt the weight of his boots behind her own on the floorboards.

"It's pretty." Mikka was a man of few words at most times, mostly when he spoke Emberan. Pia agreed with him. It was pretty. Silver outlined the talisman's everchanging jewel, the same silver as Mikka's gun. Pia decided she would take this talisman and wear it for good fortune. At least, she hoped it would grant her good luck. The girl turned it over to look for the price, but there was none. It felt potent in her hand as if it possessed more magic than a shopkeeper's lie. She would believe in its counterfeit magic, for good things were few and far between in times like hers.

Rodrigo and Lara had collected the barrels on a small cart, which they fully intended to steal. They weren't going to carry the barrels on their backs. Only Mikka had enough strength for that. Mikka had four bottles of *raska* under his arm. He would hardly be able to ration them until they reached the next nation in another few weeks, but there was some mead in the cart in case he failed to do so. Rodrigo had packages of vegetables and salted meats, and he was determined to make them taste good despite how shriveled and rotten they were. They rang the small bronze bell.

An old haggish woman trundled out of a tiny side room, her back hunched over with the weight of many long-suffering years. Her eyes were paler than Murray's, white as snow but still seeing. Her hair was a copperish red, grey only sprouting from her roots.

"You rang?" she asked, her tone teetering. Her sleeves were the color of flesh, and they hung down to her hips. Then, with horror, Pia realized they were pockets of loose skin, not sleeves.

"Yes. We'd like to purchase these goods. Thanks, ma'am," Rodrigo answered with blitheness. The old woman arched a quivering eyebrow at Rodrigo.

"He's a little too perky to be a soldier. Is he a new recruit? Lord knows I hate new recruits," she groused.

"Sure he is. Got anything to say about it?" Pia asked gruffly. She was only playing the part. Still, she felt a twinge of guilt in her chest.

"Oh no, I just hate new recruits. I used to have freedom of speech, but that's been taken too, I suppose. Damned Marzinians," the woman griped, shaking her head and counting up the prices. She eyes the talisman suspiciously, the glimmering gem making her squint. "Why do you want this?"

Pia's lips turned into a thin line. "How much?" she countered. Her fist still wavered on the bookkeeper's post.

"For this? I'll give it to you for free… I'm glad someone's finally going to take this cursed thing off my hands…" She sighed to herself, playing with strands of her own wispy red hair. Pia ignored her. She hadn't believed in the supernatural since her first battle in Sleetal.

Mikka tossed a small bag of silver coins over the table to the woman, a glare in his eyes that told her not to question it. He assumed that the troops around here didn't pay much for goods, the selfish bastards. The woman was thrown but nodded agreeably. She cradled the meager sack in her wrinkled hands as if it were her firstborn child. Once they'd paid, they took the cart and wound their way around the hole in the porch. The man with the black eyes was gone.

Mikka wheeled the cart because Rodrigo wasn't strong enough. They patrolled through town, trying to remain blank as they heard jeers and cries. They wended their way back down their previous route, each house more run-down than the last. Pia breathed in fully. She smelled a tinge of sea salt in the breeze, the cloying scent of low tide as well.

The group found their way back to the alley in which they'd left Murray and the prince. Pia peered around the corner to ensure they were still safe and sound as they had left them, no thanks to Mikka. She could just make out their dark shapes slumped atop a few crates near to the back. One by one, they filed in.

Pia heard a gasp from Lara. She wound her way through the labyrinth of crates and barrels until she finally reached the others. The sight left her as shocked as Lara. In fact, finding the prince dead and Murray missing would've been less of a surprise. Murray held a finger to his lips to silence the scolding that would follow. The prince had fallen asleep. And most strikingly, his head leaned on Nic Murray's shoulder. Mikka pushed his way through the crowd of his comrades.

"Christ, what do you think you're doing?" Mikka asked angrily, his tone subdued despite himself. But Nic Murray only spoke for good reasons, and he didn't have to answer to Mikka, at least not then. He smiled wryly instead. Mikka held Cornelius' nose until he woke up, and as soon as Cornelius opened his eyes, Mikka felt like knocking him over the head. The feeling was mutual.

"Oh, *hello.*" The prince's phrase was biting, breathy. "I had the strangest dream. We were all having a lovely little picnic on my most favorite *cliff* in Marzine. Rodrigo was making his soup. Pia was drinking with her drunkard. And by drunkard, I mean you, Mikka. Lara was studying with my betrothed. And Nic Murray was sitting with me." Murray plummeted off his crate as he heard his name.

"Can you guess who I pushed into the snapping waves below the cliff? Can you, Mikka?"

Mikka crossed his arms and squared his shoulders.

"It was you. And guess who laughed as you fell to your demise. Everyone but Murray and Rodrigo, for Murray was silent, and Rodrigo was crying. That's right, Pia laughed. Lara too. My betrothed as well. Because everyone laughs at the schoolyard bully at the end of the day." Pia was taken aback. Finally, she looked at Mikka. His eyes were ablaze.

"I would never," she swore, her stare withering. Mikka's eyes flickered, the deep violet flecks disappearing into the unwitting blue.

"Why do you feel the need to justify?" he asked, hurt imminent against the strength in his rasping, *raska*-burnt tone. Nic Murray watched as he always did, and all he wondered was how they could be so obtuse. It was a dream Cornelius had described to peeve them. It was a trivial insult, a common affront.

"Stop," Rodrigo uttered, inserting himself into the makings of an argument. "Listen to yourselves. It was a dream, only a dream. Mikka didn't die. Lara, Pia, and whoever his betrothed is didn't laugh. I didn't cry. Murray wasn't silent. He's messing with our minds. Now, keep a level head and move forward. You don't want to indulge yourselves with a meaningless argument." It seemed that with each word, he shrunk a bit.

"We're leaving," Mikka growled. "Rodrigo and the siren will wheel the cart as punishment for their disrespect. Murray's in charge of those two. Pia, we're drinking tonight. Lara, do whatever it is you do. I don't give half a damn. And you, Cornelius, you sniveling little bastard, I'll have Rodrigo roast your severed tongue over an open spit if you happen to run that mouth of yours again. And I really hope you do. It would bring me such great pleasure to silence you. Your father doesn't need to know you can't speak to hand over the gold." Mikka's knuckles were white against the collar of Cornelius' disarrayed shirt.

And so… it was as Mikka had commanded. They reached the ship by nightfall, blisters forming on Cornelius' blisters from carting the supplies. And Pia and Mikka drank by moonlight. There was an air of resentment between them as they did so. The talisman hung on her neck like how the thick fog in Orenia hung in the air. Rodrigo slept. Lara read, this time on the psychology of storytelling, a bit on the tyranny of royalty. She would never fail to be fascinated by things that could ruin her.

CHAPTER 8

A storm. Murray could smell it in the heavy, waterlogged air. It was the scent of windswept peril, and it was approaching rapidly. This storm would be quick but deadly. He already saw blackened billows on the horizon. He stood abruptly from his chair in front of the large, ornately carved wheel. Could *The Vault of Heaven* withstand a storm like this one, a storm that made the air thicker than the waters? If they were to survive this, he needed everyone's help, even Cornelius'. It was late afternoon, and darkness would fall as the storm broke. But Murray honestly didn't know if he would live to see it.

He conversed with his three hired mariners, and though prying open his lips was painful, it was necessary. Usually, he didn't have to talk to anyone. He would navigate with sea charts and answer a crewman's questions with a simple nod or shake of the head. He would help raise the sails and adjust the knots and ties, working alongside his crewmen, not above them. Now, he needed to work as an authority. He was not an outspoken person, needless to say, but working in a commanding role was necessary for their collective survival. He'd anticipated this. They were getting closer to Wilkinia by the day. Wilkinia, land of a thousand scrolls and a thousand perils.

Mannon, an Orenian man like himself, was sent to collect Cornelius and Rodrigo while he went to find Lara, Mikka, and Pia. Joan, a girl from Sleetal, and Tolmas, a boy from Embera, were left to prep the sails. They would check the knots and begin tying down the mast. He could already feel the winds at his back.

Murray careened down the damp corridors. He burst into Lara and Pia's quarters. Lara was pouring over a faded manuscript by lantern light while Pia was splayed across the top bunk, snoring. The metal door slammed against the corridor wall, the bang resounding throughout the bones of the ancient ship. Pia woke with a start, and Lara stood apprehensively.

"Hell, Murray! What are you doing here? Shouldn't you be, you know, behind the wheel?" Pia yelled, climbing down from the top bunk.

He drew in a breath and released it, his eyes cold and unnerving. "A storm is coming, and I need your assistance. Come with me immediately. Pia will help secure knots. Lara, you'll help me with the wheel." He didn't take time to gauge their responses. They were being dragged closer and closer to the blackhearted billows by the moment. He hurried down the corridor with the sojourner and the soldier in tow.

"I don't know how to navigate by sea!" Lara protested weakly, fear an underlying component in her voice.

Murray had no reply for her.

"How hard can it be? Just hold onto the wheel!" Pia spurned, fearful and furious "I have to do something I don't know anything about, not even remotely!" she concluded. Pia and Lara glared at one another as they reached Mikka's quarters. Pia figured he'd be asleep, waking with a hangover worse than the storm itself. She felt the effects of hers setting in, sharp, pointed headache. Her vision was blurry, and colors seemed too bright. She tried to ignore it and square her shoulders as Mikka did. The silence was what had made her drink so much. Many a night, they had sat in silence, but that silence was far different from last night's. Last night's was imposing and contrite, regret as thick as the air in Orenia. Pia clutched her new talisman close to her chest. She remembered how close he was in the Orenian store, how his eyes were light and flecked. Indeed they had been close, but he was as distant as Embera. She needed him to try. She had tried for so long, and she just couldn't any longer.

Murray hesitated before entering Mikka's quarters. He was apprehensive around the angry man, but everyone would die horrific deaths if he didn't act soon. Mikka was not asleep, to Murray's surprise. He was sitting in his chair, fully clothed, staring out the porthole. Deep purple rings hung beneath his eyes as he turned to stare at them.

"What do you need me to do?" he asked, his mouth an even line.

"There's a storm coming. You'll help get the mast down, and once it's secure, you'll help Rodrigo and Cornelius bail water," Murray instructed. Mikka nodded and stood to join them. They ran back through the corridors the way Murray had come.

They left through the galley door and clamored down to the main deck where the rest were waiting for them. Heavy rain had begun to fall, coating the deck in ribbons of water. Cornelius had scrubbed himself clean in the lavatory since the last time they'd seen him. He wore one of Rodrigo's white undershirts, and his hair was slicked back from the sponge bath he'd given himself. Mikka, Lara, and Pia fell in line with the others as they awaited Murray's instruction. He stood before them like a leader, like Mikka.

"Rodrigo, Cornelius, you'll bail water with those buckets. Mikka, Pia, you work with the mariners to bring down the mast and secure the knots. They'll instruct you when you're not sure of what needs to be done." A howling wind knocked into the ship, and Rodrigo squeaked. "Lara, you're with me on the bridge." His tone became lower and more ferocious as the boat rocked unevenly.

Cornelius seized the bucket, for he didn't dally with death. Another wave burst struck, knocking him to his knees. He turned and caught a fleeting glance of the sky's blue, a momentary, hopeless patch of sun. Then, the storm commenced.

It came in great waves, soaking through his shirt immediately. The rain was solid. Water began to pool on the main deck, and there was no headway to be made. Each bucket bailed was replaced with four more. Mannon, the Orenian, was shouting something unintelligible over the wind, but Mikka got the general gist of it. Hold fast. He gripped and clenched his teeth, gripping the rope. They'd gotten the mast down, now they were securing it. The raging waves of the beneath made it hard to keep a steady grip. Pia was having as great a struggle as he was, but her arms were more accustomed to strain. The ship moaned and splintered as they scaled their first of many waves. The sound of it roared in his ears. Joan had to start bailing water as soon as they were finished. It was ankle-deep. Another wave swept over the deck. When it had passed, Mannon wasn't on board. Nobody could hear Mikka's "Man overboard!" over the howling winds. Mikka stared into the roiling waves with all-consuming fear. Mannon had been beside him one moment, gone the next.

Murray and Lara stood on the bridge, the wheel clutched between them. They held on for dear life, Lara crying, Murray stone-faced. The ship shrieked like a banshee as they braved an even taller wave. Each surge they survived seemed like their last, but somehow the old *Vault* kept sailing through the writhing waters. The entire world was soon dark, save for the greenish light of the flashes of lightning. It was a watery hellscape. None of the crewmembers could see, hear, or say anything.

Cornelius was standing, his face split into a fathomless smile. There was nothing more exhilarating, nothing more awe-inspiring than this. This was where he belonged, soaring atop a massive wave's crest. The storm was a thing of beauty.

Then, with sudden, deafening silence, it was over.

The waves evened out. The storm clouds vanished. Their waterlogged mass of wood and metal floated into the setting sun. But the storm had not gone without taking its toll. Mannon had been swept off to meet a watery grave somewhere far, far below, the drink becoming his final resting place. No matter how they scoured *The Vault of Heaven*, they couldn't find him. It was a day none of them would ever be allowed to forget. And just as Murray had predicted, the storm had been quick but deadly.

Lara returned to her quarters, finding her manuscripts and tomes intact, if not a bit damp, and spilled across the floor. Mikka went to his quarters to drink alone, for his wits were lost along with Mannon. Pia sat in the galley, waiting for Mikka to come and hold her so she could cry. She needed him, but he never came. She was shivering, her face in a hastily made bowl of her brother's soup. Of course, Rodrigo had made soup, lots of it, all while sniffling. She felt like screaming at him to be quiet, and she ended up doing just that.

Nic Murray remained on the bridge beside the wheel, alone. The sun had set, and the aftermath of the storm had been dealt with. He'd moved up a chair from the galley to sit and watch the purple of twilight fade into blue. Stars ornamented the sky as diamonds ornament the garments of the rich. The night sky was a fair court lady with all the sparkling jewels she could ever desire. Murray wanted to go drink unholy amounts of raska with Mikka, drown his sorrows as the sea had Mannon. Instead, he remained. Remained as he always would.

The only thought he couldn't put to rest was a silly, childish one. He'd never had his first kiss. He could've died like Mannon, and he would've never had his first kiss. There were many things he hadn't done, in fact. He'd never been truly happy, for one. He'd never been to the moon. He'd never lost a bet or even gambled at all. He'd never had a best friend. He'd never... he'd never... he'd never had his first kiss. Murray gritted his teeth as he tried to close his mind to the thought, but it was ever-present. *He'd never had his first kiss.* He didn't care who it was with. It could be with Lara for all he cared. But it was Cornelius he would kiss. Cornelius would kiss him back.

It may have been the fear that remained with him from the storm, it may have been the shriveled vegetables he'd had the night before, it may have been the loss of Mannon, it may have been anything at all, but Nic Murray decided that he wouldn't deny himself this. He'd denied himself so many small happinesses, but not this. The sentinel stood. He was down the stairway and in the corridor leading to the crew quarters before he knew it.

Cornelius had decided to leave Rodrigo be for the night. The small, reverberative room they shared was filled with the sound of Rodrigo's sobbing, and Cornelius needed silence to sleep. He crouched just outside their room, clothes still soggy from the storm, but didn't enter.

He wanted his viola more than dry clothes and his yellowed mattress. During the low moments of his captivity, he'd let his fingers thrum over the strings, drawn the bow across them as well. The hum filled both his ears and his heart, warming him to the bone. He needed it more than ever as he shivered, sinking lower to the floor.

He heard footsteps approaching. Good grief, was that Mikka? He tried his best to sink through the wall. The last thing Cornelius needed was another kicking after a night like the one he'd had. But it wasn't Mikka coming to beat the sense out of him. It was Nic Murray. Nic Murray with his sentinel eyes and statue-like demeanor.

He glanced up. Something about his eyes was off, wavering like one's reflection in a lake. Mannon's death must have scared him witless.

"My condolences. If you need someone to talk to, it's Rodrigo you're looking for. He's rather understanding, and I hardly knew Mannon," Cornelius said.

Murray stared at him stonily. Cornelius rose to his feet. Why was Murray just standing there? "What do you need?" Cornelius asked, flushing.

Murray took a halting step forward. The lanterns flickered with the air's apprehension. It was suddenly warm, too warm.

"I've never had my first kiss," Murray choked. "I want you to kiss me."

Cornelius felt a spasm in his chest. Kissing Nic Murray? Even though he was reasonably sure he was suffering a heart attack, his heart was still beating. In fact, it was beating all too fast. He wanted to resist. But alas, he didn't.

"What an inopportune way to have your first kiss," he said casually, leaning closer. He knew how to kiss down to the very detail. Which way to turn his head, where to place his hands, where to put his tongue… he knew to wait a few seconds before their lips met.

He lifted a hand to touch Murray's cheek, pleasantly surprised to find his skin warm. He ran a finger down his jaw, stopping beneath his chin. They were closer now, closer than they had ever been. Cornelius pulled his face nearer still, and… he kissed him. It was long, longer than Murray had expected. It had been everything he'd wanted. Murray had his hands against the corridor walls beside Cornelius' head. They stood there for a moment, looking anywhere but each other. Cornelius felt a fluttery feeling above his heartbeat.

"Good enough for your first try, Murray. Find me alone for your second kiss."

Murray's face flushed red, and he stalked back the way he'd come. Cornelius smiled and retreated into his quarters, minding the sobbing less for some reason.

CHAPTER 9

A h, Wilkinia. The land of storms and less innocuous things. Peril upon peril, danger upon danger crowned by the world's largest center of knowledge. Lara had lived there before the continental war. She'd never known her parents. They'd succumbed to one of Wilkinia's perils. She was instead given up to a scholar who had raised her in their stead. She would have joined her parents in their fate had it not been so. However, she was not beholden to the man. He had never told her her own last name and never told her his name, first or last. He had raised her as a ward, not a daughter. A pupil, not kin. She would call him "teacher." It was a tragedy to her, having a single name. All the greatest authors, travelers, musicians, and artists had at least two names, if not three. Some had more still.

Still, she was eager to return to her land of peril. It had been a little over a month since they'd set out from Wilkinia. So much had happened in such a short span of time.

It would be an afternoon and a night before they reached the sea cave where they would harbor. Luckily, she had something to occupy herself with until they arrived. Or someone, for that matter. Someone being Cornelius.

Cornelius had been put to the task of mending the lower mast on the upper deck. Mikka had watched him for an hour, and after one too many remarks from Cornelius, he was making her take his place.

She climbed the precarious ladder, hoisting herself over a broken rung with the help of the rigging. The sky was a powder blue, wisps of clouds draped over it. As she climbed higher, she heard an unfamiliar sound. It was a hum, a vibration that filled her ears with sound. It made her skin tingle with its vibrant melody. Lara leaned into the bittersweet tune, letting the melody wrap around her.

Her eyes were first enthralled by the beauty of the formerly torn mast before her. Cornelius had been meant to mend the sail passably. But instead, he'd sewn a pattern into the material. The string was wound so finely that she could hardly see it in the shadows. But when the sun shone on it at just the right angle, she could she saw a forest of trees spiraling across it.

Then, she saw him. He was standing atop the far end of the mended mast. His eyes were closed, his golden hair tousled the wind. He cradled a viola in his arms, his chin near the tailpiece, a bow poised over the strings. It was a beautiful instrument, carved from the reddest cherrywood she'd ever seen. He drew the bow over the instrument with a sense of finality.

"My apologies. I thought I was quieter. I decided to pass the time with some practice," Cornelius explained, his smile dimmer than usual.

"That was lovely," she complimented.

"I suppose you would know of lovely things." He beamed. Lara's eyes were blue in the sunlight, but when she stepped forward, they were hazel.

"I came here not only to supervise you but to inquire about Andria and the other continent. Mikka cut our discussion short in Orenia," Lara told him as his lingering smile faded. Cornelius nodded, suddenly coy. He began to put away his viola.

"And what do I get in return, Lily of the Valley?"

She glowered at the moniker. "Someone to talk to?" offered Lara, her shoulders rising slightly. He clicked his case shut, propping it against the rail.

"If I was in need of that, I would go to Rodrigo. I'm not, however," he said. His tone was light, playful. Grim at the end, just as his melody was.

"Playing hard to get, I see. Alright then, what do you want in exchange?" she asked.

"If I told you what I wanted, you would either kiss me or throw me overboard," he told her coolly, beginning the task of folding the mast.

"What do you want that I could give you without kissing you or throwing you overboard?" she asked again, her smile growing despite all she knew about him and his ways. Cornelius took a moment to think, circling the upper deck.

"A blanket. I'm ever so cold at night."

"A blanket? That's all?" she asked skeptically. Cornelius smiled, looking her dead in the eyes. He drank them in, heeding the shape, the color, and size. Perhaps they were simply hazel. No, maybe purple. He still couldn't tell, even in broad daylight. He was glad she was looking him in the eyes. She was being kind to him, too. This was significant progress, given how poorly their first conversation had gone.

"A pillow as well. Give me yours, and I'll give you my chest to lay your head on." Her eyes widened, and her mouth opened slightly. Intriguing.

"You won't have *my* pillow, but you will have *a* pillow. A blanket as well. I'll see to it after our conversation."

He stood away from the folded mast, his hands on his hips. "We have a deal then," he stated. The sun's orange hue set his eyes ablaze, the shallow blue tinged with vermillion. "Is it too late to press for sheets?" he asked daringly.

"We've already made the deal. No sheets for you." She laughed, her voice breezy.

"Rude."

"Indeed I am. But that doesn't make the deal any less authentic. Now, I'll begin with a general question," she began, sobriety returning to her. She sank down against the railing, her back to the cerulean sea. "What's the most important thing to know about Andria and the other continent?" She unfurled a sheet of parchment paper from her bag, flattening it out against a floorboard.

"The other continent wasn't known to us until twenty years ago when a privateer's ship washed up on Marzinian shores," he said, deciding to start from the beginning of what he knew instead of obliging her with specific details. She'd cheated him out of sheets, after all.

"Why tell me that? Any sojourner worth her salt knows about shipwrecked Samuel Gray," she said impatiently, a dimpled frown on her face.

"Every story has its beginning. I only wish to honor that. We'll arrive at the unknown's beginning soon enough. Be diligent and take your notes until then, alright?"

Her frown deepened, but she remained silent. He told her the tale of the man, Samuel Gray, and his privateer ship, its strange design, of his language. It was discovered later on that his crewmembers had perished during the ordeal. He was from Andria, his hair gold, his skin fair, his build slim. He taught them of the land of ice and shrieking winds, not so different from Sleetal or the northern region of Wilkinia. He told of unimaginable colors and the royal court, of their beholding of beautiful things. He spoke of the common languages, stark literature, and art. Of the classics and people of fame.

Lara was familiar with his spiel, yet she listened with interest as the sun fell to an idle point in the sky. The tale he weaved from simple facts kept her attention.

After an extensive description of the centralized government and exports, Andrian sovereigns, and their evident corruption, he arrived at the twenty-year war between Andria and Walsia. He spoke of how similar it was to their own continental war and gave a quick comparison between their continent's strategics and the other continent's. The moon had risen by the time he was past the war. She realized it had all been quite vague, vivid language added to fill the cracks. She didn't care, though. He didn't know much about the other continent. He had only a notion of the place. But she felt as if it were a pleasure just to hear him speak. But then he came to a halting stop. Her ears rang with the sudden silence, his words echoing through her mind.

"I'll go find the bedclothes you're owed," she told him waveringly, almost as if it was wrong to fill the earsplitting silence. She backed down the ladder, forgetting the broken rung and almost falling to her death. The rigging again saved her, though she scarcely noticed it. His words had put her in a trance.

The effects wore off as she entered through the galley. She should've known not to trifle with him. Cornelius was a man of many games, and bargaining with him was like bargaining with a wealthy merchant.

Murray had been acting strange, more so than usual. He didn't confine himself to the bridge or his quarters. Instead, he wandered around the ship as if he were a wraith, a ghost sentenced to haunt it for an eternity. She passed him as she walked to her quarters. He was staring straight into her eyes, half his face illuminated by the moonlight, half shrouded in shadows. Lara chalked up his strange behavior to him being fazed by Mannon's death. But he was daunted by something far more trivial: his first kiss.

In fact, it was all he could ponder. All he could hear was the sound of Cornelius' voice, all he could see were the shallows of Cornelius' eyes. But Lara would never know that. He was a mystery to her, and she was consumed by her own Cornelius-related problems. She would bring him his unfairly traded bedclothes and get on with her life. But... her life somewhat revolved around him. She sighed, rounding the corner of the dim corridor. Hell, this place really did seem haunted, Murray or not.

She was relieved when she arrived at her quarters. The small comfort of a door between her and the rest of the ship pacified her. She lit her lantern hastily, for she disliked the darkness. But when she did, she cried out.

"Mikka? What the hell are you doing here? Our quarters are private for a reason!" she exclaimed, her face ghastly in the lantern light. Mikka was sitting on her bunk, the bottom bunk, his hands clasped together. She could smell him from across the room. *Raska.* She lit the wall lantern as well, bathing the room in warm light. "Mikka," she said as he staggered to his feet.

"Pia… Why weren't you in the galley?" He asked, his voice cutting into her like a dull blade. He was speaking in Emberan, poor Emberan. She knew only knew the language rudimentarily and was lacking in it herself. Still, she got the sentiment. He was learning the language for Pia.

"Mikka, I'm not Pia. I'm Lara," she explained slowly. He wore a stained undershirt and loose trousers. He was the epitome of a drunkard, at least from her perspective. All the drunkards in the novels she'd read were described as such. And what was the drunkard for? His purpose was to stir up the plot and cause conflict. As he stumbled closer, she could see his face. His eyes were a deep, northern blue, clouded from drinking. His olive skin was sweaty.

"Pia… I'm so sorry. It's just that Rodrigo's as frail as my mother. And she's dead," Mikka said with a snort. "He's just so… so delicate. I can't help but complain about him."

Lara's eyes narrowed. He was speaking in Sleetalian now, but his words were still slurred.

"Mikka," she said calmly. "I'm not Pia. I'm Lara." Her back was against the metal wall now. His hand was up against the panel beside her head. The smell of *raska* was so strong that it burnt her nostrils. Surely he could tell she wasn't Pia when he was this close. But his mind was muddled. She was someone else to him. She was Pia.

"Pia… I love you."

She met his stare with shock.

"Mikka…" Her eyes widened. He then kissed her in the

lantern light, his body baring down on hers like a wolf on a lamb. His kiss was unwanted. Worst of all, it tasted like *raska*, and Lara hated *raska*. It was like swallowing death itself to her, and Mikka was just drenched in it. She pushed against him, and though she was taller, he was a large Sleetalian man. He wouldn't relent. Finally, with the slice of the door cutting through the stale air, he stopped. They stood, Lara cowering away from him, staring at the doorway. There Pia was, her jaw set, her eyes bathed in anguish.

Mikka looked around stupidly, first at Lara, then at Pia. He squinted like a farmer standing in his fallow field. He then staggered slightly, knocked a few scrolls off Lara's desk, and toppled to the floor.

"I see," Pia said, her voice unbroken. Her fists were clenched at her sides, wavering. She wanted to punch Lara square in the eye. She wanted to kick Mikka's unconscious form. But… there was no reason to. The realization was as cold as a dagger's blade. Mikka had never been hers. He was free to kiss whoever he pleased.

"Pia, this isn't what you think it is." Lara knew the phrase well. It was used at least once in every great romantic drama she'd read. She even held the same defensive stance that all the mistresses had. No, she wasn't a mistress, was she? He'd kissed her, not the other way around. Why was she covering for the drunkard? She glared righteously, only to see Pia smiling.

"We should get him back to his quarters. I hope it was a fun night for you two. A little bit too much fun for him, huh?" Pia laughed.

"Pia…" Lara said, reaching out a hand. Pia recoiled from her, and Lara was paralyzed. She stuttered a few silly lines about Mikka's drunkenness, but Pia was staring down at Mikka, too devastated to hear her. She and Lara carried Mikka's limp body back to his quarters, laying him on his cot. They blew out his lantern. Pia even went so far as to pull his coverlet over him. It seemed as if she were following a routine. And she was. She took care of him when he got too drunk to take care of himself.

Lara removed herself from their quarters that night. She snatched a pillow and one of her many woven blankets from her bunk to sleep on, but she passed Cornelius and Rodrigo on their way back from the galley, and she didn't have the heart to explain herself. She handed the blanket and pillow over, face downcast. Rodrigo noticed nothing, but Cornelius was suspicious. In most cases, he would have asked about it, but the seared trout and brown herb bread in his stomach told him not to. Rodrigo's spiced nettle tea had made him tired. He had a blanket and pillow now, and all he wanted to do was sleep. So, just once, he held his tongue.

Later that night, Lara sat alone at the ship's prow, gazing off into the sky. Her mind was too tired to think, but she didn't have even a pallet or a horse blanket to sleep on. Her mind, however, was not too tired to imagine. And she would escape that way, away from her troubles, if only for a night. She dreamed she was the queen of the moon, residing in a sprawling bronze tower that sunk far into the atmosphere in a land that only had night. She was sovereign to all the twinkling stars. And the other land, just beyond the sea's horizon, was ruled by the sun king. And he was Cornelius. And there were no thoughts of Mikka or Pia or the war or Andria or the kidnapping. And no pain or emptiness that needed to be filled by volumes upon volumes of knowledge. She was home—home, away from the world.

CHAPTER 10

Pia couldn't sleep. And she didn't want to, knowing she would dream of him. How had she let this happen? How had she let her own affinity for Mikka escape her? Her walls reached far above her head. But as Mikka had proved in Marzine, even the most impregnable walls could be violated. She pressed her face further into her pillow, suffocating her own idiocy.

Soon she would have something to distract her from Mikka, though. The *Vault* would dock in a sea cave of Lara's choosing. Pia would have to focus only on what lay ahead, removing all other thoughts from her mind. They weren't in Wilkinia for a supply run. No, they were in the land of a thousand perils and a thousand scrolls to meet with Shadrach and other members of the Masked Birds. The eminent Shadrach, former king of Sleetal. *Former king.* It was a laughable title, but Pia knew better than to laugh at it. He would kill her and make a damn good stew out of her if she dared to do so. And besides, he was the leader of the resistance, a very acceptable title in certain circles, the circles she swam in.

Suddenly, the gentle swaying of the waves against the ship's underbelly deadened. It was almost too still, too silent. Murray had successfully navigated them into the sea cave with his two remaining mariners' help. Mannon's death had left only Joan and Tolmas, but they were managing. Pia sprang off of her bunk. Oh, to see the land again, unyielding and whole, even if underground. The relief was like a breath of fresh air.

Shadrach and a few other high-profile Masked Birds were

scheduled to meet them in a secluded monastery in the wildlands beyond the sea cave. The monks that communed there had stopped receiving funds from the church after the war ended. All assets were given to the Marzinian monarchy to make up for the "deficit." It was unfair, unholy, and tainted with ignorance. In a nation that valued knowledge above all things, this was a direct affront. The monks could survive without charity for food and drink, but they wouldn't stand being denied the funds to record and preserve texts. That was why they'd made the ill-advised choice to aid the resistance in their endeavors, seeking funds in return.

Pia put on her outer garments and wrapped her knuckles with strips of cloth as a forethought. She never knew when her anger would spill over, compelling her to punch someone or something she shouldn't. Leaving her quarters, she slung a pack of clothing and necessities over her shoulder. They would be staying at the monastery for a week, allowing them time to make plans with Shadrach and his associates. Pia momentarily wondered how the meeting between the Siren Prince and the Raven King would go but put the thought to rest after concluding that at least one of them would die. Someone always ended up dead when it came to Shadrach. She could only hope it wouldn't be her.

She roamed silently through the corridors, trying to clear her head and focus on the dim future instead of the pitch-black present. The galley stank of old soup as she passed through it, making her wrinkle her nose. Rodrigo really needed to have some variety, make solid foods for once. She couldn't complain, though. They would be feasting on hardtack and salt cod if it weren't for him.

As she marched out onto the main deck, surprise stole her breath away. There was a night sky above, but not one she'd seen before. In the sea cave, a broad stretch of blackened rock was above them. Luminous crystals were peppered between the rock, making the cave glow a soft green. She vaguely remembered Lara prattling on about this very cave, a cave from a folktale or a legend or whatever. Pia didn't care much for its antiquity, only the beauty she could see in the moment. She breathed in the salted scent of the underground rocks and the sea and a tranquility filled chest.

She saw Lara slumped against the prow, snoring, and the tranquility was gone. Had Lara really slept there all night? She didn't care. Pia shook herself and climbed a ladder to the ship's bridge to sit with Murray. He glared at the rock above them, his face turned away from the smell.

"Murray," she said, taking her place beside him. Then she fell silent, though Nic Murray was an amazing listener. The skill was credited mainly to the fact that he never spoke, but nevertheless, he was helpful when she needed to vent, and Pia needed to vent a great deal to keep herself from breaking someone's face.

"Mikka did something," Murray stated matter-of-factly. He shifted on the balls of his feet, awkward. Pia's ears rang with the sound of his voice. He'd been talking a lot lately, at least compared to the total silence of before. Sometimes, she wished he would return to muteness. His voice was just so strange, vocal cords atrophied. It made her shiver.

"He did," Pia found herself confessing. Murray knew everything anyway. She wouldn't disagree with the truth. Mikka *had* done something. There was no more said, but an understanding passed between them. It felt good to be understood, especially when Mikka felt like a stranger to her. An hour or so passed in silence. Murray was rocking back and forth eerily, mimicking the effect of the waves. Tolmas and Joan emerged from the crew's quarters and began work with the anchor and the rigging, making sure the ship was prepared to be left alone for the week.

Pia fidgeted with her cloth wrappings as Mikka finally

drifted out, his pack slung over his shoulder. He wore a frayed undershirt and an overshirt that hung well over his trousers. It would be blustery as they left the sea cave, cold as well. The warmth of Embera was only a faded memory to Pia. Even so, she missed it. At least she had her talisman, she thought, clasping it in her hand. Perhaps she would find her good fortune in Wilkinia.

Mikka had roused to the halt of the waves' lull. His eyes were blurry, and his skin felt too tight on his bones. His heart beating in his head as he tried to piece together his memories of the night before. When he couldn't, he'd dressed and packed, nursing his headache. Mikka debated filling his flask but decided against it. Shadrach, former king of Sleetal, would have the finest *raska*, maybe even some rare vodka. His cheap stuff would pale in comparison to the Raven King's.

The sharpshooter realized something was wrong as soon as he noticed Pia's absence on the main deck. She was up on the bridge with Murray, her expression stony. She ignored him, clutching her talisman. What had he done? Cursing himself, Mikka sighed and scoured his memory again. Things had just gotten back to normal, and somehow, he'd broken the peace.

Then Mikka saw Lara. She seemed frazzled, having just risen from a doze against the ship's prow. The girl was already glowering at him. Had he paraded around the *Vault* naked? Had he murdered Cornelius? His latter thought was soon disproven. Rodrigo and Cornelius marched out onto the main deck. Cornelius had his viola case strung over his shoulder, as well as a small knapsack he'd fashioned from leftover mast. Crafty little creep. His glower deepened. He should've filled his flask after all. If he was to deal with a day like this, he'd rather be drunk while he did.

It was only a quarter-hour before Tolmas and Joan had finished readying the ship, but every moment felt like its own separate ordeal. Mikka took to pacing, letting Cornelius' continuous conversation with everyone else but him fade to background noise. The only sound that he heard distinctly was Pia's laugh. Was Cornelius that goddamn hilarious? He gritted his teeth.

"For all of our sakes, shut up!" Mikka said, turning on his heels. But of course, Cornelius didn't

"Mikka, darling, I'll only ever shut up when I'm dead. But fair warning, I may even speak then," Cornelius drawled, smiling up at Mikka.

"How would you like a punch in the stomach?" Mikka confronted.

"No, thank you. I'd rather have a pastry. That's the only thing I want 'in the stomach,' Mikka."

Rodrigo momentarily considered making pastries instead of soup to continue the joke but took a look at the sharpshooter and cast the thought over the side of the boat. Mikka sighed and turned his back to the group.

"It's all in good fun, Mikka," Lara said, not unkindly. He reeled around, his eyes dark.

"Good fun? With the siren?" Mikka snarled.

"You know what? We'll let Shadrach decide what and what not to do with the prince. Speaking of Shadrach, we should set out," interjected Rodrigo with an imploring smile. Mikka whirled around again.

"Who asked for your opinion, Rodrigo?" His hand rested on his silver pistol. Rodrigo seemed to shrink into the shadows.

"Nobody," he mumbled, turning his eyes toward his boots. Cornelius patted him on the shoulder like he cared.

"Rodrigo's right. We should leave, Mikka," Pia suggested. Her tone was guarded. Mikka couldn't see her face, but he knew she would be wearing that withering glare of hers.

"Let's leave then." Mikka sighed, motioning towards Tolmas to let down the gangplank. They clamored down to the sandbank, the soft green glow of the cave crystals guiding them forward. They navigated through jutting rocks and areas that were overcome by water. Cornelius still had his borrowed pair of boots. For them, he was very thankful. His feet would be torn up and swollen by then if he didn't have the sturdy soles beneath his feet.

Carvings on the cave walls told of ancient times, times nobody cared to know about. Lara, of course, raved about them, babbling about a cave legend for about an hour. Even Cornelius was too lost to comment.

The light of the crystals seemed to dim after another hour or so of walking. Cornelius' feet were still aching from maneuvering around sharp rocks even with his boots. He was drained of stamina and preferred hauling crates back in Orenia to this sort of travel. At one point, the crystals had dimmed so much that Cornelius was afraid they'd have to make the rest of the jaunt in the dark. That led him to thoughts of lostness. What if they'd taken a wrong turn? He took steady breaths to calm himself, as steady as one could manage while walking a thin edge with black waters rushing below.

Soon, he realized the crystals' light was not dimming because they were lost but because they were moving closer to daylight. In a handful moments, they could see the cave's ending. Light poured in, bathing the rocks in an amber glow. It was beautiful and terrible all at once, and for a moment, the ache was gone from his step. He wished he could commission an artist to immortalize this scene, and perhaps he would someday. He decided that this cave could be saved when the world burned. The thought made him smile to himself, his face dripping with sunlight for the first time since the day before.

Before Cornelius, Mikka had loved this sort of travel. He remembered when he would scale cliffs and travel through hidden passages to reach his sharpshooting vantages. He would usually travel with a few fellow sharpshooters, and they would tell stories, drink cheap *raska* from a shared flask, and laugh.

That was when Sleetal had the upper hand. After a while in the cave, he forgot about his problems and let the rhythm of walking and climbing take over, reminiscing only with himself.

But then, both he and Cornelius were miserable again as they stood at the outcroppings of a dense jungle tree forest. Lara busily pulled a map from her pack, rattling off the details of which direction they would be heading and what marks they should seek out. She even read their coordinates aloud, only a jumble of numbers to the nonmilitary crewmembers.

"Please tell me you're not going to put me in chains or cover my face with mud," Cornelius begged. He hadn't spoken in an hour or so, and the closed-mouthedness was becoming unsettling. Pia turned back and gave him a pitying look.

"This is resistance territory, hon. Everyone here knows exactly who you are, mud or not," Pia told him, shrugging.

Cornelius' eyes sparked. If they weren't going to another port town, he was being taken to meet Shadrach, the leader. Cornelius had known about him before his kidnapping. He was the former king of Sleetal, after all. Now, he single-handedly ran the Masked Birds. It would be an honor to meet the Raven King, and Cornelius would do his best to make an impression, good or bad.

The sun didn't penetrate the thick canopy of jungle trees above them, and spine-tickling winds rushed through the undergrowth like a barrage of poltergeists. The crew was cold and damp from the cave, and the wind didn't help them. Rodrigo was shaking like a leaf. He pulled his sweater closer to him and shivered silently, trying to catch up to the others.

Pia was far ahead of the group as she almost always was, but Mikka still ran to keep pace with her.

"Pia!" he shouted, coming up beside her. She bristled but slowed a bit.

"What do you need?"

"I don't know, what do you need? You're angry as hell and a

lousy actress, so you better start explaining. What happened?"
he asked.

Her step faltered. "I'm not angry, *you're* angry," she shot
back. They stood among the lush underbrush, staring at one
another. Another gust of wind wound its way around them.

"I'm angry because you're ignoring me!" he yelled, his voice
rising an octave. Pia crossed her arms and shivered in the wind.

"Oh, poor little Mikka. He needs attention all day long. Why
don't you go ask Lara? I'm sure she'll give you what you want!"
she snapped.

"What did I do? Pia, what did I do?" he asked helplessly,
throwing his arms up.

"What didn't you do, Mikka? You already did Lara, so I'm
certain you'll do Joan next. Maybe then a nice girl you find at
the monastery. And maybe, just maybe, after you're out of
options, you'll do me, although a *raska* bottle seems far better
suited to your needs!" she cried. The others stood only a few
yards from them, gawking. Joan flushed, and Lara turned her
back. It was a bracing reminder that they were all still so young,
so naive. All the older folks were dead.

"I don't know what you're talking about!" he pleaded. A
memory then struck Mikka like a bolt of lightning. In it, he was
standing close to Lara, her eyes wide with fear. The warm light
of a lantern cast an amber glow over her skin. He'd kissed her
and Pia had seen.

"Like hell you don't!" Pia's voice brought him back.

"I kissed her…" he said incredulously.

"You did!" Pia yelled, triumphant. He turned his gaze back
to her.

"I thought… I thought she was you, Pia. It's been unspoken
up until now, but I…" His eyes melted. "I love you. And I was
drunk," he explained.

"You know I could escape at any time during their strange
three-way lover's quarrel, right?" Cornelius said to Rodrigo as

they stood together and watched the spectacle.

"Yes, yes, you could. But Mikka would break your arms and your legs if you did that so you couldn't leave again." Rodrigo told him with a small smile. And Cornelius believed him. They watched the bickering together, Cornelius rubbing warmth into his arms and legs. He smiled. At least it wasn't him being yelled at.

CHAPTER 11

The hurling of curses worsened with time, though their journey did continue. Pia and Mikka walked a fair distance ahead of the group, and their outrage could be heard from where Rodrigo was, the tail end of the pack. It was obvious to anyone that Rodrigo wasn't one for confrontation, and he only vaguely knew why Mikka and Pia were arguing.

"Lara, I don't want to be rude... and don't feel obligated to answer this, but did Mikka kiss you?" he asked. She drew her pack closer to her shoulder, hastening her step. He knew very well he was bothering her, but he'd been a bother all his life and didn't let the fact hinder him.

"Yes, Rodrigo, Mikka did kiss me. He was drunk as he always is, and he mistook me for Pia."

Rodrigo's eyes widened at the mention of his sister. "I'm sorry you had to deal with that," he said eagerly.

She offered him the smallest of smiles and then joined Joan in the front of the line. He then wandered up to Cornelius.

"Did you pack any soup?" Cornelius asked, giving him a much broader smile than Lara's. Rodrigo nodded, rummaging around in his pack until he found one of the canisters. Cornelius didn't intend to drink the soup, he just thought the fellow needed something to lift his spirits.

"It's not warm any longer. I hope that's alright," Rodrigo said. Cornelius nodded, receiving the soup graciously. They heard a far-flung "You're a lousy son of a-" and Rodrigo winced.

He tumbled over a jungle tree root, falling to his knees, but righted himself before anyone saw. Cornelius had already left him in the dust by the time he got up.

The shadows grew darker as the morning yielded to afternoon. Shadrach was expecting them soon. What would the Raven King be like? Rumor had it he had skin as blue as ice, hair as dark as night. He wore a raven mask over his face, his eyes the only part of his face visible. Rodrigo had his own mask in his pack. He wasn't eager to wear it, however. It scared him to look in the mirror with it on, not that he did so frequently. Rodrigo hardly ever looked in the mirror, even without the mask. He shaved and washed, even gave himself haircuts. But always without a mirror. Pia had taunted him about being pretty and not handsome when they were younger, and ever since, he hadn't been able to look at himself in the mirror without hearing her voice.

The only person who had called him handsome was his mother. His pa always saw him as a disgrace, an effeminate man. His sister saw him as a hindrance, something holding her back from untold glory. And maybe he was a disgrace, a hindrance. But his mother saw him how he wanted to be seen.

His ma had taught him many things. While Pia was off chasing their pa around the fallow field, Rodrigo was in the kitchen. She was the first to teach him how to make spice soup. Making it on the *Vault* took him back. As the scent of Emberan spices filled his nostrils, he could pretend he was back home, making spice soup with his ma. They would stand over the stove together as the stockpot burbled. He would chop shiny red and green peppers. Then, they would add the spices. Freshly ground cinnamon that was imported from the other side of Embera where it was wetter. He would always put too much of the herb in the stockpot, but his mother would never scold him. She told him there was no such thing as too much cinnamon. For that reason, there was always a surplus of cinnamon in his spice soup. There were other spices as well, including but not limited to turmeric, lemon zest, oregano, salt, pepper, sage, and thyme.

Sometimes even paprika, though Rodrigo thought it did nothing for the soup's flavor. He carried his mother's recipe with him everywhere. It was in his pack even now.

Rodrigo looked up, roused from his thoughts by a shaft of sunlight. He stopped, drinking it in. They would reach the monastery soon. He groaned and hurried after the group, making sure to watch his step.

"Rodrigo! Hurry up! The monastery is just up ahead." Relief flooded through him as he heard Cornelius' call. He was done with Wilkinia's perils for the day. All he wanted was a basin filled with hot water to bathe in and a bed to sleep in, no matter how thin the sheets. He didn't even have sheets on *The Vault of Heaven*. Even trivial comforts would be an improvement to the way he lived out at sea. He ran to join the others, nearly falling again despite himself.

The sun shone red through the trees now. Mikka and Pia stopped their quarreling to stare at the group of buildings before them, Murray close behind. They were late, the sun already setting, casting a vermillion shade over the forest.

The monastery was a well-maintained relic. Bits and pieces of architecture were taken from each of the five nations—the smooth curves and bends of Marzinian work present, as well as the sharp edges and ridges of Sleetal. The monastery consisted of a jutting front building hewn from limestone with a small, slatted attic above it and a circular tower composing the rear. Rodrigo couldn't wait to take in the forested valley from the tower's keep. A garden was torn away from the forest's clutches, numerous vegetables and fruit trees sprouting from the plot. Maybe Shadrach would let him take some vegetables back to the *Vault*.

"It's divine," Cornelius told them. "Literally," he joked. Rodrigo wanted to laugh to humor him, but the moment felt too sacred.

"Well, we should go in. What use is a building when

nobody's in it?" Pia said inelegantly. Everyone obliged, falling a step behind Pia. Only Cornelius hung back, going back and forth on a decision. None of them seemed to realize that he could just... escape. Abscond into the forest, never to be seen again. But that would be dreadfully boring. And he wanted to meet Shadrach.

Finally, as the last strand of light faded from the sky, he followed. It had only been a moment, and the others were still standing in the entry hall, judging the interior. The hall seemed larger inside, the rectangular ceiling domed. It was a resounding room, his footsteps still echoing at the ends. Tall, wooden bookcases stood like sentries, their height extending all the way to the ceiling. And in those bookcases were books, more than Cornelius had ever seen. More than there was in the royal library. There were carts, too, individual cases for illuminated manuscripts and lecterns occupied by busy monks. The only blatantly religious object in the rectangular hall was the cross above their heads.

Cornelius turned to Lara. She looked as if she could die happy. Her eyes were alight with curiosity as she stared and stared at the bookcases. Although numerous monks were in their sack-like brown robes, ordinary people wore peasant roughspun and travelers' leather. There were monks, ordinary people, and Masked Birds in the sanctuary of knowledge. And Cornelius was their captive. He was... afraid.

"Hello?" Mikka asked, coughing as a monk teetered by carrying a stack of musty manuscripts. An elderly man with dark skin and sad eyes caught Mikka's gaze from across the room, pushing up his rounded spectacles so that they caught the light. He wore traveler's leather like some of the other non-monks. He circumnavigated the monks to meet them.

"I see you've come in search of the grapevine," the man said with a secretive smile. He was a Masked Bird; he'd used the code.

"Yes, to make wine for the birds," Mikka replied.

"Welcome, brothers and sisters," the man greeted them after a pause. He smiled warmly at the group, his eyes crinkling at the corners. "So I assume he's the Siren Prince?" he asked as if exchanging pleasantries. Cornelius shrunk into the shadows behind the group, something he seldom did. But Mikka wouldn't let him stay there. The prince was hauled by his collar to the front of the group.

"His majesty, prince of Marzine," Mikka announced smugly. Cornelius struggled for a moment in Mikka's grasp but went limp.

"You don't have to introduce me so formally, Mikka. Call me 'siren' or 'bastard.' That's what I'm usually called after all," Cornelius said with a wicked grin. The bespectacled man chuckled good-humoredly.

"He's got quite the tongue, no?" the man asked amicably.

"Yes, indeed he does. He's also right here, so you can speak directly to him," Cornelius bit back, his smile contemptuous.

"He's also a captive, so I won't be playing his games. Mr. Savva, did you not chastise him for his behavior?" The man asked, his eyes still on Cornelius.

"Call me Mikka, if you please. I tried the best I could. He's a hard horse to break, however." The man chuckled again. The chuckle broke into a coughing fit. A few monks cast him disdainful glances from their worktables.

"Alright, *Mr. Savva,* if you, your group, and your verbose prince will follow me, I'll bring you to Shadrach. He wishes to see all of you before he retires this evening. I'm sure you're weary from your journey. You'll dine with him, soothe your sorrows with *raska* and conversation," he insisted, motioning for them to follow him. Mikka released Cornelius and gave him a hard shove toward Rodrigo, giving the cook a glance that said, "deal with him because I can't."

The elderly man led them through an arched doorway to

another hall they hadn't seen from the exterior. There were rows and rows of neat bunks in this room, some occupied by Masked Birds and allied travelers. One woman woke from her sleep as they walked by. She gazed at them for a moment before recognition appeared in her eyes.

"Bloody siren. Bloody with the blood of my son!" she cried, waking the man in the bunk above her. Cornelius didn't dare to look back, but he could feel her eyes boring into his sunburnt neck. He hadn't killed that woman's son. His nation had. His father had. He'd always been opposed to war, but never had he seen the consequences of it. He'd always been hidden behind the obsidian wall, a cup of rose tea in his hand, his viola bow in the other.

"As you can see, no one here revels in your presence, prince. And though you may not like it, this is what non-Marzinians think of you. If I may be quite honest, they *hate* you. So like we did during Addison's war, close your eyes and pray for death to be quick when it comes to you," the bespectacled man said, his tone still as pleasant as ever. Cornelius could feel more stares on his neck. Clutching his knapsack and viola closer to him.

"Will we be staying here?" Pia asked as they neared the end of the room.

"No. You all have private quarters in the tower. The men will have one room, the woman another, and one for the Marzinian." Cornelius was glad to be away from the general population for once. These people would murder him without so much as a thought.

The man led them through another door and out into a small yard. A chapel lay before them, the low thrum of voices emanating from the interior. "Shadrach and his associates are waiting in the worship chapel. We have places at the table for you," the man told them, hurrying towards the stone building. Cornelius couldn't remember the last time he'd been in a chapel. He put on his best winning smile, preparing himself to befriend his adversary. Rodrigo frowned as he saw the prince and slapped his arm lightly.

"Stop with that grin of yours. Shadrach will give us a more unpleasant end if you seem like you're having fun," Rodrigo scolded, his golden eyes etched with fear.

"Right…" Cornelius rejoined, his eyes on the chapel's entrance. The elderly man beckoned them inside. It was a cacophony of strewn-about pews and wooden tables. Smoldering lanterns hung low over the massive tables, casting a glow. Well preened men and women were seated on the benches, their many faces shadowed in the candlelight, all stoic. Murray would fit right if given him a necktie. They were all dining with multiple forks. Cornelius even saw one man delicately cutting his bread roll open, his plucked brows raised a bit too high on his forehead. Cornelius was suddenly in his element. Displays like this, save the pews, were familiar to him. When Cornelius saw Rian, one of the former Wilkinian princes, he began grinning like an idiot.

Suddenly, a resounding clap quieted the privileged few. Cornelius felt him before he saw him.

"Lords and ladies, our guests of honor have arrived." His voice sounded as if he'd smoked a cigar for forty years without a single breath between. The silence became smothering. "The Siren Prince and his captors." Cornelius felt his head being tugged up by an invisible string, only to meet the gaze of Shadrach of Sleetal. His eyes were as black as the darkest depths of the untold, darker than death itself. There was an unseen hand around Cornelius' throat, and it tightened the more he fought it.

CHAPTER 12

Cornelius' eyes were still pinned to Shadrach. He was just as transfixing as the prince had imagined. Even so, he broke his stare. He was now aware of the clothes he wore and how unkempt he was beside all the well-dressed guests. Cornelius buttoned his shirt's top button, dusted off his trousers, and combed his hair with his fingers. Looking more presentable, he did what Rodrigo had advised against. He smiled.

"Well? Are you just going to stand there like mountain goats? Have your seats. Everyone but you, cook. You're a short notice guest, and you'll sit at the end."

Rodrigo felt his face getting hot. A large man with the girth of two seats motioned to the spot beside him, his smile pleasant enough. Rodrigo sighed and floundered to his seat. He was only granted quick looks from Shadrach's associates, for Cornelius was the man of influence.

Mikka squared his shoulders as he always did and led the group to the far end of the chapel, where Shadrach waited on a faded throne-like seat. It was fancy in comparison to the wooden benches the others were made to sit on. Mikka put a hand on Cornelius' collar and escorted him to an honored seat, the seat at Shadrach's right hand.

"Mr. Savva, you did well," the masked man rasped. The entire room seemed to lean into his words. Mikka nodded, a smile making his eyes round. Cornelius was utterly perplexed. Nothing about Mikka was innocent. He was a war-hardened soldier who'd seen far more than most eyes ever would. Yet here he was, basking in Shadrach's praise like a boy does his father's. Shadrach held Mikka's eyes captive for another long moment. Then, ever so slowly, he began to turn his neck. Again, nobody breathed until his stare reached Cornelius.

"Shadrach of Sleetal..." Cornelius had to compel himself to speak for once. Naming the masked man lessened Cornelius' fear. The candles flickered anticlimactically atop the tablecloth. The thuds of his heart were methodical again when Shadrach finally dignified his greeting with a response.

"Cornelius of Marzine..." Shadrach said, mimicking his airy tone as best he could with the voice he had. "I've been waiting to meet my prince. You're not as tall as I thought you'd be," he said.

"Yes, everyone fancies me taller than I actually am. I hope you'll still think of me as your peer despite my not-so peerless height." Cornelius responded, his tone warm enough. There was only one problem: he'd called Shadrach his peer. The Raven King didn't slam his fist down on the table or threaten to cut out his tongue. He only peeled the raven mask from his face, no guile in the gesture. A chorus of gasps traveled through the chapel. He had the clean-cut appearance of the king he used to be, his skin as blue as ice. His face had an inky sort of sorrow, dimness that told the tale of someone aging too fast.

Cornelius noticed the man's beauty. The beauty of a demon, the allure of a soul thief. A devil in a chapel. What a sight he was. Shadrach set down his raven mask beside the plate before him, his stare still fixed on Cornelius. The prince felt an understanding pass between. He and this man were one and the same, both living out their days orbiting an unwanted throne. But if Shadrach was anything like himself, he would die before acknowledging it.

"I am not your peer, Siren Prince. Not here, at least. Not in the pit I've carved out for myself surrounded by all my dear friends." Men and women Cornelius suspected were Shadrach's servants began to pour a flavored assortment of *raska* into each of their empty goblets, Rodrigo ignored as per usual.

"Not here. Not in the pit you've carved out for yourself," Cornelius echoed, unable to conjure up anything else to say in response. He took a long swig of the flavored *raska*, choosing only to notice its triviality. The *raska* was made of ash grains that came from the fields of Sleetal's Southern Islands. It was flavored with a hint of something he couldn't identify. Bitter raspberry? Dark chocolate even? That would certainly account for its coloring. He was intrigued. The goblet held enough mystery to tempt another sip.

One of Shadrach's servants burdened his plate with leathery meat and vegetables. Cornelius realized that this was the best Shadrach could offer without Sleetal's resources. He picked at the leathery grit politely. The prince wasn't just Shadrach's equal; he was his superior. If he took a captive for the myriad of reasons he had to do so, he would at least feed them properly. Perhaps after all of this was over, he would take Shadrach prisoner and make him live a life laden with fine cuts of meat.

He took a break from feasting after swallowing a bone and instead watched the others eat, though it was impolite. All but Nic Murray ravaged their plates like pack animals. Mikka ate the most ardently of all, as if he hadn't eaten in days. He'd already emptied two goblets of the flavored *raska*. Pia didn't try to conceal her hunger either. Lara was hiding her haste, but she was the same as the other two. Only Nic Murray hadn't touched his food. He, however, held the correct fork for the greens. From whom the sentinel learned table manners, he didn't know.

Rodrigo looked pitiful, drinking cold soup from his own canister. He met Cornelius' gaze and smiled dutifully at him.

After all of this was over, he would tell the boy exactly how sorry he thought he was. How worthless he was… how honest, kind. Rodrigo was growing on him, it seemed. The prince begrudgingly ate another bite of poorly seasoned pumpkin from his plate, feeling fortunate he wasn't in Rodrigo's place.

The silence waned like twilight. Shadrach's associates settled into quiet conversation, still casting sidelong glances at Cornelius as if he were missing his nose. Cornelius had managed to stomach the sordid salad, but not the loafer-like meat. Soon, he'd finished the entirety of the *raska* goblet. A silent servant poured more of the brew into the goblet.

"Your drink is unusual. May I ask where you procured something so offbeat?" His tone was false and well-practiced. Shadrach's eyes had a shadow of amusement that made him leery of the goblet held in his right hand. The Raven King hadn't so much as chopped into his meat or taken a sip from his cup, the prince realized.

"I brewed it myself while hiding on one of Sleetal's ash grain-growing islands. A farmer and his wife were harboring me as the Marzinians lay claim to the mainland. They owned an ash grain field. Sleetalian soldiers often passed through the farmhold on their leaves. They needed a stimulant that wouldn't be damaging to their health, so I invented yarrow *raska*. Simply grind the yarrow into raspberry juice and mix with the *raska*. It's a nice cocktail. But there's a secret ingredient in this brew that I won't be revealing to you." *Yarrow.* A natural stimulant. And something else. Cornelius had had two goblets of the now obviously doctored *raska*. That explained the film on Mikka's eyes and the shaking of his hands as he braced them against the table. In fact, all of them had had quite a bit of the brew. Pia stared at the Raven King. Nic Murray's glare was reproachful.

"I intended to sleep tonight," Cornelius told him, leaving his fear behind an acidic smile. His heartbeat was strange, and his thoughts were holding festivals in his mind—the ghost of a mischievous smile formed on Shadrach's face. This man... this demon...

"I apologize to you and your group, Mr. Savva. You left a servant girl alive when you took the prince. Did you think I wouldn't find out? I gave you clear instructions, end all witnesses and never let your heart rule your head." All the while, the phantom smile lingered on his lips. "You might still sleep tonight, but your dreams will be *wild*," he murmured, his eyes crawling over Mikka. "And prince," he said, his tone syrupy with feigned regret. "I hope your dreams are especially sickening. I want you to feel even an inkling of what my soldiers felt as they died in the war against your nation. I hope Sirensea and Addison Island burn to the ground." Cornelius could only just hear his words; his heart was thudding louder than most everything. He steeled himself, latching onto his fleeting composure.

"Herbal warfare. I never thought I'd see the day when such petty trickery would be used to condemn the sparing of life. You damn us for the lives lost in the war, yet you do this? You're hypocritical, Shadrach. And a frightful bastard. And if I'm candid, I am too. Because I want Addison Island and Sirensea to burn, too. Don't you see it? We are peers. We're the same, you and I." Cornelius tilted too far in his pew and fell off the side of it. Shadrach laughed airlessly. Hearthheads, named for their orange caps, were hallucinogenic mushrooms he'd put in the brew.

Cornelius dimly saw Mikka crouched on the floor, holding his head in his hands. He'd had six full goblets. The others were in less of a state, but still on the fritz. Lara was staring vacantly at the ceiling, and Murray was slowly standing from his chair, swatting away flies that weren't there.

The patterned tablecloth colors began to sing to Cornelius, a lovely tune he had learned on the viola. He began singing the ballad that went with the melody. Shadrach turned to the bespectacled man. Something was wrong. Yes, he'd added the hearthheads on a whim, but they were only meant to serve as a truth serum, give minor hallucinations at best.

"You only ground in a quarter mushroom for each cup,

correct?" Shadrach asked, disquiet in his voice. He glared at Mikka, who had done a cartwheel. Shadrach's guests were roaring.

"I-I, I must've misheard you, my king. I thought you said four mushrooms for every cup." Shadrach's pupils dilated.

"I believe the amount Mikka consumed was *fatal*. He could d-die. But does drinking quite a lot, and his liver may be stronger because of that," Shadrach said hopefully, wincing as Murray walked into a wall.

Rodrigo stood abruptly, panic in his eyes. Shadrach's associates yelled as Mikka stepped up onto the table, his boot on the Wilkinian prince's plate.

"Shadrach, what did you do to them?" Rodrigo cried. For once, being ignored had helped him. Rodrigo mouthed a silent prayer, turning his eyes toward the cross above Shadrach's head. Such things shouldn't be taking place in a chapel.

"Round them up before they make fools of themselves even more than they already have. Give Mr. Savva a clay tablet to swallow. It'll soak up the toxicant. Hold him down if you have to. I'll deal with the prince and the cook," Shadrach ordered his servants.

It was easier said than done. Pia, Lara, Murray, and the remaining mariners were subdued enough to be lured away by a few of Shadrach's servants. The Raven King's associates booed at their leave, but Shadrach didn't care. They'd come for a show, and he'd given them one. But the curtains were closed now. The Raven King looked at the bespectacled man, already plotting his death. Perhaps he'd force him to drink the remaining *raska* with some powdered nightshade to move things along.

Mikka lost consciousness somewhere amidst the chaos. He was splayed across the table, having hit his head against a chandelier. He'd landed on his pistol, which had fired right through his leg. Served him right. Blood was now soaking through the patterned tablecloth. Shadrach's esteemed guests fled.

"All hell!" Shadrach cried in rage, standing from his faded throne. Rodrigo had turned back and forth so many times that he, too, was beginning to grow dizzy. He decided Mikka's condition was direr than Cornelius', so he would go to him first. Winding his way around the fallen pews, he was finally by Mikka's side. The cries of the others faded to background noise. The vision he saw as he knelt over Mikka flashed from present to past. He was back in Embera, the endless fields of their farmhold stretching out before him forever and ever, it seemed. He and Pia were readying an empty barn for livestock when an Emberan militiaman stumbled through the door. He collapsed with a wheezing breath, and Rodrigo was sure he was dead. Pia had already run off to get their pa when he turned to look for her. Later, he'd found out there had been a fray in town between some Marzinian soldiers traveling to meet their regiment and some civilians. The militia had to step in, and this man had been shot in the leg.

Rodrigo hadn't known what to do, but he hazily remembered his ma treating Emberan soldiers at the height of the war. To make sure the soldier didn't bleed out before the doctor arrived, she would put pressure on the wound before anything else. Rodrigo was just fourteen. He didn't want someone to die because he was too thickheaded to do anything about it. He'd knelt down beside the man and used his own shirt to put pressure on the man's wounded leg. He remembered the heart-thudding moment when Pia came back through the open door, the sunset making a halo around her head. With her, she brought a medic.

Rodrigo tore off his shirt as he had all those years ago, holding it against Mikka's bloodied leg. As he stared down at the man, he couldn't help but feel pain. This was Mikka, after all, his persecutor. He let a thought into his head in between heartbeats. He should let go, let him bleed out in the chapel. Pia would be better off without him. They all would. But unlike Mikka, Rodrigo wasn't a murderer.

"Cook! Does he live?" Shadrach yelled out. He gritted his teeth against the pang of resentment and barked a response back.

"Yes, he does. But I need you to fetch your medic *now!* His leg is purpling!" He tore Mikka's shabby pants from the bullet hole so he could see the leg itself. The leg was bleeding from both sides, which was a good sign. Shadrach looked around, his hand on a wandering Cornelius' collar. He finally sighed and loosed his hold on him, navigating around the toppled pews and tables to fetch the medic. Cornelius sat down hard like a child and began to recite the Marzinian pledge.

The prince stopped short and began mumbling about "Gale." Rodrigo's chest began to fill with anxiety. He checked Mikka's pulse once more, alarmed to discover that it had slowed far too much. *Where were Shadrach and the medic?* Mikka would need both a clay tablet and a proper wrapping for his leg. Lack of blood flow and the toxins from whatever was in the *raska* were slowing his body.

"Gaaaale…" said Cornelius, his tone musical. "Here to take my place, I see. You'll love Rodrigo. He's so much like you and I…" Cornelius laughed. "I… sort of hate him for it. Be polite and introduce yourself." Cornelius greeted nothing, his smile dazed, his eyes filmy. He was trying to pull himself to his feet again. Dread rained down on Rodrigo. He couldn't just let the prince leave. But Mikka would die if he moved to stop him. Mikka's life or Shadrach's favor. Which would he choose? It was a moral dilemma with an obvious answer. He would just have to do both.

"Cornelius, your friend Gale is-is nice!" Rodrigo cried, his words collapsing upon one another like a house of cards. Cornelius teetered to the left, frowning.

"He isn't nice, and he's not my friend, Murray," Cornelius

insisted. Rodrigo laughed shakily. He wouldn't ever be mistaken for Murray without some form of poison. The blood from Mikka's leg leaked around his fingertips, a squelching sound coming from the shirt. Rodrigo swore for the first time since he'd learned of curse words. He removed his undershirt with one hand, staunching the blood with the other. He then used it as an additional bandage.

"Cornelius!" he cried as the prince took a wobbly step toward the wooden doors. Rodrigo could see through the stained glass windows that the sun had set. The prince would be lost in the jungle if he left. Rodrigo held his grip on his shirts. Mikka began to convulse, shaking in his sleep. He was going to die. He was going to die! Rodrigo swallowed, tears in his eyelashes.

"Rodrigo," the prince said forlornly, gripping the tablecloth for support. "I'm a terrrrrrible personnn."

Rodrigo sighed, glancing up. The hot tears rolled down his face as he fixed his gaze on Cornelius. "You and me both," he responded, choking on a sudden sob. In the end, when it came down to it, he couldn't help anyone, no matter how he tried. Pia was better off without *him*, not Mikka. He should've stayed home, let her leave him behind.

"No, you're not terrible. You're Rodrigo," Cornelius told him as if it was the wisest thing anyone had ever said. His eyes didn't seem so shallow when filled to the brim with tears, tears so similar to Rodrigo's. The cook let out another shaky laugh.

"I'm worse than terrible, but thanks for trying," he stuttered, leaning on Mikka's wound with all his weight. The sharpshooter's heartbeat had slowed to a few gradual beats every moment. It wouldn't be long now. A holy quietness filled the chapel as he knelt there with Cornelius. Rodrigo's lips moved fervently against one another in prayer.

"You're not worse than terrible. You're amazingggg, Rodrigo. You're *amazing*. You are the kindesssst, most genuine person I've ever met in my entire life. Authenticity is rare. And you're this most authentic coward there ever was. And I both hate you and love you for that. You're *amazing*."

The words rang in Rodrigo's ears. His eyes widened in shock. And at that moment, through a fit of crazed giggles, Rodrigo decided. He *was* amazing. He would not give up, not until he breathed for the last time.

"Cornelius, give me your shirt," he said. Cornelius glanced at him with concern.

"I'm sorry, who are you?" he asked sluggishly.

"I'm Rodrigo." And for once, he was the main character in the story of his life.

CHAPTER 13

The gates of hell opened when Shadrach had realized he was attractive. His appeal was dark, unnatural, but it gave him the same advantage conventionally attractive men had — the same edge as Cornelius, save the need to flaunt it half to death.

Days had been short in Palace Sleetal, its turrets and spires bathed in both sunlight and moonlight only hours apart. Frost spiraled over the windows, fracturing the fleeting daylight into thousands of vivid fragments. There was a particular window in his bedchamber that he liked to read under, basking in the light while it lasted. He missed his bookshelves and dispersed sunlight, and Shadrach wasn't one to simply lie down and let life run its course. No, instead, he would reclaim what was once his and sit under his window once again. He would have his short days and long nights, have his crown and his country. And with a will that strong, only death could stop Shadrach.

He remembered the day, the moment when he knew Sleetal would fall. It was the turning point of his life, the moment when he went from favored to fruitless. His mother and father had been dethroned two years prior, and he'd quickly taken the throne. Though he wasn't the people's choice, the outcry silenced as time went on. He did his best to rule with balance if nothing else, and that was all any Sleetalian could ask for after his father's disastrous rule. Ulrik had been an incompetent king who had more interest in harlots and *raska* than he did his people's wellbeing. It was almost a mercy when he died of sweating sickness. That was the story the papers printed, at least.

In truth, Shadrach himself had sent his father to exile in Orenia, having staged a bloodless military coup. Soon after, his mother fell asleep in the bath after one too many glasses of wine and drowned. Twenty-year-old Shadrach was left with the Sleetalian throne.

Around that time, Marzine was besieging the Southern Islands. Manefall, the largest, had already been overcome. The majority of the nation's crops were grown on the islands, ash grains for *raska* too. Shadrach had mused about the nation's quandaries over a glass of *raska*, and with the bitter brew stinging his lips, he knew the common people needed their *raska* as much as he. If the Southern Islands were taken, his people would starve. The ash grains were distilled not only into *raska*, but also ground and baked into black bread. Without the grains, there was nothing to eat *or* drink.

Shadrach remembered it was pitch-black that night, a new moon in the sky. He let the alcohol soothe his nerves for a bit longer before he undressed. There was no fire in the hearth, so he shivered as he unlaced the chemise he'd worn under his greatcoat. He'd been in court only an hour previously with his cardinals and advisors. The plaintive stares and echoey conversations left him drowsy and sore. Worries lay claim to his mind, only slightly benumbed by the drink. He'd wished the court could convene in the library instead of the courtroom with its rotunda ceiling. The library was warm, and it didn't echo. He would do his best ruling surrounded by stacks and stacks of stories. But alas, tradition was tradition. Without ceremony, life was absurd. He heard a knock on the door.

"Enter," he rasped, closing his eyes as a strand fell from the knot in his hair. He could feel the fear radiating off of Lustin, his manservant. The sleeves of his dark blue greatcoat were frayed again; Lustin had an awful habit of pulling at the strands of his shirtsleeves and unraveling the fabric. Shadrach had to order the seamstress to hem his shirtsleeves every other week. It was a bother, but Shadrach liked to keep the things around him orderly. The many bookshelves in his bedchambers hadn't a speck of dust on them.

"My sovereign." Lustin placed a hand over his heart and bowed his head low. The distress in his voice was veiled, but Shadrach was perceptive.

"Hello, Mr. Rykov. Be a dear and tend the hearth. It seems I've gotten the chills. Damn this icy hell," he said.

Lustin's eyes danced back and forth from the fireplace to Shadrach, debating whether or not to tell him the bad news before or after the fire was lit. Finally, after a sinister smile from Shadrach, he hurried over to the hearth and began his work, placing the chopped wood on the bearer. Finally, after trying and failing with the intricate fire-starting tools, Lustin used his own cigarette lighter to start the fire. He muttered an apology and stood, eyes on the floor.

"I assume you have something to tell me. Otherwise, you wouldn't be here, and I'd still be cold," Shadrach said, warming himself by the fire. His dark eyes glowed like dying suns as he looked at Lustin.

"Yes, sovereign. There is news. And I hate to be its bearer. The Marzinians have taken Stjernsvet. The capital has fallen."

Shadrach froze. He'd thought they had more time. A week, two, even before this happened. Half of Sleetal was conquered. To the present day, Shadrach hadn't forgotten how complete his failure was, how sudden and striking it was when his throne was stolen out from under him. He'd tried so hard to bring stability to his people. Tried so hard to better their lives. All to fail. But he would have his revenge, using the son of Addison to reclaim his birthright. Shadrach would never forget, never fear, and never fail again.

The Siren Prince could use his charm, use his guile, use his silver tongue all he wanted, but only death could stop Shadrach. His plan was to persuade the prince to duel his own father for the throne, the ultimate betrayal. Under his coercion, Cornelius would split the nations and give Shadrach Sleetal. He couldn't wait to watch as Marzine fell from its pedestal under the boy's ignorant hand.

The plan would only work if the prince agreed, though. But fortunately for Shadrach, his consent had already been assured. Right after he'd revealed the *raska's* doctoring, Cornelius had claimed he wanted Sirensea and Addison Island to burn just as much as Shadrach did. No phrase had ever delighted him more than that one. And if it was true, the end was finally in sight.

Shadrach smirked to himself as he sat in the loft above the chapel he'd made into his private quarters. The sun was just surpassing the horizon from what he could see out the stained glass window. His pack of war-torn strays would be waking from their fever dreams soon. He should check on them. See if they were still alive, for it was the very least he could do.

He dressed and went down the chapel's main floor, averting his eyes from the massive bloodstain at the center of the table. He strode out of the chapel and into the main monastery, passed through the sick hall like an apparition, unnoticed by the tired travelers and those on their deathbeds. If it were up to him, these people would be cast out of the monastery. But it wasn't. The brothers were loyal to the Masked Birds, but they were still faithful to their God and wouldn't turn away those who asked for help. Shadrach caught the eye of a frail old woman tucked into a corner nook. She had a copy of *The Tale of Alexander* open on her lap. The whites of her eyes were yellowed. She opened her mouth as if she were about to say something, but instead, she hacked a cough into her arm. Shadrach shivered and kept his eyes ahead henceforth.

He was relieved when he reached the workroom. It was his favorite place in the monastery, books cluttering every surface— books of every kind. With yellowed, crisp pages that contained stories, he couldn't dream up himself.

He ascended the stairwell up to the makeshift dormitories he'd set up for his vagabonds. The prince was here, even though he'd intended for him to sleep in an attic room separated from the others. Nic Murray, *The Vault of Heaven's* silent captain, had attempted to strangle the cook, calling him "father." He'd had to separate Murray from the rest and put him in the attic room. Cornelius was sleeping with the others, which worried him. He only slightly expected Mikka's throat to be slit when he arrived on the tower floor he'd set apart for the men. But luckily for Mikka, Cornelius was still in the clasps of his dreams. Shadrach nodded at Rodrigo, who was praying over Mikka by the second bed. The boy gave him a dimwitted smile before returning to his devotions. Cornelius lay on one of three hand-carved beds, splayed diagonally across the sheets. His golden curls were slicked to his forehead with sweat from a mushroom dream. Those were wild. In hiding, he'd found himself bored pretty often and had picked up a book on herblore. Long story short, he'd found himself out of his mind with mushrooms very shortly. With another nod to Rodrigo, he left for the women's floor.

Pia Reyes would be awake. She'd drank the least, which was a wise choice. She was a discerning girl. Of course she was. She'd spent two years in the Emberan military, and to live through two years in a war against the Marzinians, one had to be calculating. Shadrach had spent his military service far from the front lines, likely under a gazebo. It was customary for royalty to keep away from anything that could dampen their doilies. To be fair, it wasn't his decision. It was his father's. Pia had endured long, suffering hours in the trenches, bullets flying over her head. Even after her country fell, she'd kept fighting. Joined ranks with a Sleetalian regiment, serving his country as well as hers. He respected her most out of the four he'd chosen for the mission.

"Are you decent, Ms. Reyes?" asked Shadrach, a hand over her eyes until she spoke.

"Yes," she said curtly. The first thing he saw when he lowered his hand was her bed. It was made neatly, the sheets and blankets tucked under the military mattress style. Old habits died hard, he supposed. The sunlight trickled through the tower room's many windows, the jungle trees beyond sparkling with the remnants of a late-night rain. Pia sat on a loveseat by the stove. She'd bathed and changed since the night before, having made herself vomit to get the toxins out of her stomach before they reached her blood—another wise choice.

"May I sit?" he asked.

She only nodded. He sat beside her, staring into the blackened hearth.

"Shadrach, why are you here?"

He clasped his hands on his knees, his smile faltering. "I wanted to see if everyone was still alive. After last night, I couldn't be certain." Pia gave him a withering glare.

"Well, I'm still alive. Joan and Lara are still alive, Mika only just. So you can leave now." Shadrach's smile became satirical. "Aren't you pleasant."

Her eyes narrowed, but she didn't speak.

He gave an extravagant sigh. "You're quite obviously angry, Ms. Reyes. I suggest you tell me why."

"Shadrach, if you don't know why I'm wary of you, then you're too witless to be bothering me right now," she retorted. He angled his head down and looked up through his fringe at her.

"Indulge me, Ms. Reyes," he murmured.

"No," she bit.

He rolled his eyes. "Your brother likes to talk when he's afraid. In fact, I had the urge to sew his mouth shut last night when he was trying to keep Mr. Savva from death. But I'm a good listener. And though he was rather annoying, I did pick up on the details. You're in *love* with Mr. Savva. And you're angry because he may die, and it's my fault." Shadrach hadn't intended this conversation to go this way. He'd only wanted to see if she and the others were well, but he would go with the flow. Their affinity was dangerous. It needed to be smothered sooner or later, and the opportunity had presented itself to him.

Pia stared at him, shocked. "I-I." She lurched to her feet, but he grabbed her wrist before she could escape. He felt her pulse quickening under his thumb. She was stronger than him, unfortunately. She grabbed her own fingertips and wrenched her wrist from his hands, breathing hard. He let her regain her breath for a moment, standing.

"Ms. Reyes, love isn't for you and me. It isn't for any of us. We don't get happy-ever-afters because those only exist in stories. You are not the heroine. I am not the hero. We are only people. Now, give up on Mikka. He'll never be what you need anyway, what with his drinking." He gave her an ornery smile, his teeth glinting like a wolf's.

"I hate you. And I-I don't love Mikka," she said breathlessly, her legs locked in a fighting stance. Adorable.

"So sweet of you, Ms. Reyes. I hate you too," he said tenderly. "But you do love Mr. Savva. I'm just here to advise you to end those feelings before they end you. We can't have you jeopardizing the mission, now can we?"

"I would never jeopardize our—"

"I'm simply suggesting that you take a good look at your priorities, yes?"

After a tentative moment, she nodded. "Good, good," he said, his eyes growing a shade darker.

He left Pia alone then, returning to the workroom to read another tale about those who do get happy endings. Happy endings with love that is. He, unlike Pia, would get his happy ending. Loveless but happy. After two wretched years, the end was in sight.

CHAPTER 14

Sun. Far too much sun. If he were able, he would drown himself just to flee it. Behind his eyelids, it was white-hot, blinding. But if Murray had learned one thing in his eighteen years, it was that things weren't resolved by nonreaction. So, he pried his eyelids open. It took longer than he'd expected, and once the feat was achieved, the pain was exceptional.

He was too tired to close his eyes, so they remained open, growing accustomed to the light at a funeral's pace. He began to regain feeling in his neck, his arms, and his hands. His legs ached, hot and cold and hot again. With every rise and fall of his chest, his body was reanimated.

"Murray... Murray..." The call sounded like it was measures away. But then, it was right in his ear. "Murray..." The name blazed through his consciousness. He moved his dried lips together in an attempt to make the speaker stop. His vision was no longer a ray of white light but an array of fuzzy shapes and objects, one in particular pacing back and forth across the room.

"Ah," he reproached, trying to call for a truce.

"Good morning!" the voice called. The cheerfulness made him want to walk into the ocean. It was Cornelius, he realized. Nobody else would say good morning so loudly on a morning that wasn't at all good. "Murray, I know it hurts. It hurt when I woke up, too. But you have to get up. It gets more and more painful the longer you lie there," Cornelius explained, his voice hesitant now.

Lines identified themselves in his visions, and he began to

make out Cornelius' face. Blond locks of hair, golden skin, blue eyes… The pacing shape he'd seen earlier was Lara, wearing a long, white nightdress. Cornelius was smiling kindly, his eyes red and unfocused. What'd happened? He couldn't remember the night before. Cornelius was clothed in the same white nightclothes as Lara.

"*Ifrean. In Ifrean.*" Hell. *I'm in Hell,* he said in Orenian, too disoriented to understand he was speaking aloud. He was in hell with the prince of Marzine and Lara. He hadn't expected hell to be so bright. Sure, he thought there'd be light from the numerous fires in religious paintings, but no light from the sun. He hated the sun, so he supposed it was becoming. It was like a big, fiery eye looking down on everyone.

"You're not in hell, Murray. If you were in hell, I wouldn't be here." Cornelius coughed, losing his words to a wheeze. Even in this state, Cornelius was insufferable.

"Where?" he asked, trying to sit. Pain spiraled through his body, forcing him back down again. Lara stopped her pacing, her lips drawn into a frown.

"I haven't the slightest clue, Murray. Shadrach *stole* my maps. If I had my maps, I could tell you exactly where we are down to the very coordinate!" she snapped. Both Cornelius and Murray winced, their ears ringing.

"Shadrach gave his word he'd return them when we leave the monastery. He ordered you to *rest* this week, Lara, not study, although I do appreciate your devotion to my kidnapping," Cornelius told her, beaming brighter than the sun. "We're in the room Shadrach set aside for me. You grew nervous in your final hours of hallucinations, however, and Rodrigo was looking after you. Worse came to worse, and you nearly asphyxiated him. Shadrach locked you up in here, and you passed out."

"Rodrigo? What?" Murray asked, wheezing. The room around them had fully reappeared. It was long and narrow, the roof paneling painted peeling alabaster that made his eyes tear up. There was a small bureau at the foot of the bed he was lying on and a poorly upholstered chair in the corner, but no other furnishings to speak of. Sunlight streamed in from curtainless windows on either end of the attic. He wished someone would draw them open. The air was heavy and it was hard to breathe.

"Shadrach doctored our *raska* with yarrow and an unseemly amount of mushrooms because Mikka and Pia let a servant girl live," Cornelius explained. Lara pulled the poorly upholstered chair from the corner, sitting at his bedside. Murray stared up at her, feeling helpless.

"Why are you here?" Murray inquired, regretting having asked. His throat was already sore as it was, and he couldn't seem to hold their gazes without his vision blurring.

"We were dreadfully bored. As Lara mentioned, her maps and scrolls were taken from her. Shadrach did the same to my viola. The only difference is that she can complain, and I can't because I'm a *captive*," Cornelius said, not unkindly.

"And we also care about you," Lara said in addition, giving Cornelius a scowl.

"I'm not sure you do, but I do, Lily." He'd taken to calling her either Lily or Lily of the Valley, disregarding her given name entirely. She didn't mind it much, though, being rather unappreciative of her name. "Lily" sounded elegant and ravishing, two words she didn't think she could be described as. "Lara" sounded like a rugmaker's brand name.

"I do care, Cornelius. Shame about your viola. Wouldn't have wanted to listen to it anyway," she fired back.

Murray glanced between the two. They were friends, he realized. And it was true. Here and there, Cornelius had taken the time to talk to her. He would ask about her day or help her with her duties on the ship. He would always joke, always succeed in making her laugh. They were friends, and Lara had seriously needed a friend since her encounter with Mikka.

Mikka was alive. He'd lasted two days since drinking a lethal amount of hearthhead mushrooms. He was, of course, asleep. Rodrigo had tended to him for the past while, getting him to take clay tablets and broth. He and the medic had packed the gunshot wound well and cleansed it with healing herbs. Pia had also stayed by his side. It seemed the event had closed the rift between them. She came to after only a few hours of fever dreams.

"You know, Murray, I've been meaning to ask you something. How did you know which fork to use at Shadrach's dinner? I didn't know you were a member of polite society," Cornelius asked, knowing full well he was a pain in the ass.

Murray was far too drowsy to answer, but allowed himself a single rebuttal. "Get off your high horse, lie beneath it, and let it stomp you to death," he responded, closing his eyes once more. He'd collected quite a few insults in his mind in case an opportunity presented itself in which he had to reply.

Lara gazed at Murray's face as he fell asleep. "That wasn't the warmest thing to say, but you can't blame him. You're no better than us now," she pointed out. She'd had a proper bath after vomiting all over herself the night before. Lara occasionally bathed on the ship, but with a bucket of icy water and lye soap instead of a trimmed tub by a hearth with soap made solely of roses and tallow. Shadrach led a wealthy life after pawning off a few Sleetalian monarchy heirlooms, and Lara was glad to know him because of it.

"You're right; I can't. But he stood out, that's all. With all the reading you do, one would think you'd have learned the proper fork to use for greens," Cornelius pointed out with a half-dimpled smile.

"You swallowed a bone!" she bit back, making his ears flush red. "Don't think I didn't notice that green look on your face."

"Swallowing a bone wasn't the most embarrassing thing I did that night, trust me," he told her with a kindly laugh.

"Shadrach was in a panic after Mikka shot himself. He locked you in a room with me, and... we kissed," she admitted. Cornelius' eyes flashed in memory, and the moment was suddenly fragile.

"We did kiss..." he realized. "Well, I hope you were able to bear it."

She laughed shakily. "Yes, I survived, but it was hard with the vomit you spilled on my boots right after."

He furrowed his brow, trying to remember further. "I sincerely apologize for vomiting on your boots, Lily." The tense moment had passed, and the two of them could only stare at the sleeping Murray. He looked far less peaceful in his sleep, his features brutal.

"What do you think he's dreaming of?" Lara asked, her tone quieter.

"You, I believe. That's why he looks so disturbed. He'll probably cry out soon."

Lara glared. She clasped her hands primly and turned to him. "He's probably dreaming of you for all we know," she told him with her nose turned up.

"Many have dreamed of me, but with a smile and a great deal more noise," he said airily. They laughed for a while longer before quiet returned.

"I'm going to talk to Pia, offer to have tea with her or something," she declared, riding the wave of courage the banter had given her.

His face split into another smile as he observed her. "I wish you the best of luck," he told her sincerely. "I'll pray nobody kisses you."

She started down a small floor hatch. Nausea rolled in her stomach halfway down the wooden ladder. Shadrach had attempted to confine her to a single room for the entire week, but she wouldn't have it. Lara could endure a bit of nausea and blaring headaches if it meant free rein of the monastery. Squeaking, she plummeted down the last two rungs. Monks at the carved shelves and lecterns turned to glare at her for disturbing their silence. She shied away from their reproachful eyes, offering apologies. Monks, in general, had always disturbed her. She couldn't understand how they devoted themselves to one thing, one God. Was she the only one who wanted to be a pirate after she died, sailing between heaven and hell on her spirit ship whenever she wanted to?

Lara entered the boarding room as quickly as she could. Hardly anyone slept there during the daylight hours. There were no monks, only a fevered few here and there, and they were too sick to mind her. She eyed the narrow bunks, feeling thankful for her quarters in the tower. There could be any number of bugs crawling in the lumpy mattresses, and she much preferred her bed, made with the finest Sleetalian craftsmanship. One thing she didn't like about her quarters was how close they were to Tolmas' floor. He was still vomiting up the aftermath of Shadrach's toxicant, and she could hear his groans echoing throughout the bones of the building all hours of the night.

The sojourner wended her way around a few old chairs to the tower's doorway. She shouldered her way in, bracing herself for the stairwell climb. She was spent by the time she reached it, a cold sweat having broken over her shoulders. Upon entering the chamber, her eyes fell on the stove. A kettle sat atop it, burbling half-heartedly. Joan was asleep, and Pia was seated on a loveseat before the fire. She sipped a cup of tea. She seemed serene despite all that had happened.

"Pia, could I join you?" Lara asked, her voice demure. Pia turned her head slowly, staring at Lara in surprise. "I'm sorry if I startled you..." she amended. Pia seemed to come back to herself, softening.

"Please," Pia said, motioning to the place beside her on the faded loveseat. Lara, half hoping Pia would break down and send her away in a fit of misguided rage, sat. Pia teetered to her feet, filling an empty cup with tea from the kettle and handing it to Lara.

"Pia," she began, trying to steady her voice. "I didn't kiss Mikka. He kissed me. You love him. I know you do. And I would never try to take that from you. You'll make a lovely couple. Truly, I wouldn't dare—" Pia held a finger to her lips. Lara stopped.

"I know that, Lara. I know the kiss wasn't your fault. I've known since we arrived at this godforsaken place. He couldn't get over how it's his fault and how I shouldn't blame you. Still, there's something else he said to me that I can't rationalize away." Pia's eyes remained on the dregs of her tea. "He told you he loved me, did he not?" she asked, her tone bitter.

"Yes, he did," Lara confirmed

"If I could, I would tell him I love him, too." She sounded like a wistful young girl, but the hardened look in her eyes proved that wrong. "But he's just so temperamental. I would never be safe with him. Perhaps his love for me would die with his next drink. Perhaps it would grow and grow until he was made mad by it. He's far too unpredictable, dangerous, and the last thing I need is more danger," she said, trying to convince herself. Shadrach's words rang in her ears. She couldn't jeopardize herself and the mission with Mikka.

Lara's eyes shone. "Pia…" she said, her tone regretful. "Love is never predictable. Love makes you mad, *raska* or not. He loves you, and you love him. If you need steady, leave the Masked Birds. But if you want this life with all of its twists and trainwrecks, allow yourself to love Mikka back, even with his flaws." She laid a hand on Pia's arm. She turned to Lara with a smile on her lips that didn't reach her eyes.

"You don't know a damn thing. Apologies, but it's true," Pia said. "Hell, you've never even been in love."

"I haven't, but oh have I read about it. Every heroine has a challenge similar to yours. I'll give you a spoiler; the heroine ends up with the man she loves, leading the life she's always dreamed of," Lara explained.

The sorrow remained in Pia's eyes as she fixed her gaze on her teacup again. "My life isn't a storybook. It's rewardless, painful. A heroine's life before she got her ideal is *my* ideal. All I want is to stay alive a while longer, to serve the resistance, and someday have a bed to sleep on that's mine and mine alone. I'm not some doe-eyed heroine; I'm a soldier. And sadly, I don't believe this story will end with happily ever after."

"So what then? You'll refuse him?" Lara asked.

"I'll refuse him," she agreed. She clutched her talisman against her to ease the ache in her chest, glad Shadrach had allowed her to keep at least that.

CHAPTER 15

Cornelius was a thief, but with good reason. The white nightclothes Shadrach had given them to wear were functional, but Cornelius valued his identity above all things. He felt deprived of his personality with the uniform, and without his personality, he was nothing. Or worse still, just like his late brother.

So Cornelius stole. It was three days into their stay at the monastery. Cornelius had taken to sleeping on a small portico, for Tolmas was still vomiting, and his retches were unbearable. The night before, he'd begun vomiting up blood. Cornelius wanted to be worried, but like Mikka, Tolmas had beaten him a few times, and he could hold a magnificent grudge,

The portico was barely more than a guarded platform extending from the tower, but it was private. He could see the moon shining above his head at night, the pearly white crescent lighting up his night.

The portico had another advantage. It had a view of the front courtyard, of the crops, and the jungle that stretched out many miles before the monastery. On the night of his endeavor, he was sitting cross-legged on his bed, listening to the nightbirds' song and playing pizzicato on a viola that wasn't there. Then, a man with a large trunk loitering behind him caught Cornelius' attention. He was all things elegant, and the most outstanding aspect of him was his bright purple suit. Sleetalian-made as the latest fashions dictated, and three pieces, tailored to his slender form. Cornelius noted that he would fit well in that suit. Over the past month, he'd made do with a button-down and some of

Rodrigo's faded shirts. It was agony.

That's when he'd decided on thievery. It wasn't as if a man like him would notice a trouser or two missing from his trunk. Cornelius drew himself to his feet and strode into the chamber, cringing as he saw Tolmas' skeletal form hunched over a vomit bucket. He turned as he heard Cornelius enter. His eyes were rimmed with moisture from crying. His lips were stained red from hurling up blood. Cornelius offered a condescending sort of smile, knowing his number was up.

"It'll be alright, Tolmas," Cornelius lied. The mariner looked like he was about reply, but instead turned back to his bucket for another retch. Cornelius held his breath and hurried around the beds until he reached the stairwell, which they despised because of how it tired them.

Once he was down the stairwell, it didn't take him long to find the well-dressed man. Cornelius hunched down in the workroom's shadows and began to appraise the man. Closer now, Cornelius could see the starched button-down beneath his bright purple vest. He even wore golden cufflinks at his wrists. He was rich indeed, possibly a former Wilkinian nobleman who was supporting Shadrach with his funds. Wilkinia was ruled by a dual principality, for a brother needs his brother more than anyone else. At least, that's how it was before the war. The Wilkinians kept various noble families, more than any other nation, so Cornelius' theory was quite possible. The man dug into his deep pocket, withdrawing a bronze pocket watch. He held a monocle up to his eye to read the time properly.

A monk approached him as he studied the watch. Cornelius couldn't hear their hushed conversation, but the possible noble wore a delighted smile as they spoke. Then, quickly, the monk led him to the bunk room. Cornelius stayed back a while in the half-shadow, his mind humming. He would wait for the man to return to the room with the monk for food and drink. Cornelius hoped he was famished. Sure enough, after only a quarter-hour, the man returned with the monk. He wasn't toting the trunk anymore. Cornelius made his move.

Once he was in the bunk room, he spotted the trunk instantly. It was at the foot of the bunk farthest from the room's threshold. Of course. Cornelius huffed, trying to regain his breath. The things he would do for style. He used the poles that held up the top bunk for support as he made his journey toward the trunk. Its silver handle glinted in the half-light of the lanterns.

In the bunkroom, nobody spared him a glance. The entire monastery was ignoring the Siren Prince. And that would help him steal.

He reached the trunk as smudges began to distort his vision. When he was sure the prying eyes of those around him were elsewhere, he unlatched the trunk.

There was a bounty of clothing, his efforts greatly rewarded. He stared. Two rows of liberally colored cravats were arranged beside a stack of crisply pressed collared shirts, a necktie or two among them. There were silks and trousers, nightshirts and button-downs—anything one could desire. Cornelius coughed in surprise. He crossed his legs and considered the collection before him, knowing he should only take what was needed. So he did, limiting himself to a few button-downs, an unsightly plaid waistcoat, a blue cravat, and a pair of worn boots that were stuffed at the bottom of the trunk.

These wouldn't be missed, and he was doing the fashionable man a favor with the waistcoat. Cornelius started to stand, having put everything back the way he found it. Now, if only he didn't run into the man on his way back... The already low light in the room seemed to dim as the monocled man approached, whistling tunelessly. Cornelius' heart thudded in his chest. He had to go... but where? Nowhere to turn, and the man was approaching fast and would notice the Siren Prince standing beside his trunk holding an armful of *his* clothing. There was only one way he could go, and that was out the back doors.

His heart stopped as he entered the man's eye line. It was like walking the high wire, all eyes on him. At least the man couldn't see the stolen clothes with his back turned. Cornelius prayed that would be enough. But he was Marzinian. And there wasn't a single other Marzinian in the entire monastery. *Just keep walking…*

Finally, by divine intervention or dumb luck, he reached the wooden door. As soon as he was out in the night air, he sunk down against the wall, holding his head in his hands and setting down the stack of clothing. His eyes grew wet with tears, but no sob escaped his lips. Instead, he laughed.

"Christ, I'm an awful person," he said. The prince wound his way into the darkest patch of shadow and stripped without further ado, clothing himself in the magenta shirt and plaid waistcoat. He tucked the cravat in as well, smiling. Cornelius knew he looked absolutely ridiculous, but at least he looked like himself again.

The only place he had to go to be safe from the bugs was, regrettably, the chapel. It was just as they had left it, toppled pews and all. The table stretched from end to end, a rather large bloodstain at its heart. Cornelius groaned and placed his hands on his hips. He wasn't quite the religious type, but he knew God wouldn't be pleased with this. He even made an attempt to lift one of the fallen pews.

"Very noble of you to try, even in stolen clothing." He recognized the forty-years-in-ash voice of Shadrach. Cornelius let his hands fall limp, stretching himself to his full height as he turned to him. He glared at the former king. Shadrach had his hands folded behind his angular frame, his bottomless eyes boring into Cornelius.

"Is this chapel just where you… lurk?" Cornelius asked.

"Yes," Shadrach replied, no humor in his tone. He took a step toward Cornelius. Cornelius took a step back. He felt as if they were playing a chess game in stalemate. The cycle continued a few more paces until Cornelius was back at the chapel doors.

"Look, the stolen clothes were necessary. You wouldn't allow me my old ones. I couldn't walk around in... in these," he explained, pulling the white nightshirt from his armful of clothing.

Shadrach nodded. "Fair, I suppose." Another phantom smile pulled at Shadrach's lips. "I'm glad you're here, even if it is to evade the law. I have some things I want to discuss with you, mostly due to what you said at the banquet."

Cornelius laughed again, his back against the door. "I said a lot of things at the banquet, most of which I can't remember," he disclosed.

He and Shadrach shared an intimate smile.

"What about your desire to burn Addison Island and Sirensea? Even hearthheads couldn't cause a prince to blaspheme about his nation. Unless..." he said, drawing out every syllable of the word.

"I won't deny what I said, but I am indeed the prince of Marzine. I've given up many wants before. And I won't conspire with the enemy."

Shadrach's half-smile wavered, but only for an instant. "But am I really the enemy? Have tea with me. You enjoy rose tea, yes?" Shadrach asked.

"I do? Well, yes, I suppose I do. I don't think I want to know how you discovered that." Cornelius told him apprehensively.

"I have my ways, Cornelius of Marzine. Now come," he ordered, striding toward the opposite end of the room with the aplomb of a confidence man. Cornelius was hesitant to follow the Raven King. He'd made the mistake of accepting a drink from him three days ago, and it hadn't turned out well. In fact, Tolmas was dying because of the drink. But Shadrach no longer had any reason to poison him. Cornelius fell into step behind him. He tried not to look at the bloodstain on the table.

"Are you ever going to put this place in order?" Cornelius

asked.

"The monks will replace the pews and the table. They just haven't gotten around to it yet."

"It's sort of my fault this happened. Is there anything I can do to help?" Cornelius made himself ask.

"It's 'sort of your fault' that the nations have been amalgamated into an over-militarized hellscape, too. You should focus on that first."

Cornelius swallowed. He'd assumed the loft would be filled with holy texts and musty antiques, but instead, Shadrach had converted it into an apartment for himself. The walls were covered in black wallpaper, and a faded tapestry of a vineyard stretched across the near wall, a bed with silken black coverings beneath it. A stained glass window was illuminated by the night sky, a saint with cold eyes watching them. There was an armoire carved of blackwood, the handles wrought with silver. But the object that most caught his eye was a lamp. It was meant to be the tree of life, its porcelain roots stretching out from the base of the light. Blues and greens winked through the canopy's glass with the lamp's inner candle. Cornelius was mesmerized.

"You have a very fine apartment," the prince complimented. Every other room in the monastery paled in comparison to Shadrach's.

"I suppose..." Shadrach said. He motioned for Cornelius to seat himself in a small wooden chair by a stove in the room's corner. Shadrach already had a pot of tea boiling atop the furnace, which provoked Cornelius' thoughts. Had Shadrach been expecting him, or did he also enjoy a pot of rose tea before retiring? Clairvoyant creep.

Shadrach rummaged through his armoire for matched cups. Then, he poured the steaming liquid into the cups for them, handing one to Cornelius.

"I'm sorry, but I have to ask. Are there any poisons in this? I haven't written a will yet, and I think that's something I should do if the tea has another 'secret ingredient.'"

"I give you my word that this tea is untainted," Shadrach promised with a slight nod, taking a sip of his. Cornelius followed suit, though hesitantly. His first sip was tiny. Only after he'd named the taste did he drink freely.

"How good is your word, though?" Cornelius asked after a few more sips.

Shadrach sighed, bored by his numerous questions. "I suppose you'll find out with time." He took another swallow.

"So you want to burn down Addison Island and Sirensea. My father wouldn't be too pleased with that," Cornelius began. He wished Shadrach would laugh at something, anything besides the inside jokes he seemed to have with himself.

Shadrach downed his rose tea before speaking. "I have a business proposition for you regarding that," Shadrach told him, his face shadowed in the lamplight. Cornelius nodded apprehensively. "You're the crown prince, set to inherit rule of the conjoined nations. I propose you duel your father for the throne." He set his cup down on the stove and clasped his hands, staring deep into Cornelius' shallow eyes.

The prince choked on his tea, coughing. "I have a question," Cornelius asked, his eyes wide.

"Ask away."

"Are you stupid?" He clenched his cup.

Shadrach stood. He towered over Cornelius. "Not in the slightest. I'm quite sharp, actually." The silence was enough to asphyxiate Cornelius. Finally, Shadrach spoke again. "You would the take the throne, separate the nations, and do what you please to Sirensea and Addison Island. They're yours to burn. I'll back you and give you the means to do so. All you have to do is put me back on Sleetal's throne and some of my associates on the other thrones." Cornelius scoffed, concealing his fancy. He could rule his nation justly… allow his subjects happiness and unity. Pass laws that would put everyone on

equal terms; no one group raised higher than the others. But…
he couldn't. He would die if he dueled his father.

"Absolute power corrupts absolutely, Shadrach. How do you
know I'd separate the nations at all? How do you know I'd defeat
my father?" Cornelius asked indignantly, meeting Shadrach's
gaze for the first time. Cornelius thought of his father's eyes and
the primordial fear that coursed through his veins when he
looked into them. Then, he pictured them glassy and lifeless.
Lifeless by his hand. The killer of so many killed by only one.
He could… he could avenge Gale and be Cornelius again.

I'll have to trust your word," Shadrach replied with a sinister
smile.

Cornelius felt like he was making a contract with a demon
and putting up his soul as collateral. He had one more question
he needed to ask. "How do you know my word is good?"
Cornelius asked. Shadrach fell back into his chair, leaning back
all the way.

"I suppose I'll find out with time." But despite how he longed
to accept Shadrach's offer, despite how he longed to see Sirensea
and Addison Island burn, he couldn't. He would never be able
to defeat his father, never be able to overcome Marzine's
atrocities. His allies would turn on him, and death would be his
shadow, his only companion, his fate, even. He would never be
happy, for as he told Shadrach, absolute power corrupts
absolutely.

"Shadrach, I wish the world was good. I wish I could be the
one to right my father's wrongs, but I'm not. My name isn't my
own, and neither is my life if I take the throne. I want a few more
years. I need some more time before I surrender myself to the
crown. Before I become Gale entirely."

As Shadrach stared at the prince, his world tilted a little. The
end was in sight. But he wouldn't agree. And Shadrach could
see he wanted to. He could see just how much he wanted to say
yes. But he wasn't, for some reason.

"Get out of my sight, then, if you want to be on the wrong side of history," he spat. Cornelius did as he was told, leaving the apartment, grabbing his misshapen pile of clothing as he went. He felt dead as he returned to the tower. But it wasn't he who was dead.

Nic Murray stood over Tolm's bed, clutching the boy's hand as he breathed his last. And with horror, Cornelius realized that Tolmas had died at Shadrach's hands.

CHAPTER 16

Mikka didn't suffer fools, not anymore. They had been easy companions before, the odd ones who were so very companionless. He could craft himself armor from these malleable misfits, wearing them proudly as his shield. With them, he scaled the ranks fast, his greatcoat growing more and more decorated. Serving hadn't been his choice. But Mikka had played with the hand he was dealt. He'd survived. Thrived, in fact.

The recruits ate and drank in the cold, slept in the cold, and lived by its laws. The wintry winds cut across the mountainous terrain, leaving gouges in the deep snow. Mikka's toes were always blue, his army-issue boots made for the sole purpose of sparing Sleetal's coffers. Mikka remembered a day that deadened the cold, the day that defined his service and the service of every other drinking man in Sleetal. He was out on the range, trying to get a feel for a sharpshooter's rifle before the qualifying exam.

"Lars, you'll blow off my ear sooner than you'll hit the target," Mikka groused, turning back to look at the boy. The shadowy figure gave Mikka a curt nod before readjusting. Lars was the youngest, and Mikka hated him. His eyes, the color of a morning sky, hadn't yet seen death. And, try as he might, Mikka would never forget it when the boy fell for the very last time. Lars was only thirteen, tall for his age. The recruiters ignored his birth certificate and stole a year of youth from him. Mikka remembered the shallow grave they dug for him in the stygian sands of the beaches, those morning sky eyes eaten away. It was better to hate the kind ones; they always died first.

That evening on the range, Mikka had drawn a flask of something given to him by a nameless soldier. He'd said it would keep Mikka warm, and all he'd ever wanted was to be warm, so he was unopposed to the flask. He'd taken a generous swig, regretting his boldness shortly. The taste was bracing, and he could hardly swallow it. But he did. And sure enough, feeling returned to his toes.

"Whatcha got there?" asked Lars, the wind having parted the mist for a moment.

"Dunno, Lars. Whatever it is, it freezes on my lips. It'll do just the same in your eyes," Mikka warned, firing forcefully. The bullet struck through the target's edge, the sound reverberating off of the surrounding rocks.

"At least I wouldn't have to see your sorry shooting anymore," the boy said bravely. Mikka chuckled. He was only a few years older than Lars, but he felt like a time-battered veteran with him.

"You're smart now, are you?" Mikka whirled around but kept the rifle down due to protocol. The wind cleared the mist once again, and Mikka could just make out the terrified look on Lars' face.

"Only a joke," Lars murmured, trying and failing to be aloof. Mikka let up and gave Lars an easy smile.

"Savva! Keep your head down and focus!" cried the martinet, taking a swig from a flask of his own. He complied, for the only thing he feared more than death was the martinet.

The session continued well into the evening until the sky went dark, and the sharpshooters-in-training couldn't see any longer. Even then, they forged onward, for the martinet said they could test their senses in the dark. In all truth, the man was drunk out of his mind and didn't understand the perils of doing so. But drunk men are more dangerous than shooting blind, so Mikka and Lars obliged.

Every time the cold got to him, Mikka took a sip of the bitter drink from the flask, and as if by magic, the warmth returned to him.

"In!" The martinet ordered, marching back toward the barracks. Mikka and his peers followed, and he found he was staggering. Staggering like his father.

They had missed dinner, staying out late in the cold. Mikka didn't mind it so much, though. There would be leftovers in the kitchen if he knew which cook had the kindest heart. He found himself not even wanting to eat, though, feeling full and warm, giddy and tired. It was a blissful numbness, his paralyzing fear gone until the warmth wore away. Then he took another sip, and the warmth returned. He needed more of the drink, *raska,* he then realized. Now he understood why his father drank it so copiously.

"Mikka, you don't look too good," Lars gulped, steadying him by putting a hand on his shoulder. Mikka only chuckled. The dining hall had long wooden tables at which a few groups of men were seated, talking about the notches on their bedposts. Lars and Mikka were almost alone in the hall. There were rules regarding the times they were meant to be in the barracks and the times they were meant to leave, but they weren't reinforced. The reinforcers were either drunk or asleep, too consumed in their own misery to care. Living on the base was like a looser form of jail, and everyone knew the war was lost—only the troops seeking asylum after a battle tried to speak to them to watch their eyes light up at the stories they told.

"None of us look too good, Lars. I'm just tired. We should hit the hay," Mikka told him, swallowing in an attempt to return the feeling to his throat. He strapped his gun into its case and returned it to the locker before heading to the bunks with Lars, leaning on him for support all the way.

As time went on, it took more and more *raska* to make the pain go away. Perhaps it was a dependence that made him go back for more, or maybe it was the fact that his worries grew with every waking moment.

Mikka had always known the way he wanted to go. He wanted to be shot in the heart, to feel the pain that let him know he'd lived. Whether he'd go to hell or heaven was beyond him. And if there nothing at all waiting, he wouldn't know it. He'd be dead, after all. As it turned out, death was not finite, for he felt something even now when he was sure he was dead: pain. This was hell, he realized.

"Mr. Savva's waking," said a rasping voice. He heard the sound of floorboards creaking. Had Lucifer himself come to greet Mikka?

"Indubitably," a second voice said, cracking at the end of the objectionable word. That sounded like Rodrigo, but Rodrigo couldn't be in hell. No, the boy would go to heaven. Of course, he would, being so devout.

"I don't suppose anyone has told you you're vexatious," Lucifer said dryly.

"Well, yes, but I'm trying every day to correct myself," Rodrigo pledged. He heard a long-suffering sigh from Lucifer, and with a start, he realized he wasn't in hell. His eyelids opened abruptly. It was nearly dark, mahogany sunlight seeping through an aperture. He could just make out the silhouettes of two men, one far more petite than the other.

"Hello, Mr. Savva," the taller man greeted him, his tone grave. Lucifer was Shadrach.

"*Raska*," he rasped, his throat peeling with the effort. He heard a dark chuckle.

"Anyone else would be crying for water, but not him," Shadrach said, amused. Mikka felt an obscure sort of anger, but his want for *raska* was too great for him to care. "Fetch him a bottle, Rodrick. You heard the man."

Mikka breathed a sigh of relief. Who was Rodrick, and why was Shadrach not addressing him by his surname?

"I'm sorry, Shadrach, but I'm called Rodrigo," Rodrigo told him demurely. Mikka's headache blared.

"Your name is Rodrick now, for all I'm concerned," Shadrach said dismissively. Rodrigo's silhouette left after that. Mikka suddenly felt an acute pain in his leg and groaned.

"What h-happened?" he finally asked.

"As Cornelius of Marzine put it, there was an 'herbal warfare' mishap."

Memories slowly leaked into Mikka's mind. The flavored *raska* he'd drank a little too liberally... the singing colors... the visions... the gunshot... and then, nothing at all.

"Hell, Shadrach, you poisoned us. Bastard," Mikka choked out.

"I concur, but you disobeyed my orders. It was only a bit of fun, the most modest of punishments. And besides, it was only meant to last a night. Sadly, an associate of mine got the recipe for the *raska* mixed up. You've been out for four days. However, you consumed a lethal dose, and I'm quite pleased you even woke up at all."

"I'm going to kill you," he vowed. There was that chuckle again. Shadrach was pernicious like his poison.

"No, you aren't, Mr. Savva. You and I need each other. I'll take care of your family, and you keep your head down and do my bidding." *Keep your head down*, just like the martinet had said all those years ago. Rodrigo's silhouette appeared in his line of sight again, this time a bottle held in his arms. Rodrigo offered it to Shadrach, who took it and held it up to the light.

"Well, it's a bit seedy, but you made no specifications."

Rodrigo handed him a corkscrew, but Shadrach had already pulled the cork out with his fist. It wasn't a very kingly action, but Mikka was too drowsy to notice. He heard the soft sound of the *raska* being poured into a flask, his flask. The very same flask he'd received from the nameless soldier all those years ago. He accepted it with a wavering hand.

Rodrigo doddered around the room, lighting the wall sconces with a single match as the sun died. He could make out the faces of Shadrach and Rodrigo now. Shadrach's hair was slicked back in a knot, a few strands curling down around his face. His eyes were darker than usual in the lanterns' penumbra. Mikka took a sip of the *raska*, wincing as it slid down his throat. It stung, but he didn't mind. His pain shuddered and fell away after another few swallows.

"Mikka, are you alright? Should I get Pia?" Rodrigo asked tentatively. The thought hadn't even occurred to him. He did desperately want to say yes, have Rodrigo bring Pia to him, but they hadn't left things great. He and Pia had been arguing over a drunken mistake because... well, they were in love. But Pia had told him she wouldn't have him so long as he drank. Mikka took another sip of *raska*, this time a little defiantly. He knew he couldn't quit drinking, but could he leave her? She was his best friend in the entire world, and he wouldn't be the man he was without her influence. But without his *raska,* he wouldn't even be a man. No, he'd be a coward, dead at the sea's bottom with rocks tied to his ankles.

"No," he said decidedly. "I don't want to see her." He was only nineteen. These years were his glory years. He needed the *raska* now more than ever. The pain would steadily grow every day. Perhaps in a few years, he could stop. Perhaps, perhaps. Maybe, maybe.

"In other news, Mr. Tolmas has died. I never did learn his last name," Shadrach announced a little bit too cheerfully. Mikka felt anger rise in his chest.

"You murdered him," he said through gritted teeth. He held the flask a little tighter, then. "Only Joan remains of Murray's crewmen. He won't be able to manage the ship without at least two," he told Shadrach.

"Yes, that's exactly why you need *me* to join you. You're unruly, Mr. Savva, and you take too many risks. I'll take your place as leader and be a replacement for Mr. Tolmas."

Mikka coughed in surprise, *raska* dripping from his lips. The lantern light illuminated Shadrach's sick smile. Was he *excited*? He hadn't known Tolmas well, but they'd worked side by side during that storm. He didn't need Shadrach disrespecting the dead like that.

"Why not get someone else to do it?" he asked hoarsely. Shadrach took a tiny step toward him, his lips parted as if he were about to recite a narrative.

"To be quite honest, I'm worried about the mission. I've also taken an interest in the prince's behavior. I have a plan, and if I could convince him to take part in it, then the effects could be astronomical," he divulged.

"Why am I needed then? Am I excused from the mission?" Mikka asked, this time softly.

"No. You have a debt to pay, Mr. Savva. And though it doesn't please me to admit it, the others respect you more than they do me. I'll only be a metaphorical leader. You'll have your old duties, just more modest quarters on the ship," Shadrach explained, patting his cheek patronizingly.

"I hate you," he growled, leaning away from Shadrach.

"Mr. Savva, you can trust the feeling is mutual. But again, we need each other. If this works, then you will have more power than you could ever dream up in that small, *raska*-impaired mind of yours."

"What's your plan, then?"

So Shadrach told him. Broke it down step by step. Put Cornelius on the throne. Have him separate the nations. Place his associates in positions of power. He promised to make Mikka a noble in the court of Sleetal, a noble with special privileges. Rodrigo sat on the ground beside Mikka's sickbed as the plan was relayed. He nodded along but knew he would never be given a part of the plot. His sister would, but he wouldn't.

"You'll live in comfort all the days of your life, wanting for nothing," Shadrach promised, his tone tainted like the flavored *raska*. Mikka felt disquiet rise in his chest, but he pushed it down. This was an offer he couldn't refuse. But before he gave his assent, he had one last question.

"What of the siren? Does he keep Marzine?" Mikka asked. That godforsaken chuckle returned.

"He told me himself that he wants to burn Sirensea and Addison Island to the ground. Marzine will devolve into chaos under his rule, and he'll surely be assassinated, shot in the head while playing that cursed viola. He had it right when he said absolute power corrupts absolutely." The edges of his crooked smile growing too close to his ears.

All Mikka saw in Shadrach's eyes was power lust. The man wanted his throne back, and he would do anything for it. He nodded, a frown on his lips.

Little did they know that Cornelius was among them, listening. He had decided a few days previous to sleep on the portico. There was only curtain between him and the sleeping quarters, and Cornelius could hear them quite clearly. He clutched the bow of his newly returned viola to his chest, having been waxing the instrument as he listened, but this was far more intriguing.

The Raven King was boarding *The Vault of Heaven*, but Cornelius wouldn't make his load light. In fact, it would be hell. The prince had been dancing between whether or not this was all just some screwed-up game, and he'd come to a consensus. It was a game, but it was also war. A game, a war of chess. This would either end in stalemate, or he would come out victorious. But as the night waned and the talk ceased, Cornelius couldn't keep his mind from wandering to Shadrach's prophecy.

He dreamed of another reality where he would give in to Shadrach's plot, becoming one of his pawns. He saw himself, smiling into the chinrest of his viola for a crowd of his subjects, the crown askew on his head. But then, the crown fell to the ground. Its gold split in two, and his viola silenced. A shot rang out, and he, too, fell, broken like his crown.

CHAPTER 17

Lara looked forward to their Sleetalian sojourn. Of course she did. Her wanderlust compelled her to. But even as she looked forward to it, she was worried. Stjernsvet, the capital city of Sleetal, was crawling with Marzinians patrols. It was like a rotting carcass, that city, and the soldiers were the larvae.

Sleetal would've merely been an icy hellscape if it weren't for the fortuity it offered both citizens and immigrants. The big cities were diverse and bustling, the architecture a bizarre blend of every nation. It was only like that in the big cities, though. Funds went to them instead of smaller townships. Even during the war, most Sleetalian soldiers were drafted from the sticks because city workers were more crucial to the economy. City workers had jobs in tourism and factory work, and Sleetal needed a steady income flow to finance the Marzinian war.

Sleetal's economy was based mostly on the export of ash grains and mass produced items, and tourism. Well, any place with cheap alcohol and boarding was bound to be frequented, especially with a war raging on outside the grubby boarding houses and pubs. Soldiers often went to Sleetal during their leaves of absence for those very reasons. They could drink on their meager government salaries. Drink, gamble, philander, and die. Lara knew that when they arrived in Sleetal, they would be doing the same. They would dress Cornelius up as a prisoner and tote him around the city in chains like they had in Orenia.

She consoled herself with the thought as Cornelius talked unremittingly of court gossip. He seemed to be choosing the most tiresome words on purpose, using his silver tongue for evil instead of good—if you could call his customary charm good. They were wading through a stream, and he was laughing at one of his own poorly-worded jokes. She wished he would revert back to speaking in complete sentences and using the word "dire" less. But nobody dared to stop him. They had to endure him, or Shadrach would take their earnings.

The night before their departure, Shadrach had gathered them around Mikka's sickbed and relayed a new, higher stakes plan. He planned on persuading the prince to duel his father and take the Marzinian throne. From there, the nations would be separated, and the crew would all be put in positions of power. Even Rodrigo was promised ash grain farmland on Sleetal's Southern Islands. His sister, however, was promised a commanding role in the Sleetalian military.

"How do you know the Marzinian won't go back on his promise once he has the throne?" Pia had asked skeptically.

"I'm trusting his word," Shadrach said, giving her a cryptic smile. "You've already agreed, right, Mr. Savva?" he'd asked, turning to Mikka.

"I have. It's going to be hard to play nice with him, though. He's insufferable," Mikka grumbled.

"So being kind to him is compulsory?" Rodrigo questioned as if it wasn't a prerequisite for him.

"Yes. In fact, you'll lose your shares of the reward if you don't." Mikka seemed to die just a little bit at his words.

After the meeting, they'd returned to their beds as if nothing had happened. Lara knew Cornelius couldn't have overheard them during *that* assemblage, but he certainly could've when Shadrach first relayed the plan to Mikka. So her hypothesis was that Cornelius had overheard them and was tipping the scales by being a pain.

"And then my father said I was lesser than my brother, which, if you recall, I'm not. So that leads me to believe I was only born to replace him. But you know what they say, the second attempt is always better than the first." Cornelius went on and on until Lara's ears cried out. Mikka grunted, leaning more on Pia as they finally found their way to the top of the bank. She was helping him walk on his wounded leg. It seemed they had reconciled in the way they did best: by ignoring the issue in its entirety. She couldn't so easily forget, couldn't so easily dismiss it. She still woke up in the middle of the night after nightmares of what Mikka would've done had Pia not opened the door when she had.

Lara found herself wishing Cornelius had been the one to kiss her. Then, she would've kissed back. She'd been turning a deaf ear to his rambling for hours, but had kept staring at his lips.

Cornelius finally stopped as they found the sea cave's entrance. "So that's what's happening in the Marzinian court as of late. I must ask your forgiveness, though. I'm sure I was a bore," he said, feigning penance.

He had indeed been contriving to bore them to silence. They'd done nothing but praise him. Even Mikka had made a begrudging comment about how he laced his boots, and the one thing Cornelius couldn't stand was misguided flattery. He knew this was part of Shadrach's plan, but it was just so disturbing. He was used to such things in court, but not out here in the badlands of Wilkinia. He rather liked the crew's roguish bravado.

"You weren't a bore," Shadrach told him jauntily. His voice echoed through the sea cave's caverns.

Cornelius eyed him. "Would anyone else like a turn? Murray?" he asked. He knew Murray didn't talk idly. Mikka drew his flask from his belt and took a long-suffering sip, his eyes heavy in their sockets.

"We're going to Sleetal next," Lara interjected before Cornelius could start again. She knew they weren't supposed to tell Cornelius where they were going, but what could he really do with the knowledge? The others breathed a collective sigh of relief as she began her report. Like a good tour guide, she described Sleetal, keeping the historical details vague and the adjectives bright.

"Will I be allowed to join you?" Cornelius asked. He knew Shadrach would let him join. It was Sleetal, after all, the nation he used to rule. The cities were filled to the brim with rebels and sympathizers. That's why there was such a need for Marzinian patrols.

"We should leave him on the ship with Rodrigo. I'll give him my pistol this time, so the si-Marzinian doesn't get any ideas," Mikka said, drinking from his flask again. They navigated around a cluster of boulders. Rodrigo flushed, knowing he didn't do well with firearms.

"Oh no, Mr. Savva, we'll take him along with us. He'll dress as a prisoner, and besides, Rodrick would end up sinking the ship," Shadrach said pointedly, giving Mikka a murderous look. Cornelius hid his smile, fingers to his lips.

"Then it's decided. I'll go to Stjernsvet with you. I look forward to vexing Mikka beyond all measure."

Cornelius wanted to give Shadrach a pinprick of hope to hold his interest. "Shadrach, can I ask you something?"

"You *may*."

"Tell me, what's it like to be king?" The question made the Raven King's step falter.

"I had power beyond my all imagining, and I was loved by all. Ruling was an undertaking, but I wouldn't have given it up," he said, praising the role so falsely that Cornelius couldn't help but cringe. He knew enough about kingship without Shadrach's false testimony. It was a solitary, dreadful life that ended in untimely death. The prince thought of his mother and her insanity. He thought of his father and his... well, insanity. He would eventually go insane, too, with that much power.

"It sounds like you enjoyed your time as king. That perspective's new to me, I must admit," Cornelius said, raising false contemplativeness in his tone. He was silent for the rest of the journey to emphasize his phrase, letting it ring in Shadrach's ears.

Lara was quite pleased to be back in her quarters with familiar things around her. The old scent of scrolls filled her nostrils as she lay there on the bottom bunk, her many woven blankets draped over her. The day had been exhausting, especially with her weakened body. She'd taken books from the monastery to read but was too drowsy to light the candle at her bedside. Her eyelids were heavy, and she soon allowed herself to sleep.

Lara hated dreams. Little was known about them or where they came from. Did God send them down from heaven, or were they just something her mind conjured up? This dream was obscure as all others were, but she knew where she was, the library tower where the teacher lived. She'd spent the better part of her life here, hidden among the shelves. The teacher was gone for most of each month, only in the tower for a week at a time. She was always alone but seldom enabled to venture out without him in search of companionship. The teacher brought her new books when he came back, so she was content.

But then she'd grown tired of fantasy worlds. The real world interested her more than the imaginary. She'd wanted to leave, go where the wind took her like new seeds. Once her interest in fictional worlds died away, the loneliness loomed larger. Those brief trips to the market with him were all she looked forward to in life, the sun touching her skin directly, not through the window's glass.

The last time she saw the teacher, the war was at its height, and Wilkinia was ruled by Marzine. He'd taken her to the market but hadn't let her speak to anyone as he had other times. She'd had enough of being silent, of being alone. He'd said the curved walls of the library tower would protect her, but instead of keeping danger out, they'd kept her in. She'd run away that day, plunging deep into the wildlands.

The rest of her years up until the mission were a blur of color and light. She'd traveled all over Wilkinia with a group of nomads until she found the Masked Birds and joined the resistance, her years of study a treasure to them.

But now, back in the library tower, the biting loneliness returned. The loneliness that had driven her to the precipice of madness. She began to walk despite herself. The sky was a midnight purple, moonbeams extending across the floor like a sleek white cat. As she grew closer to the window from which the moonlight emerged, she noticed a man. He had his shirtsleeves rolled up and buttoned at the elbow. It was the teacher, she realized.

"You're back early," she found herself saying. Her voice sounded unfamiliar, high, and whiny like that of a child. His voice was contrast, velvety, and coiling like a snake.

"I thought I told you not to bother me on my first day back. Go, leave me. I don't want to see you at all tomorrow. We'll resume lessons after that."

He turned back to her when she didn't move. She couldn't make out his face, only his eyes. Bluish purple and intelligent. She would always strive to do more, be more than she could ever be because of it. "Are you deaf? I said leave!" he roared. He took a threatening step toward her, and she scurried off.

She took the twists and turns through the bookshelves that led to a lofted area, pulling leatherbound volumes off the shelves in her wake. The loft was a haven in her sometimes horrifying maze of fantasies. She heard the footsteps of the teacher behind her, his boot heels clicking methodically against the worn wooden floors.

She was afraid, for he did something worse than just screaming. It was rare, this thing, but she always knew when it was coming. Tonight felt like one of those nights. He had a special pen for it and everything, one with a sharp, inkless tip. Her blood would be the ink. He would etch things in her arms and legs. *Worthless*. *Tiresome*. And worst of all, *cease*. It was a command instead of an adjective. There was something he would spread on the bloody words afterward that smelled of herbs. The cuts never left scars because of it.

Sometimes, she wished they had.

He was closer now. The fallen volumes weren't hindering him as she'd hoped. Pure terror overwhelmed her as she felt cold fingers close around her wrist. She released a cry, wriggling free and breaking into an all-out run, not pausing to knock the books off the shelves any longer. Her loft was close now. It was where she slept, where she read, where she dreamed. It was a sanctuary. And, most importantly, she had the higher ground.

"Leave me alone!" she cried, not daring to look back at the looming shadow that was the teacher. He chuckled. The sound echoed back, taunting her.

"Do you really want that? Do you want to be left alone? If that's so, you can leave now. Go! You have no place here!" That only made the tears fall faster.

"Stupid… stupid…" she sobbed. The ladder to the loft loomed ahead of her. She almost yelled with relief, springing onto the first step, hauling herself up the next. He wouldn't be able to reach her up there. She would be *safe*. She felt the grooves in the ladder, the familiar feel of where her frantic fingers would fall on nights like this one. There were nail marks where he would try to grasp the wooden rungs. He never made it to the top, though. She would hurl books down at him, once even her own shoe.

But suddenly, as she seized the final rung, a cold shock traveled through her. She felt his hand on her leg, dragging her down. His fingernails dug into her flesh, and she whimpered in pain. She squirmed and scraped, trying desperately to be stronger, to overcome... but no. She would never overcome it. In some way, she would always be trapped in the library tower, trapped in that need to be loved, to be wanted.

Her fingers slid away, and she fell, landing on her side with a painful shock. The breath was knocked out of her, and it took her a moment to draw in air. He stood over her, shadowed like a monster from a children's tale. Still, she couldn't see his face. But she could hear his voice as he leisurely descended on her.

"Lara, Lara, *Lily*. Why do you run? Don't you want this? Don't you love me?" It was silky and melodious. Not the teacher's voice, but Cornelius'. Finally, a moonbeam struck him. It was him.

"No... no, it was him, not you!" she begged. He shook his head, that same superficial smile on his face. He knelt down beside her and put his cheek to hers.

"We are one and the same," he whispered, his lips brushing against her earlobe. The sound seemed to resound through her body. But Lara wasn't afraid anymore. She was intrigued because, of course, she would never fail to be fascinated by things that could ruin her.

She woke the following morning with only an afterthought of the dream. Her hands were shaking as she combed her hair.

CHAPTER 18

Nic Murray watched them banter. A slight smile was ever-present on Cornelius' face. Lara was working the rigging while Cornelius entertained her. Cornelius had stopped trying to bore them to death and was back to his usual charming self. And oh, Murray wished Cornelius would talk to him. But there was no point speaking to someone if they didn't reciprocate. He fixed his eyes on the horizon, the orange sun setting just below the waters. And as Murray stared at it, he finally named the fluttery feeling in his chest. It was... desire.

What had he thought would happen? He'd kissed Cornelius only because they'd defied death that day. It was a short, heat-of-the-moment choice. But now, he wanted more. Murray closed his eyes and tried not to think about it. They would be in Sleetal soon. He'd had a rather existential moment the night of the storm and realized there was a lot he hadn't done. He hadn't gotten properly drunk before, and now was the best time to do so. Previously, he hadn't had feelings to drown. Now, he did.

He turned again at the sound of confrontation from the upper deck. Mikka and Shadrach were well into an argument. Well, Mikka was doing most of the arguing. Shadrach remained silent, and Murray couldn't be certain he was human with that ear-to-ear smile on his face.

Cornelius had clearly caught onto Shadrach's plan and decided to tip the scales in his own favor. He'd asked for Mikka's quarters, something he wouldn't have dared to do before. Mikka, justifiably, was outraged. The Siren Prince in his quarters, being spoiled by his adversaries. Mikka couldn't stand the idea. Nic Murray found it all rather amusing; nobody else realized Cornelius knew. He would clean out Shadrach's coffers before the man had the time to wink one of his dark eyes. Murray could speak up and tell Shadrach, but that wouldn't be any fun at all. He'd decided to watch and see how this played out. Hell, maybe he'd end up with Mikka's quarters.

Another thing Murray could check off his bucket list in Stjernsvet was gambling. His father had been rather fond of it, though that hadn't boded well for their family funds. He always came home late, his overalls stained with sweat and grime from the mines, only to venture out again in search of a table to bet on. On the rare nights Murray was up late enough to see him return for the second time, he noticed the thrill in his eyes, the haste in his step. Even if he hadn't won, he always came back with anticipation. Anticipation to "make back what he'd lost." Murray would do all the amoral things he could in Sleetal, being neither good nor bad beforehand. He would start with all the bad things and work his way up to the good things until he'd lived an entire life.

"I've had it with this! I've had it! I don't care; just give the damned siren everything he wants! Hell, you should cast me overboard now, for he'll certainly want that. He'll laugh, in fact! But I'm alright! I've always been!" Mikka yelled, his eyes blazing into Shadrach's. Cornelius and Lara turned to observe the spectacle. Pia hurried over, looping her arm through Mikka's and whispering. He heaved his shoulders and nodded to Pia. She led him away, then, and Murray was almost disappointed. He'd expected the tantrum to last a lot longer. Shadrach seemed just as disappointed as him, and Murray wondered momentarily what torture he'd had in store for Mikka.

"It's grand of you to be so generous, Mikka. I'll enjoy living in your quarters," Cornelius said, his eyes alight with cruel amusement. Murray smiled satirically, rocking his palms back and forth on the wheel.

Even the sea itself seemed to still in anticipation. Mikka's shoulders began rising and falling as he heard Cornelius' words. His nostrils flared, and his eyes seemed to spark with red. Then, he charged Cornelius, who took the most minor step to the side. Instead of barreling into the prince, Mikka barreled into the railing. Cornelius flourished his arms, presenting Mikka's fallen body.

Well, that was another thing Murray could check off his bucket list. He'd always wanted to see a bullfight. Cornelius, the Marzinian Matador, matched up against Mikka the bull. It was the fight of the century.

His quiet laugh grew louder. Louder and louder. Everyone's eyes were drawn away from Mikka and up to him. He threw back his head and laughed some more, for the hilarity of it all was too much for him. He fell to his knees, and tears fell from the corners of his eyes. He was the spectacle now, but he could care less.

Then, a warm feeling filled up his chest like a vial of sunlight. He heard another laugh. It was Cornelius'. His laughter was not deranged like Murray's though, though. It was honey. Through tear-blurred eyes, Murray saw Shadrach prodding the others into laughing. It was only Pia and Rodrigo who needed coaxing, though. Lara had a hand on Cornelius' arm, her head thrown back.

Rodrigo pulled Mikka's motionless body into a sitting position before giving a few halfhearted laughs. Pia reproached the crew, kneeling to check Mikka's pulse. A few seconds later, Mikka came to. He was met with the horror of being laughed at. Murray silenced himself.

The others had assumed he was laughing at Mikka, but it was Cornelius he found amusing, in truth. How sad. How terribly sad Cornelius' state was. It was the mirror image of his life on Addison Island. All those in the Marzinian court appeased him and pleased him with every breath that left their lips. Life on the

Vault was the same. Cornelius was a monstrosity in a circus, quite literally the elephant in the room. And that was when Murray noticed Cornelius' eyes on him. Harmony was built between them, a bridge. They understood each other.

Mikka, instead of going after Cornelius again, was taken away by Pia. He went off sullenly like the belligerent man he was. Cornelius returned to his conversation with Lara, and Shadrach strode off with his hands in his pockets, whistling a haunting tune that was familiar to Murray. He then turned back to the horizon as if nothing had happened, staring at the sea as he always did.

Despite returning to his apathy, Murray couldn't help but notice the feeling of foreboding that had settled over him. The foreboding, the heaviness in the air warned of something... but Murray didn't know what.

Cornelius gazed up at Lara, a broad smile on his face. "Tell me, Lily, what do you find so appealing about those scrolls of yours? I do enjoy reading, but I can't stand to study books as you do."

"For me, it's not just an idle pastime. It's an exit."

Cornelius pondered her words and nodded. He had always been so very conscious of the world around him, and so he'd never been able to immerse himself in another world. There were always more pressing matters at hand. If someone, anyone around him, wasn't smiling, it was his duty to change that. Cornelius glanced at the Raven King, making sure he was listening.

"When—if I become king, I'll build you a library, and I'll fill it with more books than you could ever read," he said.

She pursed her lips. "I didn't know you were that enamored with me," she told him teasingly.

He felt his heart palpitate, but he ignored it.

The look on her face grew more sedate. "At what cost, though? Uprooting libraries all around the world just for me?

I'd rather have a ship of my own so that I could travel to those places," she said, the temperance in her voice leaking away into another smile.

Cornelius' grin only grew. "Of course I'm that enamored with you. And if it's a ship you want, then you'll have the finest. Cedarwood and all. I'll name it the Lily of the Valley."

"Would you really do that? Carve some silly pet name of yours into a ship of cedarwood?" she said with a short laugh. Her hair was glossy in the sunlight, almost like a new candle's wax. He smiled a little stupidly.

"Yes," he said softly, only to himself. He didn't know why he was speaking when she couldn't hear him. But he had said it. Yes. If he could hear that laugh again, yes. He again shook off the odd pulsing feeling, convincing himself it was a lousy helping of Rodrigo's soup or the aftermath of Shadrach's herbal warfare.

Lara bid him good evening, heading to her quarters for a late night of study. He stood there, hands shoved deep in the pockets of his stolen trousers as he watched her go. Time was strange as he stood there, like an accordion. Yawning and closing and yawning again until he heard a voice.

"Hello there, would you like to join Mr. Savva and me for a drink in the galley? He wants to apologize for his misconduct." He felt the Raven King's cold fingers fall on his shoulders, and a shiver ran through him. Even still, he put on a pleasant smile and met Shadrach's gaze. The deck was empty.

"Forgive me, but I intended to play my viola in my new quarters. I haven't had the chance to since we were at the monastery." An eerie silence draped over the ship. Shadrach raised his hand from Cornelius' shoulder to trace his jaw with his index finger. When the hand clamped down again, Cornelius knew in his soul of souls that he'd morbidly underestimated Shadrach.

"You know, *Cornelius*, there's something I can't quite grasp about you."

Cornelius noticed the way Shadrach had said his given name. Not "Prince" or "Cornelius of Marzine," but just Cornelius. He tried to remove himself, but Shadrach's grip was firm. His fingers traveled down to Cornelius' collar to get a better hold on him.

"You called me Cornelius," he said, not one to hold his tongue.

"You don't know when to shut up, do you? What you pulled with Mr. Savva today was idiocy, and you and I both know you're not an idiot. So why not embrace your intelligence and accept my offer? Duel the Siren King and become my ally. I'll make it interesting for you, I promise. There's no need to amuse yourself with these silly games."

"I do know when to shut up, *Shadrach*. I also know when *not* to shut up. I was always going to outlast you, but I didn't think it would be this easy. You didn't even give it a week. It's a crying shame, too. You should've seen what I had planned for Sleetal. Now *that* would've been interesting," Cornelius said. Shadrach's breath was icy against his throat.

"So you do know. You're everything they say and more. Gifted, handsome, save ten feet tall." Waves of panic whelmed over him as he felt Shadrach's fingers traveling up to his neck, fingers curling around his throat. Cutting off his airway. Making his words rasp.

"Well, I suppose you've given up on the idea of pleasing me. Could we revisit that thought?" Cornelius choked. His mind fluttered about like a hummingbird, searching for a way out as his vision turned red and hazy. He vaguely remembered the self-defense lessons he was given back on Addison Island. He'd hardly paid any mind to them. The knowledge hadn't seemed applicable at the time. Now the universe was proving him bitterly wrong.

"Pleasing you was only an attempt to gain your assent. I

never truly needed it. It was more of an experiment, really, to see how you'd react to the sudden attention. And as I thought, you tried to capitalize on it as much as possible, grimy little worm," Shadrach said breathlessly.

Cornelius almost scoffed. It was he who was breathless. But even oxygen deprivation didn't keep him from replying.

"I've been called many things, the most common being 'Gale' and 'darling.' But I've never been called a grimy little worm, so I'll grant you a sentence in my biography. 'Shadrach of Sleetal once called me a grimy little worm. Really, he was relating to the thing in between his legs.'" He began to struggle against Shadrach.

"Here's what's going to happen. I have a reputation to maintain, even out here. There's an ever-tightening hand around my throat."

"I think I know the feeling." Cornelius coughed, the darkness almost overtaking his mind.

"I don't want you to embarrass me in front of our friends. You'll tell them you've agreed to be my puppet. If not, you won't be as golden as you are now. You know, Cornelius, I can take it all away. The luxury, the allies, all of it. I can lock you up, cut out your tongue. You'll willingly face your father, or you'll lose your voice." Of course Shadrach threatened his tongue. Every adversary Cornelius had faced had done the same. He tapped the taller man on the shoulder, no longer able to reply. His grip let up slightly.

"Well, at least g-give me Sleetal. We can't let my decision seem t-too out-of-the-blue. Give me the days in Sleetal to 'decide' and then I promise I'll agree to the plan." The cogs in Cornelius' mind turned fast. Sleetal was only to buy himself time to make a break for it. He loved it here, out on the open sea, going anywhere and everywhere. But he refused to face his father, and he didn't fancy dying. He'd much rather vanish, make a name for himself as an actor instead of making a name for himself as a king.

"I see the logic in that. Wow, finally taking my advice and embracing your brains," Shadrach said, using his other hand to knock on Cornelius' skull. "Alright… you have until mid-next week. After that, it's your voice." The fingers left from his throat just as he thought he would faint. His knees buckled beneath him. Shadrach let him fall to the deck, gasping for breath.

"Give me your scarf. I'll need it," he rasped, praying Shadrach heard him over the sound of his own depravity. A soft fabric fluttered down beside him. He listened to Shadrach's footsteps slowly growing quieter. The only sound he heard for a while was the crashing of the waves against the hull. Then, he heard a new voice.

"Well, I suppose you'll have to face your father, Lucifer himself." It was Nic Murray. Murray propped him up against the ship's railing, carefully wrapping Shadrach's scarf around his neck to hide the purpling bruises.

"I should've known you'd see it all, standing there in the shadows like you d-do," Cornelius croaked. The deck creaked as Murray sat down beside him.

"I'll always be watching," Murray said. His words would've been eerie to anyone else, but they were reassuring to Cornelius, which was a surprise. He hated being scrutinized, loathed it. But beside him was the sentinel, and he was no longer afraid.

"There are far too many studies of human behavior. Can't we all just agree as humans that we're strange species?" Cornelius asked after an unbearable pause.

"I'm glad you see me as human now, though there will always be differences, and there will always be the people who study them. The outlier will always be hated. It's just the way of things. All we can do to help it is not to contribute to the problem, to be kind and decent to everyone that we can." Murray's voice broke off at the end, almost as if he were devolving into tears. But that was impossible. Statues didn't cry.

Watchers never had their own stories. But as the moon shone down on their faces, a single tear trickled down Murray's cheek. Cornelius slipped his cold fingers into Murray's, and they sat there in silence until the moon was overhead.

CHAPTER 19

The worst thing about Shadrach's presence on the ship was the fact that Mikka would have to bunk with Rodrigo. Hell, he'd rather bunk with the siren. But it had to be Rodrigo. Ditzy Rodrigo, always with a smile and a bowl of spice soup. He wanted to smack him back to Wilkinia.

Cornelius had relocated his belongings to Mikka's quarters late that evening. A new grey scarf was wrapped around his neck, and his voice was low and hoarse, but Mikka didn't notice. He was too busy keeping himself from beating the audacity out of the prince.

Pia was always there to hearten him, though sometimes there were strained moments. He wasn't ready to give Pia what she needed, and she wasn't prepared to accept him as he was. It was like stretching out his hand to feel her fingers in the middle of a mob, only to fall short, his hand plummeting through the air with an icy shock. He guzzled as much *raska* as he could after these disconnects. It was too depressing to acknowledge he had problems, so he decided he just wouldn't. He drank more than he ever had, then—more than during the war.

There was one night, however, that he had to acknowledge the disconnect. The elements had grown increasingly worse in the past week of sailing to Sleetal, northern winds raging against the ship with brutal force. With some help from the other crewmembers, Murray and Joan kept them afloat, Shadrach being of little service. All he ever seemed to do was stand behind Cornelius, leering down at him. He wasn't the altruistic king of Sleetal everyone had pictured. He fit the role of evil wizard better with his herblore and uncanny ability to be everywhere at once.

But one day, he found that his store had run dry, not a drop left in any of his many bottles. There was hardly any left in the mead kegs either. He was left with a bucket of corks under his cot, and so he decided to screw himself further. As the rain turned to sleet, he decided to go to the upper deck and shoot the corks into the ocean.

He stumbled out into the pouring sleet, ice running down his shirt. *Sleet.* His lips curled upwards to reveal his crooked teeth. They were close to home. In summer, it was always sleeting in his village. He remembered the pranks he and his friends played on one another, dumping buckets of sleet runoff down each other's coats. His bandaged leg ached violently as the water soaked through it.

He couldn't see properly through the mist, so he found himself bucking with every turn of the ship. Still, he pressed onward, desperate to be rid of the corks. His pistol hung in its leather holster at his belt, slapping against his thigh every time a wave crashed into the *Vault*. He wasn't wearing a coat, he realized, and he threw his head back in a laugh. Of course he wasn't. He was too busy wasting away to be practical.

Mikka was near the ladder that led to the upper deck. He felt for the rungs in the darkness, getting a hold on one after a moment of groping. Hoisting himself up with the bucket was an undertaking. Everything was coated in ribbons of ice. By dumb luck, Mikka reached the top unhurt.

Murray was the only other soul out on the deck, and Mikka knew he was watching. But he could give less of a damn. Murray was always watching. He'd seen enough of Mikka to know he was capable of stupidity of this caliber.

He hunched down, bracing his back against the railing. He was sober, but only just. The headache was worse than the drunkenness. He couldn't see straight, and he could hear his heartbeat everywhere. Mikka grunted like the man he was and brushed it off, not willing to acknowledge it yet. He was frightened of the unknown, of so many things. So scared, his only succor a flask given to him by an unnamed soldier. "It'll keep you warm," the man had said. *It'll keep you warm.* And all he'd ever really wanted was to be warm. It saddled him with so much more than warmth, though. So much more. Again, he grunted and brushed it off . Murray watched. He made sure to level his shoulders; they were raised high above his ears in anticipation.

Mikka began to shake. It was like the low rumble before an avalanche at first, only his fingers wavering. He was just shivering from the cold, the cold he felt so wholly now. Suddenly, the shaking grew tenfold. His teeth rattled in his mouth. His soul rattled in his chest. When he tried to grunt it away, all that came out was a low moan. It was the first time in a week that he could remember anything. And remember he did. His mother... his father... his years of service... he let out another moan that was supposed to be a grunt. Then, abandoning all logic once and for all, he unsheathed his pocket knife. He gingerly set the bucket down beside him, reaching down into it with his shaky hand. Murray wanted to cry out, to warn him, but no warning would stop Mikka Savva.

He began. Murray reached out a hand from the bridge as if to stop Mikka, but no words came from his lips, and his hand fell limply through the air. Murray shook his head and tried to turn away from it, but he couldn't. It was like the day an oil tanker had capsized on the sea rocks before his village in Orenia. The sinister oil curled its tendrils through the sea, choking the blue away until there was only an expanse of darkness. It had reminded Murray of the creature called the leviathan. He wasn't able to look away from that sea monster then, and he wasn't able to look away from this sea monster now.

In only a moment, Mikka's fingers were cut up. Only one

cork bullet came of it. Again, Mikka grunted away the pain. Again, it came out as a moan. It was as if he couldn't see the bleeding wounds on his hands. But he could. He stared desperately at his surroundings, trying to find blame in the ship and pouring sleet. He couldn't, for this was entirely his fault. Everything was his fault. He wiped his hand on his sweater, leaving streaks of blood along the threads. Then, to Murray's awe and horror, he reached for another cork. One could only be quiet for so long.

"Mikka! Stop!" he roared, trying to be as short as possible. His steely eyes were laden with anguish. A fine shaving of cork wound off the cork before Mikka heard. His hands were shaking so severely that the pocket knife cut his palm instead of his fingers. He hissed with pain, looking up only to meet Murray's grey gaze.

"Murray?" he asked sluggishly. He could only just make out the figure across the way. Murray shook his head, wincing as the blood poured down onto the deck.

"You'll stain the deck! Get over here!" he found himself saying even as he knew the sleet would wash it away. Mikka's mind was too wrapped in cotton to understand the wants of anyone but himself, however. Painstakingly, he began to whittle again.

Murray became more and more panicked as he watched. He wiped the sleet from his eyelashes, realizing this sort of anxiety couldn't be good for his heart. So he began his endeavor, descending the bridge ladder to the main deck. His grip was like iron, keeping him from falling even when everything was so slick.

Mikka could no longer hold the pocket knife upright, his muscles giving out due to the tremors. It fell to the deck beneath him. His hands were marked up with bloody cuts. The sleet pelted him from above, but he couldn't even move his arms to shield himself from the onslaught. Dread enveloped him, and all he could do was fall to the deck like his abandoned pocket knife. Mikka told himself the wetness around his eyes was only a bit of melted sleet. He was deluding himself, he knew. Mikka was no fool. But men didn't cry, so he would continue to feed himself lies. His leg ached, and he could've sworn he felt the trail the bullet had blazed through his flesh filling with sleet.

Then, there was a hand on his shoulder. It was as cold as the metal of his gun. Someone knelt down beside him, the deck boards creaking. Only Pia would take the time to do that. But this hand wasn't Pia's. Her hands were warm, stubby. These hands were cold and slender, with long fingers bent sideways at the proximal. He squeezed his eyes shut.

"Savva, stop this nonsense. Come back inside, or I'll get Cornelius to order Shadrach to order you overboard." His voice was sane and metallic, not betraying the slightest hint of emotion. The sentinel set down a lantern he'd lit on the main deck beside Mikka's head. The lantern light bathed the sharpshooter in a warm glow. There were bags beneath his eyes that put the night sky's darkness to shame.

"I could t-take Shadrach," Mikka said to no one in particular. Murray let out a long-suffering sigh and leaned back against the low wooden wall beside him, soaked. He would sit there until Mikka stopped sullying the deck with his hands. What a fuss he was making, like a child throwing a temper tantrum. He wished he could haul Mikka inside, but he didn't have the strength to. Nobody did.

Maybe if he could get Mikka talking, he'd be distracted from whatever was collapsing inside him. He wished Cornelius was here to negotiate for him. Cornelius would find some way to coax Mikka inside.

"Why do you hate Marzinians?" he blurted.

"Shut up..." Mikka rasped, his tone almost pleading. It took him a moment or two to respond, but Murray knew he would. "Damn it all! They took everything, my nation, my... my sanity."

Murray nodded with a quirked brow. "I know. The Marzinians hurt us all in one way or another. But not all of them are inherently evil." Murray swallowed hard, disgusted by how he'd fashioned his voice to be consoling.

"They're all e-evil. I swear it." The sleet turned into rain. The bucking waves were almost lulling. The rigging was pulled taut, and everything was in its place. Murray's only concern was getting Mikka inside and bandaging up his fingers so he didn't bleed half to hell. How could Mikka be so selfish? Mannon was dead. Tolmas was dead, and Murray was the one who had held his hand as it went cold, and Mikka was throwing a tantrum over how miserable he was.

"My brother was Marzinian. My mother had an affair with a Marzinian mariner," Murray told him. The lantern's flame seemed to dim as Mikka opened his eyes to stare at Murray.

"Adulteress," Mikka ridiculed.

Murray only shrugged, nodding. He didn't much like the woman. He wouldn't defend her so-called honor if he didn't have to. And besides, this was all a lie. A lie he would serve Mikka on a silver platter to get him inside.

"My brother wasn't evil. In fact, he grew to be quite similar to you from what I've observed," Murray told him, his voice tainted. Mikka shook his head wildly.

"I'm nothing like those damned s-sirens," he swore.

Murray ignored him and proceeded onward. "He was a very large man who joined the Orenian army. Moved up through the ranks quickly. He was a selfless, kind man who was every bit Orenian as I am. And yet he still had Marzinian blood." Murray made himself chuckle. "He went on to run a small prospecting company. He got married to the love of his life and lived in a small port town with her."

Mikka's brows knit as he listened to Murray's less than detailed description. The sentinel had decided to keep it simple for the simple man.

"You said 'lived' instead of 'live,' what happened to him?" Mikka asked, sounding surprisingly interested.

"He died of sweating sickness last year. But he never stopped fighting. He fought for me, stood up to my father, who hated me. He fought for his country and saved many lives. He fought to provide his town with resources in the mines. He fought the sweating sickness and lost for the first and last time. See, he never stopped fighting, and that reminds me of you. He was Marzinian but a good man."

Mikka groaned and made himself sit up, the lantern light mirrored in his midnight eyes. "I *am* strong, and maybe not all of them are 'inherently evil,' but I think it's their folks that make em' that way. Your brother was brought up in a different country. The rest are raised to be monsters. But you're right; I am strong, and I can't stop being strong."

The shaking had come to a stop, and Murray allowed himself the barest smile as he admired his work. The lie had been successful. The funny thing was, most lies were at least based on the truth, whereas this one was entirely untrue. He'd been without affection in his childhood.

Mikka descended the ladder, watching for the broken rung. Murray did the same and followed close behind him with his lantern. They walked at a funeral's pace across the main deck.

The galley was well lit, much to Murray's surprise. At this hour, only Mikka and Pia would be here. But Pia never came alone. The second thing he noticed was the smell of Rodrigo's spice soup simmering on the stove. He breathed the steam in gratefully, warmed to the bone. Sure enough, Rodrigo stood over the stove. The others, even Cornelius with Shadrach's scarf, sat around the metal table in silence. Shadrach sat on a new, high-backed chair beside Cornelius, who shrunk away from him like light does darkness. Pia and Lara turned around to stare at them. A drop of blood fell from Mikka's finger and hit the floor.

"You're too foolish, Mr. Savva. The windows overlook the

deck, you realize. When the sleet became rain, we were met with a sight we can never unsee." Cornelius closed his eyes as if the sound of Shadrach's voice hurt him.

"I-" Mikka tried. But when he looked into Pia's eyes, his throat closed.

"You're an alcoholic, Mr. Savva. And I would be fine with that if you were of the functioning sort, but you've proven yourself otherwise." Two empty chairs sat waiting at the end of the table. Shadrach waved his hand toward them dismissively. "Please, sit," he said, looking exhausted.

Murray took his seat, ready to fade into the background again. He set the lantern on the center of the table and resolved to watch the flame's dance until he was half-blind.

"I-I, I was stripping the corks as I always do," he pleaded. His fingers were still bleeding freely. Shadrach closed his eyes and muttered something along the lines of, "You dullard."

"I was allowing you to pay back your debt to the Masked Birds in this way because I thought you couldn't be broken. Yet here you are, standing before me, blasted to bits." He sighed and rubbed his temples. "Consider it paid. I have no need for you like this. I've lost all respect for you, Mikka. You're broken, and not even she can put you back together," he said, gesturing toward Pia. She bit her lip. Hard. Until it bled.

"Soup, anyone?" Rodrigo asked. His smile was gone, his eyes brimming with pity as he looked at Mikka. Cornelius nodded. He'd been complaining of a sore throat for the past few days and had been slurping Rodrigo's soup at the same frequency Mikka was taking swigs from his flask. Rodrigo handed him a bowl.

"We'll leave you in Sleetal. I'm sorry, Mikka, but you're just too—"

"Unpredictable," Mikka interjected, his tone wavering. He looked to Pia for support, but she had turned away. Cornelius drank down his soup in silence, staring at Mikka with aversion.

"If it's alright, I think I'll retire," Cornelius said. Before he could stand, Shadrach put a hand on his shoulder.

"No. I want you here," Shadrach told him.

"You want the siren here and not me," said Mikka, fixing his gaze on the lantern. His debt was repaid, but he'd never gotten to be with Pia. Never gotten to hold her. Never gotten to be the man she deserved. Its sting was like a slap in the face.

"Yes. In other words, you're fired. Gather your things tonight. We arrive tomorrow. You're dismissed. Everyone else remains. I want to discuss business in Sleetal other than dumping our debris." He eyed Mikka disdainfully.

The man left, stalking silently down the corridor. "You're dismissed, too, Ms. Reyes. I'll fill you in later. He help with his hands." She gave Shadrach a withering glare, and left.

Pia blinked away the tears as she ran. She was alone now. Rodrigo be damned; she was alone. Rodrigo could drown in a pot of his own spice soup for all she cared.

CHAPTER 20

Pia wouldn't be the woman she was without the war. She wasn't in any way grateful for it, and she would rather not be herself if it meant the lives swept away by the war were saved. Millions had perished, all because one nation wanted dominion over the others.

She'd always been strong-willed, even without a battle. Always wanted things her way. She and Rodrigo used to play heroes and monsters. She'd always pick the roles she wanted, leaving Rodrigo to make do with her rejections. It had always been that way. But war sharpened her, gave her perseverance. It took a once-selfish girl and made her selfless, giving up her life for others' freedom. And that was the one good thing about the war.

She was fourteen when it all began, though it took her another year to enlist in the Emberan army. Their town was tucked away in a corner of the great Emberan grasslands, the soil ideal for farming. Lives there were simple. Her ma called it 'simply sublime,' using the pretty word to cover the tedious truth. Folks married their childhood sweethearts and took over their father's farm when he grew too old to maintain the crops and livestock. The women would sit in the stuffy little kitchens and pop out children until the day they were too tattered to continue. They would go to church on Sundays, and parents would coo as their children shrieked in the choir. "Simply sublime" was too simple for Pia. She wanted more than to make soup over a gas stove and have far too many children with a tired man, too sunburnt and fatigued from plowing the fields all day long to talk to her. But that was all she knew. Until they went to the coast one summer to visit her ma's sister.

Pia couldn't remember much from the trip itself, only the suffocating heat and how their wagon bruised her back when she tried to lie down for a rest. Her ma was singing as she always did, usually hymns. Her pa was attempting to get Rodrigo to be mannish and walk along the wagon's side instead of sitting in it like she was. The donkeys brayed thirstily. Rodrigo began crying after an hour of walking, so he was allowed to sit beside her again.

It was a relief when they arrived at Riolago, her aunt's seaside city. It was a noteworthy port town with many mariners and traders taking up residence in the painted homes. She'd never been to the sea before, but when looking at the vast expanse of ocean stretching all the way to the sunset, she felt nothing but small. Insignificant, just like everyone else she knew. Rodrigo was cawing like a parrot about it, and she quite rudely told him to tell pa about it.

They spent the next few weeks there with their relatives, people Pia had supposedly met before when she was a child. They all smiled and talked to her like they knew her. In turn, she did the same, glancing to her father every other moment to see if he noticed how she was trying. She played by the sea and began to relax as the summer went on. She even cajoled her father into taking her out to fish in Rodrigo's stead. But all of that ended.

Conflict with the Marzinians had been rising over the past few months. There was more news about the dispute in every town they had stopped in on their way to Riolago. It was early morning, and Rodrigo had hauled her from her bed to see the sunrise. She reluctantly went along with him, whining all the way. They stood there, staring at the horizon for a long while. The bank was deserted, and Pia liked the silence. Only the birdsong and the waves broke the silence. The orange sun rose above the waters, soaking the city in glorious warmth.

But then, the sacred silence of sunrise was interrupted by bells tolling. Warning bells. Pia squinted at the silhouette of a ship on the horizon. Stark and regal, it soared the waves like a bird of prey. It was a Marzinian siege ship. Pia felt fear rise in her throat. Rodrigo didn't seem to hear the bells tolling; he was too mesmerized by the sunrise to notice. She grabbed him by the collar.

"Pia, what did I do wrong? Are you still angry I brought you down here?" he asked.

"That's a Marzinian siege ship. We learned about them from Pa, remember? He worked on one during the Sleetalian war."

Rodrigo's eyes widened. The ship was closer now. She released her brother and began to stumble backward, coaxing him along with her.

"We should, we should go," Rodrigo murmured, his voice wavering. The sunrise made the tears in his eyes orange. Pia tripped over a piece of driftwood, falling back against her brother. They tumbled in the sand, scrambling to get up. By the time they untangled themselves, the ship was on the sands. The metal hull whined, loud and metallic. Steam blew from pipes on the exterior, the hot blast nearly scalding them. The ship cast a shadow so dark that Pia couldn't see Rodrigo beside her anymore. She heard him whimpering, though.

Pia knew they had to run. She couldn't remember much after that, only that she dragged her mewling brother all the way up the sands and into the city before any Marzinian soldiers disembarked to claim the shore. There was a battle in Riolago that week. Pia and her family holed up in her aunt's apartment until the shooting stopped. The Riolago militia and Emberan army had defended the city, but only because they outnumbered the Marzinians. Many died in the effort. They left that Saturday, their summer holiday abruptly over. She remembered Pa's dark eyes wavering in their sockets as he packed their things into their trunks. He didn't speak a word until they were out of the city and on their wagon.

Pia, however, felt something stirring inside of her. The sight of the great metal hull sliding onto the sands kept replaying in her head as they walked the grasslands back home. It made her so angry, the Marzinians just attacking an upright city without any reason other than to gain more land for themselves. The anger ate at her for the rest of the year. She tossed and turned in her sleep, dreaming of the siege ship silhouetted by the sunrise.

Then, a recruiter came to her town. He spoke of purpose, of honor. He told of a safer Embera. He offered power, too. Both men and women were welcome, fourteen years and older. No citizen had to serve in the military in Embera, not even during wartimes. It was written that way in the nation's charter. But many chose to. She knew she would make her family proud, joining the effort. She also knew it would satisfy her need to do something with herself. So, a month after she and her brother turned fifteen, she enlisted and became Private Reyes. Rodrigo begged her not to go, but she wouldn't listen. She said a quick goodbye to her ma and pa, who were just as amazed as her brother. Then, she left for training.

Fort Hector, named for a famous general, was her home for ten weeks of preparation. Outside the fort, the tensions grew and blackened like a storm cloud above their heads. These developments only emboldened Pia's need. She excelled in close combat, her strikes quick as silver. Her uppers were impressed, but it was still bitter work. Work she didn't enjoy. She grew muscles and a spine. The night of her graduation from basic training, the Marzinians declared war on Sleetal, Embera, Wilkinia, and Orenia, every other nation that made up the continent. And so started the Continental War. It was an outrage. The sight of the metal hull sliding onto the sands still flared in her memory like a warning shot. She wouldn't forget what had happened in Riolago.

She and her regiment were deployed to the Southern Islands of Sleetal later that month. Embera and Sleetal were quick to become diplomatic allies as the war progressed. It was in their best interests to join together against the superpower that was Marzine. Pia was only fifteen when she left her home country for the first time, but she wasn't afraid. She was a soldier now, a fighter. She was *something*.

On the passage to Sleetal, she was seasick almost the entire time. That was when she discovered her hatred for the sea. Being on the solid ground her entire life had taught her to trust what was beneath her feet. Suddenly, she couldn't. It didn't help that her eyes were prone to playing tricks on her. Once or twice, she thought she saw a squid breaking up the waves. Dreams of said squid kept her tossing and turning in her bunk. When it got cold, she was even more miserable. The vomit from the seasickness froze on her face. In fact, all liquid froze when exposed to the air. It was the reason Sleetalians insulated their flasks so their *raska* wouldn't freeze. Once, she stood out on the prow for a moment too long, and her left eye froze closed. She had made the mistake of crying, the homesickness worse than ever.

Needless to say, she was relieved when they arrived in Sleetal, land of ice and *raska*. She needed something to drink after an ordeal like the one she'd had. But the worst was yet to come. It was somehow colder on the Southern Islands than on the ship, a place she thought icier than her ma's scowl. The winds were so harsh that they cut pathways in the snow. The Southern Islands were supposedly the place where the majority of the nation's crops were grown. She wondered how anything could be grown in such cold. But the soil in which the ash grains and other crops were grown was right over a magma deposit. That was why they were called "ash grains," she'd discovered. The islands themselves had been formed from a series of volcanoes, which she found somewhat ironic. She'd met her own personal volcano there, after all.

Mikka Savva was a sharpshooter in the Sleetalian military. He was far less brooding then, just seventeen years old. They stayed at his regiment's fort. Since the Sleetalian army didn't allow women to join, there were only men's bunks. Pia's bunkmate was Mikka. Fate was what she would call it, but the only thing she noticed about him then was how loud he snored. They didn't speak to each other at all for the first month. Pia, however, felt his beautiful northern eyes tracing her form when she wasn't looking. She ignored it and went about her business. He could look if he wanted to. There was no privacy there. In fact, she found herself looking at him too. He was more toned than your average Sleetalian recruit. His skin wasn't sallow but a lovely olive tone. But she couldn't forget his eyes, blue as the midnight sky.

The first time they spoke to each other was in the dining hall. The troops had just returned from a deadly fray with some sirens on the northernmost island. 'Sirens' were what they called the Marzinian combatants in Sleetal. It helped to think of them as the fish creatures that lured sailors to their deaths instead of human beings with lives and stories of their own.

"Want a drink?" he'd asked her.

"Thanks," she'd said. He'd proffered up his flask and allowed her to have a swig of the bitter liquid. Then, they returned to their own silences. Soon, they began to notice each other more often. They were put on the same patrol on the odd nights of the week. They would pass Mikka's flask and talk about their civilian lives as the foul weather froze them inside out. At least, Pia would. Mikka would nod and add the occasional one-liner. After a while, he opened up more. Mikka still didn't talk about his family, but he joked. He made her laugh in the darkest place on the continent. They were miserable there, listening to far-off explosions and wondering if they would make it another month.

When Embera surrendered, Pia's remaining regiment left as political prisoners, including her commander. But she stayed.

She became an unofficial member of the Sleetalian army, donning the dark blue greatcoats they wore. She and Mikka stuck together in the fort, but they were apart during battles. Mikka was up on the bluffs, raining bullets down on the sirens. Pia was in the trenches. It was hot in the trenches, being so close to the magma deposit beneath the Southern Islands. They would sit there and sweat out their fears. She got to know those around her, holding the knowledge that at least one of them would be dead by nightfall. At the end of the night, she was glad it wasn't her. She would march back to the fort with Mikka. They would drink. Laugh. Sigh. But they would never cry.

Soon, the Marzinians became too great a force. Pia had spent a year with Mikka by the time they were seized. They were sent to separate prison camps. Pia preferred not to remember all that transpired in there. But due to overcrowding, they were both cleared. And just as they'd planned in the fort, they met in Stjernsvet, or New Sirensea if you were loyal to the sirens. Pia wanted to go back home to visit her family in Embera and asked Mikka to join her on a passenger ship back to her nation. Mikka gave in and came with her after a few arguments.

Rodrigo sobbed until he vomited up his own spice soup when Pia returned. He hadn't changed one bit, to Pia's disappointment. Neither had anything in her town. Women still sat in stuffy kitchens. Folks still married their childhood sweethearts.

Despite their exhaustion, they couldn't get used to the peace. So, without a grain of logic, Mikka joined the Masked Birds. And with an even lesser grain of logic, Pia joined as well. An old friend from the Emberan military contrived Mikka into the group. Mikka did the same to Pia. And then, they met Shadrach. The pale, raven-haired former king of Sleetal was the leader of the Masked Birds, which came as a great surprise to the two ex-soldiers.

Shadrach, after a lot of pleading, permitted them to be a team within the organization. He sent them all over the continent together. That year was the best of her life. Never had she felt more powerful, more confident, even as the war was over. She was doing something, and she was doing it with Mikka, her best friend. Mikka, the one she trusted more than her own brother. She had loved Mikka Savva, and she still did. He was screwed up. He was quite possibly mad. He was an alcoholic. He was hers. And she couldn't let Shadrach take him from her.

CHAPTER 21

I t was meant to be a pleasant meal, just some innocent soup to bring Cornelius out of his rut. Instead of jubilant and, well, glib, Cornelius had been nervous, scarcely saying a word to anyone but Lara. He'd spent long hours in her quarters with her, sitting beside her on a faded pillow as she studied. All they had were the musty texts, the lantern light, and his quiet speech with short intervals for sustenance and viola playing. But the main surprise was the tone in which he spoke: monotone. Pia often napped during the day, but she couldn't any longer because of his droning. He just never left. To be frank, the only place Cornelius felt safe was sitting beside Lara and helping her with her studies. Shadrach seemed to be everywhere else.

Again, it was meant to be a pleasant meal. Shadrach had ordered Rodrigo to prepare a meal. They were still trying to please Cornelius, so all had to be present, save Mikka, Murray, and Joan. Murray and Joan were guiding them through a light sleet storm, and Mikka was… previously engaged. Rodrigo perfected his soup recipe down to the most minor pinches of turmeric and salt. He added as much cinnamon as he could, pouring in the precious few spoonfuls he had left of the supply he had from home. He'd been saving the cinnamon for a special occasion, and this seemed special enough. Cornelius was persuaded out of Lara's quarters. He wore that same grey scarf.

The smile he wore upon emerging was so convincing that for a moment, Pia thought their jubilant, glib Cornelius had returned. Then she remembered how good an actor he was. His eyes were locked on Shadrach's with derision. It was like he was trying to prove the Raven King wrong.

"This is resplendent," he'd exclaimed. Cornelius went for the seat farthest from Shadrach, but he was made to sit down beside him with a gesture from the Raven King himself, though his side-eye was enviable. Shadrach stared right back, a cocky smile making him look like the demon he was. Cornelius, like always, wasn't one to hold his tongue. But this time, he whispered only to Shadrach.

"Well, this is good and pleasant. Maybe this time, you'll break my fingers." There was a trace of humor in his eyes as he spoke. But Shadrach didn't seem so amused. He grasped Cornelius' hand beneath the table, and he froze. Shadrach pulled the prince's fingers back, farther and farther, almost to the point of snapping. But his hold relinquished when the pain became visible on Cornelius' face.

"Pleasant indeed. Maybe I will if you keep testing me," Shadrach ridiculed.

Rodrigo was admittedly taking his time with the soup, the recipe far too long. The windows were fogged over by the steam from the bubbling pot, and the smell was heavenly, but nobody paid it any mind. They were all fixated on Cornelius, for he'd folded in on himself like a festival booth. Shadrach's fingers were still resting lightly atop his, the slow tap of his index finger a warning to Cornelius.

Then, without a moment's notice, the window panes cleared as rain instead of sleet fell. Cornelius loved the sound of rain. It reminded him of less horrifying circumstances, so he was first to glance out the window. His intrigue bled into awe, and his jaw dropped. The others soon followed suit, having seen the look on his face.

"Damn you, Mikka," Pia had murmured to herself. They could easily see the upper deck from the safety of the galley. The bucket he kept his corks in was tipped over beside him, and Pia pieced it all together in her mind. Mikka, just out from under the influence, had found his raska bottles empty. All of them. He'd squared his shoulders like a man and told himself not to think. So, tired and thoughtless, he'd gone out to carve cork bullets in the height of a sleet storm. With the cold, his weariness, and the thoughts he couldn't grunt away, he'd started shaking. Instead of bullets, he'd carved up his fingers.

"I suppose we'll be celebrating a retirement this evening instead of the prince," Shadrach said. He patted Cornelius on the shoulder, who again shrunk away.

"A retirement?" Pia asked as she charted away the scene before her. Shadrach sighed as Rodrigo's cheerful humming reached a disturbing point.

"Oh right, I forgot you were 'girlfriend-boyfriend.' My condolences," he said mockingly.

"You'll find someone else. There are many trees in the forest. So what if one's burned down? Besides, we have our very own prince here. You could aim for him. Even that odd fellow Mr. Murray would be better than Mr. Savva."

Pia buried her hands in each pocket and slipped her fingers into her brass knuckles, knowing she would punch out the former king of Sleetal any day if he ridiculed her best friend.

"You'd be lucky to have anyone, you pitiful, spineless excuse for a man! You've had everything handed to you your entire life! Have you ever once considered *our* interests? Even Cornelius, prince of your ass, has it worse than you!" she raged, standing to her feet with a loud jerk from the chair. Cornelius stared at her with unbridled awe. She was short and stout, but she loomed larger than anyone in the room.

"My ass belongs to Sleetal, thank you very much. And I suggest you sit down, Ms. Reyes, because your ass belongs to me. And if this was at all about who has it worse, I'd win. My torture was having to endure his betrothed sob and snot all over me when we met to discuss the ransom. Now that, my dear friends, was pitiful." His eyes prowled over the room. Rodrigo's humming stopped abruptly. Cornelius gritted his teeth and cast Shadrach a sidelong glance.

"You mustn't torture her on my account," Cornelius said sullenly. But it sounded like him. It had a tone and a temperament that couldn't be mimicked.

"Why? Do you love her? Ooooo, Ms. Reyes may have some competition," he said, his smile sinister. If Pia hadn't known better, she would've called Cornelius' words chivalrous. But Cornelius himself was far from it.

"At least I know better than to use schoolyard taunts. You spent your military service reclining beneath a gazebo while I spent mine wizening in the trenches," Pia bit. But before anyone could say another word, footsteps resounded through the galley. Cornelius' eyes widened as Nic Murray and Mikka rose beyond the window panes.

The soiled pair lurched through the door, Murray's expression quite evidently bored. He looked annoyed beyond the meaning of the word. Mikka, contrary to Murray, looked scared witless.

"You're too foolish, Mr. Savva, too foolish. The windows are looking out over the deck, you realize. When the sleet became rain, we were met with a sight we can never unsee." Shadrach's words were more corrosive than Mikka's drinking habits. Pia felt like holding her head between her legs until the world stopped spinning. Mikka...gone? The thought was unimaginable, but that didn't change the fact that he *would* leave her in Sleetal. He would think of her for the last time on some raska-drowned day, and her very presence in his mind would vanish.

"But you don't want me here," Mikka whispered, looking all too lost. Pia wanted to tell him everything would be alright, but it wouldn't.

"Yes. In other words, you're fired. Gather your things tonight. We arrive tomorrow. You're dismissed. Everyone else remains. I want to discuss business in Sleetal other than dumping our debris." Pia caught the affront like a punch to the teeth. And spitting out the figurative blood without going off on Shadrach was likely the hardest thing she'd ever done. Mikka's wounded hands hung as limply, fingers twitching. Soon, he left, for Shadrach had made it clear he was no longer needed. Whatever semblance of a purpose he'd found out on *The Vault of Heaven* had been taken. And after the second-worst night of his life, he had no raska to comfort him—nothing to covet. Undressed before them like a stripped cork.

But then, much to Pia's astonishment, Shadrach ordered her after him to tend to his hands. She made sure to cast a scowl in his direction as she went. He was meant for the roils and toils of the world, not a throne.

She heard his footsteps all around her, pulsating just as fervently as her heartbeat. The dim lighting made the twists and turns seem like dark caverns, and Pia was afraid of the unknown like all others. But some part of her yearned for it. How would she ever know anything without turning the corner? She heard a muted cry up ahead, but before taking the final turn to Mikka's quarters, she stopped in the storage room and her own quarters, needing two things: a small cask of clean water and bandages— her own, of course. Her hands often got cuts while training. She grabbed her small roll of bandages hastily, the cask already slung over her shoulder. There were bloody fingerprints on the door's handle when she reached it.

At first, she leaped for the door. But when her hand was only inches from the handle, her fingers paused, wavering on the edge of a choice. Somehow, someway, she knew there was no going back if she turned the handle, bloodied and printed. She instead closed her eyes, her face contorted with tears. She wouldn't lie; crying didn't come easily to her. On a day with so much wrong, she was scared of these tears. Could she live through another moment with Mikka? Could she stomach turning her attention back to the downward spiral of his life? Could she do it all again, just for the absurd hope that she could have him back? Her legs trembled beneath her. She sighed, steadied herself, and grasped the handle. Yes, she could. She always would.

She squared her shoulders like the woman she was and entered. He hadn't even lit a lantern. Well, it wasn't like he could in his state. His body was spread over Rodrigo's cot like a scarf on a clothesline. It took her two strikes of a match to stir a flame in the lantern's cage. The warm glow cascaded through the room, and she was glad for the light.

Her graceless footsteps made the floorboards creak. She lowered herself down onto the edge of the mattress and set the lantern down beside Mikka's head. "Mikka, I need to wash your hands. Your cuts will get infected, and you'll lose fingers," she said, her tone mellow like Rodrigo's nettle tea. His whole body went limp with defeat as he heard the sound of her voice.

He moaned something like, "Mmmmnooo…" This was strangely feeble-minded, even for Mikka. He was a sharpshooter or at least a gunman, and he needed fingers to operate the firearms he so loved.

"Mikka…" she went on warningly, moving closer as he turned away. "Savva, listen here. I'm going to bandage your wounds. Then, I'll leave you to your childish moping and be on my way." Her voice rose an octave, and she took a fistful of his hair, pulling his face up from the pillow. He broke away from her grasp with jerky movements, and she recoiled. His midnight eyes cut into her like daggers, but there were tears at the corners of them. She'd never once seen him cry.

"Leave. Please, just… leave," he begged. Another tear fell.

"I'm going to bandage your hands." Her lips moved clumsily against one another. "Goddamnit, Mikka, I'm going to bandage your hands. Then I'll be out of your hair forever," she seethed, her hands clenching. With a wavering sigh, he surrendered and sat up. She yanked his hand toward her, and upon examination, she realized cuts would scar, leaving raised lumps on his skin. Instead of telling him, she wetted her washrag.

Back and forth, she scrubbed over each cut until the residual blood died away. He was silent as she went on, jaw set. This was the resolute Mikka she'd met in Sleetal. Pia was harping too long on one cut, and Mikka made his first noise.

"You're done with that one," he said hoarsely.

"Well, it's not like you can do it yourself," she groused back. She did, however, move onto the next cut. It was in the center of his palm, and its origin was a mystery to her. Had his tremors really been that severe? She made an accidental sound of disgust, and one of Mikka's fingernails dug into her skin.

"A twitch," he said in stilted Emberan.

"I'll make you twitch," she shot back.

"Will you now?"

"Yes, once I'm done with these botched fingers of yours." She bandaged his hand and tied the cloth tightly before moving onto the next. He raised his hand to admire her work, eyes sullen.

"You could be a little more gentle, you know," he said coolly. They were speaking in Sleetalian now, the conversation having exceeded his capacity for Emberan.

"I thought a big strong man could handle a little scrubbing."

"I can handle more than a little scrubbing." His tone rose vehemently.

"Whatever helps you sleep at night." They quieted for a while after that. They both made attempts to vex each other during the silent period, Mikka's fingernails in her skin and Pia's washrag lingering a bit too long on each cut. The waves sounded beneath them, the storm gaining its second wind. The ship pitched mildly at first but preceded to buck like a wild animal. Both soldiers sat rigidly, Pia hurrying over his fingers now. She finally finished the last finger, and as she reached for the bandages, a gargantuan wave lifted the ship onto its shoulders and hurled it back down again. Pia's body crashed against Mikka's as the sea's wails assaulted their ears. They were both breathing loudly, the wits scared out of them.

Pia now found herself pressed into Mikka's torso, his chest rising and falling beneath her. His hands were splayed beside him so she wouldn't injure them further. Her head was against his cheek, and she could feel a layer of unshaven stubble cropping up. He smelled of leather and raska, and this close, she could smell something else, too. Maybe it was the sea salt in his hair, perhaps the citrus from Rodrigo's soup. But no. It had a distinctive tang, blood. But she found she didn't care. She didn't care about anything, the unpredictableness even. There would never be safety for her, she realized. Not in this life, this world. And so... why resist him on their last night together.

She pushed herself up so that she was straddling him. And then something entirely unexpected happened. A smile as sweet as candy floss broke over her face. And ever so slowly, he smiled back. Suddenly, Mikka lurched forward and pressed his lips to hers.

"Mikka, your hands," was all she could say.

"Who needs them?" he said, a little stupidly. But everything was a little stupid at that moment, and a little stupidity goes a long way. And so, they kissed again, falling back onto the cot Mikka had stolen from Rodrigo. The winds howled on *The Vault of Heaven*, but the world was outside, and they were inside. The lantern went out some hours later, but they didn't need light to kiss. They didn't need anything but each other.

CHAPTER 22

All of it had been for nothing. Pia was in his arms, but not for long. Last night had been more glorious than seeing sunlight again after the storm that had taken Mannon. But now, the sky had darkened again, and Mikka felt near-dead. It was an hour before sunrise, earlier than he'd seen in a few weeks. The *raska* kept him up late and down even later. He laid on Rodrigo's cot with Pia asleep beside him. His hands were bandaged, his body taut with heartache. All these years. All his toils, all his days spent at the bottom of a bottle. They had led him to this. This moment, lying beside Pia on Rodrigo's cot. He could feel the serenity seeping away, leaking from him like paint from an oiled canvas. All that remained was dread. He would never have another night like last night if he didn't act soon.

He picked himself up, naked and cold, and his eyes fell on Pia just as a shaft of grey light from the porthole did. Her back was turned, her hair pooling over her shoulders like a river of ink. Tenderly, he draped Rodrigo's patchwork quilt over her shoulders.

He was silent as he dressed, choosing his least tattered shirt. After a few moments of standing over his trunk in contemplation, he found his greatcoat. Sleetalian army issue, a little large even now. Warm and durable, thick with sealskin. Without further hesitation, he put it on. He belted his least worn trousers around his waist and hooked his pistol into its holster at his side. He put on woolen socks and worn boots, thoroughgoing for once. The pack he'd brought with him was

soon filled with what he could salvage from his clothes and his
personal belongings. It was agony removing his copy of *The Tale
of Alexander* from beneath the pillow. His fingers flicked over his
papers and his bullet rounds, counting each before loading a
single shell into his pistol. The metallic clang was music to his
ears.

The narrow corridors reeked of mold and mildew. He glided
past them like a phantom on a lake. There were no bottles in his
leather pack. And there wouldn't be if he had any. There was
only a dry flask from an unnamed soldier. He would keep it
until he, too, could pass it onto the next unlucky soul. Unlike its
last owner, he was quitting, not dying.

Mikka knew where he was going: to talk to Shadrach, beg on
his knees for his job back, and threaten the man with his pistol
if that didn't work. He brought his pack to complete the illusion.
Shadrach would think he was only saying goodbye before
leaving. But as Mikka thought over his design, his rage blazed.
After a full year of faithful service to the Masked Birds, two
years before that in the Sleetalian military, *Shadrach's* military,
the man had just decided to kick him out. Mikka bared his teeth
and cut the middleman out. There would be no begging on his
part. He wouldn't stoop before the man who'd so grievously
disrespected him. The pistol was more his style anyway. He
wasn't one for negotiations.

He felt like a new man. This Mikka was sewn together, not
bursting at his seams. His movements were so fluid that a
corridor lantern's flame nearly went out as he stepped past.
Shadrach's quarters were just down the stairway. Formerly Nic
Murray's, but the sentinel had put up the least fight out of all of
them. He now made his bed in the galley by the stove, always
washed and shaven before the others woke. He was a mystery.
One Mikka didn't care to solve.

Even going down the notoriously creaky stairway, Mikka
was soundless. When climbing up the Sleetalian cliffs to fire on

the Marzinians, Mikka would be detected by the rocks that broke away in his wake. After a few close scrapes, he'd learned to be light on his feet.

Mikka didn't hesitate when he reached the imposing quarter door. Shadrach used to be his king, his leader, but not any longer. His debt was paid, as had been made clear to him the night previous, so no respect was owed to Shadrach. Well, unless he was accepted back. Mikka moved his gun out of its holster, wincing as his bandaged fingers closed around the grip. He cocked it without a thought.

The soldier lowered himself to the floorboards and pressed his back against the wall. He hefted the pistol up before him and entered. It was dark as night, but he'd been trained in darkness. If there was any sound, he would hear it. If there was any movement, he would feel it. And all over a vehement headache. Instead of sounds and movements, it was oddly still, oddly silent. He reached the bed with ease, locating Shadrach's jaw with his finger. Before placing his gun against the skin, he frowned. Something was off. The flesh was cold, far too cold. Surely this must be his foot. Mikka slid his fingers over the man's body until he was satisfied that it was indeed his neck. But... the skin was just so cold, and it wasn't pulsating as it should be. Then, a match blazed to life behind him, a lantern lit. He was momentarily blinded by it, but then his vision cleared.

Mikka could see the room in full color then. Shadrach could've been mistaken for a sleeping man if it hadn't been for the stream of black blood that had dried on his lips. His hands were folded on his chest as if he'd been prepared for death like one of the pious. It was chilling. Mikka had seen many a dead man, but somehow seeing the former king of his own nation dead was more daunting. His vision seemed to bend. And beside him on Murray's nightstand, a telltale bowl of soup rested, spoon sunk low into the orange substance. It had long gone cold. Mikka slowly turned. When his eyes met Rodrigo's, his blood turned to ice.

In the quivering voice of the coward, Rodrigo cried, "He's d-dead. I didn't mean to, Mikka, I-I didn't mean to, you have to believe me. I tried to help him. But all I could do was watch him die, Mikka. I-I didn't mean to. God save me." He fell to his knees.

Mikka took the round out of his pistol and put it away. Rodrigo was a murderer. And more importantly, Shadrach was dead.

CHAPTER 23

It was the first time Rodrigo had ever questioned his faith, the first time he realized every little thing didn't happen for a reason, and his failures and misfortunes weren't all a part of some grand, intricate plan. Yes, he'd always been a staunch believer in happy endings, that everyone would get to stroll off into the sunset if that's what they desired. But no, now he would never get his sunset. All because of the cinnamon in his spice soup. He hadn't meant to murder Shadrach. He wouldn't ever dream of hurting anyone. Now the only thing he dreamed of was turning back time.

He'd spent hours awake before Mikka had arrived, just sitting there outside the quarter door, knees held to his chest. He only shook; he didn't cry. He'd been too shocked to feel the pain. Dead to the world around him. Cinnamon, it was. Cinnamon. His mother had told him cinnamon makes everything just a little bit better. Rodrigo remembered the many hours he'd spent beside her, an apron around his waist. He remembered how the steam tickled his nostrils, how the wooden stir spoon felt in his hands. He remembered the spice rack, a vial of cinnamon in the top left corner right beside the paprika. Cinnamon. Shadrach had been allergic to cinnamon. Rodrigo should've asked him if he had allergies. He vaguely heard Mikka's voice but chose to ignore it, for there was no point in courtesy now.

Shadrach had asked him to bring soup down to his quarters, not having eaten because of Mikka's outburst. Rodrigo waited while he took his first spoonful, wanting to hear how he could improve his mother's ever-changing recipe. Shadrach drank, appearing to be enjoying the taste and fragrance. But then, his pupils turned to slits, and he seized his throat. There was a deafening silence, only broken up by the Raven King's coughs. He was able to utter his last word then.

"Cinnamon!" Shadrach rasped, cold eyes full of mortal fear. He'd seemed omnipotent, so divine that Rodrigo was astonished that something so trivial could kill him. He tried everything he could, getting him to hurl and lay on his side and all that. Rodrigo had even attempted chest compressions when Shadrach's heart gave out. He tried every practice, prayer, incantation, and fluke he'd ever heard of. Hope was slight. Still, he believed God would help him with his pointless endeavor. He beat on Shadrach's silent chest long after he'd passed.

Blood dripped from the dead man's mouth.

Rodrigo's entire body had gone cold, his mind frozen.

So, he'd cleaned Shadrach up. Changed his clothing, leaving his shirt off. He'd joined Shadrach's hands over his chest and prayed over him for all it was worth. Shadrach wasn't a man of faith. Rodrigo read a passage from his pocket bible, then tossed it to the floor beside the bed and left, hovering over Shadrach's body to close his dark eyes. Even then, it seemed ridiculous that he was dead.

Then, Mikka had arrived, and Rodrigo was made to realize what he'd done. He found himself wrapped in Mikka's arms. In the arms of a man who supposedly despised him. He kept sobbing then, not caring. Mikka himself wasn't sure why he was holding Rodrigo. Despite how he hated the boy, he knew he had to. It was his duty. Shadrach had been Rodrigo's first. The first was always the hardest. Mikka had stopped counting at twenty, each less painless than the last. Many more had died on his account, to be sure. These were detached kills, though. He watched from cliff tops or the underbrush as his bullet struck, and the body fell with that deathly thud. Well, at least now he had someone to hand his flask on to. If anyone needed *raska*, it was Rodrigo.

Mikka heaved him up off the ground without protest and began to carry him out of the room. Rodrigo had turned the other cheek so many times but ended up just being slapped again and again, and he was tired of it, tired of living in the example of a damned parable. He was not the Good Samaritan.

Up the stairs they went. Mikka knew he needed the sea air, something to bring him out of this delusion. He'd murdered a man, but did he have to be so sore? He thought of Pia and closed his eyes, sighing. What would they do? The crew of *The Vault of Heaven* was leaderless, and Mikka had many questions, all of which he couldn't answer alone. Would Cornelius go free? Were they all free? What was to become of the Masked Birds without the former king of Sleetal? All Mikka truly knew was that he was glad of the man's death. Rodrigo had unwittingly saved them from Shadrach's hand.

Lara awoke to Rodrigo's wails and stumbled out of her quarters, a leatherbound thesaurus under her arm. "What's going on, Mikka?" she asked, wiping the dreams from the corners of her eyes. Mikka looked over at her grimly as they passed by.

"Rodrigo killed Shadrach."

She dropped both her thesaurus and her jaw. Mikka went on his way, carrying Rodrigo to the upper deck. They cried through the galley, tears staining Mikka's one good shirt.

Meanwhile, Lara began banging her thesaurus on the doors of the crew quarters. They all emerged drowsily from their respective quarters, leaning into the narrow corridor. Cornelius put the heels of his palms to his eyes and wondered what all the ruckus was about. Was the ship being marooned? If so, it was a shame. Mikka had drunk all the mead.

"Lara, what in God's name are you doing?" Pia asked, the quilt still draped over her body. Lara took a moment to regain her breath, her nostrils swelling. Only the Nic Murray was absent. He was already out on the bridge steering the *Vault* and wasn't there to witness the madness of the sleep-deprived crew. Cornelius wasn't wearing the scarf, and Lara could see what he'd been hiding. Dark, livid bruises in the shape of fingers curled sinisterly around his neck. But there was no time to worry about that. Shadrach was dead.

"Rodrigo murdered Shadrach," she revealed. After a moment of incredulous silence, Cornelius began to smile a little. Everyone stared at him for a long moment. Lara, after the initial shock of Rodrigo hurting anything but his own dignity, did too. Shadrach was gone, and they didn't have to endure him anymore. Cornelius felt a burden being removed from his back. Shadrach was dead. He was safe from dueling his father, at least for the moment. He felt figurative fingers fall away from his throat and breathed a sigh of relief.

They were set to arrive in Sleetal that day, but they didn't have to if they didn't want to. They didn't have to do anything they didn't want to. This *Vault* was no longer Shadrach's. This mission was no longer at Shadrach's command. They could split the money for Cornelius' recovery between themselves, or they could abandon him in some port town. Hell, they could make him walk the plank, not that Lara would want that. She'd grown rather fond of him in the past weeks, the past days in particular. When his voice was low, she could really hear him.

But there was also a startling reality to the Raven King's death. The Masked Birds, the last resistance against Marzine's tyranny, was without a leader. Lara was first to follow Mikka and Rodrigo, not bothering to beckon the others after her. If they freed Cornelius, would she get her money to travel? Could she have *The Vault of Heaven* for herself? Everything was up in the air, so she went to seek answers, not even bothering to check if Shadrach was indeed a corpse. The others soon followed her. They were all still in their nightclothes, save Pia, who stayed behind to dress in something other than a patchwork quilt.

The sky was overcast with wispy yellow clouds, darker billows cropping up here and there. It was the color of the sky before a blizzard. The more northward they ventured, the more unforgiving the weather was—storm after storm, blizzard after blizzard. Rodrigo was lying flat on his stomach, rigid as a wooden plank. The others formed an oval around him, Mikka at one end, Cornelius at the other. Nobody had the slightest clue what was happening, only that Shadrach was dead and Rodrigo was the one responsible. Lara was the only one bold enough to ask about it.

"How did he die? Did Rodrigo mean to? What's to become of the Masked Birds? What's going to happen to Cornelius? What's going to happen to all of us?!" Her voice rose an octave after each question she gave voice to. She felt Pia's hand slide into hers, and she squeezed it tight. Mikka looked up, his eyes sullen. The *Vault* leveled a particularly large wave, and they all pitched, grabbing onto each other.

Lara..." Mikka began.

"Please tell us," a disconcerting voice interrupted. The soft click of bootheels sounded as Murray strode over to them. His eyes fell on Rodrigo. His hands were in the pockets of his long leather coat, his russet curls windswept.

"Cinnamon," Mikka said, noting what he'd gathered from some of Rodrigo's stutterings. "We're saved by cinnamon."

Rodrigo's shaking stopped abruptly.

"He put it in the soup, not meaning to harm him. He tried everything he could, but his soup killed Shadrach, therefore setting us free." The ice in Mikka's eyes melted as he gazed at Rodrigo. He finally had respect for him, if only an ounce of it. The cook sat up abruptly and turned to stare at Mikka, his eyes red and puffy.

"Saved us?" There was no quivering in Rodrigo's voice now. Cornelius could see his throat bobbing up and down. "Saved us, Mikka?" His face was the picture of misery, his golden eyes wide through the tears. He staggered to his feet, Mikka still dwarfing him. The sun shone through the overcast sky, leisurely making its ascent behind his back. The waters glimmered grey. He sniffed, partly from laughter. "None of us are saved. Not a single one of us." His eyes roamed over them with disgust unlike any they'd before. Then, he snapped.

"Murder is unforgivable!" he yelled. He'd been devout all his life, and this was contorting his mind. Mikka hated it when the kind ones broke. "I-I'm going to... to hell. From this life of torture, to an eternity of torture. Just pain and pain and more pain still... burning, forever and ever and then some!" He raised his arms up, only to let them go limp and slap his sides again. "I killed Shadrach. I killed him. I didn't want to, I didn't mean to, but I killed him. Everything is w-wrong and u-unfair, and I would go to the ends of the Earth to make it stop!" His eyes hardened, and he stood to his full height. "But I can't do anything, can I?"

Pia stared down at her unlaced boots. Cornelius' mouth hung open, his lips poised as if to speak. But no sound came from him. It was so, so quiet. Then, Mikka spoke. Mikka Savva, crazy enough to speak in the darkest daylight. Crazy enough to shed light on an open doorway.

"Then, I suppose we'll just have to make the most of this life before we all supposedly 'go to hell,' Rodrigo." His face solidified into a scowl, his eyes shadowed with anger. "This is what we're going to do. We're going to get rich... and get the throne. We'll have to make do with Shadrach's plan. Cornelius will duel his father and triumph, goddamnit! We'll be kings and queens of our own separate nation; everyone else be damned!" he yelled, his battle cry echoing across the waves. Then, his tone got quiet. Awfully quiet. His hands clenched into fists. "I will be the king of Sleetal. Pia will be my queen." He shot her a glare. This was the most tender he could be. "Lara, you'll rule Wilkinia. Rodrigo will rule Embera if he ever gets over his ridiculous guilt.

Nic Murray will be king of Orenia. And you, Cornelius, will be the Marzinian king. Our names will be etched in the sky. Our empires will rise and never fall. We will be the air they breathe. We will never be forgotten. And that's how we make the most of this life."

Cornelius looked at Joan, who was glowering at all of them. Her name hadn't been mentioned.

"Joan can have Addison Island," Cornelius promised. "Lord knows I don't want it." Everyone stared at him. Rodrigo began to chuckle, knowing in his heart of hearts that Mikka's little speech didn't mean a damn thing compared to the eternity of suffering he would soon face.

He let his mind wander to the dead man in Murray's old quarters, his hands joined on his chest, his ankles swollen from the cinnamon. All he felt was anger. Nothing more, nothing less. His last tear rolled off his face. He licked it, the salt tasting like cinnamon, and turned his head to the horizon. A vast expanse of nothing but ice stretched out before them, the lights of Sleetal's capital city winking.

CHAPTER 24

Sleetal, the continent's foremost industrial power. At least it had been before the war. After, it spit out even more factories, but for Marzine.

Marzine and Sleetal were almost equally matched in the continental war, Marzine only casting a slightly paler shadow. The odds were in Sleetal's favor in most ways. Stronger machinery, stronger soldiers, and stronger willpower. But Marzine was more tactical. Almost everyone had heard the stories about the plot that leveled the icy empire. When Marzine took Embera, not a single account was released about the nation's conquer. Instead, Marzine declared war on Sleetal through Embera due to some supposed "aid disputes." The Sleetalian court was focused on resolving the Emberan ruse while Marzine crept in through the cracks left in their icy extenuate. Marzine took the capital at the break of dawn when not even the most perceptive soldiers could see their ships through the city's smog. With Sleetal was breached, havoc ensued. Most troops had only just been shipped off to fight in Embera, a false battle cry yelled across the waters weeks earlier. Sleetal's capital city was taken vulnerable, and although there were casualties in Embera because of the false inquiry, Marzine's military never offered so much as a repose. The continent was soon just plain Marzine with awful little parts falsely named "Marzinian Sleetal" and "Marzinian Embera."

Now, standing on the starboard side of the *Vault*, Lara stared at the capital city before them. The factories' red glow shone through the ever dusk of the smog. These factories were all forges of war, but she was glad for them. They fed the hungry, even if it was through dismal hours and meager wages.

Every other port town they'd stopped at had been small, sun-bleached, and sand-crusted. Stjernsvet, the capital city of Sleetal, was another world entirely. It was easily the most diverse metropolis on the face of the earth. People from all over lived in stingy apartments and stately homes. There was no in-between. Stjernsvetians were either the richest of the rich, overseeing their many factories, or the poor's poorest, working long hours at one of those factories. It was like an unkempt bookcase, the city. People stuffed on either side of people stacked up to the ceiling that was the polluted sky. Stories in their eyes, hollow from the war or shining with the splendor of the good life. It was formally called New Sirensea, but the former name was used more frequently among the denizens. At least, that was what Lara had read. She loved the name Stjernsvet. It meant "Stars' Light" in Sleetalian, which was ironic. The people lived and worked in darkness, whether from the smog or one of the many blizzards. The light of the stars would never be visible in Stjernsvet.

As they drew closer, Lara could make out the shapes of the predominant buildings. All sharp edges and pointed tips, brick-and-mortar. Industrial and deteriorating to its cursory core. She could already smell the scent of factory refuse wafting from the waters. They wouldn't have to dock their ship in an alcove here. There were many bizarre, repurposed ships in the everyman's city. From barges to schooners. Yachts to dinghies. Even a canoe roped to a pier's underbelly here and there. Most were owned by patrols of "Marzinian" soldiers. Few of them were truly Marzinian, though. The majority were picked off the husks of the defeated nations to serve. They were making up the deficit, after all. It seemed everyone was.

The only reason they were stopping in Stjernsvet was for a night of indulgence before they had to act on their life-or-death plan. A night to remember themselves, to remember that they had all been people before the war, before Cornelius. Lara pulled at the scratchy blue tunic of the Marzinian soldier's uniform. They'd decided hours earlier that Cornelius could masquerade as a soldier as well. All he had to do was wrap his face with bandages and wear a cap to cover his distinct golden curls. The prince was thrilled, to say the least. His joy was a bit more subdued when he saw the overlarge tunic, though. It had belonged to Rodrigo, but the cook had decided to stay in his quarters and refused to leave. He'd explained that he wanted to dispose of Shadrach's body alone. It was disturbing, needless to say, but they were all drunk on the revelry of their borrowed time in this world.

"What do you think?" Cornelius asked Lara, his voice having regained its musical quality after far too much nettle tea. She turned away from the stagnant waters, glad for the slightly less smelly air.

The tunic looked absolutely ridiculous on him, as it did most everyone. He'd cinched a belt around his waist to appear more manly, but all that had done was make the garment look like an Emberan summer dress. At least he'd put on the customary sackcloth leggings beneath it. She had a sneaking suspicion that in warmer weather, he would gallivant around in just the shift. He was in the process of covering his face with linen, busily knotting the loose strands around his neck. She burst out laughing.

"I tried, alright? This... uniform doesn't give me much to work with. I can't believe Marzine's finest roam around in these. They should've at least provided the poor souls with trousers of some sort." he grumbled. Her laughs died down into a subtle smile.

"The peak of pulchritude," she praised, her everchanging eyes crinkling at the corners. They found a way to sparkle even in the greyest of cities.

"Lily of the Valley, using big words I see," he remarked, his tone almost approving. He strode over and leaned against the railing beside her.

"I complimented you. Isn't that what you wanted?" she asked impishly.

"Oh Lily, do you really consider me so vain? How rude," he said, feigning hurt.

"Ticket, it's your fault for not having the proper appreciation for my big words." She'd taken to calling him "ticket" in moments like this one to counter to his "Lily."

"I'll have you know I appreciate your big words. Pulchritude just caught me off guard a little, that's all."

She chuckled and turned out to the waters again. They were nearing the lower jetties now. These docks harbored only the most misshapen ships. The *Vault* wedged in beside a very large rustbucket and a very small shipwreck-waiting-to-happen. She inclined her head upward toward the bridge where Murray was standing, only to see him staring right at her. Glaring, she'd say. Glaring rather vindictively if she were to go a step further.

Moments later, all of them but Rodrigo were standing facing the dock in a six-pointed star formation they'd learned from Cornelius. It would make them less noticeable besides the countless Marzinian patrols who'd had the most basic of basic training, practically a three-week-long round of ice breaker questions and bed-hopping. Mikka stood at the head of the formation, Pia at the rear. Lara had been alone in their shared quarters the previous night again. Pia had spent hers in Mikka's quarters, which he'd taken back from Cornelius upon Shadrach's death. Mikka cleared his throat to make a speech. That's what strong leaders did, right? But Cornelius interjected.

"My turn, Mikka."

Mikka glowered but nodded. Cornelius' well-practiced smile fell away as he strode to the head of the group, hands clasped precisely behind his back. He turned to face them, a very uncharacteristic blush on his cheeks. With Sleetal's greatest success and failure behind him, he began. "It's commonplace for all of you to hate me. It would be commonplace if the feeling was mutual. Now, I don't know if you do indeed hate me, but I don't hate you. I quite enjoy you, in actuality. This," he chuckled, eyes sweeping over them. "is the first place I've been the man I've always wanted to be. I have nothing to prove here, and neither do you. I don't have to have good posture or choose whether to wear a frock with notched lapels. And if I did have to choose whether or not to wear a frock with notched lapels, my social standing wouldn't depend on it. Here, I'm free. Here, I'm determined to continue to be free, even as a captive." He nodded at them, a melancholy twinge in his eyes.

He could've cared less before. Everything could burn; nothing saved but himself and his viola. He felt Lara pull him into a tight embrace and then press a kiss on his cheek. Murray shook his limp hand and searched his eyes for some form of acceptance. But the sentinel passed by him too. The plank was set down, and he fell into formation as they marched into the lower city of Stjernsvet.

Cornelius had taught himself not to care. He'd honed his skill of neutrality with every death, disappointment, and misnaming. Honed it with every time he dared to look his father in the eyes. The palace on Addison Island was grand. He could see the moon right out his chamber window, the sea curling and coalescing beneath it. He drank rose tea and listened to the rain, fancying his loneliness romantic. He could've gone on that way forever and ever. He and his neutrality in sickness and health, till death do us part... He remembered the delicate hand his mother had placed on her chest the night he was taken, the glassy quality of her eyes. He was never enough on Addison Island. Never enough. But here, he was.

He still wasn't sure if any of them knew his name, but at least he knew his own. Cornelius, it was. Now he had his own clothes, stolen but long owed. They fit him. They weren't tailored, but they fit him. He didn't care if this was Stockholm syndrome or the misgivings of a young man's mind, but he cherished these people. He'd only ever felt this way towards one person before then: Gale. Gale had purple eyes, purple like the precious stones he loved to collect. His favorite had been the amethyst, though it was near worthless. Gale was sweet and kind, laced with all the sugar there ever was. Gale was going to be king of Marzine, but he was murdered. Now, he hated Gale, for he bore Gale's burden. But not anymore. He let the honey seep out of his eyes and breathed in. Then, he breathed out. He was done.

Mikka knew of an inn not so far into the city. It was close to the docks, and the smell was unbearable, so not many frequented it. Nobody would recognize them there. The *raska* was cheap, and Mikka swore it was the taste of Sleetal itself with a boy's big dumb smile on his face. He made sure to fall a step back with Pia, whispering a promise in her ear before heading up the formation again. Whatever he'd said left her pleased. She pulled the knot out of her hair and let her thick, dark curls frame her face.

They traversed the lower city's streets, passing a small Emberan market with gourds and corn cobs and every summer squash one could imagine. The bright reds and blues of the tents made Pia's smile grow. The smell of earth and spice soup wafted from a wooden cart only a few feet away on the uneven path. It almost covered the city's unpleasant odor. A pretty girl with thick, dark hair like her own tended it, stirring a large clay pot suspended above a fire. She didn't spare Rodrigo a single thought, not bothering to wonder if he would have liked to see the Emberan market like the ones back home, would've liked to sample the spice soup of another.

They made a detour through the Orenian District of the lower city. There were many pubs down these poorly paved streets, tiny little joints stuffed with noise and sound of every measure. She glanced at ever stoic Murray, wondering how he ever grew to be so quiet when surrounded by such noise. The voices had a continuous sort of brogue to them that she couldn't quite understand. The Orenian village they'd visited hadn't been like this in the least. It was all muted coughs and surly soldiers. She was glad that the culture had been able to take root here, a seed planted between cobblestones.

The five nations were joined at the seams here. All was in harmony in the city of Stjernsvet. Well, that wasn't entirely true. There were the soldiers. They did as they pleased, flaunting their power wherever they went. And almost none of them Marzinian. It was amazing what even the most negligible crumb power could do to someone. She never made eye contact with the recruits as they passed. Stjernsvet was lovely when one didn't acknowledge the soldiers' bloodstain.

Finally, after two wrong turns, one brief confrontation, and two rests for marveling over street performances, they made it to Mikka's inn. It was a decaying, two-story building with chipped blue paint coating the timbered exterior. But the most noticeable aspect of the building was its slight lean to the left side. An elk head was mounted above the door, which hung wide open, inviting guests inside. In a hand-painted scrawl, the sign read "The Elk's Head Inn" in Sleetalian.

"Haven't been here in months, have we?" he asked, leaning back toward Pia. She chuckled, recalling the nights after their numerous missions spent up in one of the two rooms the inn offered. They played cards and drank *raska*, doors locked and windows sealed.

"There are worse places to be," Lara offered objectively. She hefted her bag closer to her as she did whenever she was intimidated. Since nobody else dared to step through the wide-open door, Mikka did. The others shuffled in behind him, Cornelius last. He closed the door because the stench of the sea was indeed getting to him.

The first thing Cornelius remarked on was another, very

similar elk's head above a hearth. This place really had the whole elk theme down. A stewpot was on the fire, bubbling as the flames licked at its sides. With the sea out, the smell was tempting. Cornelius' stomach sighed. A few other patrons sat at a long, wooden bar, all Sleetalian and all men. They were large and beefy like Mikka, braidless as was the custom for former soldiers. In Sleetal, when a young man had to do his military service, they chopped off his braid.

Mikka led them over to a comfortable little table tucked away in the corner beside the fire, a matted elkskin rug beneath their feet. There was room enough for all of them in the overlarge chairs, made for the burly men that sat at the bar. Cornelius was conscious of his rigid posture and let his back go slack. He let out a contented sigh, trying to push away the gnawing need to straighten it again.

"This isn't the worst place ever!" Lara said with more enthusiasm, her smile growing. She was sitting right beside the prince, her eyes warm like melted chocolate. He still couldn't decide what color they were, but they were delectable all the same. He hummed in agreement, not finding any words to proffer in response. He had a thing for her eyes. Only her eyes, not her, to be sure, only her eyes. At least, that's what he was telling himself.

Nic Murray was sitting on his other side, staring intently at him. Cornelius felt the hairs on the back of his neck prickling and looked over.

"What'll you have? Perhaps I'll try my luck with your drink." Cornelius was not well versed in less-than-superb alcohols. Even the wines at the ferry dock on Addison Island had been up to par with those in the palace. He used to sneak out in a ferry boat hand's uniform to drink there.

Murray poised his lips and opened his throat. He'd rehearsed speaking to Cornelius in his mind over and over again. And now, his lips wouldn't produce sound. All he managed, in the end, was "lager." Cornelius nodded appreciatively and turned to Lara.

"Murray thinks the lager is good. I'll buy you a pint with my fictitious riches," he said, pantomiming holding stacks of bills. She laughed, and Murray sighed. He shouldn't have tried speaking in the first place. But why hadn't he been able? It'd never been out of his capacity. He'd just never wanted to.

A homely barmaid came by a while later, and they put in their orders, Mikka begrudgingly passing up his turn. The stew, however, cheered him considerably. It was a traditional Sleetalian herring stew with crusty black bread on the side. He let out a contented grunt as he wolfed it down.

While they wined and dined, blushes on the noses of those who did more of the previous, Murray thought back on his lack of speech. His lager was left untouched, and his stew grew cold after an hour. He'd never had trouble speaking before. But right as he'd looked into Cornelius' eyes, he hadn't been able to say more than a single word. His palms had been sweating, his heart hammering, but why? His brows furrowed. Was he… was he so enamored by Cornelius that he couldn't speak? Murray's eyes widened with a sudden epiphany.

Oh… It's love, isn't it?

He'd been so detached up until that moment, but sure as death and taxes, he was in love. In love with Cornelius, Siren Prince of Marzine. He smiled a little helplessly, and without further hesitation, downed his pint.

CHAPTER 25

"**W**ho is he? Well… who was he?"

"Shadrach of Sleetal. He reigned for a few years before the war. He liked his titles and formalities." The clerk smiled gravely. He knew how the death of a loved one could affect someone, but he'd never met a grieving person who'd outright lied about their loved one's identity. But knowing what he knew, he decided to be kind to the stranger.

"Very good, sir, but isn't the king," he said good-humoredly. A boy with a dead man in a cart stood in the parlor of the finest funeral home in Stjernsvet. It was a rare sight, to say the least. The bodies were usually delivered around the back, not carted in through the front.

"He is if I say he is. Now, I have a gun, so you should take everything I say as the gospel truth. You'll give him a proper burial with a priest and everything if you don't want to join him." Rodrigo placed a metal handgun on the table. The clerk stared down the barrel, his eyes widening.

"I'm sorry, s-sir, but I don't own the cemetery. I-I'm not permitted to-"

"You have arms, don't you? Never mind the priest. I'll say the prayer. I have the book anyway. Get your spade. Dig him a grave, or I'll have to dig two, and I wouldn't want to waste my fervor on the likes of you." His fingers wavered on the trigger, his grip shaky like the rest of him. It was the crazed look in his eyes that made the poor clerk comply in the end, not the handgun.

At sunset, the grave was up to par with the stranger's standards. Fit for a king. It was for a king, after all. Shadrach of Sleetal was all *primed and pretty, the beauty of new death on his face. His hair was combed, face shaved. He even wore a suit jacket and necktie. The frightened clerk lowered the dead man into a coffin of the stranger's choosing. They sold them at the funeral home to make a little extra profit. You know, for the yearly bonus. Then, just as the moon began its ascent into the sky, the coffin was shouldered rather inelegantly into the hole. The turned-over soil was ladled back in over the coffin. Pile after pile until it was full again. The clerk lowered the spade, exhausted. The top buttons of his shirt were open, and his face was beet red. His upper city hands weren't used to such hard work.*

A headstone marked "Here Lies — " loomed above the freshly dug grave. The deceased's family were meant to get an engravement beforehand, but "Here Lies — " seemed to do the trick. The stranger produced a pocket bible from his cloak and read the customary passage. He seemed to know the words well, his fingers tracing the page. There was a sort of neurotic constancy in his voice that only gave way after the passage had reached completion. Only then did he weep. Knees down beside the newly replaced soil and all. He let out a wordless sound that made the watching clerk shiver. The clerk was deeply disturbed by the end of the night, but the stranger paid him. A sock full of coins with a handwritten note. "Thanks." It read. And a little lower on the parchment, "I hope this is enough to compensate you for your trouble." It wasn't even half of what was owed to the funeral home, but he could care less. He was just glad to be alive.

Rodrigo brought billows of darkness with him as he strode down the streets of upper Stjernsvet. This area was less impoverished than the rest, and he appreciated the cleaner air for all it was worth to him now. He'd carted Shadrach's corpse under an old horse blanket for hours to reach the finest funeral home in the city, taking with him a small handgun he had from home and a sock full of coins, also from home. He'd spent a sum of the sock on a rented suit for Shadrach and a sum on a sandwich along the way. While the others were off gallivanting

like madmen and women in the dead of night, he was only just
waking from hysteria's sleep. He scarcely remembered anything
from the past hours, only that he needed to lay Shadrach to rest.
Once he had his burial, Rodrigo told himself everything would
be alright again. But it wasn't, was it?

His hands were shoved deep into the pockets of the cloak
he'd borrowed from his sister, his fingers around the handgun.
He'd promised his father that he'd only use it to protect Pia, but
it was a solace only to him now. Rodrigo could see why Mikka
was so fond of that silver pistol he carried at his belt. He felt as
if he could ward off the evils of the world by brandishing the
gun and waving through the air. Everything was his with a gun
in his hand, a gun that hadn't even been loaded when he'd
threatened that poor clerk.

The coins he had left were only enough to buy himself a large
dinner, so he would do just that. All he really wanted was some
of his own soup, but dark thoughts surrounded the galley, and
he didn't want to return to the *Vault* until he had to.

It was nearing the second hour of morning when the
streetlamps finally switched off. There wasn't enough moonlight
to see the cobblestones he walked on. It had been clearer up at
the funeral home. He could see the moon from there. The smog
was overbearing, and it stank like death even in a wealthier
neighborhood. If this was the greatest city in the world, Rodrigo
was a clucking chicken. He pulled the hood of his cloak up over
his disheveled hair and tried to disappear into its folds.

There were many food stalls in the lower city's markets. He
would find the booth with the most food for the lowest price.
Thoughts of Shadrach would leave after he had something to
eat. He was in the mood for Orenian food. Something fried in
oil and vaguely potato-shaped would do him some good.

There were more Marzinians in the upper city, and he would
be glad to go back where eyes were off of him. To them, he was
a suspicious thief swallowed up in a cloak looking for a sweet

old woman to purloin. There was too much gatekeeping in Stjernsvet. The rich didn't want their lives tarnished by the poor, and the poor didn't want their lives dictated by the rich.

Across the way, a group of decorous young men emerged from a restaurant. The warm lights from inside shone on their flushed faces. They were Marzinian. And soldiers at that. Rodrigo couldn't recall seeing a single Marzinian soldier native to Marzine during his time in the city. It was a peculiar sight. Peculiar and unlikely. *Wait...* Rodrigo stopped dead in his tracks, nearly tripping over a stray bench. He sat down hard on it and tried to silence the beating of his heart.

Even in the half-light, he could see the bold crests outlined on their tunics. He saw the imperial greatcoats they wore over their tunics as well. They were King's Guard. A King's Guard had arrived at his hometown in Embera a year and a half before to claim the land for Marzine. Now his family had to pay burdensome property taxes like serfs on a Lord's land. The door to the restaurant swung shut, and the light disappeared. Then, after a moment of bother, a lantern was lit. There was muted talk among the group of King's Guard as they strolled away from the restaurant, moving to the center of the cobblestone street. Rodrigo began to eavesdrop. He stood wordlessly, consigning his guilt to oblivion for a moment.

"We missed the procession in the plaza, but I'm sure it'll be alright considering the circumstances," the smallest of them said, only just able to keep up with the others. The tallest one grunted in response.

"We were following orders. I'm most worried about reporting back to his majesty. I don't want to tell him we lost the rest of them again." The responding soldier's voice was dismal with dread. Rodrigo raised a brow. The rest of them? What was that supposed to mean? The lantern light briefly flashed blue.

"At least we have their cook," the smaller one sympathized. Rodrigo again stopped dead in his tracks. So did the party ahead of him. "Waited for him to pass by all damn night in that seafood place."

He blinked, his lips parting in shock. The smaller one turned gradually. His face was illuminated by the lantern. Rodrigo had never seen a more scarred face in his life. Raised ridges spiraled across his golden skin, some young and pink, some old and grey. But past all the scars, his eyes were the most terrifying thing. Cold as a mariner's memories. Rodrigo shivered. Might as well surrender while he still could.

Then, with a slump, he fell to his knees and extended his wrists. He didn't even try to run, didn't even give a thought to the handgun in his cloak. He was Rodrigo, after all. These men were the highest caliber of humans. They had thousands of ways to capture and disarm him.

The scarred man leered down at him. "You're cute," he taunted. Soon, his face was thrust to the smeared cobblestones by the boot of the small soldier. He felt his wrists being put in irons. Then, the same scarred man hit him over the head with what felt like a baton, and Rodrigo descended into darkness.

On the other side of the city, the revelry of the crew's supposed "last night of freedom" was dying down. The majority of them were drunk on the cheap liquor at the Elk's Head Inn. They were the only ones left in the barroom. The bald men at the bar had long since gone, and the bartender had retired for the evening, leaving them the keys to the two upstairs rooms. Pia and Mikka were sober and discovered that a night of celebration was not nearly as fun without alcohol. They'd listened to nonsensical jokes from Cornelius. They'd watched Murray consume almost as much lager as Mikka would raska. Something seemed to have disturbed his customary stoicism. Maybe it was the lager, perhaps something else entirely. Mikka gave Pia a glance and squeezed her hand beneath the table.

"Hey, we're going to bed," he told them with an unconvincing yawn. Lara smiled and waggled her eyebrows.

"That's not all you're doing, I'm sure," she slurred. Cornelius snorted a laugh and leaned back in his chair, slouching more than he had his entire life. His manners instructor would beat him senseless if she could see him now. His nose glowed brighter than the coals in the hearth.

"You know, if Rodrigo were here, you'd have to lay off. He'd wanna room with you." Cornelius giggled.

Mikka grimaced, stood, and promptly left, taking Pia with him. Cornelius smiled suggestively at Lara. Murray watched on with evident envy. "Imagine if Rodrigo were here. He'd be a hilarious drunk," Cornelius said, not realizing he already fit the character. Cornelius turned to Murray, smiled stupidly, and took a sip of the sentinel's lager.

"This stuff is awful," he remarked with all truth intact. Then, turning back to Lara, he tried to piece together a flirtatious line from the words floating around in his mind. "They only have two beds in the rooms upstairs. We should share one."

Murray sputtered and tried to speak. It felt like the end of the world to a man who couldn't stand without nearly falling over. But of course, he said something ridiculous.

"Oh, be a gentleman. We'll share a bed. Or we could just push them all together," Murray suggested. Lara scowled at him.

"Since when do you talk?" she spat. "And besides, Joan needs to sleep somewhere. Right, Joan?" Lara glanced at the spot where Joan had been sitting. She was absent.

"Maybe she went to the washroom." Cornelius chuckled.

"I'll sleep on the floor. Joan can have the bed," Murray said sourly. But Joan hadn't gone to the washroom as Cornelius suggested. She was in Rodrigo's same predicament, being hauled into an alley by King's Guard. In her drunken state, she'd found herself very peckish and had gone out for food even though the stew pot was still only half empty. Unfortunately for Joan, she had been recognized. They were very selective in who they captured, and she wasn't needed now that they had

Rodrigo. Without ceremony, they'd split her skull open on the alley cobblestones.

Lara soon retired after a testy criticism from Murray about the dark circles under her eyes. It was just him and Cornelius now, the last ones in the barroom. The lights were lackluster and low. Murray finished off the last of the lager as Cornelius scolded him for offending Lara. Anger developed inside him. Why was Cornelius so hellbent on defending Lara?

"Why do you care?" A mad flush came over Murray's face. "Sure, she's as lovely as a spring flower and all, but I promise you I'll give you everything she's got and more. I'll even learn how to change the color of my eyes if that's what you want." He hiccuped. Murray was just about ready to cry, and all Cornelius wanted to do was laugh.

"Murray, things change." Cornelius stretched in his chair, allowing a lazy smile onto his lips. "I love all of you equally, and I would give up all Marzine's riches to be with you forever." He closed his eyes and sighed contentedly. His words were slurred, but the meaning was there.

Now, Murray wasn't one to ever share how he felt unless it was essential. But this seemed absolutely necessary to him, especially with a gallon of lager sloshing around inside of him. "I wish you loved only me, Cornelius; the rest of the world be damned," he admitted, sobering if only for a second. He looked down in regret. He found his lips moving to their own accord for a second time. "Would you kiss me again if you had the chance?" His facial expressions were more fluent than Cornelius had ever seen them. He'd gone from angry, to stoic, to vulnerable. His eyes were so pure now.

"Murray, I want to kiss you too. But I... I don't want to hurt you. This is all so new to me, and sometimes, I'm terrified." He gulped. Cornelius raised a hand to cup Murray's face. He slid a lock of the sentinel's russet curls behind his ears. They were both very tired and very drunk. The tautness of sea travel, criminality, and the war itself weighed heavily on both of them. Murray had just woken from a long, grey dream. Now he wanted to live. Cornelius wanted to live too. Differently from how he had on Addison Island.

"I don't care if you're afraid, and if you don't want to hurt me. I'll gladly hurt for you," Murray whispered, so close he could smell the perfume of Cornelius' hair. He kissed Cornelius slowly at first. Then, after a moment of astonishment, Cornelius kissed back. Time seemed to slow for the two of them. Murray felt euphoric. When they were through, Cornelius left without a word. And then there was just Murray in the barroom alone. He sat there, blushing madly, scolding himself for being so foolish. There would be repercussions in the morning, and he would deal with them then. As of now, he would sleep.

Rodrigo slept too, the sleep of a guilty man. He was passed out on an imperial ship on the way to Marzine. On that very same ship, Addison of Marzine resided. Addison wasn't one to wait for his prey to be delivered to him, so he'd left Marzine on a supposed "tour of his domain." The crew of *The Vault of Heaven* didn't know that they had been followed since their time in Orenia.

CHAPTER 26

The sway of the waves was soothing, and Rodrigo was snug beneath the silken sheets. His body was warm, and his face was cold, chilling air biting at his nose. His head hurt, and all he wanted to do was go back to sweet, sweet unconsciousness, but he had his morning duties to attend to. Try as he might, he knew he would wake Cornelius on his way out. The prince woke at the sound of a hair fraying.

"Ugh..." he moaned, shifting up out of the sheets, his eyes still closed. But then he realized something. There were sheets on the bed. Rodrigo, to his own dismay, didn't have sheets. His eyes flew open, and his head hurt like it had been rammed in with an axe. Momentarily, he thought he was in hell. To be fair, most of *The Vault of Heaven's* crewmembers woke up in the morning thinking they were in hell. It was an exceptional occurrence for Rodrigo, however. He was always rather chipper in the morning.

Something cold kept his wrists in place. Cuffs, he realized. Suddenly, he was submerged in memories. And with memories came pain. He remembered the night of Shadrach's extempore funeral. That night had been more galling than the death itself. He hid it in the back of his mind for fear it would destroy him if he dwelled too long on it. Another set of chains kept his feet immobilized beneath the sheets of what now appeared to be an almost offensively lustrous bed.

The room was quite luxurious overall. According to his muddy memories, he was in the King Guard's custody. He shouldn't have expected any less from an imperial Marzinian ship. Everything was gold or at least gold-threaded, and most of the room's furniture was unnecessary, such as the overly upholstered chaise lounge and the elegant desk in the corner. There was even a bookcase with numerous volumes behind the glass covering. Everything was bolted to the floor to keep it steady, in fact. It was the most luxury he'd ever laid eyes on. Rodrigo loosed a breath. He'd started this journey crying after his sister, and now, he was on an imperial ship, strapped down on a feather bed. All he could think was, *How did I get here?*

He lay there for a very long time, trying to be as unobtrusive as possible. After another scan of the room, he found his cloak and other clothing folded on the armour in the corner. He could see the violent bruising on his face and stitching on his forehead from a particularly deep gash in the mirror above the armoire.

The silence ended as he heard a polite knock at the cabin door. Who would knock on a captive's door? What was he supposed to do, give his permission? He was in chains, for heaven's sake. Struggling against his irons was all he could do.

"Uh, come in?" he called in accented Marzinian, clearing his throat beforehand. It seemed to be coated in a fine layer of dust as if it had been without disturbance for centuries.

The door turned open without a sound. Everything was well oiled on an imperial ship, even the hair of the staff members. Rodrigo stared at one such staff member, who was likely the most interesting-looking man he'd ever seen. His hair was as blond as pastry dough, and his eyes were the purest blue Rodrigo had ever seen. He was comically tall, so tall that he had to duck when entering the round cabin door. An Andrian man, he realized with a start. The Andrian smiled warmly, an affability in his eyes. When he spoke, his accent was unlike anything Rodrigo had ever heard. His Emberan was laughably sharp and enunciated. Rodrigo wondered why he didn't speak Marzinian.

"Greetings, sir. Good day to you." He folded his arms behind his back and licked his lips. "You must be very disoriented, and this will all be explained shortly by the king himself, no less!" Despite all the austerity of his demeanor, the Andrian man seemed delightful. Maybe it was how foreign he was, but Rodrigo sensed a peculiar kindness in him. He gave up struggling against the bindings and sunk back down into one of the many pillows with an eyebrow raised.

"The king?" was all Rodrigo could say, nonplussed. His heart began to race. The man leaned in, and his eyes crinkled in a smile.

"Yes, the king. And my business here is to prepare you to have an audience with him. My apologies, but his majesty only wants the most beautiful people in his presence. In total, I'm here to make you... beautiful," he finished excitedly. Rodrigo's headache worsened. He was handsome, *handsome*. He wasn't some maiden flouncing around in a frilly dress. Pia would always brag that she was the more handsome twin despite being the girl, which made him insecure. His more diminutive stature did nothing to help that.

"Excuse me, but I can't help you with that. This all *seems* lovely, albeit terrifying, but I'm not adjusted to having audiences with kings; I'm just the cook. Do you have the rest of us? Am I the only one? Did we all, well, survive?" He became more and more anxious with every question that remained unanswered.

"Ah, always first to ask about your friends. Unfortunately, that information is restricted. I know nothing in the way of their whereabouts. All I'm allowed to tell you is that you're safe here. Well, safe for the moment, at least," the Andrian explained apologetically.

"Alright, t-then. Is there any chance you could get me out of these cuffs?" The man seemed to ponder it for a moment, adjusting his coattails as he did. His uniform seemed very starched, and Rodrigo wondered if he would have to wear something akin to it. Looking like a crow was not something he fancied.

"Well, you do appear very fragile. If need be, I could subdue you myself. I suppose it's alright." The man began to search through a wardrobe by the cabin door. The outfit he gathered was far too ornate for Rodrigo's taste. It was all very tailored and form-fitting and had about four pieces. There was a black overcoat, a vest of the same color, an undershirt of the contrasting color, and a paisley cravat. And the trousers, oh Lord, the trousers. The hilarity of it all was too much for him to bear. He began to hyperventilate. This was precisely the opposite of what happened to Cornelius; he was getting treated to the finer things in life due to a crime he'd committed, and Cornelius had committed no crimes and was forced to slum it aboard the *Vault*.

The Andrian man paused and offered him a bemused smile. "Not accustomed to Marzinian wear, are you."

Rodrigo began to chuckle. "Oh no, I'm very 'accustomed' to these sorts of things. I get captured and forced to wear the finery of another nation every other week, in fact. Bold of you to assume I wasn't as well-traveled as yourself."

The man's laugh was short and polite. His eyes were almost as enthralling as Shadrach's, and he certainly had the same mannerisms, but everyone reminded him of Shadrach nowadays. Everyone. It was the guilt that made his laughs die away.

"The bathhouse is across the hall. The door to your wing is locked, so you won't be allowed to go farther than your parlor. You'll be expected to bathe and dress. If you need assistance at any point, call for me. My name is Winston."

Rodrigo snickered again. His name fit his demeanor like a glove. And what was a bathhouse? A house of baths? And on a ship? Oh, bother. Marzinians and their money.

"Thank you, Winston," he said as the man undid his restraints.

The Andrian man watched him for a moment, something darker in his eyes, but then Rodrigo began to rub his wrists and ankles, and Winston left. His left ankle had been bound a little too tightly, and the blood had pooled above the cuff. The ankle itself was purple and swollen. Rodrigo grimaced and massaged circulation back into it. Everything was sore, and Rodrigo briefly wondered how long he'd been chained under the sheets. Had the others noticed he was gone? No, not likely.

Then, an unholy relief swept over him, a cool breeze to calm him down. He couldn't hurt anyone he cared about here, not if he was caged in. At least he could find out if Pia was alive and keep the king from sentencing her to death. He wasn't dead, so evidently they wanted something from him. Perhaps he could bargain for her life with that something. If only he had Cornelius' skill of persuasion.

There was some difficulty to be had in bathing and clothing himself. The bathhouse was just as it sounded; a house of baths. It was larger than the bedchamber, and the walls were hewn from stone to trap the steam heat which rose in great clouds, blinding Rodrigo as he stepped into the depths. There were foamy soap bars to wash with on shelves carved into the stone walls at the end of the pool. There were towels scented with lavender lain out after he was done. He was on edge the entire time, not knowing what to feel. But apparently, the promise of hell hadn't killed off his religious beliefs, for he was praying to a nauseating point the entire time.

After about an hour of trying to dress correctly in the suit, Rodrigo finally found his way through the many buttons, ties, and cinches. It was like navigating a new language, and Rodrigo wasn't fond of it. The morose excitement of it all had finally left him, and he was alone with his anxieties, trembling as he always did. As a final touch, he slicked back his hair properly like his mother had taught him and shaved his face clean. A pubescent beard had been cropping up on his chin and cheeks for some time now, and he was glad to get rid of it.

Rodrigo called for Winston, his voice shaky. As if he'd summoned a spirit, Winston appeared beside him. Again Rodrigo marveled over how strange he looked. His eyes were just so transfixing. So clear, so blue.

"I see you've dressed." He moved to readjust the cravat, and Rodrigo almost flinched away. "Just in time as well. You're expected quite soon, and the king doesn't take kindly to poor punctuality." His tone of voice was only subtly frightening, lulling Rodrigo into a false sense of security. Winston stepped back to admire his work and proffered a charming smile. "Well, you clean up nicely," he complimented. With his anxiety, Rodrigo could only conjure up the dimmest of smiles.

"Yes, uh, so you'll escort me to, uh, his majesty?" Rodrigo was visibly shaking. Winston nodded and put a stabling hand on his shoulder.

"You'll be just fine, I'm sure." Winston's eyes grew empathetic, and Rodrigo gave up on trying to understand the man. The Andrian strode toward the door to the parlor and motioned for Rodrigo to follow. Of course, he obliged; what else could he do?

Before leaving his supposed "wing," the cuffs were placed on his wrists again. Winston told him it was protocol, but he didn't need any explaining. There was a multitude of reasons for securing a prisoner, even one made to wear a paisley cravat.

The corridor they stepped out into was nothing like those of *The Vault of Heaven*. For one thing, they weren't the industrial grey color of the *Vault*, but a sky blue with the same crown molding of the bedchamber. Gold intricacies spiraled up the wallpaper from floor to ceiling. The portholes were tinted a tangerine color, so they appeared to be drifting through tangerine juice. It was a pleasant sight for his extremely sore eyes.

They continued on. The corridors had smooth curves for

turns instead of the sharp edges one would customarily find on a ship. But this was an imperial Marzinian ship. Everything was made in the Marzinian fashion. There were too many bureaus to be practical, he realized. No number of objects would fill all of them.

After finding the maze's end, Rodrigo was relieved. His ankles were already tender, and walking didn't help. The suit was unpleasantly tight, and his wrists hurt from being in the chains for so long. The delicate decor made his eyes burn after staring for too long. He never imagined that too many intricacies would be a bad thing. Every door filled him with adrenaline, but those only led to other wings.

Now, these doors had purpose. They were large, square, and wooden. It was uncommon to see such a thing on a ship, but this ship was the most uncommon vessel there was. Winston sighed and grasped the gilded handles, but before he could open them, he suddenly stopped. "We've arrived at the great hall." He turned to Rodrigo, his eyes flaring. "You are not to speak unless spoken to. You are not to move unless told to. You are not to eat or drink anything unless the king himself orders it. Don't so much as breathe in his presence unless you desire pain of the finest thread count, clear?"

Pain had a thread count? Rodrigo had a keen sense of déjà vu. This sounded very similar to what they'd instructed Cornelius to do, and Rodrigo didn't like it. He nodded.

"As a m-mirror," Rodrigo said a little stupidly. Winston removed his chains and then proceeded to open the doors.

It was like strolling into heaven itself. The light of the many windows just about blinded Rodrigo. After a few moments, he adjusted to the brilliance. He remembered his wing as a cheap upstairs room at a pub compared to this. But the most prominent part of the throne room was the throne itself, gilded and shining. And on it sat a very prestigious man. More expensive than the room itself. Addison of Marzine, king of Marzine.

Rodrigo knew he wasn't meant to move, but he gave a steep bow anyhow. He felt it was necessary, given the grandeur of it all. Winston pulled him up by his shirt collar immediately. The king frowned, his eyes lined in darkness and profoundly unnerving. The prince wasn't one to deny the opportunity to talk, so Rodrigo had learned this man was a murderer in cold blood. He'd murdered his own son. But Rodrigo was a murderer as well. An unintentional one, but one all the same. He and this man were alike.

"Sit," the king commanded, his voice booming. Winston had to pull him to the seat at the table's second end, which was about a half-mile from the king. A plate of some kind of seafood and a goblet of white wine seemed to simply appear before him, both of which he didn't touch. The room felt austere once Winston left.

The king cleared his throat. "Rodrigo Reyes of Embera. I've heard little of you compared to your companions. Your title is humble: cook. Your crimes are extensive, aiding in the capture of the Crown Prince. You're an odd one indeed."

Rodrigo gulped but didn't respond.

"Do you answer to this title and crimes?" the man bellowed.

"Yes, y-your majesty." Rodrigo worried over each of the three words he'd spoken.

"Despite your flaws, I have a use for you. Tell me what you think it is."

Rodrigo didn't know. He didn't have a use. He'd helped capture the prince. The best he could give was information on his whereabouts. Then, he remembered his reason. They would get to go home together someday, see the sun setting over the bronze hills. He would do it for her, even if hell was all there was waiting for him. She deserved this life, even if he didn't.

"I can tell you where the crown prince, your son, is," Rodrigo said, fully intending to lie and either give up his life because of it or jump ship before his visit to the guillotine.

"I know where he is," the king proclaimed, a measure of mirth in his voice. Rodrigo's eyes widened. Addison of Marzine clasped his hands together, a regal ring adorning one of his fingers.

Rodrigo's eyes met his, and he felt a twinge of fury. "Why haven't you taken him back, then?" There was a rage in his voice that Rodrigo couldn't conceal.

The king smiled wanly. "My son is a weak, simpleminded human being who is adamant on being a failure. Both of my sons were. I killed the first one because he was weak, and Cornelius had bested him in all aspects of life by age eleven. He's still the scum of the earth, though. I gave him his brother's name three years ago, and he disregards my command by going by his previous name. I'm giving you the courtesy of calling him by 'Cornelius' so that miniature head of yours won't spin too much. I can't kill both of them. I need an heir. No, I need some way to strengthen my heir, to smother those delicacies in him—a good king rules with his mind, not his heart. From what I've observed, he's very fond of you. At the former king of Sleetal's trick soiree, he told you you were 'amazing' and such. He cares about you. He cares about you, and to lose something he cares about will shatter him."

Rodrigo swallowed. "You're saying…"

"As your king, I'm commanding you to duel my son. If he loses, you'll be my new son, proving yourself stronger than he'll ever be. Stronger than the majority of people. If he wins, he'll rise from the ashes of his suffering, a new, perfect crown prince. And only in those hands will I leave Marzine."

Anger. Anger like Mikka's. No, anger like his own. The outrage of years spent being stepped upon. Of years turning the other cheek. Of years of being good. And now, he was being forced to kill or be killed. Kill *Cornelius* to live. How dare this psychotic man pick and choose his children? How could he suddenly just accept Rodrigo as his son? No, he wasn't that crazy. He simply expected Rodrigo to lay down and smile sweetly as his throat was slashed from ear to godforsaken ear. But he was more than a fatal duel.

He stood silently and pushed in his chair behind him. The king raised a brow. "I'm afraid I'm useless to you, your majesty. I refuse."

"Oh my dear boy, you can't refuse. You will duel him. You've already killed, haven't you? I thought you were the one who killed Sleetal's former king. I suggest you reconsider your refusal."

Rodrigo's heart felt as if it had been pierced by the blade of a sword. He clutched at his chest as the king's eyes bore into him. He continued to smile that horrible, horrible smile. "I'll even spare your sister. Knowing you, that's the only way you'll be bought." And with that, Rodrigo's anger vanished into cold, abysmal shock. He was going God knows where with Lord knows whom, being made to jump through hoops for his sister who didn't give half a damn about him. And the worst part was that he didn't know who even gave a whole damn about him.

CHAPTER 27

D awn was breaking over the Elk's Head Inn when Murray realized what was making him so ill at ease. Joan wasn't in her bed, nor was she in the barroom when he stuck his head out the door of their upstairs room. What's more is he had the feeling she was dead, not just missing. First Mannon, then Tolmas, now Joan. All three of his mariners had died or were in the process of doing so. He cast a sorrowful glance at the folded sheets of the bed. If she'd given him notice of her death beforehand, he could've slept in her bed instead of curling up on the softest floorboard and shivering under his long leather coat all night. His back ached.

Murray didn't know why she was dead or how he knew it. He just did. He had an intuition for the more morose things in life, having lived like a dead man for what felt like centuries. Cornelius was unmoving in the narrow bed beside the one Joan would've occupied, Lara's sleeping form shivering beside him. He'd pulled the blankets off of her during the night. Leaving her out in the cold wasn't the most romantic thing to do. He shrugged on his too-large overshirt and coat, straightening the collar in the mirror and thinking of the letter he'd write to Joan's family, who lived in rural Sleetal.

Well, it would be best if he tiptoed out and woke Mikka first. Cornelius and Lara could sleep a little longer. After the best day in months, this one would be one of the worst of their lives, Murray could just tell. He'd had the same feeling of foreboding before Shadrach had choked Cornelius halfway to hell; God rest that disturbing man's soul. The sentinel looked in the mirror one last time before leaving. His unruly russet curls stuck up oddly, and he patted them down. He would prefer his bearer of bad news to be somewhat presentable, and he'd give Mikka the courtesy in hopes that one day the same would be given to him.

The corridor between the two rooms was hardly a corridor, more of a landing, actually. There weren't even five feet of floorboard to tread on to reach the other room. The walls were paper-thin, so thin that a wall sconce would tear through if hung. Because of this, every sound could be heard across the way. Needless to say, they hadn't gotten much sleep. He yawned, not bothering to knock.

As he'd suspected, they were wrapped around each other like scarves. At least they'd taken the liberty to cover themselves with the sheets. Murray stared longingly at the bed on the opposite end of the room. If only they hadn't gotten together, he could've slept on that bed. His back concurred. There was a candle still burning on the flimsy nightstand. It was only a stub now, but the flame was still bright as ever. What a fire hazard. Those reckless teenagers had a complete disregard for safety. Then he realized that he was one of "those teenagers." Of course he was. He'd done reckless things too, but only just recently. He'd kissed Cornelius. Twice. Murray's brow knit involuntarily.

"Mikka, Pia, wake up." Mikka stirred, groaning and uttering a curse to himself in Sleetalian. The absence of *raska* was likely the first thought in his mind. Mikka's eyes finally jolted open, red and bloodshot. He looked thoroughly crazy.

"Joan's dead," Murray said nonchalantly, betraying none of the loss he felt. His eyes roamed to Pia, who was still dead to the world, her head on Mikka's exposed chest. Mikka scowled at the slouching sentinel.

"Eyes on mine, pervert," Mikka snarled, pulling the sheets over her shoulders. Murray was amused that lust was his concern after what he'd said. He sighed and looked up at the ceiling, a trace of a smile on his lips. It was strange that everyone thought men couldn't control themselves at the sight of a woman's shoulders. The supposed "inability to keep it in his pants" was hilarious. Any decent person should be able to do that, not just someone who preferred men to women. But that was neither here nor there.

"Joan's dead," he said again. There was another twinge in his chest. Mikka must've finally understood the meaning of his phrase, a long silence following. Murray waited patiently for a response, keeping his eyes locked on the ceiling.

"How... how do you know?" Mikka asked accusingly as if Murray himself had killed her. He tried to find the logic in his intuition.

"She's not in her bed, nor is she downstairs, and she wouldn't leave without instruction. She was either arrested by Marzinian authorities, someone else, or was killed by an unknown on the street," he informed him. Murray finally took his eyes off of the ceiling but stared straight at Mikka instead of his bedmate. His expression was all too simple, and it took the best of Murray not to laugh at him.

"I think you're right."

"Now, if there's even the slightest chance she was arrested by the Marzinian authorities, we should take our leave while we still have the opportunity. Cornelius took his bandages off at the end of the night. He needs to put them back on." Murray's mind was working frantically. Mikka grumbled to himself for a moment.

"You're right. Get the others ready and make sure Cornelius is wearing his bandages. We'll meet you downstairs in a quarter-hour." He was his soldier self immediately, sharper than ever without the *raska* making him sluggish. For the tiniest moment, Murray was proud. A smile lived and died on his face.

He followed the sharpshooter's orders and woke the others. It took a considerable amount of shaking to wake Cornelius, who customarily woke at the drop of a pin. Lara woke soon after, and he explained their situation. The room was grey with grimness as they dressed and packed away their strewn-about belongings. Lara wrapped Cornelius' bandages again. Murray, despite himself, was a little jealous. He blocked out his feelings as soon as he recognized them, though. It was a foolish thing, falling in love with Marzine's prince. Cornelius tried to give him a few meaningful looks, but he never met his gaze.

From the look in his eyes, Murray knew that he did remember last night. He finally acknowledged Cornelius' pleading looks at the room's door. He grabbed Cornelius' arms securely, his fingers pressing into his skin. Lara was already downstairs. "I don't know," he whispered, for he didn't know. There was too much at stake to think of trivialities such as love and drunken kisses. But to Murray's immediate shock, he smiled that sweet smile of his, and all Murray wanted to do was make the same mistake he had twice before. Before he could, Cornelius slipped out of his fingers and down the stairs. Murray followed, dazed.

The owner of the Elk's Head Inn was startled as Mikka handed over the coin for their stay with a glower, but there was no time to apologize for his actions. Mikka's hand was on his gun holster, shaking with fear or anger or lack of *raska*. Only God knew what kept him going without his *raska*. He led the group out of the inn, and they stole down the filthy streets, trying to blend in with the workers on their way to the Industrial District. Little did they know they were already being watched. The watchers left them alone, though. The king had explicitly ordered them to leave the "pitiful children" alone until they reached their ship.

The sun rose to its midmorning position in the shrouded sky when they reached the Emberan market from before. The soup smelled heavenly and inspired hunger in all of their stomachs, but there was no time for stopping and marveling over the city's spectacles. There was no time for anything but walking and looking suspicious while trying not to look suspicious. Murray found himself sarcastic after the loss of yet another mariner. Again he thought of the letter he would have to write—the third one.

The streets grew more crowded in the lower city as the day progressed. Workers walked in groups. Merchants called from carts. The crew fell into a leisurely pace. Half of them were convinced everything was in order. Joan might be gone, but maybe she'd turned back to the ship or just run away, free of obligation now that Shadrach was dead.

Murray wasn't as convinced as the others. He was skeptical by nature, but he trusted his intuition, for it had gotten him out of many unsavory situations. In his mind, she was dead in an alley. He frowned and delayed, walking two steps behind the others. Joan wasn't their concern anymore, though. All they had to do was get back to the ship and get out to sea.

Honestly, if it were Mikka missing, they would waste the entire day looking for him. But if it was one of the nothings of the group, they wouldn't bother. Murray knew he wouldn't be looked for, at least not for too long. His replacement could be hired easily. So could mariners like Mannon, Tolmas, and Joan. Joan was worthless to them and Rodrigo even more so.

His frown bent into an all-out glower. They were a group of self-serving, egotistical children living off of the hope of a stroke of luck. They were all damaged, too set in their ways to care for anyone but themselves. The fortresses they'd built around themselves for protection were keeping them in, caught inside with the darkness the walls were meant to keep out. Mikka and Pia were the closest thing to love anyone post-war could hope for, and even they were twisted. He certainly wouldn't have it as good as them. All the love he would ever have to his name were two desperate kisses shared with Cornelius, Siren Prince of Marzine.

Even as he thought of Marzine's crimes, he wished Cornelius

would fall into step with him. He wished Cornelius would promise him that they'd look for him if he was lost. He wished Cornelius would hold his hand. He wished... he wished... but they were all just wishes in the end. None of his wishes would come true, no matter how he wanted them to. Instead of wishing more, he looked up and felt his stomach flip. Cornelius was holding Lara's hand. Of course he was, because he was an egotistical, self-serving kid, just as they all were. No tears would fall from Murray's eyes over this. Instead, he hardened his face and sighed.

But something else caught his eye while he was looking up. Bits of the bandages were falling off Cornelius' face. And because the universe hated them, a group of Marzinian soldiers were striding down the street opposite them. They would recognize Cornelius. His face was on the damned coins. The head soldier, a stout Wilkinian man, was staring directly at Cornelius.

The Wilkinian man and his troops stopped as he ordered something obscure, eyes still fixed on Cornelius. Mikka noticed the development too. He put his hand on his holster for succor, not having his flask for that purpose any longer. The patrol began to wind their way through the crowd, clearing a path through the common people who looked on with apprehension.

"They know it's me!" Cornelius whispered. He turned to Mikka, his eyes wide. If it was only a few weeks ago, Cornelius would've run right into the arms of the nearest soldier. But he had another purpose now, and he knew more about the Marzinian soldiers' loyalties. They would either kill him or try to get the king to pay for his return as Shadrach had. He didn't want to die and didn't want to feel like a captive again. "What are we going to do?" he asked, his tone laced with concern. Lara squeezed his hand. Mikka squared his shoulders, and Pia clutched her talisman as the soldiers advanced.

"We're going to scatter. If you have any loyalty to this group, you'll be back at the *Vault* by sundown."

His gaze seemed to penetrate Cornelius' soul. "I'm trusting you. Just this once, I'm trusting you."

Murray sighed, knowing he would be inconspicuous on his own. He would be just excellent if he took off his soldier's uniform. With the coins in his pocket, he could get himself some espresso and enjoy silence for the evening. Mikka grabbed Pia's hand and pulled her along with him down an alley. Cornelius and Lara broke off in an all-out run. Murray lamely crossed the street and joined a line of workers waiting for their train to pull into its station, pulling his tunic over his head and folding it into his pack. The soldiers probably hadn't even noticed him in the group. He was similar to those around him, a man who simply fit into the background.

The train would take him where predestination intended him to go, plausibly the industrial district if he took note of the coveralls adorning the folks before him. The one good thing about Marzine's occupation of the continent's nations was free public transportation. With the king's abundant wealth combined with Sleetal's many technological marvels, they'd been able to implement a train system throughout the city of Stjernsvet. Murray wasn't simple enough to believe only bad things came from war.

After what felt like hours of waiting, the patrol finally lost interest in the area and moved elsewhere in their search. At long last, the workers' line was allowed to climb the metal steps up onto the platform as the train pulled into the station. A wonder of human advancement waited before him. He wouldn't have cared much for the steam engine in the months before Cornelius' arrival, but something had changed in him, and he still didn't know why.

People went through periods of change, but never this quickly. It was like he was waking from a long dream. He was talking, walking, *moving,* not standing still any longer. And most of all, he was making memories he actually wanted to remember. Vivid, colorful memories. Life was beautiful, changeable, and worth living.

The sentinel had seen the railways cutting a path through the city before. On them traveled great grey steam engines that let out puffs of water vapor every now and again. They boarded the train's fourth car. The benches inside the train car were wooden and upholstered with red cushioning. He sat in the very back where he could be alone and closed his eyes, leaning his head against the window. It was quiet, quiet despite the people. They all kept their heads down, all too weary to worry the one beside them with a bit of conversation. He was tired, too. This metamorphosis, though vivid, was unwanted, he realized. He'd been comfortable in his cocoon. Comfortable by himself.

Murray let his drowsy eyes survey the cityscape from behind the window. Buildings upon buildings stretched out as far as his eyes could see. The train had ascended a bridged railway. From the raised platform, everything was in view. Murray wondered how many lives were led in Stjernsvet, how many stories were beginning and ending on the maze of streets and passages. Murray closed his eyes again, overstimulated. He pulled his coat collar up around his ears, clutched his pack to himself, and began to doze with his breath fogging up the glass.

He was woken by the blaring sound of the loudspeaker announcing the train's stop. Murray didn't have the slightest clue where he'd ended up. His neck was sore, and his head throbbed. He stood sluggishly, shouldering his pack and stumbling toward the train car's exit. He had to wedge himself between two old women to join the line. One smiled sweetly at him. The other smacked him with her purse.

Murray made it out onto the platform and looked over his surroundings. It was afternoon. That was all he could tell, for the sun was almost overhead. He was somewhere in the heart of the city, unable to see neither the water nor the factories.

There were only poorly-paved streets and gloomy apartment buildings, residents looking over the city from their tiny verandas. Murray shoved his hands deep into the pockets of his leather coat and looked around indiscriminately. There were only a few shopfronts and no carts, horses, or even automobiles in the street. He enjoyed the silence, only disrupted by distant sounds of the more populated areas of the city. It was nice. And the air was fresher.

He chose to head left, hoping to come across a cafe or bookstore. The position of the sun in the sky bathed everything in purple shadows. Some of the buildings were draped in ivy and vines, summer's flowers blooming among the thorns.

After a bit more strolling, Murray came across a cafe. Like the shops before it, flowering vines covered its alley side. His eyes fell on the sign. It was called "Nutty Njal's." The door was ajar, and Murray could smell the espresso beans roasting from within. His mouth watered, and he realized he hadn't had espresso since an awkward breakfast with Shadrach in Wilkinia.

He turned the door open, an entry bell clinking merrily. The barroom was small but pleasant. The floor was tiled in a black-and-white pattern and appeared to be freshly waxed. Darkwood tables of two or three seats were up against the far wall with an array of framed, hand-drawn sketches over them. The cafe bar itself was made from the same dark wood, and the barstools were uneven heights as if made by a novice. It was a gawky little place, and Murray liked it.

"Hello there! I haven't had many customers today. Thanks for stopping by, friend." A skinny Sleetalian man popped up from beneath the bar with a steel canister in his hand. His long hair was tied back in a ponytail, signifying his lack of military service. Murray attempted to smile at the man, taking a seat atop the tallest of the barstools.

"Espresso," was all Murray could manage. The barkeep's smile faded.

"Yes, uh…"

"Murray. You can address me as Murray," the sentinel said. The man's jovial smile returned.

"You can call me Njal." So this was *the* Njal of Nutty Njal's. Njal made himself busy preparing Murray's espresso. They had the place to themselves, and Murray was nervous around the overly friendly man. After another few moments of bustling, Njal turned back to him with that same smile. He watched on with particular angst as Murray took his first sip. No wonder he hadn't had many customers.

Murray's face brightened as he tasted the coffee. It was rich and dark and everything he needed. He closed his eyes and sighed contentedly.

"How is it, Murray?" Njal asked earnestly. Murray looked up at him with a frown, disappointed that his moment had been interrupted. He was well aware he was being rude, but Njal could wait until he finished his cup.

After a moment of silence, Njal sighed so wistfully that Murray almost felt guilty. "What's on your mind, Murray?" he asked. This time, Murray answered. It was mainly to shut Njal up, but he found himself telling the truth.

"A man and times long past," Murray muttered into his espresso.

"Delightfully cryptic. Who is this man, and what does he have to do with your past?" Njal continued on. Murray took another sip of his espresso and found words on his tongue before he could stop them.

"If I told you who he was, you wouldn't believe me. And I haven't known him for long. He just reminds me of everything I wasn't in my formative years, that's all."

Njal nodded as Murray took another long sip, and his mind began to hum.

"What is he that you weren't?" Njal asked, leaning closer as Murray leaned back. He downed the remainder of his espresso, dregs and all, quite ready to leave after the numerous questions. He met Njal's eyes as he spoke the following phrase.

"Proud. He's proud in the best way. Tenacious and peculiar and... and... damn. He's just so pretty. He loves his life and himself and finds beauty in everything. And I... I'm just starting to live because of him." Murray, to his own horror, felt a tear trickle down his cheek and into the espresso glass.

Njal had finally shut up. He stared at Murray. Murray stared right back. Finally, the sentinel sighed. He sifted through his pockets for some coins and slapped them down on the bar. Then he stood, shoulder his pack and traipsing to the door. But before he could leave, Njal called out to him.

"Wait!"

Murray looked back warily, his eyes red. Njal gave him a wavering smile, and Murray finally noticed that Njal's eyes were also wet. "Murray, I hope you end up with the man who allows you to live. And I hope you enjoyed your espresso. Come back again someday and tell me what happened, alright?"

Murray felt his lips spread into a smile. "Alright, Njal. Thank you," he said. The merry bell clinked again as he left.

Murray had learned three hard lessons in his youth. He'd learned how to hold his own hand, how to hold his tongue, and he'd learned that no love was unconditional. But as he strolled back to the train platform, he realized that all three rules had been broken. Njal had held his hand for him, even if only figuratively. He'd listened to Murray. He'd helped. And Murray hadn't held his tongue for once. The sentinel wasn't quite sure if the third rule had been broken yet. But this love he felt, this mad, glorious love, seemed vast to him. It seemed unconditional.

The Vault of Heaven was empty of both Shadrach's corpse and Rodrigo when Mikka and Pia arrived back at the docks. Only a note remained, and from its contents, they knew the Marzinian monarchy was onto them.

Bring the crown prince to Addison Island by the end of the month for a duel. You will not be inciting the division of Continental Marzine. Instead, you will be rewarded ransom money. Rodrigo Reyes has been kidnapped because there are ramifications for capturing the crown prince. He will be dueling the prince of Marzine for the crown because there are also ramifications for conspiring with the enemy. The duel will be to the death, and either party will be pardoned of his crimes upon victory.

The note was written in every language to get the message across. They had all returned at sunset to read the note dooming either Rodrigo or Cornelius to an untimely death.

CHAPTER 28

F ew things got to Cornelius as much as Murray. When looking at the man, he felt as if his heart were being held captive by Murray's slender fingers, beating out of control because it so desperately wanted to escape his grasp. But try as he might, Cornelius couldn't shake the sentinel. After their drunken kiss, Cornelius had had no other choice but to go lie beside Lara on the narrow bed and pretend his affections for the both of them weren't the only thing occupying his mind. He'd flirted with Lara as they'd fallen asleep, whispering sweet nothings to her through the lager's haze. Murray had only entered the room when he was on the precipice of sleep. They'd stared at each other, and then Murray had removed his leather coat and laid down on the floor. And that was that. There was no further discussion on the topic until Murray woke him the following day, convinced Joan was dead.

Cornelius wasn't persuaded. Had it not been for his affinity for his captors, he would've done the same thing as Joan, escaping into the night while everyone else was still in the hold of their drunken dreams. Because Shadrach wasn't there to torment them anymore, she'd felt no obligation to stay and had taken the first passenger ship out of Stjernsvet. That was the logical explanation, at least, but Murray was hell-bent.

Despite the madness of Joan's disappearance, Cornelius couldn't help but cast come-hither looks at Murray from across the small room as he dressed and as Lara bandaged his face again. As it turned out, Murray was adamant about ignoring him until it was only them in the room, Lara leaving to go meet the others downstairs. But then, his steely eyes were back on Cornelius, and that familiar over-beating of his heart returned. To his surprise, and oddly his pleasure, he found Murray pushing him against the frame of the door, those slender fingers pinning his arms to his sides. There was an unmistakable glint of desire in his eyes, and Cornelius remembered all the others that had looked at him similarly. But Murray was entirely contrary to them. Murray knew his name.

"I don't know," Murray had said then said, and Cornelius knew he indeed didn't know. Didn't know what to make of their situation. They'd kissed twice, once while intoxicated, and yet the air between them smelled of roses and rain. Cornelius didn't know what to make of it either. It was a fantastic feeling, not knowing. In his previous relationships, he'd always been the one to know, the one to have experience. Well, except for with the man who'd taken his virginity, a dark-eyed King's Guard who, to this day, worked for his father. They still had the occasional tryst when life behind the obsidian wall became dull again. Murray was the first since him to make him feel vulnerable, to make him feel inexperienced. And the feeling was mutual. They were both vulnerable, both bemused by their predicament.

Maybe he even felt a little bit insecure, for when Mikka insisted they leave the Elk's Head Inn early, he'd extended a hand for Lara to hold as they perused the streets of lower Stjernsvet. She'd taken it willingly, and he'd wondered again what color her eyes were. Today, they mirrored the sunlight that painted the mist golden. But tomorrow, they could be dark as a moonless night. She was ever so changeable. But not with him. With him, she was consistent. She let him speak to her, and she listened, humoring him. Others listened for pleasure. But she— she was something else entirely. She was fascinated by him. And he didn't know if that made him favor her more than Murray or the other way around. There was that vulnerability again. The not knowing, the absurdity of the rock and the hard place he'd gotten stuck between.

A patrol of Marzinian soldiers caught onto them when they were nearing the docks. Of course they did. While trying to be inconspicuous, they'd made themselves conspicuous to those around them. And Mikka, to Cornelius' delight, told them to scatter. Since he was holding Lara's hand, he ran off with her instead of Murray. But as they stole down the sodden street, he gave a backward glance to Murray, hoping the sentinel would know that he would've preferred to spend the afternoon with him, discussing the weather and doing... other, less innocuous things to each other. It was he who Cornelius had last kissed, after all.

The afternoon was pleasant enough anyhow. Lara brought him down to the docks, where they could more easily blend in with the masses. To help with their hangovers, she bought them each a cup of piping-hot black coffee. It wasn't the nastiest he'd ever had, but it was undoubtedly on the list. It was the kind of drivel sold to factory workers who hadn't the coin for anything more expensive. But it eased his headache. Did the job, just as the factory workers did their jobs. Sleetalians and their mass production. Industrialism had failed the ancients, so why had they thought it would work for them?

After coffee, they crept into one of the shabbier theaters of the lower city without paying for tickets. They saw an Emberan romance about a woman who'd fallen in love with her father's second wife. Scandalous, but well worth the mischief of sneaking in. Cornelius rather enjoyed it, in fact. He was used to only the highest quality performances in the most prominent theaters in the world, and the change of pace was nice. What he enjoyed more than the performance itself was Lara's laughter during it. Her laugh was as eloquent as her speech, something he appreciated about her. She'd laughed all throughout their voyage on the *Vault*, laughing when the hand around his throat hadn't allowed him to laugh with her.

The sunset was blood-red and glorious as they strolled down to the docks together, arm in arm. The smog colored it that way, and he marveled over how something so foul could look so gorgeous when it floated into the sky. He kept his cap pulled low over his face so he wouldn't be recognized, and she teased him for how his nose stuck out. He took it off and pulled it down on her head, having to stand on his tip-toes to reach. This was the epitome of throwing caution to the wind, but workers were just getting off their shifts, and no one was paying attention to anyone but themselves. The Marzinian patrols had found bars to haunt for the evening, and all was listless in Stjernsvet.

That is, until they boarded the *Vault*.

Cornelius' heart didn't stop when he read the letter from his father. No, it curled up and died, aging a century by the time he read the last word. The page wrinkled in between his fingers, and if it weren't for his years of practice with restraint, he would've torn the parchment to ribbons. But no. This little letter would be a keepsake for when he left his father to rot in a prison cell. He would frame this letter, hang it right above his bed so that he could look at it every night and feel righteous about never letting his predecessor see the light of day. This letter, after all, sentenced either him or Rodrigo Reyes to death. And Rodrigo, he found, was more of a brother to him than his actual brother had been.

It was just like Addison of Marzine to make punishment a spectacle. He'd done it since Cornelius was a child. If he were too unruly at the dinner table, his father would make the servants tie his hands behind his back, put him on the floor with whatever dish they had that evening, and eat on his knees, like an animal. And that's where his restraint came from.

He could feel the others' eyes on him as he read over the letter again and again.

"Cornelius… I had a crap father, too. But my old man was nothing compared to this." It was Mikka who spoke to him,

Mikka of all people. Trying to console his inconsolable rage. He burned with it. Burned like he wanted to burn Addison Island and Sirensea to the ground, his father along with it.

"What did yours do to you? Was he too there, or too not there?" he asked, eyes still flitting over the page. The galley's floorboards creaked as Mikka took a step closer.

"He beat me sometimes. My mother, too."

Cornelius, despite himself, smirked. "Same with mine. Until my mother's mind escaped her. Then he let her be, for she was too far away from herself to cry out in pain how he liked." Finally, he set the letter down on the galley table and turned to face the others. Each of them seemed wary of him, as if they hadn't known how laced with poison the Marzinian line was up until then. The sunset filled his seemingly soulless eyes, making them bleed red.

"Ah, a wife-beater. We don't take kindly to those where I'm from," Pia said slowly. Cornelius gave her an appreciative look, burying his hands in the pockets of his tunic so he didn't reach for the letter again. He took a seat at the head of the galley table. The others followed suit until they were gathered around a single lantern.

"Let me tell you the story of my name. Or names, as it were. I want you to know just exactly who we're up against. And by who, I mean the wretched little man I call Father," he said. And so, he began.

Only the finest for the elites of Marzine. The finest for the finest. But how did one reach this status of finery? How were the food and decor deemed worthy of these few fine slaves of hierarchy? Cornelius could ponder such questions for hours, but he had a job to do. A lesser prince would lie back and allow someone else to do this particularly grueling work for him, but not him. His grueling work was of the social variety, to put a smile on the face of every guest by the end of the evening, and in return, the monarchy would gain each noble's backing for the impending war.

Being only fourteen at the time, he was seen as a sort of pet. A young, handsome hound eager to be scratched behind the ears and left dinner scraps. His hair was coiffed, none of his unruly curls showing beneath the layers of perfumed grease. His smile was as superficial as ever, eyes filled with reflections of the palatial ballroom around him. But that was the same for every young party-going gentleman in the room. His individuality was brought about by his suit. The other young men were clad in dark frocks and cravats, whereas he wore a dapper Sleetalian suit the color of a cloudless sky. He would be recognizable even without the suit, though. At these revelries, it was customary to wear something to display one's status. He wore his crown, which shone atop his head. All eyes were on it, not the wearer beneath. And Cornelius preferred it that way. He *was* the crown. He was the symbol of Marzine itself.

Cornelius prepared himself for the impending trial, preparing to become whatever his associate wanted in an evening. He would do it for his father, an insane despot who ruled with an iron fist. Whenever he thought about his duties, he was reminded of the dog-like quality he possessed. A young, handsome hound sent to fetch his master's slippers. In truth, Cornelius was the most powerful man in the room, save his father. He was merely masquerading as a mutt. If it pleased him, the prince could have even the richest duke executed in a matter of moments, and those who questioned his judgment would follow. But he wouldn't do that. His father still reigned supreme, and unfortunately, he would follow his victim to the grave if he used his powers as prince.

"How shall I play the game of guile this eve?" he murmured to himself, surveying the room for the most interesting target. The people wining, dining, and dancing among the festooned tables and silken curtains were all valuable, but who had the most value of the lot? Ah, his mark was his father's brother, the

Archduke of Sirensea. The richest duke, as in the one he could execute if it pleased him.

While Addison of Marzine had a large frame and an end-all glare, Adrian of Marzine had a fragile frame and a deflowerer's simper. Other than those differences, they were very similar. They had the same arresting blue eyes and untamable hair. He was undressing a group of young ladies-in-waiting with his eyes when Cornelius strode forward. He took two goblets off a server's tray as he wove through the revelry, not bothering to check the contents. It all tasted like urine anyway.

Unobtrusively, he seated himself beside the sleazy man, setting the goblets before him. Adrian glowered at the drinks, ready to pummel the person who'd disrupted his ogling. But when he turned to see Cornelius seated beside him, his manner changed entirely. A smile spread across his face, and his plucked eyebrows rose in surprise. He looked like a clown without makeup.

"Hello, m'Lord," Cornelius said. "Would you be so kind as to share a drink and regale me with a story? I've heard you're a grand raconteur, and I would be obliged to hear your tales." He feigned regard. Adrian would surely tell an unbelievably dull anecdote as he always did at these soirees.

"Ah, it's good to see you, nephew. I appreciate your company. Now, which one are you? Gale or... I can't quite recall the other prince's name, but his majesty made no mention of his other son appearing at this little gathering," he said, gesturing around at the finery as if it were all made of smoke and mirrors.

Cornelius kept the frown off of his face by smiling wider. It was just so odd. His brother had died almost three years prior. There was a large funeral procession and everything, but no matter. Adrian had the tendency to be distracted, and with all the wine in his belly, forgetting the first prince's death was to be expected. So Cornelius would just have to play the role of Gale. He was already a practitioner of this role, given his mother's obsession with her less-than-alive son.

"Yes, my name is Gale. I would tell you my full Christian name, but I'm sure you have no interest in such trivialities. This is a revel, after all. We're here to share stories of intrigue and gaze on pretty things." He used the man's perversion to his advantage with the last remark, creating a common ground. To be safe, he threw in a rakish look at the ladies-in-waiting. Adrian chuckled boorishly.

"I suppose you're correct. I'll tell you a tale of my time in the royal military. I was a fine young man, strong-willed, and..."

Cornelius put on his mask. He nodded earnestly, laughed, and gasped at the correct times. The prince paid attention to the general story so he could recount it to another if he was ever asked to, but ignored the details because of their dastardly unimportance. Nobody needed to know about the many women who had supposedly clung to him in Embera or the betrothal he'd fled in Sleetal.

After Adrian of Marzine, he moved onto the duke's daughter, his cousin Constance. He knew the other five names she had in addition, but again, he wouldn't pay attention to such trivialities. This was a revel, after all, and she was sulking. She wore a calamitous purple gown that was sure to burst or suffocate her sooner or later. Her hair was equally as disastrous. The golden strands seemed to have been woven into a donut-like shape atop her head, and the style wasn't flattering, given her pointy face. He brought her a drink as he had her father, but changed his tune. She was quite the gossip, so he gave her an exclusive piece of knowledge concerning a maiden's affair with one of the Wilkinian princes. She also thought he was Gale, which made him a bit wary. She had been there at Gale's funeral. He clearly remembered her beet-red face as she wept.

Most of the people he spoke to knew him as Cornelius. Most had been to Gale's funeral as well. What was this? Another one of his father's games? Addison of Marzine had a penchant for public embarrassment. His advisors were often put in the stocks naked after giving him false testimonies. Even Lyra, Addison's own wife, was made to sleep in the stables after falling off her horse during a royal procession. But bringing esteemed court members into his joke was going a little too far, even for him.

The prince moved uncertainly onto the following eminent figure, and again he was met with misnaming. The Lord of Bluebay also thought he was Gale. Cornelius asked the man about his political views on a failed attack on Riolago, one of Embera's major ports, for he knew the man made outrageous proclamations about politics. He took a sip of a drink every time he spoke to a person, wagering he'd be drunk by the end of the night.

He passed from noble to noble, maiden to maiden, waltzing and drinking and discussing polite topics of conversation. After a while, the finery began to rot. The silks and velvets folded, powders melted off faces. No one knew he was Cornelius. They all addressed him with "Prince Gale" or "My prince" or a similar title. While dancing with the dull daughter of some noble, Cornelius caught his father watching him.

He hadn't noticed the king's presence in the room, which was surprising, for the man loved grand entrances. He sat soberly upon his jewel-adorned throne at the end of the ballroom, sipping a goblet of something. His eyes moved as if chained to Cornelius, studying and pondering him as if he were... as if he were a spectacle at the circus. He was and always would be a spectacle at the circus, watched by all—the elephant in the room forevermore.

That was when he realized that the waltzing music had quieted. The dull daughter had stopped dancing. It was quiet enough to hear poison coalescing in blood.

Cornelius let go of the damp hands he was holding and turned in a slow circle, his heels chafing against his new leather boots. Then, his father stood. The throne was up on a pedestal at the end of the hall, and a mobile stairway had to be pedaled over by a servant. He stepped down onto it. His mane of silvery gold hair was tucked away in a braid that would make any other man appear effeminate. His crown was poised perfectly, not lopsided as Cornelius' was.

"My son. As you can tell, there's no legitimate purpose for this event. I commanded you to strengthen my connections, and that is what you attempted to do. But this wasn't a test of your social faculties. It was a test of something else. I wonder, would you answer to only Gale if I told you to?" An amused smile spread across the king's lips.

Cornelius went rigid. Finally, *he* was the one being humiliated. He'd avoided it up until then, being flexible enough to bend before his father's daggers struck him. But now, he was frozen, and a dagger had stabbed right through his heart.

"What is the meaning of this, your majesty?" he asked, a pinprick of anger in his tone. That was all he allowed them to see. A pinprick, nothing more, nothing less. He looked up from the plated floors, only to meet his father's gaze. Everyone was watching. Everyone was staring, scrutinizing not the crown but the one beneath it—his father most of all.

"I couldn't help but take heed of your recent misnamings. The queen already calls you by my first son's name, and so do most of our dear compatriots. So I've made a decision. If it's a first son they want, it's a first son they get."

All Cornelius could think was, *He's finally gone completely mad, hasn't he?*

"You are now Gale of Marzine. Cornelius of Marzine is no more. He perished three years ago in an unfavorable accident. Gale survived, and, as I said before, you are Gale."

Cornelius, not Gale, was a marker on a war map. A piece moved to display a strategy, not a person. They were all staring at him, scrutinizing him. They were all in on his father's plan. He had to say something. He couldn't sit back and watch himself crumble. Because, as always, Cornelius wasn't one to hold his tongue.

"Public humiliation. I knew this would happen sooner or later. But surrounded by our intimates? That's very low, even for you. If you find this appropriate, why didn't you simply kill my brother in public? You could've sold tickets and made a fortune. Everyone needs a little gore here and there. Jogs the liver," Cornelius said bitterly. The king held up a hand.

"Gale-"

"No! I'm not Gale! I'm Cornelius!" He was well aware that it was within the king's rights to have him killed on the spot. At least the blood that exuded from him would be his own.

"Gale!" Addison declared in response.

"You're a peddler of pains, not the king of Marzine! You build walls around the elite with the sufferings of the common people. I'm nothing to you, nothing! And you're nothing to me!" His breathing was forced, his eyes red with fury. Finally, endowed with enough confidence to meet his father's primordial stare, he sighed. He spoke the final phrase in monotone, not wasting any more breath on his father.

"I'm Cornelius of Marzine. And when I'm king, I'll burn your every accomplishment, monument, and memory to the ground. You *will* be nothing. And I'll be everything." Then, the astonishment of all who watched, he smiled. It was a ghastly smile that drew the corners of his lips all the way up to his ears. "You will burn."

He left. That fated evening defined him. He was not nothing. He had words that nobody could silence. He was Cornelius.

More than anything, he told the crew his tale because he had a plan, dreadful as it was. After Rodrigo, if he could stand to end him, they would go for his father. Cornelius had enough courage to finally look him in the eyes and defeat him, and it was because of Rodrigo. Because of the one with the pretty, tired golden eyes. Eyes nothing like his father's. The one who consoled and condoned with every breath in his lungs. The one who made them soup when they were hungry for solid foods. Even though he would die at his hands, Cornelius knew the world's future would be sculpted by his many kindnesses, and that was enough. There would be a future for the five nations because of him.

Little did he know, Rodrigo was no longer their sweet little soup cook. No, he was going through a metamorphosis that, much like Murray's, was unwanted. And it made him bitter, cold. Cold enough to claim the crown for himself.

Both parties were so focused on their destinations that they didn't notice their own decay. Pia most of all. She hated Cornelius, *hated* him for what he had to do to her brother. And he hated her right back, despised her for how she'd behaved towards her brother when his life was a sure thing, and his soup was only just annoying and not precious.

Mikka shook during the night, trying to keep the memories of wartime from haunting him too badly. He knew that just a few glasses would put him to sleep. But because he had Pia now, he abstained. Murray was still trying to get accustomed to seeing the world in color, and Lara was trying not to allow her fascination with Cornelius grow into something more. If she let him have her, then her goals would never be accomplished, and she would never be satisfied. But it grew harder and harder with each glance he gave her, each time he called her "Lily" and not "Lara." And above all of that, the *Vault* itself was falling apart, only one mariner left to care for it. It seemed the ship mirrored its crew.

CHAPTER 29

Every morning, Rodrigo was startled awake. And every morning, he looked around to find himself in foreign surroundings.

Before all the traveling and hostage-taking, he'd rise with the sun, a particular well-known sunbeam landing on his closed eyelids. His bedroom back home was humble, but it was his. He was sure everything was just how he'd left it—neat as a pin. His bedframe was hewn from an oak tree that had fallen on his and Pia's birthday. It was tucked into the corner, across from a window overlooking the bronze fields. His mother had knit the quilt and had taken extra care to include his favorite colors, purple and red. Rodrigo had similar stories about everything; each possession was beloved to him. It was the same for each person back in his hometown. Of course, he was sorry to leave, but his sister was in danger, and he'd had an obligation to her. She'd come back from the war broken. It was the disturbing void in her eyes that most affected him. How foolish he'd been back then, caring for her when she would put him in a wheat grinder for kicks and giggles.

Everyone around him was suffering, it'd seemed. He had to help them all; no one was left behind. In Embera, he'd genuinely wanted to be like the Good Samaritan, the poor sod who decided to be good and godly instead of keeping his head down like everyone else. And so he was. No need was left unmet. How foolish he'd been to care so obsessively. It wasn't like a damn was given about him in exchange.

His efforts were taken for granted, and he was seen as a

scapegoat. Precious few cared for him, but he was set in his ways. Pia became his main priority when she returned home a war hero. He'd saved her, pulled her kicking and screaming back from the brink of insanity. But even after all he'd done to persuade her to stay, she joined the Masked Birds and went overseas on death mission after death mission, returning home more fragmented than before. He hadn't been enough for her. Instead, she needed Mikka Savva or Shadrach of Sleetal to take care of her. But, being the wretch he was, he'd followed her when one of her missions seemed too absurd to live through. He should've just let her die if that's what she wanted. *How foolish he'd been.*

Now he was here. He never had to turn the other cheek again, never had to take their scorn. Nobody would ever hurt him again, leave him again, or use him again. Only because he wouldn't let them. He was finally, finally being who he wanted to be, living under no one's jurisdiction but his own. Free. But still foolish.

Upon arriving in Marzine, he discovered something that undid this sense of intoxicating freedom. It was the night before their voyage ended, in fact. Rodrigo was overcome, soaked in gold and jewels and excess of every sort. He didn't care for the riches, didn't care for the little cakes he was offered or the golden cufflinks in the wardrobe. He would often turn out the gas lights before entering his rooms to keep the gold from blinding him. Overcome, indeed. And angry too. Angrier than he'd ever given himself permission to be. After turning out the lights the night before the voyage ended, he collapsed onto a woven rug in the wing's vestibule.

The day had been challenging. The damned Marzinian king was making him train for hours every day. Rodrigo was flabby, which made the task even more challenging. Sometimes he wondered what the point of this education was. He obviously wouldn't surpass Cornelius in terms of fitness or skill in time for their duel at the end of the month. His teacher was a stern, older Marzinian man who declined to speak to him in anything but Emberan because he assumed Rodrigo didn't speak any other language. Coincidentally, he could only speak a few Emberan words, so Rodrigo never understood his instructions. Stupid Marzinians with their stupid pride. Stupid golden wall sconces. Stupid Wilkinian rug. Stupid.

It was all too much, but he had improved in the time it took to return to Marzine on the swift imperial ship. He learned combat skills and basic swordplay. Also, on a strict diet of lean meats and greens he hadn't ever heard the names of before, his muscle tone developed. But beneath all the absurd dining and strict teachings, he was still his sister's brother. It was all too much. That he could say, but too much was what he was used to. And now, he wanted to win. He wanted to surprise the king of Marzine and become the prince. And with no prospect of heaven, this was all he had. This was all he was.

Fallen on the rug, gasping, he realized this. In a life built on accidents, a meaning had found him. His fists curled at his sides, and he measured his breaths. Nice and easy. Focusing on the darkness around him, the light in his heart went dormant, and the biding rage erupted.

Gently, he picked himself off the floor and wiped the tears from his eyes. The king of Marzine didn't think he was capable of victory over his son. Rodrigo was only a pawn to him, one he would run ragged over the chessboard if it meant victory for his bishop. But Rodrigo was determined. He would show the king he wasn't a pawn anymore. Rodrigo stood there in the darkness, breathing heavily. Then, he opened the gilded door and escaped into the hallway.

He wasn't supposed to go anywhere without Winston, but Winston be damned. He *would* win, and the king needed to finally comprehend that. His footsteps echoed through the high, curving hallways.

"Sir, what are you doing at this hour? You're not allowed to leave your wing unattended. You know this!"

As if out of thin air, Winston appeared. Rodrigo didn't pause to listen to the rest of his scoldings. He buried his hands in his pockets and felt for the close combat knife he'd stolen from the training win to defend himself with if someone tried to silence him before the duel. He moved his thumb over the blade, slicing it into his finger. Then, he lifted his bleeding thumb out of his pocket and turned to the man.

"I cut myself. I was going to go ask the king for bandages." Winston stared at him in astonishment.

"No, no, no! You don't ask the king himself for bandages, sir. He's the king! That's ludicrous. Did you... did you hit your head as well? I can bandage your finger and attend to your head wounds, too. The king doesn't need to know of this!" Winston exclaimed with alarm.

Rodrigo's smile was true now. He drew out the knife so slowly that the shaking of his hand was not only visible but brazen. His conscience was begging him to stop.

"Tell me, Winston, where does the king retire to at night aboard an imperial ship? I do desperately need a bandage from him. Take me to him, Winston." With the agility he learned from training with the Marzinian man, Rodrigo soon had the close combat blade pressed to the Andrian's jugular. His conscience withered away.

"Sir, I-I..." Winston said.

"Winston, I know you value your neck, so take me to him. Get me past his guards and whatever else there is," Rodrigo said, his voice wavering. He had to admit, this newfound immorality had a thrill to it. And the best part was that they'd never expect it from him.

If Winston so much as swallowed against the blade, his life would end. He'd had a disturbing human anatomy lesson with his Marzinian teacher, who hadn't spoken more than a word the entire time. From it, he'd learned where the critical veins were.

"Yes, sir," Winston finally said, his tone grave. Rodrigo's smile grew. He would show the king. He would show them all what years upon years of mistreatment could accomplish. But amid the glory of Winston's capture, he forgot to maintain his knife's posture. His grip was loose, one that Winston could easily escape from. And so he did. Why would the king of Marzine hire an ineffective man to watch over the continent's most wanted chef? How foolish Rodrigo was.

Winston disarmed him in one fluid motion, overtaking him with an elbow and the twist of the wrist. His flushed cheek was thrust against the floors, and Winston had his arm pinned against his back. Rodrigo immediately began to flail, struggling until he tired himself out. Winston waited patiently beside him. His yelling quieted down until he was only crying. If he were as strong as Mikka or as charming as Cornelius, he would've made it to the king by then. But alas, this had been his very best attempt.

"Just you wait... Just y-you wait. I'm going to kill him! I'll kill him... I swear it," Rodrigo said.

Winston sighed, slid the bloodied knife into the pocket of his trousers, and relaxed his grip. "Oh, no, sir," he said.

Rodrigo couldn't comprehend his words. "No, sir, you won't kill him. This 'duel' is not a fair one. Even though my life belongs to the king, I must tell you the truth now that I realize exactly you are. You're a fighter. You almost slit my throat, after all." Winston kept a light grip on the collar of his tunic to keep him down.

Rodrigo finally began to understand the meaning of his words, and he went rigid. "You can't mean... no, you don't mean that. It can't be a lie, can it, Winston?" The gas lights went out entirely as the ship's curfew enacted. The doors were mechanically locked unless one had a master key like Winston.

"This training you've been given, this promises you've been

made… it's all fake, sir-Rodrigo. The hope inspired in you is a distraction, a wolf in sheep's clothing. Dueling the prince, you'll be overtaken easily just as I overtook you now. You don't have a chance in hell," he said. His grip on Rodrigo's collar tightened. Rodrigo felt dread make his blood go cold. "And," Winston continued, "if you did have a chance in hell, the king would dispatch it. He means to poison you before the duel. It's all smoke and mirrors, my dear friend."

Rodrigo rotated his neck to look back at Winston, wide-eyed. "I-I don't believe you. You wouldn't tell me this if it was true, would you? You're… y-you're lying!" Rodrigo screamed, thrashing some more. "Please, tell me you're lying."

"I wasn't planning on telling you originally because I thought you would just lie down and die. I thought you *wanted* to die. But from what I've just witnessed, you aren't one to just accept the poison. You're a fighter. You used to fight for others, but everyone you've ever loved has abandoned you, and all you have left to fight for is yourself. And I'm sorry for that. But you still have to die because Addison wishes it." Winston's voice collapsed at the end.

Rodrigo couldn't fathom it at first, but slowly understanding streamed through his mind. He was a lamb for slaughter. He was supposed to be convinced he could be victorious over the prince of Marzine for the sake of conciliation. But he was the loser, the pawn. His fate was decided, and he would indeed die. That meant there was no reason for the rage, no reason for the fight. There was no reason for any of it. And just as it had always been, no matter how he tried, nobody loved him. Well, not truly, at least. Maybe out of pity, maybe out of obligation.

Halfway across the continent, the one who loved him out of obligation rested on *The Vault of Heaven* with the one she loved truly. Two shattered souls sat together on the upper deck, staring up at the moon. Mikka's eyes were bloodshot, and his face was unshaven, but for once, he didn't stink of *raska*. He'd been sober for the longest extent since his brief stint as a political prisoner. There was no *raska* in Marzinian prison camps without bribery, and Mikka didn't have any money.

Pia sat cross-legged beside him, unraveling the bandages on his hands to clean the wounds. She put fresh ones on his fingers every few days to keep the infection from taking his hands. The night was clear, illuminated only by the light of the moon and a thimble full of stars. The air was cold, but the winds were taciturn. Mikka's eyes were fixed on her as she worked at the pus-filled scabs with her washrag. Her scowl was too obvious not to notice, but he wasn't good with feelings. He'd made a promise the morning after their first night together that he'd try, however, so he would.

"Pia... are you... are you alright?" he asked awkwardly. She stopped her washing abruptly and gave him one of her patented withering stares. Then, she returned to her scrubbing. Mikka glowered, wondering what he had said.

"I hate him, Mikka." Who did she hate? Ah, Cornelius. He hated Cornelius too. This would be easy. The one thing he knew how to talk about was his hatred for Cornelius.

"I hate him too. Vain, pompous Marzinian. He thinks he's the best thing the world's ever known," Mikka said. Pia's scowl grew more grey as he went on. She shook her head and began to work on his wounds.

He bit his lip at the pain to keep from crying out. He was mystified.

"No, not the Marzinian. It's Rodrigo I hate," she said, her pupils turned to slits like a demoness.

Mikka shrunk away, suddenly disliking their choice to leave the lanterns behind. "I hate him as well," Mikka said, trying to be agreeable. But Pia only raged against his cuts in response. He cringed.

"I just... hate him. He's such a waste of breath. All he knows how to do is make soup and smile without reason. I mean, he's a walking wisecrack. He murdered Shadrach with cinnamon!" A hysterical laugh followed close behind. It echoed across the silent waters. Murray watched them from the bridge reproachfully, but she didn't care. Then, without premonition, she began to cry.

"Oh… *oh*," Mikka said, stupefied. He pulled her into a flimsy hug, taking care to leave his unwrapped hands up in the air. She buried her face in his chest and cried more furiously. She shook in his arms, and the only thing he could do was cradle her closer.

"I hate him, Mikka. I hate him!" she cried, her voice softening against him. The silence was unendurable. Finally, she spoke again. "But I also love him," she whispered, stilling finally. Murray sighed on the bridge, pulling at his leather coat collar as he watched. It was all too much. But they were used to too much.

CHAPTER 30

"We arrive tomorrow." It had been too silent before Cornelius spoke. *The Vault of Heaven's* remaining crewmembers sat attempting to confer around the metal table in the galley. They were failing, none of them knowing how to broach the topic of the plan. A chill circled around the room, and there was no steam from Rodrigo's soup to ward it off. It had grown more and more painful to ignore his absence after weeks of Rodrigo-less sea travel.

For one, the food was absolutely atrocious. It turned out Pia did have a conscience. Or somehow, she'd grown one overnight. She suddenly felt bad for neglecting her brother, and she'd taken over the cooking as penance. What had once been fresh ingredients turned into a blackened mess. Still, the others stomached her lumpy courses. They'd all had worse, with the exception of Cornelius, who ate it anyway. He could be very agreeable when he wanted to be.

"We do arrive tomorrow, don't we…" Lara said, her tone grey as the sky beyond the galley window. They all jounced from side to side as the ship braved a particularly violent wave.

"I hate the sea," Pia said, closing her eyes. The dark circles beneath them made her look like she had no eyes, only sockets. Cornelius averted his gaze, his stomach too overworked to bear the unsettling thought.

"Me too," Cornelius and Mikka said simultaneously, then glared at one another. The only one who didn't share in their hatred of the sea was Murray. He was utterly enamored by it, even more so than he was with Cornelius. It was a large expanse of nothingness and it reminded him of himself. He loved to stare out at the waters, the waves ever-changing.

Mikka cleared his throat. The big man squared his shoulders, ready to do some much-needed leading in Shadrach's absence. All that remained of the Raven King was a grave marked Here Lies –. The lantern in the center of the table slid to one side before coasting back to the center as another wave crashed into them.

"We should go over the plan one last time," he suggested. It was more of an order, really, for Mikka made no suggestions. Murray hid his amusement, his eyes pursuing the lantern as it slid.

"Yes, sir," Cornelius said sarcastically, giving a beleaguered salute.

"Oh, you mean the limp bit of excrement we've labored over for far too many hours?" Lara asked. She picked her head out of her hands to scorn Mikka. He ignored them.

"It'll work. It has to. If you recall, it's either this or death," Mikka said. He braced his fingers against the edge of the table and cleared his throat. "So, when we arrive in Marzine, we'll act as separate parties. Us against Cornelius."

"It shouldn't be too difficult for you to play your role, Mikka. You already despise me, after all," Cornelius said, giving Mikka a scathing smile. But before the sharpshooter could prepare a response, Cornelius continued. "I can take it from here if you don't mind. I'm told I'm a fantastic speaker. And if we continue on with your gruff voice and even gruffer demeanor, I'm certain all hope will be lost."

Mikka gave him a dead-eyed stare. "The only thing fantastic about you is the fact that one day, you'll die," he muttered to himself.

"And when I do, I'm sure you'll be the most teary-eyed. You have to admit; I am growing on you. But at a funeral's pace,"

Cornelius said, the dark circles beneath his eyes seeming to lighten after ridiculing Mikka. "Anyways, we'll have to stop our flirtation for now. As you said, our plan needs reviewing. So, after proving our *passionate* hatred for each other, you'll claim the ransom my frightful father promised in his letter. From there, you'll leave me on Addison Island to face his wrath." Cornelius shivered. "It pains me just to think of it. But when it comes to you all, I'd give up my left—"

"Don't. Finish. That. Sentence," Lara said, voice low and dangerous. She'd taken out a leather-bound notebook and was taking diligent notes.

"Eye, Lara. I was going to say eye. Get your mind out of the gutter. Or my trousers, for that matter." Cornelius smirked.

She huffed and scribbled something down on the page. "After abandoning me with my father, you'll sail the *Vault* across the bay to our lively capital city of Sirensea. Please, have some lobster for me while you're there. It's been ages since I've had Sirensea lob—"

"Get on with it, please," Murray said through gritted teeth, eyes still on the lantern.

"Only a joke, my dear. You won't have the time nor the reticence to dine at a sit-down restaurant. You'll go to the peninsula instead, where you can best conceal yourself. It's what we consider the slums of Sirensea—you'll be surprised to find the peninsula's quite a bit like upper Stjernsvet," he said as Mikka's fingers clenched into fists.

"Get off of your high horse," Pia said, eyes alight.

"And let it stomp me to death? Right. Murray already told me that one," Cornelius countered, giving Murray a sidelong glance. To his astonishment, a wan smile spread across Murray's lips.

"Speech has its benefits," Murray said, and Cornelius flushed.

"Couldn't have said it any better myself," he said. "Now, we should get back to the matter at hand. Our lives are at stake, after all. You'll hole up on the peninsula for a week or so and return to Addison Island the night before the duel. Try not to be late."

"Wouldn't dream of it," said Lara, and Cornelius smiled dimly at his clasped hands.

"Like Mikka and Pia did before, you'll scale the obsidian wall—no small feat, but doable as my capture's proven—and rejoin with me in my tower. You'll subdue my servants and pose as them, confining yourselves strictly to the tower, so you're not recognized. On the day of the duel, you'll finally leave the tower after a night with yours truly. All servants will be occupied then, for duels are a public affair in Marzine. They weren't thirty years ago, but because of my father's perversion, all are permitted to watch the combatants... er... fight for their lives." Cornelius seemed actually disturbed by the prospect, the smile melting off his face.

"What a degenerate," Lara said to herself, eyes becoming bitter.

"He'd say the same about you, fine folks," Cornelius said, brightening up again. "To continue, you'll take your posts at Palace Marzine's weakest points, which we've already gone over. By each wing's doors to the central courtyard, yes?" he asked.

There was no response. It seemed everyone had sunk back into puddles of their own sullen wonderings.

"This is so that if I don't hold up my end of the deal and... win the duel, you'll still be able to assassinate my father. Assuming I am victorious, we'll continue on to the next phase of the plan. But before that, there'll be a day to recollect in the tower. You know, get our bearings and all."

Pia's shadow became a shade darker. The part Cornelius was omitting was that Rodrigo would be dead, and the supposed "recollection" day was really just a day of mourning. No one could assassinate the king of Marzine properly after losing their twin brother. "I'll supply you all with the weapons you couldn't smuggle in from the *Vault*. I have many, many decorative swords gifted to me by opportunistic lovers. You know, there's something inherently sensual about swords..." Cornelius mused.

Mikka shot him a glare to end all glares, and he chuckled.

"After the recollection day, you'll again take your secondary posts at all the exits to my father's wing, the king's wing, as we in the business call it."

"Real imaginative," Pia grumbled, and Cornelius laughed.

"The Marzinian Monarchy is known for its tyranny, not its creativity, Pia darling."

Pia rolled her eyes, and he went on to the next step. "With her blade, Pia will make a small incision in my father's neck while he sleeps. Coating the knife will be sumac poison, brewed from the recipe book of the late Raven King. His debauchery is finally working in our favor. And that's the biggest middle finger we could give him." Cornelius chuckled, his hand instinctively to the bruises around his neck, now a few shades lighter.

"Indeed it is," Lara agreed. Murray's eyes narrowed as he stared at the lantern, and he knew in his heart of hearts that if Shadrach were still alive, he'd be the one to murder him, not Rodrigo.

"So my father will have an unceremonious death, choking on his own tongue and swelling up like a balloon. In the morning, his servants will find him lying alone in his great, four-poster bed, and they'll decide my mother's too infirm to take the throne in his stead. I'll be given the crown, and I'll address my people in Sirensea, claiming my birthright. We'll wait a month before the division of the nations so I can gain the trust of the nobility. But then, all will be made right, and the continent will be in harmony. If you still desire the thrones of your respective nations, I'll hand them right to you. But if not, there are stewards and former royalty to rely on."

Mikka and Pia's eyes met from across the table, knowing that Mikka had been lying when he'd said he'd rule Sleetal. He'd do just as Cornelius said and put a steward on the throne. Then, he and Pia would travel together. Perhaps after a couple of years, they'd settle down and get hitched in Stjernsvet.

"It's so long a shot that our arrow will have to land on the moon to hit its mark," Murray said after a moment of heavy silence. The remaining crewmembers turned away from their grim ponderings to look at them. The barest sliver of a smile appeared on his face.

"I mean, he's not wrong," said Lara.

"Here's to dying together." Cornelius laughed, raising a fictitious goblet to the sky.

"Cheers!" they cried in unison, raising their own fabricated glasses. The galley table cleared. First Pia, then Mikka. It was effectively their last night together, so little sleep would be had between them. After the pair, Murray left. He said nothing in the way of an explanation, but Cornelius knew he would be out on the bridge. He was always there. There, or his coffin-like quarters, though he never went down there anymore. Shadrach had died in his bed, after all. Nobody wanted to sleep on someone else's literal deathbed.

Lara and Cornelius were alone together, and the only light was that of the lantern left in the center of the table. Lara's eyes were as nebulous as ever, but he still hadn't given up on trying to name the color. That evening, they were the color of plums with tiny flecks of gold and silver near the pupils. She was reading over the plan again, her brows knit in concentration. She would mutter little details here and there, and Cornelius was content to watch the cogs in her mind turn. He didn't want to go to bed yet, for this could very well be one of his last nights alive. He closed his eyes and leaned back in his chair. Lara looked up from her work.

"What's wrong with you?" she asked in that eloquent voice of hers. He gave her a strained smile, and the flicker of the lantern's flame made it look like the sun was setting in the shallows of his eyes.

"Lily of the valley..." he sighed.

Her smile had a mischievous edge now. Was there perhaps some green in her eyes?

"Ticket..." she said, mimicking his listless tone.

"When will you stop calling me that?" He laughed.

"When will you stop calling me Lily? It isn't my name, just as 'ticket' isn't yours," she said testily.

His smile took on a conspiratorial look. "What does 'ticket' mean anyhow? I use Lily of the Valley as a term of endearment for you because I think you're resplendent. But I'm sure ticket has another meaning," he said, leaning in and balancing his chin on clasped hands. Neither one of them broke eye contact.

"Do you really want to know?"

The silence was almost absolute, save the wailing of the waves. Cornelius nodded. All warmth left the galley.

"You can tell me," Cornelius mentioned. He swallowed, his mouth growing dry.

"You're irresistible, you know that? Well, almost irresistible. Otherwise, I'd be in your arms right now behind locked doors."

Cornelius' eyes widened. He didn't have a witty retort waiting on his tongue. Then, he blushed. "Lara, why do you call me a ticket?"

She clasped her hands and avoided his gaze. "Cornelius, I call you 'ticket' because I want to see the world. Every inch of it. But I didn't have the means before I met you. No ship to sail on, no coin to spend. Cornelius, you're my means. You're my 'ticket' to see the world. Well, not you, but the money made at your expense."

His eyes fell limply from hers.

"I've been cursed with wanderlust. I can't be caged in like an animal. I love you, Cornelius, but you're just another tower to be locked away in. I love you, and so I have to remind myself that you're my ticket and not... not mine."

A shadow came over his face, and she could see how his fists clenched, how his lips trembled. He gritted his teeth, and he bore an uncanny resemblance to the teacher.

"Wait, Cornelius, please don't trouble yourself. We can still be good friends like we are now," she attempted, trying to undo the damage.

"Of course," he whispered, only to himself, but she heard. "I'm not Cornelius to you either. I thought I could love one person and only one person. The more time I spent with you, I thought that you were that one person. The person I could be with forever. I was sorely mistaken. And I... I love you. But when you said you loved me, you lied. I know because I've told that lie so many times before. You don't love me, you love what you can have because of me, and I respect that. I respect you, Lara. I wish you the best of luck on your travels, but after this is all over, we should part ways for good." Tears lined his lashes as he finally looked up at her. His eyes were iridescent and so... so profound. "Perhaps we'll meet in the next life," he whispered. And then, abruptly, he left.

Lara felt a chasm-like void open in her. She was the sojourner with the plans. But right now she didn't know what to do and feared she would never know what to do again.

Cornelius was Gale. He was Lara's ticket. He was an animal in a circus, the elephant in the room. A chip to bet and barter with. He was many things, but he wasn't himself. He was a lover. He was a friend. A hostage, an enemy, a prince... but never just himself. He left the galley late that night and stalked out into the frigid air. So many faces he'd worn, he didn't know which was his any longer.

He was the prince of Marzine with a father and mother who didn't know the name they'd given him. He was the hostage of a resistance group he'd befriended out of fear. He loved a woman who called him a ticket. And maybe, just maybe, he loved a man who stared at him like his father. He would soon become a spectacle in a duel against the one person who cared for him not out of pity or obligation. He laughed at himself. He laughed, but like his faces, he couldn't distinguish laughing from crying.

He fell to his knees on the deck. His legs wouldn't support him any longer, and it was lovely just to let go, just to give up. He hugged his knees to his chest. His tears were silent, but he knew Murray heard him. The sentinel watched from the bridge. His steely eyes were pained as he watched Cornelius weep over Lara. He'd heard it all, seen it all, but he wasn't angry nor discouraged. He was simply sad to see Cornelius suffering. Golden Cornelius, sitting alone in the center of the sea.

Murray felt inclined to go to him, leave the bridge's safety and console him, but now was not the time. *Later,* he thought to himself as he watched. Later, when Lara was off his mind. Murray loved Cornelius, and he knew Cornelius could love him too, but not if the makings of their love were built on the grave of another. He closed his eyes and took a breath, then fixed his gaze on the expanse of the sea before them, staring at the horizon as he always did.

Besides, it would be hard to love Cornelius if they died tomorrow.

CHAPTER 31

"I think I might be sorry I have to do this, Marzinian," Mikka said in surprise as he stared down at Cornelius. The prince gave him the most contemptuous smile he'd ever received, looking up through his curls.

"Well then, you can imagine how *I* feel about this arrangement," he said.

Murray smirked, lurking in the corner of the galley behind the other crew members. He looked like a charcoal drawing, black and white in a world of color.

Lara was spellbound by the pages of a book and wasn't engaged in the affair. She was the only one, save Cornelius, who was seated. Contrary to Murray, she was color in an all-grey world. So vivid that it made his heart palpitate. Mikka looked down and smiled somewhat menacingly, but Cornelius wasn't menaced. Sure, he was about to be roughed up a bit, but it was necessary if he wanted to wear the guise of "wounded hero." Like his mother, too far away from himself to cry out in pain how Addison liked.

"Let's get this over with," Mikka said. He ran his fingers through his hair. "I'll be gentle," he lied.

Cornelius hoped Mikka's fingers would be cut on his jawline. "For your sake, I hope you are," he said, his words scraping through the air.

Mikka's fingers curled into fists at his sides. The first strike was to his face. He took the blow with a gritty smile. Mikka hit him square in the jaw next, and his head spun. The pain was extraordinary, but he took it all in stride.

"Oh, for me? Thanks, Mikka," he choked, spitting bloody saliva onto the floorboards. The sunlight streaming through the galley window made his face glow. Mikka smiled viciously. Then, he slogged Cornelius again, this time on the arm, and the chair almost tipped over. His head swam, but he bit the bullet.

"As I live and breath! Look everyone, I've found the world's last man-wolf!" Cornelius exclaimed. "I'm just so blessed to have—"

Mikka interrupted him with another blow. "I lied. I'm not at all sorry I have to do this," Mikka confessed.

Cornelius' cheek was beginning to swell, and he had to blink to keep himself conscious. "You're a barbarian, Mikka," Cornelius said, all seriousness intact. Pia chuckled. "Thank you, thank you. I'll be here all week." Cornelius glanced at his three audience members.

Lara looked up from her reading for a moment. She smiled vacantly at Cornelius and then looked back down. In the light, her eyes had blazed blue. Would he never know what color her eyes were? It didn't matter. As a rule, he didn't pursue what he couldn't have. *Don't cry, Cornelius.* Oh Lord, everything hurt. His chest, his arm, his face. His face, his face, *his face.*

The unpleasantness went on in that manner for another few moments. Mikka's strikes were met with clever remarks. Cornelius spoke even when Mikka punched him in the mouth. He simply smiled bloodily and lectured Mikka about how he should've hit rougher, rougher like how he was with Mikka's mother last night. It was a lovely performance Cornelius put on, but his eyes were polished over in pain. He was gasping by the end, though he was glad for the hurt. It would all help him play the part of "brave-faced prince" better. The pain he felt then was only a fragment of what he would feel soon. Paired with the sentimentality, the physicality of his confrontations with his father was also something to consider. His brother had died at his hands, after all. Gale's last words had been, *Run, Cornelius!*

And of course Cornelius would grant his last request. He wouldn't be caught dead dying like a hero.

Mikka, Pia, and Lara left to tie down the sails and check the rigging. The last of the Wilkinian winds had been raging against their two sails for the past week, but the winds had just about run dry. Keeping the sails up any longer than necessary would damage them, and the last thing they needed was a weak sail. It was difficult to keep the ship in shape with only five crewmembers, but they were managing. The *Vault* was designed for such circumstances, after all. It was a small, triple-leveled Sleetalian warship built narrowly enough to fit into the Marzinian canals. The downside of its size was that it impaired their ability to go long distances without heavy maintenance at ports. But again, they were managing. Only Murray remained in the galley with Cornelius, who sat shivering with his eyes closed. The smile still hung on his lips, a morbid habit of his. The sentinel watched Cornelius forlornly.

"Oh dear Lord, Murray," Cornelius said, licking his bloody lips. The prince leaned forward and held his head in his hands. Murray took tentative steps toward him until he was right behind Cornelius. "There's no use crying about it, is there?" he asked. That sentence alone disconcerted Murray more than the bruises Shadrach had given him.

"There isn't…" When all else failed, Murray told the truth. He put a cold hand on Cornelius' shoulder. The prince couldn't help but be reminded of Shadrach, who'd nearly choked him all the way to hell after innocently putting a hand on his shoulder. He knew Murray wouldn't do that. Murray was a good man, even with all his shrouds and silence. He was steadfast and lovely and… and… Cornelius couldn't think. He couldn't think about how his father would demolish him once they were reunited. He couldn't think about the suffering his nation had caused, couldn't think about how his closest friends were belligerent bastards who'd kidnapped him for money.

He couldn't think about Lara and how she'd looked him in the eyes and told him he was simply a means to an end for her. Nothing more, nothing less. He couldn't think about tired, sweet Rodrigo and how he would have to end his life. He couldn't think about the before, the after, or even the now. And he certainly couldn't think of the sentinel behind him. Stoic and far too good for the likes of him. His head was heavy. Murray was kneeling before him now. His brows were knit together, his grey eyes tender. Murray cupped Cornelius' cheek. He used his calloused thumb to wipe away Cornelius' tears.

"Oh, Murray," he said breathlessly. He could smell salt in the sentinel's hair. He could feel Murray's pulse in his hand.

"It'll... be alright," Murray promised. He was about to say something else, but he stopped and embraced Cornelius, holding him close. Cornelius cried without sound, and Murray marveled over the moment. Collectively, he'd believed he wouldn't feel this much in his lifetime, let alone a handful of seconds. But all his walls had been reduced to rubble.

"Why do you care? What d-do you even want from me anyway?" Cornelius faltered.

"I have no answer," Murray responded. Then, a moment of clarity struck him. "What if it's just you I want? What if I cared for the sake of caring?" he asked. Cornelius drew away from his grasp, and Murray felt colder than the darkness between the stars. Cornelius' lips were still bleeding, and the blood had gotten on his collar.

"Impossible, my dear sentinel. Everyone wants something, and there's no love without condition."

Murray retook his hand. "That's true. But, why does it matter *why* I care *if* I care?"

Cornelius let a sob take his body. "Because you'll leave me if... if I don't meet your conditions..."

Murray, despite himself, drew Cornelius back into his arms. Words appeared in his mind. Words he knew he had to say.

"I'll be here as long as you want me," Murray vowed. Cornelius hadn't lied when he'd said love without condition didn't exist. Murray had learned that a long time ago. But his love was damn near close to unconditional. And *he* wouldn't just disappear, for he wasn't a lost soul any longer. He kissed the place where tears fell from Cornelius' eyes and stood. Cornelius stood as well, his vision momentarily leaving him.

"You should bathe and put on clean clothes before leaving," Murray said, looking down at Cornelius. The change in tone was abrupt, and Cornelius gave Murray a grisly smile. He knew why they hadn't continued. If they died that day, all of the promises and honeyed words would be in vain.

"Yes... I should," Cornelius agreed. Murray walked out of the galley and onto the deck, inevitably returning to the bridge. Cornelius stood there a while longer, looking after him almost fearfully. He then went in the opposite direction. He walked down the corridors he'd come to know so well until he reached the lavatory.

He didn't like to spend long periods in the lavatory. It was shared by the entire crew, and Rodrigo had cleaned it regularly before his capture, but now Rodrigo was captured. There were two toilets for a reason unknown to Cornelius, a sink with a simple looking glass suspended over it, and a bath behind a curtain that was little more than a basin with piping and a drain at its belly. It stank like low tide.

Cornelius turned the bath pump all the way to the left, which supposedly made the bathwater hot, and watched as a bit of the water store from the ship's gut was emptied into the basin. While the bath filled, Cornelius went to collect some fresh clothing from his and Rodrigo's cabin. He hadn't touched any of the cook's belongings. Everything was still neat as a pin, albeit covered in a layer of dust. Cornelius traced the patterns in the woven blanket he'd gotten from Lara. With the thought of their evening together, his face fell. He yanked the blanket off of his mattress and threw it to the floor violently. Then, he collected his clothing and returned to the lavatory.

The bath was full when he arrived, and Cornelius turned the pump off. The piping whined. The ship's plumbing was old, but it worked, and that was all they could hope for. Cornelius began to unbutton his shirt. Halfway down, a button got stuck in the loop. A bout of anger overcame Cornelius. A button, of all things, was hindering him. He grabbed both sides of the shirt and pulled as hard as he could. The remaining buttons, including the offending one, snapped off the shirt with rhythmic little *pops*. The buttons scattered to the tiled floor, congregating in the corners of the room. Cornelius didn't care. The shirt slid off his shoulders. He'd simply been sullen before, with good reason too. Now he was furious. Cornelius disrobed fully and stepped into the bath. The water was cold as he'd expected, but he eased the rest of the way in. He let his head lull under the water, and all light left his eyes.

Cornelius didn't want to die. He wanted to live. He was the happiest he'd ever been, but also in the most anguish. It would be so much easier to give in and let the water solace him. But he couldn't do that, could he... Cornelius needed to live. There was so much left for him to do. He had friends, even if they had kidnapped him for money. He had a nation to rule. He had Murray to fall in love with. And he had Rodrigo to... to kill.

CHAPTER 32

Two men, one Marzinian, one Sleetalian, walked the bluffs of Addison island. The Marzinian was smaller, and bruised and beaten. His wrists were in chains, his golden hair longer than it ever had been. The Sleetalian was big and sturdy, clean-cut, and patched up. The bandages on his fingers told of the hell he'd been through. He guided the Marzinian, lingering a few feet behind him at any given time. They were a half-mile away from the palace compound.

Mikka was trudging to his own execution. At least that's what it felt like. But if all went as intended, he was walking into a windfall beyond his wildest imaginings. It was best to believe that while his future looked like a dead end, it was really the last turn in the maze. All he had to do was look at it from another standpoint to see the way out. But here, marching behind a disheartened Cornelius, he couldn't quite see the loophole anymore. He truly felt like there was a noose around his neck, and the floor would fall out from under him at any moment.

Cornelius was in a worse mood than Mikka. His disposition was less than sunny, and his fists clenched in the restraints. His bruises and bindings were costume makeup to put on a show for the Siren King, but the panic in his eyes was real. He'd changed since his last supper with Addison, and change wasn't something the man appreciated.

The pair were alone on the northern shorefront. The crew had concluded that it would be safer if only one of them went with Cornelius. And Mikka, being the leader of the pack, had to step forward. He'd argued that the animosity between Cornelius and him would be more believable than if Lara or Murray delivered him. It was the safest bet, and none of them fancied dying, so they allowed him to go alone.

The day had an abundance of clouds, and the visible sky looked like a vanilla toffee that had been stretched too thin. It was warm on the illustrious Addison Island. Mikka was accustomed to the frigidity of the northern sea and was sweating like a pig. An instinctive hand reached for his flask, but it wasn't there. The heat wasn't the only thing provoking him. There was also fear. Fear and the memories of wartimes and the fatigue of weeks at sea. He was in constant, excruciating pain. The world seemed flat and endless without Pia beside him, his own personal purgatory.

"Mikka, I'm sorry," Cornelius said, drawing him out of his cesspool. He sounded like a child that was being made to apologize by his mother. Nevertheless, Mikka was startled. Cornelius, no matter how much Mikka wanted to fault him for every problem he had, was faultless. He'd been forced into their plight, taken from his cushy life behind the palace compound's obsidian wall.

"What for?" he asked begrudgingly. He pitched over a protruding rock, steadying himself before he could fall into Cornelius.

"For giving you such a hard time. I mean, you did kidnap me, but even still. I was a pain in the ass."

Mikka chuckled dryly, a smile revealing his *raska*-stained teeth. "That's the kindest thing you've ever said to me," he reflected, his words without contempt.

"It will forever be the kindest thing I've said to you, Mikka," he responded.

The lightened mood darkened soon after. The obsidian wall rose as they ascended a small hill. It shone in the fragmented sunlight, and Mikka had to squint as they drew closer. He'd only ever been here at night, and this was a side of the palace compound he hadn't seen during his first break-in. It was farther away from the shore and far more threatening. There was no lull in the security for this side, for the compound's door was here. He felt nervous electricity crackle in his fingertips. If Pia knew how wrong it felt to be sober, she would let him drink his weight in *raska* every night. He couldn't wait to return to the *Vault* and hear that laugh of hers again. It would all go away then. They would sit in the galley and tell lewd jokes until morning. But... none of that would happen if he was gunned down on his way back. He closed his eyes and remembered how he'd seen Marzinian soldiers before opening fire on them from the cliffs. They were inconsequential black dots on the horizon. And now he was being put in their place.

"You should probably draw your pistol now. If worse comes to worse, hold it to my temple and drag me out of here. I'll pitch a fit, but don't be hindered. I trust your judgment." Cornelius said darkly. Mikka did as he was told and drew his pistol from its holster. He saw armed bodies in the distance and tried to ascertain just how armed they were. His sharp eyes honed in on the most decorated one, and with a start, he realized it was the king of Marzine himself, out to greet his accidentally prodigal son. The King's Guard must've seen the *Vault* approaching and informed the king of the matter. Of course. Their second plan was relatively freehanded compared to the first.

"Father dearest..." Cornelius said to himself. Then, he put on his most coveted mask: Gale. The change was instant. His eyes began to shine. His lips parted in a smile that practically shrieked, "putting on a brave face." He arched his back and puffed out his chest valiantly and Mikka, who now stood beside him, even noticed his chronic curls begin to flatten. The change was uncanny, and Mikka shivered despite the heat. Cornelius was carved of clay, he realized. In a world of wooden figures, Cornelius was clay-made.

A procession of cavalry trotted out of the obsidian wall's

main entrance. Mikka swallowed. The sounds and smells of an army occupied his ears and nostrils. This was unquestionably a power play. The king of Marzine was showing off his means for a single man and a prince who may or may not be Cornelius; it depended on the moment. Mikka's knuckles were white on the grip of his pistol. It was fully loaded, and he wasn't afraid to use it. But shooting would get him shot, and he would refrain from doing so for as long as possible. He was still recovering from one gunshot wound. He didn't need a thousand more.

Addison of Marzine and a few associates stood before the ill-fated pair, backed by the soldiers and the whole of the King's Guards. Addison's hands were folded behind his back. He wore a brilliant royal blue coat that fell to his knees. It was all very kingly, very noble. Mikka despised it. And what he despised more was the look in the man's eyes. Just as Cornelius described, they were somehow more vast and ambiguous than the entirety of the ocean's waters. The king's oiled lips broke into a smile as he saw his son, beaten and bound with that brave-faced smile on his lips.

"My dear boy, my dear son. Gale, how I've missed you." His tone was slippery with lies, lies Cornelius recognized but wouldn't acknowledge. He looked Addison dead in the eyes. Before, he would avoid his father's stare like the plague. But his acting was as polished as ever. He wasn't at all frightened, only furious, and the anger drowned out all else. Now that he'd seen the state of the nations, the suffering his father had caused, he understood that he had to earn his fear.

"As have I, your majesty." He made a show of struggling against his bindings.

Mikka gave him a sidelong glance, half miffed and half proud. Then, Addison of Marzine gave his attention to Mikka. The soldier felt it in his bones. Every fiber of his being begged him to run now before this... this *thing* took his life. He just couldn't be human. He just couldn't be. In his peripherals,

Mikka saw Cornelius tense up.

"I suppose you're owed ransom money, Mikka Savva. And a word of advice, don't use that pistol. You'll be dead before you have the sense to pull the trigger. And in turn, your security is guaranteed on the way back to your vessel and forever afterward. I have no desire for conflict. My son could be wounded in the fray, and none of us want that." The men and women standing around him nodded in agreement. "So take your ransom and be on your way. We won't follow you; you have my word."

Every word thudded into him like a dull dagger. Mikka nodded his understanding, and Addison snapped his fingers.

A sack of coins was brought forth by a servant and tossed across the divide. In return, Mikka unlocked Cornelius' chains with the key in his greatcoat pocket and gave him a gentle push. Cornelius stumbled into the between, wide-eyed and out of breath. He looped the sack of coins onto his pack, aimed his pistol at Cornelius, and began to back away just as they'd planned. Then, the unthinkable happened.

Addison's face contorted into an ugly glare. He seized his son by the shoulders, thrust him away from himself, and smacked him hard across the face. A moment of trivial shock passed over Cornelius' face before he fell to the ground, cowering beneath his father. The king's regal veneer fell away. He kicked Cornelius in the gut and spat on him. The King's Guard and soldiers watched on blankly, making no moves to stop him.

"Bravo, oh bravo! What a great show you put on! Did you really think I wouldn't know of your relationships with your captors, Gale? This man isn't your enemy; he's your friend! You've befriended the bottom feeders of the world and gallivanted around the continent, making a mess all because you were given *freedom*. You've put on a great show, you've had your fun at sea, but it's over now. You'll never leave Addison Island again as long as I live. Hell, you'll never step outside your tower." The king was poised as if to kick groveling Cornelius again, but he sighed instead. He licked his lips, readjusted his posture, and folded his hands behind his back, once again refined and proper. "But, *bravo,* my dear boy," he murmured.

Mikka fled. It wasn't like he could stop the king of Marzine from maltreating his son without an entire battalion of soldiers gunning for him. But seeing Cornelius being kicked right before his eyes triggered something in him. Sure, his old man had done the same to him. But it was Cornelius with that look of shock on his face. Cornelius, the Crown Prince of the Marzinian empire.

The king kept his promise. Mikka wasn't prevented from leaving in any way. His breathing was labored as he ran, and his back was aching with the weight of the coins when he arrived back at the northern shorefront. He could see the others gathered on the deck of the ship, awaiting his return. The vessel was unanchored as they'd planned, floating steadily away from the shore.

Pia shouted something incomprehensible. His head was pulsating with adrenaline, and his blood reached its boiling point as he dove into the water. It was hard to keep his head up with the sack of coins knotted to his pack. A coil of rope slithered down the side of the ship, and Mikka clutched its end. He looped it around his left leg and tied a knot through his belt. The others heaved him up onto the deck, soaking wet and sputtering.

"Mikka, tell us what happened," Lara ordered. Mikka took a moment to recover himself, ignoring her.

"I know why Cornelius was so petrified of facing his father," Mikka murmured. "He's not lying about those eyes. They're... consuming, nothing like Cornelius'. And what's worse is he hit Cornelius. Right there with me watching. But he let me go without so much as a scratch! I have the coins and everything! We should get out of here. He might just be giving us a head start."

"Of course his father would get into a physical altercation with him with you watching. He knows how Cornelius cares for us, and he hates it. The crown prince of Marzine, traveling with his adversaries and liking it. It frustrates him to know that Cornelius is out of his manipulation. So he made a spectacle out of his power to console himself. At least that's how I see it," Murray explained.

Pia helped him stand, and his bad leg ached treacherously.

"Murray, get us out of here before the king decides he wants his gold back. We'll handle the sails, you steer," Lara said. Murray ascended the bridge and navigated them away from the northern shorefront as the others put up the sails. It was testing with only three of them on the sails, but they had been learning mariner's work under Murray's charge for a few weeks then. They were lucky that afternoon as well. They caught a southern wind that carried them out to sea.

Fortune wasn't smiling on Cornelius, though. He'd seen the horrified look in Mikka's eyes. And though he had expected a welcome like this one, he was embarrassed. And in addition to embarrassment, the welcome hurt like hell. He made himself cry, for that's what Gale would've done.

"I-I thought you were pleased to see me, your majesty! I promise I'll do my best to amend my trespasses." He would have the King's Guard doubting their loyalties by twilight. He broke into a sob to add insult to injury.

"Someone get him to a medic. He'll need these injuries and any others he has treated," The king of Marzine said, disregarding Cornelius' pleas.

"Oh, father, please don't leave me! I haven't seen you in so long! I-If I may, I don't need a medic! I'm alright!" Cornelius knew the consequences, but he just couldn't resist. He sat up a little and groped at his father's boot heel, only to be kicked harshly in the face. A nasty spiral of pain made his mind go white.

"Oh, and treat him for the broken nose I just gave him. I want it set so it heals properly. We can't have the crown prince looking less than immaculate, can we?" Cornelius couldn't hear the rest. The pain was victorious over all else.

He was hoisted onto a stretcher. A cotton blanket was draped over him, and a pillow was placed beneath his head. The world was running left. He knew that it would've been more prudent to shut his mouth on his knees before his father, but alas, Cornelius wasn't one to hold his tongue.

He was unconscious for the setting of his nose and the stitching of the cut his father's fist had left on his face. But when it was all over, he found himself sitting in the place where it had all began: his bedchamber, on his bed. He remembered the night he was taken. He'd been lying in bed after a lukewarm cup of rose tea, his shirt open, his viola clutched to his chest in place of a lover. The moon had been whole and pearly, and he had been drunk on the evening's tragedy, fancying himself some sort of wounded hero. The night was spent dining with his father, mother, and betrothed. His mother had misnamed him one too many times.

"My name is Cornelius, the name you gave me," he repeated now, months later. He happened to look out the enormous, half-curtained window—a full moon. The undulating waves caressed the shore. The moon illuminated it all. It was marvelous, but also grippingly sad. His months-long journey had come to an end, and he was back here. He'd been freer as a captive than as a prince, he realized, and stood abruptly. His nose smarted, but he proceeded toward the window anyway. It was nights like this one that made him feel like the last person alive. He stroked the glass lovingly and extended his fingertips over the moon. It was the size of his palm, and it looked like he was holding it in the sky with his fingertips.

This time, he knew he wasn't the last person alive. He hadn't been sure months ago, but now he knew there were others. He had *them*. They were out there, biding their time.

And there was also Rodrigo.

He was somewhere in the palace compound, alone like Cornelius. They were all apart from each other, but oh so together. This bond and the coup that was about to occur because of it was built on the sacrifice of Rodrigo Reyes, a cook who made soup and nothing else. It was built on the love of two soldiers and the eyes of a sentinel, always watching. It was built on wanderlust, rose tea, and rain.

CHAPTER 33

Even great glittering metropolises like Sirensea had shadows. And in those shadows, those needing to disappear can hide.

For *The Vault of Heaven's* crewmembers, hiding where the light didn't reach was a wise choice. They didn't want to be found, at least not for another week. And the shadow of Sirensea, their hiding place, was the western peninsula. It was there they would disappear. In essence, the western peninsula was a little island joined to the mainland by a land bridge that vanished at high tide. On the branch was a hospital for the deranged, a prison, and a grouping of ugly brick-and-mortar buildings used to house those under the prison and hospital's employ. The peninsula land was still stately, a custom for Sirensea. The capital city was the king's prized possession, and he wanted to keep his favorite things neat and organized so he could control them. It was, however, the most neglected place in Sirensea Lara could find.

Conveniently, there was a lodging house for visitors there. All the crew had to do was pretend they were friends of a Marzinian soldier who'd been sent to the hospital. They would be hidden in plain sight. The ship was stowed safely in a sea cave beneath the bluffs of Sirensea. And without the clunky old *Vault*, they were unrecognizable.

They had to cross the central city to reach the peninsula, though. And that necessitated being more vigilant than they ever had been. The king had ordered the crew to leave and never return, and they were disobeying him by stepping foot in

Sirensea. All they could do was keep their heads down and hope the king was complacent enough to lower surveillance.

Unlike the other nations, Marzine didn't maintain many patrols of soldiers. The people of the gilded city didn't need to be observed. This was both a service and an obstruction to the crew. They had to wear stolen finery to meld with the masses, keeping their chins up and their voices hushed. Lara was offended by it all, and she was sweating down the back of her gown. She'd seen the poverty and suffering of the other nations. She'd seen the starved people, the illnesses that ran rampant in the countryside. If only a little was culled from the royal treasury, many bellies could be full. If their coup somehow resulted in victory, she would feed the hungry. Then, she would leave on a ship of her own design and see Andria for herself. Being the queen of Wilkinia didn't appeal to her. She would restore the dual principality and be on her way. All her bindings would be raised, and she would be as free as the wind itself. And slowly, but surely, she would remember why she wasn't with Cornelius.

There were only four of them now, so they were less evident as a group. They were only stopped three times in the center city, which was far less than they'd expected. After all, they were from the outside. Precious few from other nations lived in Sirensea, and the continental war had made the citizens suspicious of outlanders. Their minds had been poisoned by war propaganda, and they would dirty the hems of their finely tailored skirts and trousers to cross the street and confront the strangers. But as always, the former Masked Birds got through it, telling the concerned men and women about their friend in the hospital on the peninsula. The individual, still wary, would cross back over to the other side of the street, have a spot of tea, and complain to their shrink about the encounter later that evening. Lara couldn't wait to shake the city's drivel off her stolen leather boots.

They made it to the peninsula with four more confrontations. The story about the ill soldier they knew with began to chafe their ears. With each new person, Lara added something new to the story. He'd lost a leg in the war. He had a sweetheart here in Sirensea. He was the former Sleetalian king's illegitimate son and so on… Awfully trivial things like that. The last man stared at them for a full minute in silence after Lara was done with her account. As they went on, they realized that the king had raised his surveillance, not lowered it. There were patrols of Marzinian soldiers swimming through the mainstreams of people. But fortune was in their favor. The larger thoroughfares kept them hidden because of how they were filled with people. But even in less populated side streets, they found ways to avoid the augmented defenses. They hid in the shadows, cowering and praying to remain unnoticed. It was a stroke of luck, making it through the city without any less-than-trivial confrontations.

The peninsula was almost entirely forsaken, the residents locked away in cells or hiding out in their brick homes. They passed only one man as they walked the waterlogged stretch of land that served as a bridge to the peninsula. He didn't approach them, but offered a sort of haggard smile as he crossed over to the mainland.

Back on the mainland of Sirensea, there'd been carefully manicured hedges and trees around every sunlit, painted corner. There'd been gas lamps and every modern contraption available to make life easier for the privileged few. But on Sirensea's western arm, the trees weren't in engineered little lines. The street was still cobbled, but it was uneven in places. There weren't gas lamps, but only the occasional lantern. Not even Lara commented on the change of scenery. The four were tired of talking, of planning, and trying to grasp the fleeting future. She knew she should save her breath for her last words anyway. They wouldn't give her so much as a trial if the King's Guard found her. Only Cornelius would. They would give him that courtesy, or pardon him altogether. Lara wondered what Cornelius would say on the stand. Murray caught a glimpse of her smile and cocked his head curiously.

"Cheerful, are we?" he whispered so the lovebirds wouldn't hear them.

"I was just imagining what Cornelius would say if he was put on trial: 'I'm too handsome to be on a stand made of cherrywood, I demand oak!'" She mimicked. "But that's an exaggeration; he's not that self-important. At least, I hope not." Murray's eyes were no longer unbearable.

"No, he'd say, 'I was only trying to share the glory of my good looks by sharing the glory of the resistance. Some people just can't handle my beauty.'" They shared a smile. The wind whistled through the underbrush. The sun glowed orange above the turquoise waters. Murray had to admit it was beautiful in Sirensea. The silence they fell into was genial. Murray knew Lara loved Cornelius too, but she couldn't bear to be a queen, couldn't bear to be trapped under the tines of a crown.

"You love him too, don't you?" she asked softly. He was surprised by how unlike herself she sounded.

"Yes," he admitted, unable to say more than a single word. She stopped and turned to him. Murray looked her in the eyes, and he wondered what color they were. Magenta? Green? He couldn't tell. She was warm and entrancing. Everything about her was welcoming, and everything about him was cold. His eyes turned people to stone. Hers thawed the hardest hearts. A smile to sob over made dimples in her cheeks.

"He's yours. I'm going to leave after this. I'm going to go… everywhere, Murray, everywhere. You have to take care of him, though. You have to help him make the nations whole again. I know he loves the both of us, but you're what's best for him, even if you're one of two fools. We're both fools, see. We fell in love with the Siren Prince of Marzine and were quite literally bewitched by his siren song."

Murray looked up at her, teardrops wetting his lashes. "You were never meant to be kept, Lara, never meant to belong to someone. See the world. And someday, come back. Tell us about your adventures. And we'll tell you of ours," he said, his lips parting in his sentinel's smile.

The crew got situated in the boarding house. All they had to do was wait for the week to end.

Across the bay, on Addison Island, a chance encounter was about to take place. Cornelius was miserable in his chambers. Whenever he looked up from his own picked-at nail beds, he hated himself for choosing such a livid color scheme. Who would ever think scarlet and mint mingled well? In fact, the ghosts of his decisions before the kidnapping haunted him. He had an entire closet full of garments left behind by his lovers. He found himself wondering why he'd had such hobbies. He knew there was no shame in it, especially given his circumstances, but his habits still made him realize how much he'd changed.

After collecting the courage to leave his bed, Cornelius found himself perusing one of his many ambry vaults. This one held all of his discarded and unused instruments. It was the size of a small prison cell, and the dust lining the walls made him cough. He turned on the gas lantern, and amber light cascaded over his collection. There was a wide variety of instruments. But one he loved more than others: his first viola. He'd been made to learn the principles of almost every instrument, but favored the viola the others. He'd taken it up seriously after his classical training was complete, but this was his first viola. He hadn't seen it in years, let alone held it close and played it. His favorite viola was back on *The Vault of Heaven*. Cornelius took a step toward the student's viola, navigating around the strewn-about parts of a tenor clarinet.

"Hello, old friend," he said contritely, sweeping the dust off the case's maker's mark. He picked it up carefully. He hadn't played it since he was twelve. It was a welcome distraction from the feeling of impending doom in his chest. His fingers instinctively felt for the clamps that held the case closed, but he hesitated. No, he shouldn't play it in a musty closet. He'd neglected the instrument enough. Instead, he would take it to the music room.

Cornelius had used the music room for many things in his life. Most of which had to do with social entertainment, but he'd also cried there, performed recitals for ghosts there, and practiced for hours unending. He'd go back there and stand in that one patch of sunlight that warmed his face and pretend he was the hero in a tale. That would do the abandoned viola justice.

Cornelius would have to get past the guards his father posted by the stairway down to the palace's main level, but that would be effortless. He knew each guard by name, knew what to say and what to do. Many a time, he'd snuck out of the palace compound to have some time away from the eyes of Addison.

Before he left, he stopped before the mirror in his room. It was undoubtedly ornate, which he'd never understood. Why were so many mirrors decorated? It was only the picture in the glass that interested the onlooker. He smiled at himself and plucked the crown off its little velvet pillow. There was a myriad of reasons why he'd chosen to don it. The most likely was that he wanted to mock his father by fleeing from his chambers, even with the crown on his head.

The damned thing couldn't hold him back.

Descending the stairway down to the main level with the viola tucked under his arm was almost surreal. There'd been few moments of happiness in his childhood, the majority of which made solely of music. And circling down the stairway, all he felt was the ecstasy of the few bright moments of his childhood.

He almost didn't notice the guards as he sped past. One of them grabbed his shirt collar and hauled him back into the stairwell. Cornelius identified the man quickly from the oiled handlebar mustache he wore. It was a point of pride for him, and he stroked constantly. The man raised an eyebrow and poised to speak, but Cornelius began his charade before he had the chance.

"Lyle, how's the girlfriend?" Cornelius asked jovially. He recalled his last encounter with the man in which he learned of the barmaid he'd been talking to. Lyle's eyebrows raised. He released Cornelius' collar and set him down.

"Quit the small talk, prince Gale."

Cornelius chuckled and took a step toward the threshold arch. Two other guards stood a few feet away from them, obstructing the doorway. They exchanged nervous glances, knowing what he was capable of. After a moment of awkward silence, Lyle spoke again. "She's, er, she's not my girlfriend anymore." So his mustache wasn't the only thing he was stroking.

"My apologies," Cornelius said, placing a hand over his heart. Lyle only nodded in response, flustered. Cornelius turned to the other two. They were shaking in their royal tunics. One had a hand on the hilt of his sword. Cornelius smiled.

"Good day to you as well, Janan and Julius. How's your mother, Janan? Did the treatment work? I'd be happy to put in a good word with the court doctor if it unfortunately failed. I have only one condition," he said, furthering compassion in his throat. She blinked, confounded at his fast words. He realized he was pushing the limits a little.

"I-It didn't work... You would? And your condition?" she asked. He smiled indulgently, a little sickened by himself for offering such a thing for an evening in the music room.

"Yes, I would. You just have to let me through," he told her lightly. Julius put a hand on her wrist, but she gave him a pleading look. He opened his mouth, closed it, and nodded. Cornelius' smile grew.

"Much obliged, ladies and gents." Cornelius strode right on

through. His routine had worked like a charm, and many parties had benefited from it. Janan's mother would indeed get seen by the court doctor. He never broke his promises.

His favorite place, the music room, was a turret that bridged off from the second floor. Cornelius was flattered by the patrols of guards on the main floor, pleased that his father knew what he and his tongue were capable of. His broken nose was throbbing, but he still forged forward. The viola deserved to be played.

Avoiding King's Guard was easy enough, but he was stopped once. He played the same trick on this guard as he did the ones posted by his door and was on his way, emboldened. Everyone could be bought, and he had many favors he could call in as the prince.

The gas lanterns grew a shade dimmer, signaling the approaching night. A summer sunset bleeding into twilight was perfect for his playing. He loved a touch of the dramatic. He climbed the carpeted stairway to the second floor without disturbance and waltzed down the turret's corridor. There were no guards on the second floor. His father had underestimated him after all. It was what he always did, reducing him to Gale instead of letting him live up to Cornelius.

Finally, his fingers closed around the handle of a dark wooden door. A plaque read "Music Room 4." It was the least-used music room in the palace. There were, in total, twelve music rooms. But music room four was neglected, so he gave it his attention. It overlooked the palace gardens and had a direct view of the sun as it set into the sea. One could hardly see the hulking obsidian wall from so high up, only the great beyond. But when he opened the door and stepped inside, he realized he wasn't alone. At first, he thought it was his mother, the queen. He knew he was bound to see her where she shouldn't be. But it wasn't. There was a stranger in music room four.

A boy wearing a dapper Sleetalian suit stood facing the

curtained window, toying with a harp he had no skill in. A blue fire was hissing in the hearth, and the room was bathed in the pink glow of early sunset. There were various other instruments and midnight blue decor that Cornelius had spent many hours lounging upon. The ceiling was domed for acoustics, a depiction of twilight draped across it.

The boy didn't seem to know the prince was there with him, so an offended Cornelius made his presence known with a sarcastic knock. It had all been a flight of fancy up until that point. But his dance had come to an abrupt stop. The boy turned, and they shared a look of awe. It was Rodrigo before him, after all. Rodrigo, who he was just now realizing was his most intimate, best friend.

"Rodrigo," Cornelius choked.

"Cornelius. You d-don't know how glad I am to see you." Rodrigo smiled sweetly. He still had his smile, but he'd changed. His frame was wider, his jaw sharper. He'd grown muscles somehow. And most surprisingly, dark circles were beneath his eyes. Eyes that had grown darker, poisoned by injustice after injustice. Cornelius was rooted to the spot. Addison's ordeal had changed Rodrigo. But even though his change was evident, his kindness hadn't left him. There was no rhyme or reason for it, but it would never leave him, so there was no point in fighting it off. Rodrigo crossed the room to stand before Cornelius. Then, he embraced the man who was to murder him.

Rodrigo led Cornelius over to the chair by the hearth and helped him sit down. Cornelius was in a trance. He'd dropped his viola by the door once he recognized his friend, and now he had nothing to hold onto but the chair's arms. He stared at the fire in rapt attention. Stared at it like Murray did the sea. The sunset faded to twilight and then into night without words. Cornelius let the realizations crash over him like ocean waves. Rodrigo was here. Rodrigo was his best friend. He would soon be the cause of Rodrigo's untimely death.

"Cornelius, I have to tell you something. I've been searching the palace up and down for you since yesterday." He inclined his head towards Rodrigo slowly.

"Tell me," Cornelius replied. Rodrigo closed his eyes and smiled. When he opened them, tears had collected in his lashes. It looked like sapphires were dripping down his face in the light of the blue flame, and he realized how appropriate it was that Rodrigo would cry jewels.

"Cornelius, I don't want you to feel guilty about… about e-ending me when the time comes. The king, your father, means to p-poison me before the duel. He's doing this to… make you a better sovereign, I believe," Rodrigo explained.

"But, that's not fair at all…" Cornelius felt far away from himself. "Why aren't you trying to escape? Why are you wearing their suits?"

Rodrigo smiled tenderly.

"Why are they just letting you roam free like a lamb for slaughter? Rodrigo, why aren't you fighting? Tell me! Tell me right n-now!" Cornelius yelled, his eyes filling with tears as he stared at Rodrigo. He gripped the arms of the chair.

"Oh, Cornelius, my life isn't worth the suffering of the continent. I'll die so you can bring down Addison. That is your plan, right? I figured the crew would come up with some way to do that." He looked down at his lap. "Winston was wrong. I will take the poison willingly." He clasped his hands together. The sun was long dead under the sea.

Cornelius didn't know who the hell Winston was, but he didn't care. He just wanted Rodrigo to stop being so good. "Stop being the damned hero, Rodrigo. Just s-stop it. I-I can figure this out. I a-always do!" Cornelius begged.

Rodrigo shook his head. "Maybe I'm not the hero. Maybe I'm pitiful like Pia always told me. But if I have to die, this is the best way to do it. I may not be a hero, but my death will have been heroic," he told Cornelius. The prince swallowed and looked up.

"You're amazing, Rodrigo. Amazing." Rodrigo recalled the evening in the Wilkinian monastery when Cornelius had said the very same words to him. "But just this once, be the c-coward we thought you were."

"Thank you."

A sob wracked Cornelius' body as he realized the extent of what was to come. Rodrigo watched him for a long while.

"Rodrigo, will you make me soup, just one last time? I can get us into the kitchen. And then I'll take you out to the garden, and we can have a meal together. And t-talk. I'll try to get you to escape, and you'll laugh and tell me again how you're not the hero, even though you are," he said. And so, they did. They snuck into the kitchen. The chef and her proteges had retired for the evening, so they were all alone. Rodrigo made his spice soup one last time. There wasn't a pinch of cinnamon in this recipe. He ladled it into canisters, and they fled into the gardens. They sat on a stone bench in the center of the flowers, the sweet, nauseating scent overwhelming them as they drank the soup. The moon had risen high into the sky. It was late, and the remaining soup was cold.

"You know, you're my best friend."

"And you're mine."

"And I care if you die. So please don't."

"Do you care because you pity me, or because you feel obligated to?"

"No, I don't care for you because I pity you. I don't care for you because I feel obligated to."

"I'm glad you care if I die, not out of pity or obligation. But that doesn't change the fact that I will."

CHAPTER 34

Nic Murray wore stolen sovereign servant's attire, though his demeanor was nothing like one of these foreshadowed few. From birth, every aspect of their lives was planned to shape them into immaculate drudges. Spending so much time on a waterlogged ship with Lara and Cornelius had forced him to learn things about the royal family and their servants that he would've rather not known. Knowing all that the sovereign servants went through, he wasn't too pleased with the idea that he was dressed in a vestment that had belonged to one of them. But it was necessary, and the one he'd stolen it from hadn't been killed. In fact, he and Cornelius' other personal servants were hidden away in one of his vaults. The crew would return for them after the coup was over and set them free.

Though his attire troubled him, it didn't worry him half as much as the empire they were about to take down. Before Cornelius, he'd been too cautious to take such an immense risk. After all, he would die if this went wrong. But Cornelius was worth the risk.

He hadn't seen any King's Guard yet, and he was sure he wouldn't. Every guard, resident, and servant on Addison Island was preoccupied with the duel. It was the event of the century because the king told them it was. The duel itself wouldn't be all that exciting to anyone but the king, who loved the raw sentiment of compelling his son to murder. The duel was just two young men fighting an ordinary match in place of gladiators and war prisoners. That alone wouldn't interest a bloodthirsty, aristocratic audience. Murray deplored Addison for the circumstances surrounding the duel and would cut the man's throat ear to ear if he were given the chance. But alas, that kill belonged solely to Pia. It was her brother who would die, after all. And by blood, it was her right to take revenge.

Murray's position was by the third wing's doors out to the central courtyard. Pia occupied the first wing, Mikka the second, and Lara the fourth. They surrounded the king's wing, and if all else failed, they could take it, barricade it, and negotiate an end from there. Murray hoped it wouldn't come to that, though. Mikka and Pia would rather use their fists than negotiate, and Lara's vocabulary was far too large for peace talks. And he, well, he would be comically bad in negotiations, seeing as he'd only just started speaking after years of refusing to do so.

Despite his many flaws, Mikka was the most resourceful of the lot, the best under pressure, too. He was their backup plan if they found themselves cornered in the king's wing without any hope for negotiation—the backup plan to their backup plan. The king's wing had a circular tower at its center with a window overlooking gardens. Mikka had his sharpshooter's rifle strapped to his leg beneath the vestment. From the window, he could assassinate the king with his rifle.

As time passed, Murray tried not to admire the magnificence of the hall. The wallpaper was a dark mauve with little golden intricacies spiraling all the way to the ceiling, which had a stained-glass skylight, something he'd never seen before. The light that filtered through made the wooden floors shine with each coat of wax applied. With the rich decor, all of this was enough to make an appraiser soil her pants. But the smell also added something to the ambiance. It smelled of lemon zest and old parchment and something else. Whatever it was, it was genteel, and it made him feel like more of an impostor than he actually was.

In his marveling, he had neglected the distant reverberation of footsteps. Now he heard it, clinking the baroque wine glasses hanging upside-down behind the hall's bar. Murray's entire body tensed. There were many, he realized, the footsteps of an entire outfit. He drew Mikka's pistol, borrowed for his protection, out of its holster. The footsteps grew thunderous. It now seemed like thousands were descending on him, though he knew that couldn't be true.

Something swept over Murray. A cold, unnerving sense of dread. So without an inkling of the reasoning he was known for, he hid. He made for the bar in the corner of the hall, his footsteps muted as he leaped from one Wilkinian carpet to the next. Just as the intruders entered, Murray ducked under the bar, almost smashing a vintage vase on a low shelf with his shoulder. It was dark, hidden away beneath the bar. The shadows were painted a variety of colors from the stained glass ceiling, and he tried to measure out his breaths. The footsteps stopped in what he estimated was the center of the hall.

"The King's Guard announce ourselves. We know an enemy of the empire resides in this room. Reveal yourself, and we will spare your life," an airy voice threatened. Murray's steely eyes shot back and forth, searching for an out. Lord, he didn't know what to do! He didn't want to die, not when he'd just learned to live again. Not when he promised he'd never leave Cornelius...

The King's Guards began pacing the hall, overturning tables and chairs to find him. He heard "all clear" every other moment as more crannies and crevices of the room were found unoccupied. He didn't know how much time he had left before he was discovered, and he still couldn't think of anything to do. Finally, Murray peered around the bar. He locked eyes with Mikka, who was in chains along with Pia and Lara in the room's center beside a tiled fountain. Murray's heart sank. Mikka and Murray stared at one another for a few seconds, and Murray noticed a cut along Mikka's cheek. It was nasty and beginning to swell, and he could only guess at what hysterics Mikka had gone into when they'd finally caught him. All things considered, he was lucky to be alive.

"Reveal yourself, criminal!" The King's Guard beside his crewmembers called, his face stony. Mikka nodded ever so slightly as if to encourage Murray to give himself up. Murray spent a few heartbeats, considering. It was the logical thing to do, and maybe it would make up for his illogical choice of seeking sanctuary beneath the bar. He slid Mikka's pistol between two white wine bottles, committing the spot to memory so they could go back for it if somehow they escaped. Murray raised his hands above his head and stood.

"I submit," he said, his eyes cold. Each King's Guard turned from their respective areas to stare at him. They drew their guns in unison. He'd lost the ability to feel fear other than trivial shock long ago. But now, all that well-practiced deadness was gone, and he was terrified.

"Approach slowly, criminal," the one between his crew members called. Apparently, he was the Cornelius of the King's Guard, the speaker. Murray did as he was commanded. If only he had his Cornelius here. The prince could surely talk their way out of this. As soon as he was within ten feet of the speaker, he was seized from behind. A King's Guard thrust his jaw down on the floor, and he nearly bit his tongue off. His wrists were put in cuffs, and his feet were shackled together. Then, without a moment to let him recover from the attack, he was hoisted to his feet by the chain between his wrists. He could already feel the bruise forming along his jaw.

"Committing a crime against the empire has divested you of your rights," the speaker told him. Murray only nodded compliantly. They could take his rights. So long as they let him live, he'd be just peachy.

Soon, they were being seated on the upholstered chairs of the hall. Their feet were rechained to the legs of the chairs. Murray couldn't see Lara and the lovebirds' faces, their backs turned to one another. The King's Guard handling Murray was a young Marzinian man with a clean-cut, brooding appearance. He wouldn't look directly at Murray, always avoiding his steely gaze.

"Sir, are we going to interrogate them right here?" Murray's man asked.

"Yes. We don't have the time to bring them elsewhere. The duel commences in two hours. We need to know their motives so we can successfully shut down their operation," the commander said. Unlike his ward, the commander did look Murray in the eyes. Murray made himself demure out of habit. But like a cruel professor, the commander set his sights on the quiet one. His eyes were like pebbles, dark and petty. There was something that felt familiar about him, an empathy between them Murray couldn't quite name. But despite it, Murray knew he was being challenged. So he lowered his shields. He made his gaze audacious. And then, he did something he thought he'd never do: negotiate, embodying Cornelius as he did.

"You don't have any rights either. You and I, sir, are the same. Don't act high and mighty when you're low, low like the vermin you eat," he said in accented Marzinian.

The commander's eyes lit up, surprised the vermin could speak. But yes, could speak. And yes, he would choose to speak now of all times. After a life spent in silence, he was ready for a chat.

"What?" the commander asked, his dark eyes narrowing. Murray shrugged, a flicker of amusement in his eyes. Like a bear stepping in a steel trap, the man grabbed Murray by the collar of his vestment. His face was so close that Murray could smell the remnants of a cigarette on his teeth. "Speak, or we start shooting," he threatened. Murray made like Cornelius and smiled at the most outrageous time. The smile was dripping with venom.

"What's your name?" he asked idly, clasping his hands

together in the chains. The commander's grip on his collar loosened in surprise. Murray watched the telling emotions pass over his face. First shock, then uncertainty, and finally anger.

"Rat!" The commander raised a fist to smack him, but Murray's sigh stopped him. The sentinel looked ever so bored.

"Tell me your name, and I'll tell you why we're the same," he said with Cornelius' appeal. Every other King's Guard watched intently to see what their commander would do. After a moment, Murray knew he'd won.

"Nicholas Rose-Delisle. Seven years as a King's Guard Commander." He took a step back, almost affronted.

Murray shook his head and colored his smile wry. "We have more in common than our rights. Our names, too. I'm Nicholas Murray, though my friends called me Nic Murray or Murray, never just Nic. You can call me either. In fact, please do call me Murray. We're friends by namesake."

Rose-Delisle crossed his arms and scrutinized Murray.

"Murray, what are you doing?" Mikka whispered in Sleetalian. Murray only laughed, again mimicking Cornelius' mannerisms. Cornelius would laugh in the face of death, flirt unabashedly with it.

"Sir, what *are* you doing?" Murray's brooding King's Guard asked suspiciously, still aiming his gun at Murray's head.

"Let the man talk," Rose-Delisle ordered, shaken. "Now, *sir*, tell me why we're the same."

"The king probably has you fetch his slippers. What a good little soldier you are, Nicholas. He never tells you that, though, does he? He glowers and sends you off on another death hunt or yells at you for another's mistake. You take one step forward and about a hundred steps back, right?" Murray said, smiling like a ray of damned sunshine.

Rose-Delisle gritted his teeth. "I'm steadfast in my role. I live only to serve the king. Now give me a substantive reason why we're the same unless you want your death now rather than later," Rose-Delisle said.

Murray shrugged again, and this time Rose-Delisle seized his shoulders. His dark gaze was imploring, and Murray knew he was desperate for a reason to doubt his loyalties.

"Murray, stop before you get us all killed. You don't want our deaths on your conscience, do you?" Lara asked. Murray disregarded her and continued on.

"Oh, repeating your oath, are you?" Murray replied. He felt giddy, watching Rose-Delisle squirm. But alas, he was tolerant and would tell Rose-Delisle the truth.

"I admire your adamance." Murray licked his lips. "Alright. Here's why we're the same. My life belongs to the Marzinian empire, and yours does, too, Nicholas. You live to serve the king, just as your oath dictates. You don't have rights because your life is Addison's, and when your life belongs to another, your rights also belong to them." Murray turned his head to look at the other King's Guard. A few lowered their guns, looks of disquiet on their faces. He was tempted to quit while he was ahead, but the culmination of his speech was just too enticing.

"You all have dreams. Everyone does. And those will never be realized under such a depressing rule. Let me ask you this: Is this the nation you put on a pedestal as children? Did you really want to serve a blood-stained, disunited Marzine? Probably not. As I see it, you aren't the villains. You were only doing as you were told, and I *commiserate* with you. Nicholas, and all the rest of you." Murray's eyes gleamed.

Rose-Delisle's lips were quivering traitorously. In fact, all the King's Guards were frightened by his words. He'd made them out to be the victims, and that's all any self-serving human wanted. And though he didn't believe a word of the story he spun, it would let him and his crew make it out alive.

"You... you're wrong, Murray," Rose-Delisle accused. It was the most delightful thing to hear his own name spoken by the enemy.

"No... no, I'm not, Nicholas. If you really think so, shoot me," Murray said evenly. Rose-Delisle's grip loosened, and Murray felt feeling flood back into his shoulders. Murray's brooding King's Guard handed over his gun after being indicated to do so by Rose-Delisle. Murray knew he wouldn't shoot, so he smiled again.

Lara interjected, and he could hear her thrashing against her restraints. "Don't shoot! Please, he doesn't know what he's saying!" Lara cried from somewhere behind him. His other two crewmates were soldiers, and were trained in the art of keeping their mouths shut. Murray could only imagine what was going through their minds, though.

Rose-Delisle bared his teeth. One with a keen eye would notice the slight wavering in his arm as he held the gun, wavering the elite King's Guards were trained against.

Rose-Delisle cocked the gun. Murray's heart thudded despite his conviction. He closed his sentinel eyes then, for he didn't need to watch to know the outcome.

"I-I am steadfast in my role. I live only to serve the king."

Murray smiled consolingly, eyes still closed. "Yes, you do, Nicholas Rose-Delisle. And that's the issue. That's why we're the same. We have no life outside of this empire, no rights. Dreams are dead, and so are we, roaming the earth with no rhyme or reason for doing so." He heard Rose-Delisle's labored breathing. Murray felt as if any second he'd be blasted to hell, but he kept talking, kept smiling. "Do you want to know why we're here? To serve a new king, a new empire, ruled by Cornelius of Marzine, or as he's more commonly known, Gale. I'm in love with him. And more importantly, I *know* him. And because I do, I can swear that he'll rule justly and that you and I will have rights. He'll restore the nations. And if he doesn't, Nicholas, you can shoot me when we both realize it. I'll die willingly then." His smile fell, and he opened his eyes.

Rose-Delisle slowly began to lower the gun. He looked ever

so reluctant. He didn't want to believe Murray. But he had to, because every other King's Guard in the hall did. Rose-Delisle put his gun on the carpet along with many other guns that had been lowered during Murray's speech. The mariner was shocked. He'd done it. He'd convinced the King's Guard.

Rose-Delisle unlocked his chains, wrist, and ankle. The first thing Murray did was shake the man's hand. "A new king, you say?" Rose-Delisle asked, his dark eyes wet.

"Cornelius of Marzine. He's dueling our other friend as we speak. We were the ones who took him a few months back, planning to hold him for ransom. But Cornelius could sell a fox its own pelt. And so, he became our friend. Now we're assassinating his father together like friends do," Murray explained. He trusted Rose-Delisle, the man who hadn't shot him when he'd asked so nicely for him to do so.

"Don't assassinate him," Murray's brooding King's Guard called. "Wouldn't that just usher in an era of unrest? The theoretical coup would have to be bloodless. We can convict the king of numerous crimes, and death is an easy out. We should lock him away instead," he suggested. Every other King's Guard murmured in agreement.

"When do you suggest we do that, good sir?" he asked expectantly.

"Right now, when everyone can see it," he responded with a savage grin. They were all just people anyway. Victims. And suddenly, Murray believed his own lie.

CHAPTER 35

Cornelius' hands would soon be painted red, blood dripping from his fingertips until the day he died. He felt weightless as he and Rodrigo stood together on the chessboard. It felt as if it were only them, and there wasn't a bloodthirsty audience forming a perimeter around the arena. The chessboard was what the king called the dueling ground. Addison took great pride in his red arena, having loved a good game of death-for-sport since childhood. He'd had great slabs of marble and obsidian carted in from Orenia and laid over the soil in a chessboard pattern.

The arena was in the center of the seaside gardens. The fated pair had drunk their soup just outside the chess board's seating. In retrospect, Cornelius realized just how morbid their last supper had been. It was like a requiem for a living man.

His long, fine-pointed silver sword wavered in his grip. His leather armor weighed him down. Without it, he was sure he would float up into the clouds. Rodrigo was clad in the same gear, but their opportunity wasn't equal. It was a lie, a conjuring trick. If Cornelius wanted to, all he had to do was stand there and watch. Rodrigo's death would do just as his father had intended: shatter him. But this was the plan, and he'd always found a way to put himself back together. So many lives would profit from Rodrigo's death, too. He would die nobly, and Cornelius would make Rodrigo into a saint, a martyr.

They heard the simultaneous jeers and praises of the audience. Rodrigo hadn't realized how far he was leaning to the left. He only just caught himself before falling to the ground.

He locked eyes with Cornelius as the beginning symptoms took hold of him. Then, excruciatingly, he smiled. Cornelius felt tears collect in his eyelashes, but he blinked them away and squared his shoulders like Mikka. His sword began to shake in his hand. Rodrigo was close, so close Cornelius could hear the prayer he repeated under his breath. A lesser man would be cowering in fear.

"And the curtain rises, Cornelius. They came for a show. Let's get on with it." He nodded encouragingly.

The past week had been torture, even though he'd spent every day with Rodrigo. They had discussed all sorts of topics, from the exact shade of a sunflower's petals to the end itself. And through those hours of discussion, they came to a decision. When it happened, they were lying on the floor of the music room, staring at the painted-on twilight above their heads.

"Theatrics," Rodrigo had murmured under his breath.

"What do you mean?" Cornelius asked in response, yawning. He'd rolled over so that he was on his stomach and propped himself up on his elbows.

"We have to put on a show. Your father can't know you know the predetermined factors. As much as you'll want to, you can't just stand there and watch while I die. You have to attack. And I have to provoke your attack. We have to perform for our audience, or Addison will know that I didn't go insane and choose to attack you despite the poison." Rodrigo loosened his cravat and closed his eyes. "I don't know if I'll ever get used to wearing these things." He was quiet for a moment.

"You'll never get to," Cornelius responded without humor. His face darkened, but Rodrigo only laughed. He still hadn't come to terms with his own death, but he was pretending he had, and his countenance was almost perfect. Cornelius could still see the telltale circles beneath his eyes, though. He still noticed when Rodrigo withdrew into himself, staring into the distance for long periods of time.

"You're right. I never will. But frankly, we should really rehearse it. The end, I mean. We should script our actions to make the duel easier for ourselves. I think doing improv in that death arena would kill me sooner than the poison."

It was Cornelius who laughed this time. But his laugh was terse. He hadn't come to terms with Rodrigo's death either, and he wasn't even trying to pretend he had.

"That's morbid, Rodrigo," he said. Cornelius' eyes had dark circles beneath them, too. For the prince, it was guilt that kept him up, not the fear. It wasn't he who would take the poison, after all.

"I know. But it's for the progress of the continent. Now, will you rehearse my death with me?" Rodrigo asked. Cornelius sighed and pushed his cheek to the floorboards.

"You bastard. Didn't I tell you to stop playing the hero?" he mumbled into the wood.

"Thank you, Cornelius," Rodrigo said, his tone solemn now. And so they rehearsed his death. Rodrigo scripted the figurative closing of the curtains all that night, hidden away in the palace's guest wing with a bottle of chardonnay and a silk kerchief. He gave Cornelius the script the following day, and they acted it out in the music room using wooden practice swords for props. Turning it into a performance lessened their suffering considerably. After hours of rehearsal, they almost believed it was only a show, just some artful deception and sleight of hand. But there was one part they could never get to, that being Rodrigo's death. It was just too terrible to think of, let alone rehearse.

More than a performance, it was a dance. A dance with swordplay. They would parry and strike and strike and parry until Rodrigo's eyes grew glassy. Then, it would be over. In the script, Rodrigo didn't detail the stabbing. He simply wrote, "*The end.*" But strangely, Cornelius' script continued for one more line.

Cornelius will cry out in horror. At least, Rodrigo hoped he would.

Cornelius had smuggled Rodrigo into his tower during the final night to see his sister. The others sat behind closed doors in Cornelius' bed-chamber, listening to the agonized voices in the parlor. Pia was crying, not Rodrigo.

Cornelius was disheartened, and he wasn't the only one. Mikka's eyes were red as if he'd been crying, but they all knew better than to ask. He had a hand on the doorknob as if he was going burst in and save Pia from her sorrow. That night, after her visit with Rodrigo, he held her. Cornelius let them have his room. He wasn't going to sleep anyway. Lara retired to one of the three guest chambers he'd prepared, but Murray sat beside him all night silently. Cornelius found his hand slipping into Murray's. The sentinel squeezed his fingers every so often to let him know he was still there. The only other thing Murray did was stare at a candle on the table before them. He stared at it the way he stared at the sea.

The others donned sovereign servants' attire early in the morning and took their posts, leaving Cornelius to prepare himself alone. His hands were shaking violently as he tried to force the buttons of his shirt into the proper holes. That was when he realized why mirrors were made ornate. He had something to look at other than the bastard with the soulless blue eyes. The bastard who was failing to dress while Rodrigo Reyes was taking poison in his place.

Rodrigo was indeed drinking the poison. In the early hours of the morning, it was administered. It was Winston who brought it. He came alone, for the Andrian man could stop Rodrigo if he tried. He came with a case full of all the tools and tubing needed to force the toxicant down Rodrigo's throat, but the cook, with that damned smile of his, downed the small vial is one fatal gulp. He said nothing to Winston, only gripped his arm on the way out of the chambers. His fingers left bruises.

Winston then realized his error. Rodrigo Reyes was a fighter, just not the sort he'd suspected. A smile spread over his peculiar face as he stoppered the vial and placed it back in his case.

The soon-to-be-dead man went straight to the arena, escorted by King's Guard. He walked purposefully as he began to smell the putrid scent of death within himself. It all felt detached, distant. This wasn't his life, or his death, for that matter. No, it was only a dream. He couldn't be dying. It was that lie he told himself as he finally met Cornelius out on the chessboard. Yes, only a dream. He was asleep in his bed back in Embera. Soon, that well-known beam of sunlight would fall on his eyelids, and he would wake to the smell of steam from spice soup wafting up through the floorboards. He would go downstairs and eat with his family. Then, he would do his chores and feel the sun on his back. Stare out of the fields and feel his heart beating solidly in his chest.

Rodrigo felt tears prick at the corners of his eyes as his eyes met Cornelius'. "And the curtain rises, Cornelius. They came for a show. Let's get on with it," he said. Cornelius, after a long breath, nodded. He wiped the tears from his eyes and tried to mimic Rodrigo's ever-present smile.

"Onguard, my dear friend." And so, they danced. All of Sirensea was watching, all the fine people with their powders and cufflinks and cravats. All with their own lives and loves and losses. But none of them mattered. Only the pawns mattered in this game. The audience faded away, faint like an old painting left out in the sun for too many hours. Even the king's eyes were nullified, holding no power as the duelers circled. Rodrigo smiled to himself. *This is only a dream. I'm going to wake up soon,* he thought.

Cornelius thrust his blade at his opponent's stomach, but Rodrigo evaded the attack. He parried and held Cornelius' blade hostage for a tense moment. The pressure of the two blades made sparks fly. It was all scripted, all well-practiced. The crowd cried in approval, stamping their feet. Addison sat in rapt attention, compelled to watch for once in his godforsaken life. The boy, Rodrigo, wasn't giving up.

Addison had thought the duel would be short and sweet. But it was as if the cook hadn't even realized he'd been poisoned. He took out a pair of bronze opera glasses and peered through them. The boy was whispering something under his breath. What was it, an incantation? No, a prayer. Of course, he was praying for deliverance because he knew he would soon die. Satisfied, Addison replaced the opera glasses back in their case and settled down, crediting the display to human denial. Still, there was something off about the display.

Rodrigo forced Cornelius back into the leftmost corner of the chessboard. They were panting on the square where the black castle would stand. Cornelius made a show of ducking under Rodrigo's blade and tripping him up by grabbing his boot heel. A collective gasp sounded from the outskirts of the arena, the noble people of the continent in shock. The prince of Marzine against a nameless cook. This was the fight of the century only because they were told it was.

The sun beat down on their leather-clad backs, making them sigh and sweat in moments of respite. At the present moment, Rodrigo and Cornelius stood in opposite corners of the chessboard. They could lunge at one another at any moment, like bishops gliding down diagonal squares. Rodrigo felt a sort of numbness spread through him as he stood there. The poison was circulating through his bloodstream faster because of the exertion. He put on his best impression of a murderous smile and leaped forward. *This is only a dream. I'll wake up soon.* The final moment of his life was approaching quickly. His heart pounded in fear, his hands began to shake, but he wouldn't let it show. He would never let them see just how afraid he was. After all, hell was waiting for him. His prayer went on like a fervent poem. He repeated it over and over again. *God save me...*

God save me... God save me... A broken verse of hope he didn't believe. Damned was he, even though he looked to God. Finally, he was back in the moment. It wasn't a dream, and it never had been. He was dying. But... on with the show.

"Gale of Marzine!" he called in a tone he deemed epic enough for a martyr. "My sword will be through your gut soon enough!" The crowd erupted in protest, and Cornelius feigned fury. A wine goblet was thrown into the thoroughfare. His blade met Rodrigo's with a clang that left their fingers crackling with electricity. Cornelius felt sweat spill into his eyes. He stared at Rodrigo and realized how labored his breathing was, how flushed he was. The poison was coalescing in his veins, and his heart would give out soon. Cornelius sneered at him, as was proposed in the script.

Finally, the prince responded. "So much for being friends!" he cried.

Addison of Marzine smirked as he watched from the viewing box. He took a sip of his wine, the taste as sour as wrath itself.

Rodrigo knew it was his time when his veins began to show beneath his skin. They were a dreadful, bright scarlet color that seared into his dying mind. He felt the paralysis spread into his torso. Cornelius waited, sword poised.

Rodrigo faded in and out, trying to stay conscious. He could taste blood and the remnants of the *raska* shot Mikka had poured him that morning. Cornelius was drenched in sweat and gasping, waiting for the next move.

As was rehearsed, he charged Cornelius, each footfall thousands of agonies. His lungs burned, his life drained away. His blade sliced through the air... but as it fell, Cornelius deflected it with his own. The sword ricocheted away from them, knocking to the opposite end of the chessboard. Cornelius kicked him down, tears mistaken for sweat streaming freely from his eyes. He put a knee on Rodrigo's chest to keep him down. He sobbed, but Rodrigo only smiled. His tired, pretty golden eyes were glazing over bit by bit as the poison took hold of his mind.

"I always knew you w-would be the death of me, y-you and y-your silver tongue." He gripped Cornelius' collar he knelt.

The prince's masks fell away. All the guises he'd ever worn were gone now, and he was bared before Rodrigo. "Please don't go," Cornelius choked.

"I-I don't want to. But you have t-to let me."

Cornelius still had to stab him. It was the last act. It had to happen, or all of this would've been for nothing. His death would be in vain.

"I-I can't..." Cornelius whispered to himself. Rodrigo moaned and closed his eyes.

"See you in h-heaven," he said.

"That's a l-lie, Rodrigo," Cornelius uttered.

"I know, but it's a k-kind one." Then, Rodrigo took Cornelius' blade in his hands and plunged it deep into his own chest. Blood spurted from the wound, but Rodrigo was already dead as the blade pierced through his skin. The world tilted, and Cornelius shattered right then and there, his fragments more numerous than the stars in the sky.

Cornelius hadn't realized how loud the roar of the crowd was until Rodrigo's blood began to dry on his face. The ghost of Rodrigo's last smile was still on his lips. Blood was drying. It looked so, so *wrong*. Then, Cornelius felt something searing into his back. He turned his head sharply and met his father's stare. Evil. The most unadulterated evil was in the king's eyes. Cornelius then did as the script proposed: he cried out in horror. It was so loud that it overcame the audience. So loud that Rodrigo could hear it from heaven.

CHAPTER 36

No. Somehow, something wasn't right.

The boy was dead.

This was the outcome he'd intended, right?

His son had been shattered again. Shattered to pieces. He was even in tears, kneeling over the dead boy. If Gale held onto his sentiments, he would surely go mad—a good king rules with his mind, his intellect, not his heart. A good king is cold and calculating and makes sacrifices to better his kingdom. Addison knew this well. His own father, the previous Marzinian monarch, had prioritized the crown above all things. He was doing the same, presenting Marzine with a better future by preparing his son now.

Addison had felt wrong many times before. The most recent wrongness had led him to kill his firstborn son and then conquer half of the known world. Before that, his feelings of wrongness took place at the Ruler's Councils. The Ruler's Council was a convention held in Wilkinia at which the rulers of the continent would meet to discuss international threats and dealings. He'd always felt that wrongness when looking into the stygian eyes of Sleetal's king. Shadrach, the Raven King, was called. Addison had known Sigrid, his mother, and had gotten a similar sense of wrongness from her. There was something about the inky quality of their eyes that made him feel so sad, hopeless, so wrong. The young king and his haunting eyes were just too far out of place for detailed Addison. So, he'd waged war.

Now, afflicted by the wrongness again, he was vexed. He gripped his marble throne's arms, the veins in his wrists throbbing beneath his skin. If he were gripping his wine glass instead of the arms, it would shatter instantly. He gritted his teeth.

Something was missing. Something was wrong. But what, exactly? The people in the crowd were as lovely as painted figures. The sky was clear, the air pristine. The dead boy had stained the chessboard red with his blood. The young prince cried in suffering, the sound sincere. Everything was indeed just as he'd intended it to be. Then, the puzzle pieces finally fit together in his mind. The Reyes boy had taken the blade and thrust it into his own chest. It was as if they'd had a… a plan. But he was too cowardly to plan his own death.

He glanced around and finally noticed the lack of the King's Guard. They usually haunted him like wraiths. They had since he'd taken the throne from his father. He clenched his teeth. All hell! He didn't need them to hold his hand while the wrongness ran its course. He could figure this out himself.

Gale's eyes met his. There was no deception in his misery. He should've felt oh so triumphant at that moment, but he still felt that gnawing disconcertion. Addison stood abruptly, his throne toppling. Knowing him, his servants should've bolted it to the ground. Insolent fools. He would yell at them if any were around, but curiously, there were not. The audience was growing quieter. Their eyes were fixed on him, their dainty handkerchiefs over their lips to hide the surprise. He and his son were locked in battle.

Cornelius, not one to hold his tongue, spoke. "You killed him!" The phrase was off-script, but the script had ended with his horrified cry. He wished he could just hold his tongue for once because the plan wouldn't work if he kept speaking. But seeing his father leering down at him, listening to the jeers of the crowd, was too much.

The audience members were visibly doubtful now, gossiping amongst themselves. The gory ending had been impressive, but now they wanted to return to their homes in Sirensea. Cornelius was just standing there like a wretch, soaked in his best friend's blood, crying and screaming at the king of Marzine. Despair encroached on his rage, and he stumbled, choking on another curse.

"You rotten bastard! Come down from your ivory tower, and I'll cut your heart right out of your chest!" The plan was unraveling more and more with every word he spoke. When his father returned his ridicules with silence, much to his horror, he spoke again. "Alright, alright! Let's make this exciting, *father dearest*, since you're obviously not interested in petty brawls!" His tongue had a mind of its own. The king took to the stairway aisle. The clipping of his bootheels seemed to resound through the arena. The King's Guard weren't following him, Cornelius realized. In fact, he hadn't seen a single crest-laden soldier throughout the duration duel. It was only the king, his subjects, and his bloody son.

"What do you propose?" the king asked. The audience hung on every syllable he spoke, their attention spans renewed. Cornelius exhaled, thinking back to only months ago. He used to be the golden son. He would drink rose tea and listen to the rain. Now, he was bloodstained. Ugly. Broken beyond all repair. He'd spoiled the plan, and all that was left was Shadrach's proposition, his deal with the devil. He would claim his—no, Gale's birthright.

"The throne!" Cornelius roared. A collective gasp rose off the crowd, and Cornelius breathed in the scent of fear. Rodrigo was still smiling, pretty, tired golden eyes seeing nothing at all. "If you die, everyone has to honor me as king of Marzine! If I die, you no longer have a threat on your hands. You can go and sire another poor, godforsaken son to be your heir!" A few court ladies cried in outrage. There had never been such a display.

Addison of Marzine descended the stairway in long, elegant strides. Audience members reached out and touched his flowing robes as he went by. He didn't even take a sword with him into the arena, expecting his presence to resolve the issue. Cornelius gritted his teeth, ready to draw blood. But with a single cruel word, the man stole all hope of another duel.

"No," he spat. His primordial eyes finally silenced Cornelius. "My counter-proposal is that we go back to the palace for the victory banquet." His voice was soft now, so soft that the audience couldn't hear.

Cornelius opened his mouth to speak, but his words were stopped by a hand grabbing his bloodstained collar. A hand, but it wasn't his father's. At first, Cornelius thought the King's Guard were there to drag him away. But there was something familiar about the hand. He'd held it the entire night before the duel, after all. Murray. So silent he wouldn't be noticed even if he strolled into the arena unannounced. So silent, and without the King's Guard to stop him, he was invincible.

"You won't be doing that, Addison."

The sun shone down on a silver pistol, Mikka's pistol. Cornelius saw Murray's fingers curling around the grip, his finger on the trigger. There wasn't a single tremor in his body. A statue with steely, piercing eyes. Eyes that had the very same quality as his father's. The only difference was that he didn't fear Murray's eyes. No, he loved them, loved them more than he would ever care to admit. With one hand on his shoulder, one hand holding Mikka's pistol, Murray began to speak, something he would've never done had he not met Cornelius.

"Addison, I wish we could've met under other, less unpleasant circumstances." He gave Rodrigo's corpse a grave stare before looking back at the king. "You see, I love your son. In another life, we could've been friends, you and I. Family. But not now, seeing I've got a loaded gun pointed at your heart. And I do intend to pull the trigger if you decline the generous offer we'll be making on Cornelius' behalf."

Cornelius heard footsteps behind him, but he didn't dare look back. Murray had appeared out of nowhere. He could understand something like that. But the others? This was off-script—way off-script.

"Murray, don't do this. Surrender yourself, and maybe he'll let you live," Cornelius whispered.

Murray shook his head, and Cornelius could hear the smile in his high, offbeat voice. "You have many enemies, Addison. This morning, we were captured by the King's Guard. Instead of locking us in some tower, we were interrogated into telling them our plans. As it turns out, you're very disliked. Hated, in fact. And a shade too careless for the nation's taste. We have the King's Guard now, and they honor Cornelius of Marzine as king, Addison. And most likely, all of your 'Marzinian' soldiers will as well. They don't have that grand an opinion of you either, seeing that you burned their homes to the ground and picked them off of the corpses of their nations." He was smiling that odd, tight-lipped smile of his. Addison went red in the face, and then, to Cornelius' horror, he withdrew the blade out of Rodrigo's chest. The sound of the sword being removed was sickening. Cornelius clutched at his throat, trying to keep the bile down. Murray looked back and nodded at the others. Mikka, Pia, and Lara joined ranks with them. Pia was crying.

"I know a bluff when I see one," Addison said, eyes locked on his son.

"You might want to get your eyes checked, then. A coup that would've taken years to construct was staged in a matter of hours just because someone was bold enough to try. We'll be putting Cornelius on the throne and putting you in either prison, or the ground. Your choice. Surrender the throne, and you'll have a comfortable little bastille tower to retire to after this is all over."

Cornelius was in a stupor. There were still so many

unknowns. Where was his mother, and who was taking care of her? How had the King's Guard betrayed his father so quickly? There was supposed to be an oath to prevent that. They'd won, it seemed. Despite all odds, despite all the tragedy, they'd won. Murray's grip on his collar tightened.

"Don't address him as Cornelius. He is to be called Gale under my decree," Addison said through yellowed teeth. He was running out of time, and he knew it.

"I'm sorry, what was that? Your... *decree?*" Murray asked incredulously. His fingers began to tap a methodical rhythm of Cornelius' shoulder. Methodical like Murray himself. It was always Murray, standing vigil, looking after the group. It was always Murray, listening when someone needed to be heard. It was always Murray, seeing them through the worst of storms.

"Yes, my decree!" Addison snarled. Murray smiled guilelessly and fired the pistol twice into the air. With the shots, the audience went from bewildered to wild. None of them had sought death when they came to Addison Island to watch others die.

The King's Guard were securing the palace compound and sending word to Sirensea. From there, the spark would grow into a flame. All subterfuge of the former king's benevolence would fall. Everyone would know of the king's dethroning. And yet Cornelius was catatonic.

"Addison, I would like to inform you that your son's name is Cornelius Addison Lyra Anpiel and not Gale Addison Lyra Raziel. He died at your hands years ago. His name is, in fact, Cornelius," Lara said. Finally, a beleaguered smile found its way onto Cornelius' lips. His name was Cornelius. Not Gale, but Cornelius.

"You killed my brother, Addison," Pia added, giving him her withering glare.

"And you'll kill yourself if you don't accept Murray's offer," Cornelius advised, dead tired. He looked down at Rodrigo. It was a while before Addison put down the blade, but when the King's Guard arrived, proving the coup, he did.

Murray squeezed Cornelius' shoulder as he watched his father being taken into custody. Nobles who'd pledged their loyalty to Cornelius arrived a few moments later. The others were planning to fight the coup, but Cornelius couldn't comprehend that. Only Murray's hand kept him from floating into the clouds as his father walked away with two King's Guard beside him. He was dignified to the end, going without a fight.

Addison smiled. It was he who'd won. His son, *Gale*, had been shattered, and was beyond repair. Even if he took the throne immediately, he would be a righteous king. Ruling with his mind, not his heart. Finally, Addison was satisfied.

The end was bitter-sweet. They'd lost Rodrigo. And somehow, Cornelius knew he wasn't in hell. He hadn't lied with his last words, after all. Murray was finally speaking, Mikka and Pia were in love, and Lara would be able to go where the wind took her, free. But Cornelius, like an exotic bird, was trapped in a gilded cage yet again.

That evening, after all the proper funerary arrangements were made for Rodrigo, after the account of their coup was penned by Lara and handed off to couriers, Cornelius realized the full ramifications of the past hours. He realized what he was now: the king of Marzine. The Siren King of Marzine, as Mikka had said on the *Vault's* deck after Shadrach's death. He'd be a good king, but he'd never wanted to be a king at all. Not truly. It was a lonely, lovelorn life. But he had Murray, so that was yet to be seen.

As the night began, Cornelius collected his friends in the music room. They sat in a circle around the metal table that Rodrigo had served meals to them on. Cornelius had brought it to the palace out of sentiment. They were dirty, tired, and consumed with glory. Cornelius smiled dimly, his senses still subdued. The gasolier was set on low, and the golden intricacies looked crimson.

"So, our names will indeed be etched in the sky," Mikka began with a roguish smile. "I told you." He chuckled.

Cornelius smiled lazily, his posture bending. Murray held his hand beneath the table, still keeping him anchored.

"Yes, Mikka, our names will be etched in the sky," Pia agreed. Her eyes were dark. "We'll etch his name in the sky too, right? Rodrigo will be remembered for all he's done, right?" Tears were in her eyes before she could square her shoulders. "We'll make him a saint and build monuments to him all over the continent. Lara will tell his story wherever she goes, won't you Lara?"

The sojourner nodded. She searched around in her bag for a scroll and smoothed it out on the table, and they stilled as they realized that nothing was written.

"I'll write his story, and I'll give it to the world. It's also our story. A story about a prince and his silver tongue, the sharpshooter, the tough-as-nails soldier, the silent sentinel, a girl plagued with wanderlust, and a kind cook." A tear fell from Cornelius' eye. Pia leaned her head on Mikka's shoulder, and he pulled his soldier's greatcoat around her. He didn't reek of *raska* as he had for far too many years. Lara wrote a title at the top of the page.

The Tale of Rodrigo Reyes

EPILOGUE

Murray had taken to drinking rose tea with Cornelius in the evenings. It was a lovely practice. Sometimes, when their thoughts were particularly dark, they would add shots of *raska* to their rose tea, unflavored and undoctored to be sure. But other times, when Cornelius was done with his tea, he would play the viola for Murray. He would play a haunting piece he'd titled "The Mariner." Cornelius told him every time that the song was written for him. It was the only piece he'd ever composed. The new king preferred to play by the score, honoring the composer's work instead of his own. One evening, Murray was listening to "The Mariner" as he always did. He closed his eyes and absorbed the melody, taking great pleasure in his next sip of rose tea. Before he wanted it to be, the song was over. He sighed and opened his eyes again.

"How was I?" Cornelius asked him, a smile hidden in his voice. They were on a terrace overlooking the tossing waves. The moon was brilliantly full, dusting a silver path in the waves.

"Oh, you played terribly. I couldn't stand to listen," Murray responded, his tone rich with well-practiced emotion. He'd become quite expressive, though he still didn't speak unless he needed to. Or now, wanted to. Cornelius smiled and gingerly set his viola down on its stand. Then, he went and sat beside Murray. Their armchairs were right on the edge of the terrace, only a thin rail keeping them from plummeting into the sea. It was nice to just sit on the precipice together. Murray could stare out at the sea as much as he wanted from that vantage.

"Murray," Cornelius began, his voice taking on a

conspiratorial tone. Murray hummed in response. "What do you think would've happened had Shadrach lived? Would you have given up a place in the Orenian court to be with me? Would we even be together at all?" Murray pondered it for a moment. He looked stoic even now, drowsy from the *raska* and rose tea. Then, he began one of his famous speeches. Speaking only when necessary had taught him to be purposeful in discussions, placing the meaning of his words above all things.

"You and Lara would be married, though she'd be unhappy in the Marzinian or Wilkinian court, whichever she chose. She would want to be in Andria as she is now. You would try all you could to satisfy her, but your efforts would be in vain. She'd either commit suicide or disappear. I would either be at sea or in Stjernsvet, not in Orenia. My life would be spent at the bottom of a bottle, gambling until my death day. Mikka would have been abandoned in Stjernsvet and would either be almost dead, or dead by now. Pia would have run away from her place in the Emberan court, depressed and unable to see life's luster. She'd search for him, and maybe, just maybe, she'd find him. We all know Pia would follow him anywhere. Shadrach himself would be doing God knows what with Lord knows whom. And Rodrigo would be... alive." Murray's stoic eyes saddened. "He'd go back to Embera and make soup for his family until the day he died." Cornelius took Murray's hand in his and put his lips to it. There were moments like these in which they couldn't help remember all they'd given up for these evenings, for this tainted happiness.

"It's better this way, my love," Cornelius said gently. He drew his fingers across Murray's cheek, but the sentinel looked away.

"But is it?" Murray asked. That was a question they would never answer.

Mikka stood at the prow of an Orenian cargo ship, the air syrupy as it had been during his first trip to Orenia. The gloom was disheartening, and all Mikka wanted to do was take a drink from his flask to warm himself. The crew had buried it with Rodrigo during his funeral in Embera. He heard footsteps behind him, Pia's footsteps. She slid her arm through his.

"What are you doing out here all alone? Aren't you cold?" she asked, moving closer to him. He bent down and kissed her cheek.

"I would be if it weren't for you," he said in accented yet well-spoken Emberan. He'd learned enough from her in the past year to speak in full sentences. The pair stood arm in arm for another few moments, the silence a solace. And Mikka was warm with her beside him. Still, something was gnawing at the back of his mind.

"Pia?" he asked.

"Hmm?" She closed her arms around his waist.

"Do you think he'll be there? He was just a wanderer, right? He wouldn't stick around for an entire year just because of a promise from a counterfeit soldier... would he?" The pair were on an Orenian cargo ship because, in Conaire, Mikka had promised a man with dark eyes that he would come back the following year. If he made good on his promise, the old man had sworn he would repair the dilapidated porch Mikka had fallen through.

"I have a feeling about this, Mikka. He'll be there; I know it." Pia's golden eyes glowed in the half-light as she looked up at him. She felt for the talisman around her neck.

"Alright," he said, staring down into the black waters. It was another hour before they finally moored in Conaire's main harbor. They weren't criminals this time and didn't have to hide their ship. Conaire had flourished into quite the port town since the last time they were there. Not a single Marzinian soldier patrolled the sodden streets, and the broken-down shacks that lined the thoroughfares had been repaired. Nobody lay dying in side streets, and the people that bustled about didn't look sickly and malnourished. It wasn't deathly quiet either. There was laughing, song, even. The continent's five nations had almost entirely returned to their former prosperity with some careful coordination with Cornelius. Everything was improving, and the future was far less bleak. Mikka and Pia themselves had nothing to do with the changes. They'd given up their thrones to stewards and ran off to seek thrills that could match *raska*. It was foolish, but if the war had taught them anything, it was that life was short. They would seek happiness while they could.

The sun broke through the clouds midday, and Conaire was finally bathed in sunlight. They'd stopped for potato scones from a street stall. After their meal, they were finally ready to face the dark-eyed man. The farther they traveled into town, the more they could hear the birdsong. The melodies could match any great composer's masterwork. Only silence was shared between Mikka and Pia as they stood across the street from the shopfront.

The porch had already been repaired, but the man was nowhere to be found. Mikka squared his shoulders and exhaled.

"He repaired the porch. Or someone did, at least," Mikka said. Pia squeezed his hand. There was another long period of silence.

"I think it was him. He knew you were coming back," Pia insisted. The talisman around her neck seemed heavier, if only for a moment. Mikka was suddenly staring at her. He raised his free hand and tucked a lock of her hair behind her ear.

"I always come back," he said.

Lara bowed low to the velveted floor, kneeling before Alexander of Andria. She wore a gown of white and carried a satchel over her shoulder. Her hair was in a loose braid, and her eyes were as nebulous as ever. The Andrian king motioned for her to rise, and she did. His greying black hair flowed down his back like a silk stream. His daughter, Isabel of Andria, knelt beside his throne.

"State your business in the royal court, sojourner. You're

from the other continent, yes?" he asked, voice subtle.

"I am, your eminence. My name is Lara, and I come from the nation Wilkinia. And as for my business, I've come to tell a story if it's a story you'd like."

A coy smile drew the king's lips tight. "Please, the Andrian court would love to hear your tale. But first, please tell us what you've named your story."

"The Tale of Rodrigo Reyes, your highness."

ABOUT THE AUTHOR

Holly Pfeiffer is fourteen years old and basks in the glory of raised eyebrows from baristas when she orders the doubleshot espresso. But her age eccentricity doesn't only apply to copious coffee drinking.

She also writes books. Books with vivid characters and captivating plots. I know. Shocking. Our Holly does some age-appropriate things, too. She attends high school and sits up all night nose-deep in a good young adult fantasy. She frets about her acne and lives with her parents, brother, and two cats, avoiding them all in a very teenagerish manner, except for the grey cat. She likes the grey cat.

ABOOKS

ALIVE Book Publishing and ALIVE Publishing Group
are imprints of Advanced Publishing LLC,
3200 A Danville Blvd., Suite 204, Alamo, California 94507

Telephone: 925.837.7303
alivebookpublishing.com